# Blood Passage

*a Donaghue and Stainer Crime Novel*

# Michael J. McCann

The Plaid Raccoon Press
2011

This is a work of fiction. All names, characters, institutions, places and events portrayed in this novel are either the product of the author's imagination or are used fictitiously. Any resemblance to actual persons, living or dead, events or locales is entirely coincidental.

ISBN: 978-0-9877087-0-0

# Blood Passage

**Also by Michael J. McCann**

*The Ghost Man*

For Lynn

# 1

The day that Lieutenant Hank Donaghue walked into the alley beside the Biltmore Arms Apartment Building on 121st Street in South Shore East was the day the alleged soul of Martin Liu departed its body and began the next segment of its journey from nothingness to eternity. It was a warm afternoon in early June four years ago and the wind was blowing in off the river. Summer had not yet completely settled in, but the heat was right behind the door, waiting to come through.

Uniformed police officers shifted from one foot to the other at each end of the alley, their presence preventing onlookers from ducking beneath the yellow crime scene tape for a closer look. Detective Joe Kalzowski stood off to one side, questioning the elderly African-American woman who had called 911. She lived in a two-bedroom apartment on the sixth floor of the Biltmore Arms and had spotted the body from her bathroom window. A second witness, the elderly woman's 14-year-old grandson, waited with one of the responding officers, staring at the body on the ground with a mixture of shock and fascination. Dr. Jim Easton, the Assistant Medical Examiner, crouched beside the body, withdrawing the long thermometer with which he had measured the temperature of the corpse's liver. Members of the crime scene unit had already claimed the victim's wallet, containing his driver's license, credit cards and sixty-five dollars in cash, and were now taking photographs and bagging scraps of trash to be brought along for further study.

Hank knelt beside Easton, who grimaced up at him over his glasses.

"Looks like cause of death is going to be exsanguination, roughly five hours ago," Easton said, putting the thermometer away.

"Not much blood."

"Right. Your primary scene is somewhere else. This is a dump site. Shot somewhere else, died here."

Hank looked at the bullet wound in the body's left leg, just above the kneecap on the inside of the thigh. "Sloppy work. Shot from the front?"

"Yeah. Through and through, very close range. He wasn't running away."

"Self-inflicted? Accidental discharge, maybe?"

Easton pursed his lips for a moment and then shook his head. "Awkward angle." He shuffled around behind the body and held his own hand out so that his wrist was twisted back on itself. "Have to be something like this, but only if he were struggling with someone, and there are no contusions on his wrist that would suggest a struggle for a gun. We'll test his hands for GSR, but I'll tell you right now, someone else did this to him."

Hank looked at the nose, which had been bloodied and broken, at the split upper lip and at the bruises on the forehead and both cheeks. He shook his head. "Worked him over first."

"Felt like some broken ribs," Easton agreed, smoothing his blond mustache. "Maybe internal injuries."

Hank noticed that the young man's clothing was nearly new. His hair was neatly groomed and his hands looked soft. The scattered packets of merchandise and paraphernalia suggested a drug deal gone bad. It was definitely the wrong part of town for a 24-year-old Asian with little street experience to be selling junk, as the neighborhood, from 118th Street all the way south to Kensington, was territory claimed by the African-American R Boyz gang.

Hank frowned. A CSI had already done a field test on one of the packets that indicated heroin, but it wasn't a heroin kind of neighborhood. If the kid had been selling, he definitely didn't have a clue as to how to go about it. Something didn't add up. If the kid had been shot somewhere else, then he wouldn't be here trying to sell—

Hank's cell phone rang. He stood up and moved a few steps away from the body before taking the call, then he put the phone away and went over to Kalzowski, who was wrapping it up with the elderly woman.

"Joe, I gotta go."

Kalzowski frowned. "What is it?"

"Jumper downtown. There's no one else. You okay here?"

Kalzowski's eyes flicked to the packets and syringes scattered on the ground near the body. "Yeah, pretty cut and dried, I'd say. Go ahead, I'll handle it."

"All right." Hank ducked under the yellow tape and peeled off his latex gloves as he approached one of the uniformed officers, a sergeant named Booth.

"Can someone give me a ride downtown?"

Booth squinted at Hank. "The jumper?"

"Yeah."

"No problem." Booth snapped his fingers a couple of times. "Jamieson! Take Lieutenant Donaghue downtown, will you?"

As Hank waited for Jamieson to unlock the passenger door of the police cruiser, he glanced back at the alley. Another wasted life. Between the buildings the late afternoon sun flickered and cast its blinding light across his face. Hank closed his eyes for a moment, aware of the warmth on his flesh and the glowing redness behind his eyelids. Then he slipped on his sunglasses and got into the cruiser.

By the time they were flying across Harborfront Bridge into Midtown he had already forgotten Martin Liu's name.

# 2

Four years later, on a Monday morning in the middle of May, Hank sat in front of his computer in the homicide detectives' bullpen working on a report. He'd assisted in an arrest this morning and liked to get rid of administrative chores as soon as he could. He and Detective Jim Horvath had gone over to Chinatown to interview a witness in the fatal shooting of a grocery store owner. Horvath was in his early thirties, tall and slender with neatly combed straight black hair. He'd been with Homicide for two years now and was showing an aptitude for the job. His partner, Detective Amelda Peralta, was attending the autopsy of the victim and was unavailable, so Hank agreed to fill in.

Horvath parked the car in front of the four-plex on Fremont Street where the witness, John Li, lived. According to Horvath, Li was the victim's son-in-law.

*We proceeded around the north side of the building to the door at the rear serving as the entrance to Unit C,* Hank typed. *Detective Horvath knocked loudly on the door, identifying himself and asking Mr. Li to open the door.*

What happened next happened quickly. As Horvath pounded again on the door, Hank took a few steps back to see if he could see anything through an upstairs window. He heard the door at the front of the building open and close. His angle of view being better than Horvath's, he caught a glimpse of someone peeking around the corner at them. Before he could open his mouth to say anything, Hank saw a gun. He yelled and threw himself down as a shot punched into the vinyl siding of the house next door. The gun disappeared as Horvath bullrushed the shooter, chasing him around the corner and down the street. Hank caught up with them in time to see Horvath grab the kid around the shoulders and steer him into a row of garbage cans on the sidewalk. The kid fell among the cans as Horvath danced aside. By the time Hank reached them Horvath had secured the gun, cuffed the kid and was searching him for other weapons.

*During the course of said search I saw Detective Horvath find a plain white envelope in the front right pocket of the suspect's jeans,* Hank typed. *The unsealed envelope contained eight (8) small paper packets sealed in plastic. Consistent with the appearance of single-use bags of heroin, each packet bore the inscription "Flyer" stamped in red ink. I telephoned Detective James Schein in Narcotics and—*

A clatter at the desk across from him pulled his eyes away from the monitor.

"Goddamned lawyers," Detective Karen Stainer growled. She slammed her leather portfolio down on her desk and dropped into her chair.

9

Hank looked at her, saying nothing.

"Goddamned court." She wore a crisp white blouse and a black skirt suit, and had removed her jacket to drape it over the back of her chair. She carried her weapon, a Browning Hi-Point C9 nine millimeter, in a leather holster on her right hip. Also clipped to the belt of her skirt were her departmental identification and her gold shield. "I don't get why they don't go straight from arrest to the fuckin' gas chamber without all the bullshit in between."

Her Texan drawl, which made "get" sound like "gee-yit" and "between" sound like "bit-wayuhn," would be charming if it weren't coming from a mouth that looked like it might bite a chain in half at any moment. Karen was 36 years old and a fifteen-year veteran of the police department. A Tai Kwon Do black belt with a mean streak, she was five feet, three inches tall, weighed one hundred and five pounds and had fists like a pair of shoemaker's hammers, small and very hard. Her face was sharp-featured, her blond hair was carelessly chopped short, and her eyes, a lovely pale blue shade, tended to fix on people in a laser beam cop's stare.

"Excuse me," said a voice behind Hank, "I'm looking for Lieutenant Donaghue."

Hank looked down at his hands, still poised over the keyboard. "Donaghue?"

"Uh, yeah. I thought his office was over there, but Lieutenant Jarvis said his desk is out here in the bullpen. Do you know where he sits?"

Hank turned around and looked at a young detective in his late twenties. His hair and beard were neatly trimmed and he wore jeans and a blue corduroy jacket over a yellow patterned shirt. His glasses had thin black frames and narrow lenses. His skin was the color of chestnuts. Hank looked at the departmental identification that hung on a lanyard around the man's neck, he looked at the departmental accordion file in the man's right hand with the white and red CCU label on it, and he looked down at the man's shoes: three-hundred-dollar Reeboks. Now what would a twenty-something up-and-comer from the Cold Case Unit want with him?

"He's Donaghue," Karen snapped. "I'm Stainer. What do you want?"

"Uh, Detective Waverman, CCU. Okay if I sit down?" Waverman sat in the visitor's chair beside Hank's desk. Next to his elbow was a nameplate with Hank's name on it. He looked at it and hummed softly while opening his accordion file.

Patience is a virtue, Hank reminded himself. With a small movement of his hand he tapped the mouse button to minimize his half-finished report.

"I'm sorry to bother you, Lieutenant." Waverman removed a manila file folder from the accordion file and set it down on the corner of Hank's desk. "I just wanted to ask you a few questions about the Martin Liu homicide. It was a case that belonged to Detective Joseph Kalzowski four years ago. It

10

was transferred to CCU a year later, I believe after the retirement of Detective Kalzowski, and recently assigned to me."

Hank picked up the manila file folder and opened it. "Liu?"

He flipped through the documents inside the folder. They were copies of various items from the murder book kept by Kalzowski during the original investigation. If CCU had received the case they would have the actual murder book, which was the entire file covering the case, so this was just a "show and tell" excerpt Waverman had put together to carry around with him to interviews.

There wasn't much there. He looked at a couple of crime scene photos and nodded as it came back to him as clearly as if it had been yesterday.

"Yeah, I remember. Kalzowski had the lead. I got called away a few minutes after we got there and Joe did all the leg work. We were pretty short-staffed back then." He closed the folder and put it back down on the corner of his desk. "Not much I can tell you about it. Why?"

"Do you recall any connection between the vic and out-of-towners, maybe from a university or college somewhere?"

"Nope. Anything in the book about it?"

"What's this all about?" Karen interjected.

Waverman shook his head, still looking at Hank. "No, there isn't. I got something today, though." He took a piece of paper from the accordion file and passed it over to Hank. "An incident report filed by a beat cop early this morning relating to an assault near end of shift yesterday afternoon. A guy by the name of Joshua Duncan, a student from Thomas Gaines University in Memphis, was found beaten up in an alley over in Chinatown. He told the cop he was investigating the death of Martin Liu, or words to that effect."

Hank scanned the document. An incident report was an electronic file sent through the department's computer network. This one stated that the semi-conscious victim had been found by city sanitation workers who called 911. The responding officer questioned the victim, who said, quote, "I'm investigating Martin Liu, who was killed here four years ago."

The victim's wallet was stolen from his pocket, netting his assailants two credit cards and a couple hundred dollars in cash and travelers checks. The victim's knapsack was found at the entrance of the alley. Missing were a notebook, an iPod, a hardcover book on early childhood development and a return airline ticket to Memphis. The victim told the officer he was a graduate student studying child psychiatry. He described his assailants as two Asian males, one wearing a dark blue sports jacket and red sneakers, the other wearing a black leather jacket and cowboy boots.

Hank leaned forward and fired the document across his desk at Karen, who snatched it up and looked it over.

"The officer ran the Liu name," Waverman explained, "saw it was flagged in the system as a cold case file and made a mental note to send a

11

report to me first thing this morning. I'm on my way to the hospital now to see Duncan before he leaves but I thought I'd look you up first to see if you had any idea why a college student would be looking into a four-year-old homicide."

"We appreciate you bringing this to our attention," Karen said. "Just have the paperwork done to transfer the case back to us."

Hank looked at her, amused.

"Hey, I'd be happy to," Waverman said, standing up and quickly returning the manila folder to the safety of his accordion file. "I've got a full plate, believe me, but it's not that easy, Detective. The CCU doesn't hand back files that have been turned over to it. Politics and funding, you should know that." He leaned forward and took the incident report from Karen's hand. "I have to get over to the hospital before he takes off. He's already been discharged. Thanks anyway."

"We'll both go," Karen said, standing up and pulling her jacket off the back of her chair.

Hank saved his work, logged off the network and stood up. "We'll all go."

Waverman looked from Karen to Hank and shrugged. "All right. I'll drive."

They trooped down to the elevator and Waverman pressed the button for the lower level where his car was parked. When the elevator arrived Hank stood at the back and looked at their reflections in the mirror-paneled interior of the elevator car. Waverman was short, about five feet nine inches, and weighed about a hundred and fifty pounds. He stared at the buttons on the control panel and quietly hummed something under his breath. Standing next to Hank, Karen caught his eye in the mirror panel and winked. Stay tuned, Little Ms. Mischief is in a mood.

Hank towered behind Waverman at six feet, three inches. He weighed a pound under two hundred and was a little round-shouldered. He had long arms with long, slender fingers, size thirteen feet, and a size 34 waist. He had frizzy brown hair that was starting to show some grey, he was clean-shaven with a dimpled chin and fleshy lips, and his heavy brow gave his brown eyes a brooding look. He was 44 years old and beginning to feel every last day of it. He remembered Liu clearly now, remembered staring into those sightless green eyes and thinking that something was wrong with the set-up. He remembered being a little surprised at the color of the victim's irises. He remembered moving out into bright sunshine, aware of being alive while Martin Liu lay dead in the alley behind him. He remembered putting the sight out of his mind during the ride over the bridge back into Midtown.

He rode in the back of Waverman's Subaru Outback while Karen sat up front in the passenger seat. As soon as they were out of the parking garage and into traffic she glanced over at Waverman.

"How long you been on the force?"

"Three years," Waverman replied, eyes on the traffic ahead of him. "Graduated from the academy, finished probation, rode patrol for a while and then passed the detective exam."

"Where'd you go?"

"Anti-Terrorism. Then an opening came up in CCU, I applied and got in. The Martin Liu file is part of my case load. This is the first time anything new has broken on it."

Karen was not going to be diverted into discussing the case until her other priorities were satisfied. "Elspeth Williams is your captain there, right? What's she like?"

Waverman shrugged. "Not bad. A little distant. Spends most of her time in meetings."

"I hear she's a bitch. Can't turn your back on her. The only six she cares about is her own."

Hank watched in the rear-view mirror as Waverman's eyes widened a little behind his glasses.

"I don't know," Waverman said cautiously. "She seems okay to me."

"Y'all got five detectives in the unit, right?" Karen shifted in her seat to look at him. "Bill Ireland still there? He's the only one I know of."

"No, there's Amy Chin, Edgar Roberts, Sami Verdan, Maureen Truly and myself. Sami's been there the longest."

"Must be boring," Karen opined, "sitting around all day waitin' on something to happen to cases that are deader than a fuckin' doornail. I just came over to Homicide last fall from Family-Related. Christ, you haven't seen anything until you've done a stint in Family-Related Crime. Can't catch your breath."

Hank listened to them swap a few more names until Waverman stopped at a red light. He leaned forward and asked: "What hospital is the Duncan kid in?"

Waverman glanced at him in the rear-view mirror. "Angel of Mercy."

The light changed to green and Waverman accelerated smoothly through the intersection.

"I see you carry the Glock 22," Karen said, nodding at the holstered firearm that Waverman had unclipped from his belt and put in the well of the center console within easy reach of his right hand. "How's that work for you?"

"All right," Waverman shrugged. "I'm not much for guns."

Departmental policy gave officers the ability to choose their service weapon from an approved list that included the Glock 22 and a number of other alternatives.

13

"Off-duty weapon?"

Waverman hesitated and then understood her question. "Oh, I only have this one." He glanced over at her, knowing he was expected to reciprocate. "What about you?"

Karen shrugged blandly. "My court gun is this Browning High Point nine mil with burl wood grips I'm carrying right now, since that's where I was at this morning. My normal duty weapon is the SIG Sauer P226, more expensive but a lot more gun for your money. I fire the forty S and W with that, and it's a very nice piece. My oh-shit backup is a Kel-Tec P11 nine mil, the little 10-plus-one shot, my off-duty is a Beretta Px4 Storm and my barbecue gun is an ass-kicking Smith and Wesson M66 .357 magnum revolver with ivory grips. Mean-assed sweetie."

Waverman frowned. "Barbecue gun?"

A smile flitted around the corners of Karen's mouth as she rolled her eyes and looked out the side window. This was too easy.

Hank leaned forward again. "A barbecue gun is a gun that you carry to barbecues in order to show it off. She's from Texas. Barbecue guns are big in Texas."

"Okay," Waverman said perfunctorily.

He was obviously not very interested in the subject, so Karen pressed it.

"What'd you score on the academy course?" she asked, referring to the shooting course that all academy participants were required to pass with a minimum score of 280 out of 400 in order to graduate.

"Three thirty-six," Waverman replied. This score was middle rung but good enough to qualify him for the minimal marksmanship bonus on his bi-weekly paycheck.

"Did you shoot the bonus course?" It was possible for departmental officers to shoot an additional course after graduation in order to improve on their academy score and qualify for a higher paycheck bonus. Very few of the newer officers bothered with the bonus course these days, though, as the department had instituted an annual requalification system a few years ago despite vigorous resistance from the union. The requalification test was a "no miss" pass or fail course that almost everyone found either very stressful or a nuisance, and since it took priority over the academy bonus course, very few officers now bothered with the latter.

"No," Waverman shook his head. "Did you?"

Karen scoffed. "Hell, yeah. I shot a 396 academy, but I was hung over that morning and felt like shit. Shot a perfect 400 next time."

Waverman raised his eyebrows. "Wow, Four Hundred Club."

"Yeah, membership currently at five." Karen nodded at Hank in the back seat. "The Lou back there shot a 397 academy but never shot the bonus. I've watched him practice with that boring Glock 17 he carries and he's definitely Four Hundred material. Won't shoot the bonus, though."

"I don't like to play with guns," Hank said.

Karen laughed and looked out the window.

The car remained silent until they turned into the hospital parking lot. Karen had had her fun, and was now probably brooding about the case from her previous assignment that had dragged her off to court this week. It was a child molestation case that had taken an ugly turn, and despite her hard-boiled exterior Karen was upset. Just the same, Hank was grateful for a little peace and quiet.

They went into the hospital and up to Josh Duncan's room. As they approached the door, Hank glanced at the glass of an emergency fire hose cabinet. It was a habit developed over a lifetime, finding and using reflective surfaces. He caught a glimpse of Waverman's left hand and saw that it was clenching and unclenching, betraying his nervous tension.

They found Duncan sitting on the edge of his bed, already dressed, zipping up his knapsack.

Waverman went through the door first. "Joshua Duncan?"

He looked up apprehensively. "Yes?"

"I'm Detective Waverman; this is Detective Stainer and Lieutenant Donaghue." Waverman held up his badge. Karen pushed in behind.

Hank, bringing up the rear, slipped off to the side and up along the bed to the wall so that he was positioned on Josh's left. He put his hands on his hips, moving his jacket aside so that the young man could see the ID and badge clipped to his belt. He saw Josh glance at his sidearm and then look down at his feet.

"We'd like to ask you a couple of questions about the assault yesterday," Waverman said. "I understand you suffered a mild concussion. Are you feeling okay this morning?"

Josh nodded. "Yeah, I guess. My head still hurts, though. They gave me something to take for it. I feel pretty woolly."

"I'd imagine," Waverman said, looking at the bruise on Josh's cheek and the cut on his eyebrow which had taken four stitches to close. "What were you doing down in that part of town?"

According to the report, Josh was 24 years old, which made him only two years younger than Waverman. He was African-American, about two inches shorter than Hank, maybe ten pounds lighter, and had a build like a basketball point guard. There was a definite athleticism to him that could not be missed beneath the shoulder-length dreadlocks and casual clothing, but Hank was a little surprised by the nervousness, betrayed by a difficulty in making eye contact and the way he held his knapsack close to his chest.

Josh hesitated before answering Waverman's question, and that was all Karen needed.

"Got a problem with authority, kid? Don't feel like answering questions today?"

"No, no, not at all. Please, ask anything." Josh touched the side of his head. "I just feel a little woozy."

"We understand," Hank said, "but Detective Stainer's right, Josh. The answer to Detective Waverman's question is pretty important to us. What were you doing in Chinatown asking questions about Martin Liu?"

"It's part of my responsibilities. I'm investigating a report of a previous life."

"A previous life?" Waverman repeated. "I'm afraid I don't understand."

"Yeah, I know. Most people think it's a lot of bunk."

"You're a student, Josh?" Hank asked. "From Memphis?"

Josh nodded. "Thomas Gaines University. I'm a Ph.D. student specializing in child psychiatry. I'm an assistant researcher with the Division of Supplementary Studies."

"Who's your research advisor there?"

"Dr. Maddy Walsh." Josh made eye contact with him for the first time. "She's the Director of the Family and Child Psychiatry Clinic at the university."

"Uh huh. And you do research for her, is that it? Research that brought you up here to Glendale?"

"Yeah. Dr. Walsh and I were here last month to interview the family of a child whose case we've accepted. Now I'm here to investigate the previous personality."

"Previous personality."

"Uh huh," Josh nodded. "Martin Liu."

Karen cleared her throat. "You sure the doctors said you were okay to leave?"

"We don't understand the connection between you and Martin Liu," Waverman said.

Josh shook his head. "The connection's between Martin and the child whose case we're investigating. The child who said he was Martin Liu in his previous life."

"What child are we talking about here?" Karen asked.

"I'm not sure if I can say right now," Josh replied uncertainly.

Karen looked at Hank. "Well, this isn't making a hell of a lot of sense."

"Detective Stainer has a point, I'm afraid." Waverman removed his BlackBerry and glanced at it. "I have to get back for a one o'clock meeting. Can you come by the station a little later and give a complete statement?"

"I guess so," Josh said. "Sure."

"Where are you going now?" Hank asked. "Back to your hotel?"

Josh nodded.

16

"Which one?'

"Airport Inn."

"Not exactly walking distance. How about if I spring for a taxi and you let me ride with you. You can tell me a little more about your work at Thomas Gaines."

"Okay, thanks," Josh said, managing a small grin. "They took all my money."

"I know. Karen, can you come up and get me in about an hour?"

She sighed as though it were the end of the world. "Yeah, sure."

"Give me a call when you get back, okay?" Waverman asked Hank with a meaningful look that said, *It's my case and I want any information you get from this person.*

"Sure, no problem," Hank replied.

As they watched Waverman and Karen file out of the room, Josh turned to Hank. "I didn't know cops attended meetings and stuff. I thought it was all just riding around in cars and arresting people."

Hank smiled. "Actually, police departments can be just as bureaucratic as any other organization. You'd be surprised at all the time-wasting nonsense we have to put up with."

"I had no idea."

"Got everything?" Hank watched Josh ease down from the side of the bed and pick up his knapsack. He was obviously sore from the beating he had taken.

"Yeah." Josh held up his knapsack. "Not that they left me much."

"Mind if I take a look?" Hank held out his hand. Josh gave him the knapsack without hesitation. It felt empty. Hank unzipped the top and looked inside. Couple of pens, a pencil, a Sharpie marker, a wad of yellow Post-It notes, a small metal pencil sharpener and a few wood shavings from the pencil. Hank held the bag up close to his face, as though trying to see into the bottom, and inhaled slowly. Nothing. He lowered the bag and quickly unzipped the side pouches. Empty.

"Cleaned it out, didn't they?" He handed the knapsack back and decided that he wasn't being protective of the bag; he was being protective of himself.

They left the room and slowly walked down the corridor to the nurses' station.

"This patient has been discharged and is ready to leave," Hank said to the nurse on duty.

"Oh, you can't just walk out," she said to Josh, standing up. "What's your name?"

"Joshua Duncan," he answered politely.

She consulted a sheaf of papers on a clipboard and nodded. "Yes, I have your signature, but you have to be taken down in a wheelchair."

"A wheelchair?" Josh looked embarrassed.

"Hospital policy. Wait here a moment." The nurse disappeared through a doorway into a back room and a moment later a volunteer came out with her, a white-haired African-American in jeans and a plaid shirt with a name tag that said *Bob*. He grinned at Josh as he brought a wheelchair around into the corridor.

"Ready to go, are you? Have a seat."

"Yes, sir." Josh sat down in the wheelchair.

Hank followed Bob and Josh into the elevator and they rode down to the ground floor.

"Here you go," Bob said, stopping just short of the sliding front doors.

"Thanks very much." Josh got out of the wheelchair with a wince.

"No problem. You take care of yourself now, son."

There was a bank of pay phones along the wall inside the front doors. The one at the end connected directly to the largest taxi company in town. Hank called for a taxi and then strolled back over to join Josh at the door. The kid didn't have a problem with authority, he decided, because he had been deferential to the nurse and the volunteer. He seemed polite, well-mannered and respectful. Not a problem with authority; more likely a problem with police.

"Have you dealt with the police before in any of the other cases you've researched, Josh?"

"No." He shook his head. "This is only my second case. In the other one, the previous personality was in his fifties and died of a heart attack. Which is unusual, actually, because the age of previous personalities at death tends to average about 34 to 38 years old."

"I see. You seem nervous around police."

"No, I'm okay."

"Have you ever been arrested?"

"No, I haven't."

"Okay, that's fine. I'm not trying to hassle you."

"I understand that."

"You seem a little nervous."

"I'm okay."

"Some kind of problem before?"

Josh hesitated, then nodded. "Yeah, I suppose."

"When was that?"

"Last summer, outside a bus station in a town not far from Rayville, Louisiana. I was visiting a friend in Shreveport and was waiting for a connection back home."

"And?"

"Sheriff saw me leaning against the wall of the bus station while he was waiting for a stoplight. I saw him look over, then come around the corner into the parking lot and right up in front of me. Got out and asked me what I thought I was doing in his parish."

Hank waited.

Josh looked at him. "He had a problem with my hair and the color of my skin. Said he didn't need my kind of trash coming up from New Orleans into his parish. I tried to tell him I was in transit, but he wasn't interested in listening. Said if I was going to hang around the streets of his parish with dreadlocks or whatever you call that druggie hairstyle I could expect a visit from one of his deputies. Said if I wasn't gone in half an hour his deputy would be back to arrest me."

"Bothered you, did it?"

Josh frowned. "Of course it did, it scared me. I've never had any trouble before in my life. I grew up in Knoxville and I've lived in Memphis for a while now and never had any trouble with the police. But that was definitely a wake-up call. It reminded me of how much intolerance there is out there and how powerless we are when the police decide they want to make our lives hell."

"The guy sounds like a pretty big asshole to me," Hank said.

"Well, yeah."

Hank stared until Josh made eye contact with him. "Lot of assholes out there."

"Yeah, I guess so."

The taxi arrived and they got in. The hospital was located in Granger Park and Josh's hotel was at the north end of the city in Bering Heights, so the taxi ride was going to be somewhat long. The city of Glendale was divided into districts in a hub-and-spoke configuration with the river dividing it diagonally from northeast to southwest. The ocean was five miles downstream from the city limits. Midtown was the hub and Bering Heights, Granger Park and Springhill were the spokes on the west side of the river, with the heavily industrialized districts of Strathton and Wilmingford on the east side. Glendale's international seaport was located in Wilmingford. The districts of South Shore East and South Shore West straddled the river at the south end of the city. Bering Heights, in the north, contained a college and an international airport that serviced the national headquarters of a number of large corporations. Granger Park, where Hank had been born and raised, housed the upper class on large estates on the edge of the municipality and morphed into suburban sprawl farther south. Springhill, having once been a separate municipality that amalgamated with Glendale forty years ago, was a mixture of residential, commercial and municipal properties that included State University and the stadium of a Class A baseball team currently affiliated with the Pittsburgh Pirates.

As the taxi ground its way north through heavy traffic Hank asked Josh a few questions about his studies. Josh explained that he liked to work with children. As an undergraduate he took courses in early childhood education and worked part-time in the day care center on campus. In his senior year he attended lectures delivered by Dr. Walsh and learned about the research being conducted by the Division of Supplementary Studies into reports by children of past life memories, but he shifted first into child psychiatry before seeking admission into the Division.

Hank noticed that as Josh talked about himself and his career interests his body language became less tight and self-protective, and his face showed more expression.

At the hotel he badged the clerk, explaining that Josh had been mugged downtown and had lost his room keycard along with his wallet. The clerk expressed his concern but explained that there would be a nominal charge to replace the keycard which would be added to the final bill. Josh nodded and the clerk produced a duplicate. They went up to Josh's room on the eighth floor, where Josh found his laptop, Personal Digital Assistant and other belongings undisturbed. Breathing a sigh of relief, he slipped his PDA into his pocket and thanked Hank for the taxi ride.

"I'll arrange for replacement travelers checks and pay you back for the cab fare," he said.

"No, don't bother," Hank said. "Come on, let's go downstairs and I'll buy you lunch in the restaurant. I want to hear more about this case you're researching."

"All right," Josh said, gratefully. "I guess I am a little hungry."

They rode the elevator back down to the main floor and went into the restaurant just off the front lobby. They were seated at a table along a wall of tinted windows that gave them a clear view of the lobby and elevators without being seen by anyone in the lobby while they ate. Josh ordered a chicken Caesar salad and unsweetened iced tea while Hank asked for a club sandwich with extra mayo and a large Coke.

Josh glanced at the time on his PDA and took another of the painkillers given to him by the doctor at the hospital. Hank asked him about his movements after arriving in town.

"I flew in on Friday afternoon," Josh explained. "On Saturday I interviewed the mother of the previous personality, Meredith Liu. She's actually Caucasian, despite her last name. She's the only surviving parent. She goes by the name Meredith Collier now. Her maiden name, I guess." He took a mouthful of salad and swallowed before continuing. "On Sunday I went to the apartment building where the previous personality lived."

"By previous personality you're referring to Martin Liu, I take it?"

"Mm hmm," Josh nodded. "Sorry. Dr. Walsh insists that we be very precise in our terminology. Actually, no one that I talked to apparently lived there when Martin Liu did. So it was kind of a dead end."

Hank was thinking that any tenants who'd lived in the building when Martin Liu was murdered probably lied to Josh to blow him off. Few people were interested in talking to a complete stranger about a four-year-old violent crime.

"Then on Monday, uh, yesterday, I went down to the Golden Dragon, the place where Ms. Liu said her son liked to spend time. I wanted to see if I could talk to any of his friends there, and also I was hoping to run into Martin's cousin Peter. Mrs. Liu mentioned that Martin used to meet his cousin there quite often."

"But it didn't go too smoothly, I gather."

"It was kind of a strange place," Josh admitted. "I was very uncomfortable. It was like some kind of gaming room, downstairs under a hairdressing salon. I went down and saw a sign that said 'Members Only' but there was no one at the door so I went in to find someone to talk to. There were a few men sitting around playing a game with dominoes and dice in a cup."

"Pai gow," Hank said.

"Pardon me?"

"The game's called pai gow," Hank said. "Go on."

Josh explained that as he approached one of the tables he was intercepted by a middle-aged Asian man in a rumpled white suit who took him by the elbow and steered him back toward the entrance.

"Sorry, pal, didn't you see the sign? Members only."

"I'm a student from Memphis," Josh said to the man, who was apparently a waiter. They passed a small bar at which two men were drinking tea and looking at newspapers. "I'm doing research on a person named Martin Liu who used to come here four years ago. Was he a member?"

At the mention of Martin Liu's name the two men slid off their barstools and came over to where Josh and the waiter stood in the doorway. One of the men wore a blue suit jacket over a pale green shirt, blue jeans and red sneakers. The other, who was heavier and looked older, wore a black leather jacket and sunglasses despite the low lighting inside the club.

"We don't talk about members here," the waiter said, lightly pushing Josh's elbow in the direction of the stairs.

"I understand," Josh said. "That's okay. Let me give you this." He reached into his jacket pocket and took out a business card, realizing belatedly that the sudden movement had caused the man in the leather jacket to reach into his own pocket, possibly for a weapon. It began to dawn on him that it was not such a good idea to have come here.

He held up the card for everyone to see, then handed it to the waiter. "I'm also looking for Martin Liu's cousin, Peter. Maybe you could give him this and he can get in touch with me. I'm staying at the Airport Inn, or he can call me at the cell phone number on the card. I just want to talk to him about Martin."

The waiter took the card without looking at it. "Good idea if you leave now. *Now.*"

"All right, no problem." Josh realized that the clicking of dice and the clacking of dominoes had ceased in the room. Everyone was watching him with expressionless faces: old men, young men, and the two tough-looking individuals who now stood on either side of him.

"Martin's mother mentioned that he liked to come down here," Josh said lamely. "I just wanted to talk to some of his friends."

"Out, gangsta," the man in the blue jacket said. "Now."

Josh nodded and began to leave. Behind him, Blue Jacket snatched Josh's card from the waiter and followed Josh up the stairs. Leather Jacket brought up the rear. They went outside and the two men walked on either side of Josh along the sidewalk.

"Pretty stupid for one of the Boyz to think he can just walk into a 14K club and start bothering people," Blue Jacket said.

Josh frowned, wondering if they thought he belonged to a local gang or if it was just a racial slur. "You don't understand," he said. "I'm not in any gang. I'm a student from Thomas Gaines University in Memphis. I'm doing research."

"Yeah, well, research this." Blue Jacket pushed Josh into an alley. He grabbed the strap of Josh's knapsack and swung him against the corner of a dumpster. Josh staggered and Leather Jacket stepped up and punched him in the face. He fell to the ground and was kicked repeatedly in the chest, buttocks and thighs. Through half-closed eyes he could see a pair of grey cowboy boots swinging back and forth, striking him with shocking force. A kick in the face drove his head back against the brick wall of the alley and he momentarily blacked out. When he regained awareness he felt his knapsack being pulled away and heard one of them conducting a brisk inventory of its contents. Then he was hazily aware that Blue Jacket was leaning down to peer into his eyes.

"Go home, stupid. Don't come back here no more."

The cowboy boot kicked him in the stomach and Josh curled up, retching. After an eternity he realized that he was alone. He closed his eyes and slid down into a black well of unconsciousness.

"I *was* stupid to go there," Josh admitted, staring at his fork. "I didn't realize it was a gang hangout of some kind until it was too late."

"You have to understand that when someone's murdered, people stay upset about it for a long time afterwards. It's not something you can just show up and start asking questions about."

"Yeah, I get it. With my other case it was just a matter of talking to family and friends to develop a profile to compare to what the child was saying about his previous personality. No crime was committed, and no one belonged to a gang, that's for sure."

Hank finished his club sandwich and wiped his mouth with his napkin. "Maybe you can explain to me a little more about what you and Dr. Walsh are researching."

"All right." Josh pushed his half-finished meal aside.

"You okay?"

"Yeah. My stomach isn't ready for too much food yet." Josh folded his hands. "The Division of Supplementary Studies is the name of the area I'm in. It was created at TGU to study the phenomenon of reports by children of memories of past lives. You'd be surprised how many cases have been investigated in the last forty years, starting with the first program at the University of Virginia. Over two thousand from all over the world, and those are just the ones that have been documented. Anecdotal evidence suggests there are hundreds of other cases that have never been researched."

"You're talking about reincarnation?" Hank said. "That a person's soul or whatever moves into another body after death to start all over again, and then the child starts talking about his previous life as that other person?"

Josh nodded. "I know it sounds sketchy and New Age, but bottom line, yeah. There are many possible explanations for past life statements by young children. Paranormal causes have to be considered among them."

Hank raised his eyebrows. "And your university actually gets funded for this kind of work?"

"You'd be surprised. Over the years we've received a number of huge endowments from very wealthy people with an interest in reincarnation. It's a lot more important to people than you might think." Josh tapped the table with his finger. "Studies have shown that at least twenty-five per cent of Americans believe in reincarnation."

"Hindus and Buddhists?"

Josh shook his head. "The same studies have shown that over twenty per cent of American *Christians* believe in reincarnation."

"That's a surprise," Hank admitted.

Josh spread his hands. "There you go. Once you get past the initial barriers of skepticism and cynicism, there's some very interesting ground to explore. These children tend to be precocious and begin to talk at an early age. They start speaking about past life memories between the ages of two to five and stop talking about them between the ages of five to eight. In some cases they eventually forget these early memories, which is not unusual since five to eight is the age span when children begin to forget most of their early childhood memories anyway. During the period when they do recall these memories of a previous life, seventy-five per cent of these children recall the manner in which they died when they were the previous personality, and in seventy per cent of these cases the death was violent and unpleasant."

"A con job," Hank said. "They're fed their lines by parents who want little Johnny to be something special."

Josh nodded. "Our investigations are designed to root out this kind of fraud, and it does happen. We have a lengthy checklist that we go through with a whole scoring system to analyze the case. We consider the accuracy of the information, unusual behavior in the child such as specific phobias or preferences, birthmarks or birth defects that somehow connect to the previous life, the intensity or spontaneity of statements, exaggerated claims by the parents, and all that."

"But you're telling me that in some cases you've proven these kids were reincarnated?"

"No, you have to remember we're not trying to prove that reincarnation actually happens. That's not our objective. We're not True Believers or anything. We're conducting objective, rational research into a surprisingly recurrent phenomenon among children and letting the evidence suggest possible causes. Reincarnation just happens to be one of those possibilities."

"Nicely put. Sounds like a direct quote from somebody's dissertation."

Josh grinned. "Okay, busted. But like I said, Dr. Walsh insists that we be very precise in how we say things. We're scientists."

"So that's what brought you to town," Hank said casually, taking out his notebook and pen. "Somebody's kid started remembering stuff he couldn't possibly know, and you came up here to check it out."

"Yeah, that's right."

"You understand, don't you, that when you start poking into an open homicide case the police are going to want to know why you're interested, right?"

"Yeah, I get it. I didn't before, but believe me, I do now."

"I'm going to need to know the identity of this kid, so we can look into it. If somebody has information about a homicide, even a three-year-old kid, we're going to need to check it out."

Josh nodded.

"So who's the kid?"

"His name's Taylor Chan. He's actually three and a half."

Hank jotted down the name on a fresh page of his notebook. "Parents?"

"His father's Dr. Michael Chan, an assistant professor of economics at State University. His mother's Grace Chan. She's a real estate agent in Springhill. They live at 46 Parkland Crescent. I think that's the right address." He looked down and grimaced. "Oh yeah, my notebook was stolen. Wait, it's in my PDA." Josh took out his PDA. His thumbs rocked back and forth and he nodded. "Yeah, 46 Parkland."

"Thanks." Hank wrote it down. "How'd they come to get in touch with you about their son?"

"After Taylor started making all these unusual statements about having been someone named Martin Liu, Dr. Chan spoke to a friend of his in the Psych Department at State. His friend referred Dr. Chan to Dr. Walsh, and that's how we got involved."

24

"I see."

"Mrs. Chan captured some of the statements on videotape, the day of Taylor's third birthday. He said his name had been Martin, that his mother's name was Merry and that he'd had green eyes. Mrs. Chan showed the tape to her cousin Peter, and he also seemed to think the statements were significant. Then apparently Taylor told Peter that two men named Shawn and Gary had hurt him."

"So what happened next?" Hank asked.

When Josh didn't answer, Hank looked up from his notebook.

Josh was staring through the tinted glass into the lobby, his eyes wide.

"What?" Hank asked. "What is it?"

"It's them," Josh whispered, face rigid.

"Who?" Hank slipped his notebook and pen into his jacket pocket.

"Walking to the elevators. See them? The Chinese guy in the leather jacket and the other guy. He was wearing a blue jacket yesterday."

Hank looked through the glass and saw two Asians sauntering casually through the lobby toward the bank of elevators. One wore a black leather jacket and cowboy boots and the other wore a plum-colored sports jacket, a pale green shirt, faded blue jeans and red sneakers. The guy in the plum jacket was younger, thin, and stylish in a brainless sort of way. The guy in the leather jacket was stocky and tough-looking, like someone accustomed to making a living with his fists.

"The guys that attacked you?"

"Yeah," Josh whispered. "My God, they've come back for me."

# 3

"Stay put," Hank said, getting up. "Give me your room card."

"Room card?"

"The replacement key card for your room," Hank said, holding out his hand.

"Oh, yeah. Right." Flustered, Josh passed it over.

"Don't move." Hank started toward the restaurant entrance. Edging between a group of people clustered around the cash register at the front, Hank took out his cell phone and punched a number.

"Stainer."

"Karen, I'm still at the Airport Inn. I have a visual on the two goofballs who assaulted Josh Duncan. What's your twenty?"

"En route, Lou. ETA ten."

"They're at the elevators. Might be going up to the kid's room, since they took his keycard. I'm going to have a little word with them."

"I'll be there ASAP."

Hank closed the phone and shouldered his way into the lobby. The two men got into the elevator. The one with the leather jacket leaned forward and punched a button. The doors slid silently closed.

The guy wearing the plum jacket and red sneakers looked familiar to Hank, but he couldn't place him at the moment. He walked over and pressed the button for another elevator. The doors opened, three people got off, and Hank got on. He pressed the button for the eighth floor and the doors closed.

They're a little slow getting here, Hank thought as the car rose smoothly. The assault happened late yesterday afternoon and only now they're paying a visit to the kid's room. They work for someone who has to tell them what to do. The guy in the plum jacket, who the hell does he work for? Hank racked his brains without luck.

The elevator reached the eighth floor and the doors opened. Hank drew his Glock and peeked left and right down the corridor. Empty. He turned right and started down toward Josh's room, 824. He walked slowly, heel to toe, with his gun extended in a low ready position. He could see that the doors of 824 and 822, the next room up on the same side, were both open. A housekeeping cart was parked between the rooms.

He reached 822 and paused, lifting his gun close to his sternum. He looked into the room and saw a woman in a housekeeper's uniform making the bed. He lowered his gun and passed the doorway, eyes flitting between the cart and the open door of 824. He reached 824 and paused, gun elevated again. He looked into the room and saw the two men inside, poking around. The guy in the leather jacket was tossing stuff around on the desk while his partner watched, exuding boredom.

"Police officer!" Hank stepped through the door and raised the Glock in his right hand in a relaxed Chapman stance, right arm stiff, left elbow bent, left hand cupping the fingers of his gun hand.

"Show me your hands, now! On top of your head!"

Plum Jacket turned to look at Hank with a slightly puzzled expression on his face. Leather Jacket froze in the act of opening the desk drawer, then slowly turned, hand creeping toward his pocket.

"Don't do it!" Hank called out. "Hands on top of your head!"

At that moment a housekeeper stepped out of the bathroom in front of Hank to see what all the noise was about.

Plum Jacket lunged forward and shoved her into Hank, knocking him down. As the woman floundered and rolled over his head, Hank felt the two men rush past him out of the room. He struggled to his feet, grabbed the housekeeper around the waist and hauled her upright.

"Stay here!" he ordered. "Don't move!"

"They said they were friends!" she complained.

He quick-peeked out the door, saw the two men running down the corridor away from him, and hurried out.

"Freeze!" he shouted.

As luck would have it, the housekeeper in 822 chose that moment to step out of the room to see what was happening.

"Get out of the way!" Hank yelled.

Plum Jacket turned and squeezed off a shot that punched into the ceiling a few doors away.

Hank pushed the housekeeper into 822 and followed her into the room. "Are you okay?"

She nodded at him wordlessly, eyes wide.

"Stay here!" He quick-peeked and dashed back out of the room in time to hear the two men crash through the stairwell door at the end of the corridor.

Hank ran down the corridor as a bell chimed and an elevator door opened. It was Karen.

"Stairwell!" Hank shouted. "Go back down to the lobby!"

"Yep!" Karen punched the elevator button and the doors closed again.

Hank opened the stairwell door and heard their footsteps echoing below. He started down. He went down one floor and paused. Their footsteps continued to boom up at him, so he went down another floor, then another. As he passed the fifth floor landing the stairwell door flew open, hitting him. He careened into the far wall shoulder-first and rebounded into the metal railing, striking his back with a sharp blow that drove the wind from his lungs. He sat down hard on the top stair, mouth open. He gasped for breath, then struggled to his feet and listened. Nothing in the stairwell. He pulled open the door to

27

the fifth floor. No one there. He hurried to the elevator and pressed the button, rubbing his aching shoulder. When the elevator arrived he got in and pressed the button for the lobby. He leaned back gingerly against the wall of the elevator and concentrated on breathing.

The doors opened onto the lobby and he stepped out, eyes flicking around. Plum Jacket and Leather Jacket were nowhere in sight. Karen emerged from the stairwell and saw him. She shook her head.

"Damn it," Hank said, holstering his gun.

"Backup's on the way," Karen said. "Where's Duncan?"

"Restaurant, hopefully," Hank answered. "They fired one shot into the ceiling. There were two housekeepers. I don't think either of them was injured."

Karen nodded again. "Check on the kid, I'll go back upstairs." She punched the elevator button and turned to look at him. "You okay?"

"Couldn't be better."

"You sound a little winded."

The elevator doors chimed open. "There's your ride," Hank said.

Karen got into the elevator, chuckling at him.

Josh was still in the restaurant at their table. He said he'd tried to leave but they wouldn't let him, because the bill had not yet been paid and he had no money. Hank settled the bill and took Josh over to the front desk, where he arranged to have him moved to another room on the third floor. Josh agreed that as soon as he replaced his stolen traveler's checks he would pay his bill and move downtown to a hotel not far from police headquarters that was often used by the department to sequester witnesses. Hank jotted down the telephone number of Josh's PDA and said he'd call him later.

As Hank went out the door to rejoin Karen upstairs, he glanced back and saw that the painkiller Josh had taken at lunch was beginning to make him drowsy. He lay stretched out on the bed of his new room, hands folded on his chest, eyes closed. Hank quietly closed the door on his way out.

# 4

At eight forty-five the next morning Hank was sitting in a comfortable leather chair in the office of Douglas Barkley, commander of the Detectives Services Bureau, feeling distinctly uncomfortable. Sitting next to him at the oval meeting table in the corner of Commander Barkley's spacious office was Karen, looking equally as uncomfortable, and next to Karen was Captain Ann Martinez, looking very pissed off. It promised to be an unpleasant start to the morning.

"I suggested this pre-meeting," Commander Barkley began in his rumbling baritone, "because I thought you might wish to clarify things a little before our meeting at nine."

A 51-year-old African-American, Barkley was built like a nose tackle and had the mentality to go with it. Tough, aggressive and unmovable, he had steadily acquired power and influence in the department after parachuting into the organization five years ago along with Chief Bennett and several others from the FBI. As commander of Detective Services he was in the hot seat in a city that had seen the homicide rate rise each year over the last three years. Barkley loved the pressure and he loved to pass it on to his subordinates.

"I appreciate the opportunity to clarify the situation from our point of view," Martinez said.

"Your detectives appear to have interfered with a case belonging to one of Captain Williams's detectives, Captain."

Martinez shrugged. "The file does currently belong to them, but it's my understanding that the detective from the Cold Case Unit was the one who initiated contact with Homicide. Isn't that right, Lieutenant?"

Hank described Waverman's visit to the Homicide bullpen yesterday, their trip to Angel of Mercy hospital, his trip with Josh Duncan to the hotel, the appearance of Josh's two assailants and Hank's unsuccessful attempt to arrest them.

"If the Lieutenant hadn't interrupted them," Karen chipped in, jumping to Hank's defense, "they probably would've stolen Duncan's laptop from the room and hauled him off to work on him some more."

Barkley glanced at her, frowning. When in the presence of the commander, lowly detectives were expected to be seen and not heard. "That's fine," he said in irritation, "I get it. Nonetheless, Captain Williams is well within her rights to insist that the case remain in CCU." Barkley glowered at Martinez. "Don't expect me to play referee between the two of you."

"No, I understand," Martinez replied. "The last thing anyone wants is a pissing match between Major Crimes and Special Investigations. I don't think at any time we gave them the impression that we wanted to take over the case. Correct, Stainer?"

Karen shrugged. "I may have said something like that at first, but Waverman had to leave only a few minutes after we got there, and Hank pretty much saved his ass by going with the kid back to the hotel."

"And yet," Barkley complained, "Captain Williams will no doubt feel that her detective has already been excluded from information obtained from the assault victim at that point."

Martinez shrugged elaborately, knowing full well that Elspeth Williams had already called Barkley to complain bitterly about the intrusion of Homicide into a CCU investigation. Williams and Martinez were fierce rivals and there was no love lost between them.

"We have no interest whatsoever in keeping anything from Detective Waverman," she said dismissively.

"Hank got some additional stuff on the student's connection to the Martin Liu case," Karen said. "He would have passed it on to Waverman except for the fact that the shooting at the hotel made us both late getting back. Waverman was off duty by then." She wanted to make it clear that it was Waverman's bad luck if he hadn't gotten an update on current events.

Barkley harrumphed and shifted his considerable weight. "What position do you intend to take vis-à-vis CCU in this meeting, Captain?"

Martinez spread her hands on the surface of the table as though reluctantly showing her cards. "I'd like my people to stay involved."

"Captain Williams won't be happy with that."

"Given their case load, some sort of compromise should be possible."

"Compromise." Barkley seemed dubious. He looked at his watch and turned to pick up the telephone on the corner of the desk behind him. "Cheryl, have Captain Williams come in now, please."

The door opened and Captain Elspeth Williams and Detective Waverman entered the room. Williams sat down in the vacant chair on Barkley's right and Waverman took the chair on her right, next to Hank.

Waverman had exchanged his blue corduroy jacket for a Harris Tweed edition that he wore over a white shirt open at the collar along with black denim pants. He carried a briefcase in one hand and a cup of coffee in the other. He sat down, nodded to Hank and Karen, positioned his coffee cup on the table close to his right hand, opened his briefcase on his lap, removed the red CCU accordion file that contained his show and tell photocopies from the Martin Liu murder book, placed it on the table in front of him, then followed that with a pen, a notepad, and a black three-ring binder that Hank guessed must be the complete Liu murder book. He closed the briefcase and put it down on the floor against the wall behind him. He opened the notepad, clicked his ballpoint pen, and smiled at Barkley.

"Good morning, Captain," Barkley was saying to Williams, with a brief nod of acknowledgement for Waverman. "Captain Martinez has been providing me with some of the background related to the Liu case. I see Detective Waverman has thoughtfully brought the file along with him, but I understand you have some concerns about Homicide's involvement in the case you'd like to discuss."

Williams nodded curtly, shooting a look at Martinez. "I certainly would."


Twenty minutes later, Karen dropped into her chair and threw a half-empty container of coffee into her waste basket. "Christ, I hate meetings. And what kind of sadist has a meeting to *prepare* for a meeting? Jesus."

Hank said nothing as Captain Martinez crossed the floor to stand at the point where their desks met. "All right, you two. You wanted in on this case, you've got it." She handed Karen the black three-ring binder Waverman had brought to the meeting. "It's a copy, of course. This guy apparently does everything in duplicate and triplicate."

Karen dropped it on her desk. Opened and maintained by each detective during the course of a homicide investigation, a murder book contained every document relevant to the case, from the autopsy report to lab reports, interrogation transcripts, notes, and even news clippings and media transcripts. This murder book, of course, had been maintained by Joe Kalzowski and was relatively thin, as they normally go. Nonetheless, it contained every piece of paper Kalzowski had been able to generate while the file was in his care.

Karen leaned back. "I still don't get why the case wasn't just transferred back to us."

"Politics," Hank said. "Their budget depends in large part on how many cases they work and how many they close, but as soon as Waverman said he was too busy to work the case full time he gave us an opening you could drive a truck through. We do all the heavy lifting, Waverman's name stays on the front of the jacket and CCU takes the lead with the media if we're able to close it. But we're spending CCU's money instead of our own."

"Yes," Martinez said, "remember to inform Detective Waverman when you're going to incur expenses on this thing. An e-mail's good enough."

Karen unclipped her shield from her belt, rubbed it vigorously on the sleeve of her blouse, and clipped it back on again. "I tell you what; I think this Duncan kid's a couple cards short of a full deck."

"The research might be genuine enough," Hank said, "but somebody wants things to stay quiet. We need to talk to him more about it."

"Yeah, well, whatever." Karen rubbed her forehead. "I just wish I was finished with this other thing."

"I thought your testimony wrapped up yesterday morning," Martinez said.

31

Karen sighed, the weight of the world on her shoulders. "Yeah, I got through the cross yesterday, but in the afternoon there were a couple of motions they had to dick around with. I haveta show up again before noon in case there's a redirect. I didn't hear anything, so I have to go on over and check. Goddamned lawyers, in a world of their own. It'd break their neck to text a cop, for chrissakes."

"All right." Martinez crossed her arms, looking at Hank. "You said you were going to move the kid downtown?"

"Into the Ramada, yeah."

"So get that done. Captain Williams agreed to resubmit the drug packets and syringes from the crime scene to the lab for retesting, so stay on top of that. See what you can get out of the student about this research of his."

Hank nodded. "We'll start working the victimology. Talk to family, friends."

Martinez spread her hands. "So go to it."

Hank watched her walk back to her office, then grabbed the telephone book from the bottom drawer of his desk. "I'm going to get the kid moved now. I'll call you later."

Karen stood up and headed for the elevator. "Later, Lou."

He picked up the phone and reserved a room at the Ramada down the street, then looked up the number of Josh's PDA in his notebook and called it. Josh told him he had just received his replacement traveler's checks. He had also cancelled his credit cards and new ones were being arranged for him. Hank told him to check out and take a taxi down to the Ramada.

"I'll meet you there."

"All right, Lieutenant."

Hank spent some time chasing down names, addresses and telephone numbers from his notebook. Then he called Waverman.

"I'm moving the student downtown into the Ramada," Hank said. "I'll put in an expense claim for it and send you an e-mail. All right?"

"All right."

"I'm going over there shortly to ask a few more questions. Want to come along?"

"I wish I could," Waverman said. "We're having a brainstorming session on another case. Everyone attends."

"No problem. You told Barkley you haven't had a chance yet to redo the victimology, so Detective Stainer and I will get started on that today."

"Great. Take care of that, and I'll check on you later."

Hank smiled to himself as he cradled the receiver. Waverman had suddenly gone from driver to passenger in the Liu cold case and Hank knew he was finding the change a little disconcerting. Of course, Hank mused, if Waverman treated Hank and Karen like hired help he could rationalize the situation much more easily in his own mind. It wasn't every day a detective could dump work onto the desk of a lieutenant.

Hank read through the documents in the binder, then went to the photocopier and copied a few selections, which he put in a manila file folder that would serve as his own show and tell file. The file folder went inside a manila envelope. Then he went back to his desk, sent an e-mail to Waverman about the hotel expense, locked the binder in his bottom drawer, got up, lifted his jacket from the back of his chair and, manila envelope in hand, took the elevator down to the main floor. The hotel was four blocks away and he was looking forward to the walk.

# 5

Hank looked out the second-floor window of Josh's new hotel room downtown and saw nothing unusual in the parking lot below. Cooper Street was busy with lunch-hour traffic. He pulled the heavy curtains together and sat down across from Josh at the table in the corner of the room. Josh was powering up his laptop while finishing off the last of his late breakfast. Looking at the ugly bruise on the student's cheek, Hank flexed his sore shoulder. His back was still a little stiff as well, but the walk had helped shake out a few of the kinks.

"Okay," Josh said, swallowing the last bite of his sandwich, "I talked to Dr. Walsh and she told me Dr. and Mrs. Chan signed a limited waiver that allows us to disclose information to the police in situations where a crime may have been committed. What do you need to know?"

"Take me through this thing from the beginning," Hank said, removing his notebook and pen, "starting with the child's name."

"Taylor Chan." Josh crumpled up the paper wrapping from his sandwich and fired a three-point shot into the trash basket next to the bed. "And the crowd goes wild."

Hank smiled. "Played some basketball, did you?"

"Yeah. Thomas Gaines was the only school to offer me a full athletic scholarship. Vanderbilt was my first choice, but they didn't come through. Hey, I was starting point guard my last two years at TGU, and we were conference champions my senior year. Not bad, even if it was Division II."

"You didn't want to walk on at Vanderbilt and take your chances?"

Josh shook his head. "I wouldn't have made it. Too much talent ahead of me. And I needed the scholarship. My dad's a dentist and my mother's his dental hygienist, so we were okay for money, but Dad has a thing about me paying my own way. So I took the full scholarship. It was the right thing to do."

"Apparently it led you into research you find very interesting," Hank said. "Tell me about Taylor Chan."

"As I said, his father's Dr. Michael Chan, an economics professor at State University." Josh moved his cursor around, looking at his laptop screen. "I'm just opening the file with my notes in it." He tapped the touchpad. "His mother's name is Grace Wong. Grace's father's name was Warren Wong and her mother is Anna Liu. Anna Liu is the sister of Stephen Liu, who was the father of Martin Liu."

Hank wrote down the names. "So the boy's mother was related to Martin Liu, is that what you're telling me?"

"That's correct. They were cousins."

"So you're saying that Martin Liu was supposedly reincarnated after

34

his murder as the son of his cousin Grace Chan."

Josh sat back in his chair and folded his arms across his chest. "As many as 25 per cent of documented cases involve alleged reincarnation into the same family. Often while carrying her child the mother has a dream in which a deceased family member announces to her that he or she will be re-incarnated as their child. These are called announcing dreams. More than 75 per cent of all documented cases involve an announcing dream of some kind. Grace Chan had an announcing dream in which her cousin Martin told her he was returning to life as her son."

"A dream," Hank said.

"That's right."

"Did she tell anybody about this dream?"

"Her husband."

"Did her husband tell anyone about the dream?"

"No, according to him he forgot about it. Apparently it happened in her fifth month and stayed in the back of her mind until Taylor was born, but Dr. Chan completely forgot about it until Mrs. Chan reminded him last fall when Taylor started talking about being Martin Liu."

"How'd she feel about this dream at the time? Did she say?"

Josh looked at him. "What you're actually asking is whether or not Mrs. Chan *wanted* her child to be the reincarnation of her cousin. Was her state of mind positive or negative when it came to the possibility that it might be true?"

Hank smiled faintly. "Yeah, that's what I'm asking."

"Dr. Walsh questioned both parents in this regard tangentially," Josh said. "It's part of the interview process. It's important to see whether the parents are pre-disposed to *wishing* that the reincarnation of a family member might happen. Dr. Walsh's technique involves indirection. Her conclusion was that Mrs. Chan was distinctly uncomfortable that her child might be the rein-carnation of her cousin."

"It's not something she particularly wanted," Hank said.

"That's right. It was creeping her out."

"What about the father?"

"Dr. Chan told us he didn't believe in reincarnation. He was con-cerned there might be some clinical reason his son was making these state-ments. He talked to a colleague in the Psychology Department at State, a pro-fessor named Dr. Isaacs. Dr. Isaacs spent some time with Taylor and felt there was nothing clinically wrong with him and recommended to Dr. Chan that he contact Dr. Walsh at Thomas Gaines. Which is how we got involved."

"Okay." Hank leaned back. "So you said the boy's three and a half years old, correct?"

"That's right."

"And how old was he when he started talking about being Martin

35

Liu?"

"Mrs. Chan shot some video last November 15 on the day of Taylor's third birthday when he made a number of statements about being Martin," Josh said. "She told us there were a few other things before that, but she didn't really pay much attention to them at the time. It was only when she thought back that she realized the significance of those earlier statements."

"So this birthday video is the earliest evidence of the kid making these statements?"

"Yeah, that's right."

"I wouldn't mind seeing it some time."

"How about right now?" Josh gestured at his laptop.

"Now?" Hank got up and moved around behind Josh's chair.

"Yeah, I've got all the relevant video documentation here."

Hank raised his eyebrows. "Must be some hard drive in this thing."

"This is my working laptop. There aren't any games on it."

"Not even Solitaire?"

Josh made a face. "It's a Mac. Here, take a look." He used the touch-pad to move his cursor and tapped on an icon on the desktop. A window opened on the screen and the video began to play.

The picture bounced around a little and then steadied. A small Asian boy sat at a kitchen table eating cereal from a bowl.

*"Looks like the battery's okay, Taylor," a female voice said.*

*"Okay, mama," Taylor said, spooning in another mouthful.*

*"It's your birthday today, Taylor. You're three years old. Do you feel all grown up now?"*

*"Not all growed up yet," the boy said.*

*"Uncle Lee and Aunt Mia are coming over today to see you," Grace Chan said, zooming in on her son's face. "You've never met them."*

"That's Dr. Chan's brother and sister-in-law," Josh explained.

*The boy said nothing, eating. The camera zoomed out again.*

*"Aunt Mia says she has a really nice birthday present for you."*

*"Is Aunt Mia Chinese?" Taylor asked, chewing slowly.*

*"Yes, of course she is," Grace Chan said.*

*"When you were a little girl," Taylor said, carefully dipping his spoon into his bowl, "you came over to my house one time and you said you didn't like my mama because she wasn't Chinese."*

*There was a moment of silence. The camera dipped and steadied.*

*"What do you mean, Taylor?" Grace Chan asked, her voice a little high.*

*"When I was Martin," the boy said firmly, playing with the cereal in his bowl, "you didn't like my mama because she wasn't Chinese."*

*"When you were Martin?" Grace Chan repeated, sounding upset.*

36

*"You're Taylor, not Martin. You're Taylor, sweetheart."*

*The boy looked up at her, his expression serious. "When I was Martin you didn't like my mama because her name was Merry and she had blue eyes. And I had green eyes."*

The video abruptly ended.

Hank straightened and put his hands in his pockets. "That was interesting."

Josh nodded. "Yeah. Martin Liu's mother's name is Meredith. She's a Caucasian with blue eyes. Martin's father was Chinese, of course, but Martin did have green eyes."

Hank gestured at the laptop. "How reliable is the video? Did you consider that it might be a fake?"

"We had a low level analysis done and we can't find any evidence that the clip was fabricated or tampered with. No breaks, no audio dubbing."

"The kid might have been following a script."

Josh shrugged. "Maybe. Bear in mind that we don't see it as proof of anything definitive at this point. It's simply a piece of evidence to be considered."

"All right," Hank relented. "So what happened next?"

Josh returned to his notes. "So after the video was taken, the next incident was, uh, well, the same day. Mrs. Chan's cousin Peter visited Taylor. She said that he only comes around on Taylor's birthday to give him a present. It's the only time they see him. According to Mrs. Chan, she was still upset about Taylor's statements on the video at breakfast and she mentioned it to her cousin. She played the video for him and according to her, her cousin became quite concerned."

"Concerned how?"

"I'm not quite sure," Josh admitted. "Mrs. Chan said her cousin began to question Taylor about what he had said that morning. Usually he gives Taylor his present and leaves. Dr. Chan doesn't like him. But this time her cousin asked for tea and sat down with Taylor. After a few minutes, according to Mrs. Chan, the conversation got a little strange."

"How so?"

Josh pointed to the screen. "This is a clip from our interview with Mrs. Chan. I excerpted it from the complete video so I could reference it easily. It's her recollection of Taylor's statements to her cousin Peter." He tapped on an icon and the video began to play.

A young, well-dressed Asian couple was sitting on a sofa in a living room, presumably in the Chan residence. Mrs. Chan was speaking.

*"Peter asked Taylor if he liked to play video games and Taylor said that he did," Grace Chan said. "He has an Xbox. He's quite advanced for his age, and he already can use a computer. He learned his ABCs from a computer*

37

*program over the winter. Anyway, then Taylor said to Peter that he was sorry he didn't tell Peter about the secret bad thing he found out about."*

*A female voice off-camera said, "He said this to Peter?"*

"That's Dr. Walsh," Josh said.

*"Yes," Grace Chan said. "He said, 'I'm sorry I didn't tell you about the secret.' I said, 'What secret?' Taylor said, 'something bad.'"*

*Off-camera, Dr. Walsh asked: "How did Peter react to this?"*

*"He said, 'Who, Taylor? Who was doing it?' Then Taylor said, 'My friend. He played a game where he took people's money but he gave it to these men. They hurt me when I found out. They wanted to know if I told anybody about it and they wouldn't believe me when I said no. I wanted to tell you about it but I didn't have time.'"*

*"A game taking people's money," Dr. Walsh repeated, obviously puzzled.*

*Grace Chan nodded. "That's what he said. Peter asked him again who the friend was but Taylor wouldn't say a name. Then Peter got a very strange look on his face and said, 'Ah, that's all right. I'll find those people and make sure they don't bother you any more.' Taylor said, 'Okay,' and then didn't say anything else about it."*

*"Was there anything else that Taylor said to your cousin at that time that may have related to these memories?"*

*"Peter asked him a question."*

*"What was the question, Mrs. Chan?"*

*Grace Chan looked down at her hands in her lap and said nothing for a few moments. Then she said, "He asked Taylor, 'do you remember who hurt you because you found out about the game?'"*

*"Did Taylor say anything to that?"*

*Grace Chan kept staring at her hands. Her chin trembled slightly. Finally she said, "Yes, he said that Shawn and Gary hurt him."*

*"Shawn and Gary?"*

*"Yes." Grace Chan looked up at Dr. Walsh off-camera. "Peter asked if they were Chinese and Taylor said, no. He said Shawn was a black man and Gary was a white man."*

*"All right. Was there anything else?"*

*Grace Chan glanced reluctantly at her husband, who was obviously unhappy about what his wife was saying.*

*"Anything else?" Dr. Walsh prompted.*

*Grace Chan nodded. "Taylor asked to see Peter's pictures."*

*"Pictures?"*

*Grace Chan wrung her hands in her lap. "Peter said, 'what pictures?' and Taylor said, 'the pictures on your tummy.'"*

*"What did he mean by this?" Dr. Walsh asked.*

"Tattoos," Grace Chan said. "Peter has tattoos on his chest. But he didn't show them to him right away. He asked Taylor what the pictures were like."

"And?"

"Taylor said, um, he said, 'birds, two funny birds with fire. Fire in their mouths.'"

"I don't think we need to go into this at all," Dr. Chan interjected. "This is not relevant. Can we discuss something else? Do you have any other questions, Dr. Walsh?"

"Does your cousin have tattoos on his chest, Mrs. Chan?" Dr. Walsh persisted.

Grace Chan nodded.

"Dr. Walsh, my wife's cousin has absolutely no relevance whatsoever. Can we—"

"Did he show them to Taylor at that time?"

Grace Chan nodded again.

"Dr. Walsh—" Dr. Chan tried again to interrupt.

"How did Taylor react when he saw them?"

"He laughed. He came up to Peter and touched them, and he laughed. Peter said, 'another little secret, right?' and Taylor said, 'another secret.'"

"Had he ever seen them before, Mrs. Chan? Had Peter shown them to him before or mentioned them to him before?"

Grace Chan shook her head. "They're secret tattoos, or whatever. Dragons. To do with Peter's, um, affiliations. He doesn't talk about them with anyone."

"Had anyone ever mentioned them before to Taylor or discussed them in Taylor's hearing?"

"Peter is not talked about in our house," Grace Chan replied, looking miserably at her husband. We don't discuss him around Taylor. So, no, Taylor had no way of knowing that Peter had tattoos, let alone what they looked like."

The video clip ended.

Hank went back to his chair and sat down. He picked up his pen and jotted a few notes in his notebook.

"This cousin Peter have a last name?" he asked, still writing.

"Yeah," Josh said. "It's not Liu. Just a second, I'll find it in my notes." He tapped the touchpad and studied the display. "Here it is. Mah. M-a-h."

"Peter Mah," Hank repeated.

"Yes, that's right."

Hank wrote it down, although he didn't need to. He knew about Peter Mah, and he knew about the significance of the dragon tattoos on his chest.

"There's another one you may want to see," Josh said, tapping again.

"Oh?"

"Dr. Walsh interviewed Taylor on-camera with his mother," Josh explained, "but he wasn't saying anything at all about the previous personality. So she closed it down and we talked about it in a sidebar. She thought maybe I could get him to say a few things if we made him feel more comfortable away from the camera. So I asked him to show me his room. We went into his room and I got him to show me his toys. We left the door open so his parents could hear what was going on and so he felt he could leave whenever he wanted. We just sat down on the floor, the two of us, and played with his toys for a while. I used my PDA to record our conversation."

Hank got up and came around the table again so that he could see the screen over Josh's shoulder.

The video began to play. It was a little grainy, but Hank could plainly see the little boy sitting cross-legged on the floor surrounded by action figures, die-cast cars and other toys. There was a dark shadow on the left edge of the frame.

"That's my knee," Josh explained. "I put my PDA up on top of a dump truck. He didn't really pay any attention to it. I think he considered it one of my toys and wasn't interested in playing with it."

*"Now I'm going to drive home," Taylor said, pushing a car across the carpet.*

*"Where have you been?" Josh asked.*

*"At work," Taylor replied. "I work at a big school, like Daddy."*

*"So do I," Josh said, playing with another car. "It's fun."*

*"Yeah." Taylor left his car behind a pile of books. "Now I'm at home."*

*"Okay. Now what are you going to do?"*

*"Play, before supper time." Taylor picked up an action figure and waved it around.*

*Josh picked up another figure and pointed it at Taylor.*

*"Bang, bang. Gotcha."*

*Taylor stiffened, staring at Josh, and dropped his action figure. He said nothing for a moment, then slowly reached for a colored block. He took several blocks and started making a pile in front of his crossed legs.*

*Josh picked up the action figure that Taylor had dropped and held it out, but Taylor ignored it.*

*"Come on, Taylor. Let's play guns."*

*Taylor shook his head emphatically, adjusting the pile of blocks in front of him.*

*"Don't you like playing guns, Taylor?"*

*Taylor said nothing, looking down at his blocks.*

*"Do you have any toy guns, Taylor?"*

*"No."*

*"How come? Are you afraid of guns?"*

*Taylor said nothing for a few moments, playing with his blocks. Finally he murmured, "He hurt me. In the leg."*

*"Who hurt you?"*

*"With his gun."*

*"Who hurt you in the leg, Taylor?"*

*"That man."*

*"Who, what man?"*

*"Shawn. He was a black man, like you, but he didn't have no hair."*

*"No hair?"*

*"Yeah."*

*"Shawn hurt you?" Josh asked.*

*"Gary was yelling and Shawn kept hitting me with the gun and it went bang and hurt my leg and there was blood."*

*"That's terrible," Josh said. "Where did this happen, Taylor?"*

*Taylor did not reply. He stared down at his blocks, not moving.*

The video clip ended and Josh looked over his shoulder at Hank. "That was it. He didn't want to talk about it any more."

Hank realized he'd been holding his breath. He sat down again and jotted in his notebook. "So that gives the two names coming from him, not just from the parent. Interesting. There seemed to be emotion behind it."

"Yeah. Dr. Walsh has had a number of experiences with children who've been coached by someone in what to say," Josh said. "She feels very strongly that Taylor's statements are spontaneous."

"I have to admit," Hank said, still writing, "this is very strange stuff. You've seen children make these kinds of statements before?"

"Well, only the one time before personally. But I've watched a lot of video of other interviews as part of my dissertation research and a lot of it's just like this. It can give you the chills. It's like another person, an adult, speaking through the mouth of a child." Josh laughed nervously. "Which is what it may actually be, another person speaking to us about their past life and their death."

Hank set aside his pen and looked at him. "It's hard to swallow. I mean, rationally, there's nothing in our modern culture to prepare us for this kind of concept. People want to believe in life after death, but the fact of the matter is that we live in a scientific age with a very mechanistic view of existence that prefers to explain phenomena in purely physical and biological terms."

Josh looked at him speculatively. "You sure you're a cop?"

"Hey, I went to school too, you know."

"Police Academy, right?"

Hank pointed at him. "Don't be condescending."

Josh looked stricken. "I'm sorry."

41

"Fact is, son, I earned three university degrees and passed this state's bar exams by the time I was 22 years old," Hank said. "*Then* I went to the academy."

"Sorry, I didn't mean to insult you or anything."

"So do you have anything else I should see?"

Embarrassed, Josh deliberated for a moment, poking around in the files on his computer. Then he nodded. "Yes, there is, actually. I was just looking at my notes again. It's not a video clip, just a piece of information. Actually, a couple of photos. Hang on a sec."

"Photos?"

"Mmm." Josh tapped the touchpad. "Taylor has a birthmark. Two birthmarks." He looked at Hank. "This part of our research is really quite amazing. Sixty per cent of reported cases of past life memory by children include a birthmark or physical defect that corresponds in some way to a wound or blemish or other physical characteristic of the previous personality. These marks are checked against post-mortem records whenever possible."

"You're saying these children have the same kind of birthmarks as the person they're supposed to have been in the previous life?"

Josh shook his head. "No, what I'm saying is that the child often has a birthmark or other physical defect that corresponds to the cause of death of the previous personality. If the previous personality was shot, they have a birthmark where the bullet entered the body. Sometimes they have two birthmarks, one for the entrance wound and one for the exit wound."

Hank stared at him. "I find that very hard to believe."

"I know, when you see the photos, it freaks you right out. I've looked at files with post-mortem photos of gunshot wounds right next to photos of a child's birthmarks, and it's uncanny, the resemblance between the two."

"I don't see how that's possible."

"It's very strange," Josh acknowledged, "and very hard to explain. Dr. Ian Stevenson, who pioneered this field at the University of Virginia beginning in the 1960s, did a lot of work in this area. In a book called *Reincarnation and Biology* he documented 225 of these cases. He compared the birthmarks to the Stigmata, the wounds people can develop that resemble the wounds of Christ, and he also compared them to known cases in which people develop blisters or burn marks through hypnotic suggestion. His point was that the mind can do things we really don't understand very well. I could lend you a very interesting book by Dr. Jim B. Tucker that explains it a lot better than I can."

"I still don't understand what you're driving at. You're saying that a person's mind can somehow subconsciously reproduce wounds as birthmarks in their next life?"

"It may be possible."

"But when a person dies, their mind dies too. I mean, blood stops flowing to the brain, the brain dies, it's game over."

"The brain dies," Josh agreed. "In a *mechanistic* world view this means that whatever went into the makeup of the person also dies. But it's possible that the mind is not the same thing as the brain. What if the mind is a phenomenon that interacts both at the physical level with the brain and at the metaphysical level with the soul or some other mode of being that we don't really understand very well right now?"

Hank shook his head. "I don't see how anyone can answer that question."

Josh leaned forward and gestured with his hands. "See, it could be that in some cases where the personality is very strong, the soul or the spirit of that person somehow holds on to self-awareness from one life to the next, long enough to articulate certain memories in early childhood after gaining the power of speech. Memories of a violent death would be particularly vivid, and it may be possible that these traumatic memories play themselves out in the new mind, while still in the womb, in such a way that wounds are reproduced as birthmarks just as burns or blisters can be produced through hypnosis, by the mind acting on the body in ways we don't completely understand. Dr. Tucker refers to this as trauma transfer, the carrying over of traumatic emotion from one life to the next and the manifestation of that emotion in certain physical characteristics."

Hank shrugged. "Pretty far-fetched. What does this have to do with Taylor Chan? Are you telling me he has a birthmark that matches the gunshot wound of Martin Liu?"

Josh turned the laptop around so that Hank could see the screen. "These are two pics of birthmarks that Taylor has on his left thigh. The one on the left is from the front; the one on the right is from the back. The one on the left looks like a round puncture wound, like an entrance wound, and the one on the right, on the back of his leg, is larger and more ragged, like a severe exit wound. Is this where Martin Liu was shot?"

Hank stared at the screen.

"See, that's what I was originally supposed to do today, come down and see you guys."

"See us guys?"

"Yeah, the police. To request access to Martin Liu's autopsy report. It's something we try to do in each case where there's some kind of physical defect or birthmark. To match them up. Can I do that?"

"I'll see what I can do," Hank said after a moment. "Can I get copies of these pictures?"

"Sure," Josh said. He leaned down, dragged over his computer bag and removed a small photo printer not much bigger than his hand. He set it up on the table and plugged it into the laptop.

"You guys must have some budget," Hank said.

"Oh, it's just a little direct printer that runs off a USB port."

"Right, you can also use them with digital cameras."

"Yeah. This only prints four by six. I hope that's okay."

"No problem."

The printer came to life and began printing the first photo.

"So when do you think I'll be able to see the autopsy report on Martin Liu?"

Hank took the first photo from the printer and examined it as the second one began to print. "I think maybe we should do this in a particular order, Josh. First comes the active homicide investigation under the jurisdiction of the police and then afterwards a research case into reincarnation once all the shooting and assaulting and fun and games are cleared away. All right?"

Josh's eyes fell. "Sure. I understand."

"Once the dust settles you can see whatever's in the file that's relevant to your research."

"Thanks."

Hank nodded. "All right, then." He tucked the photos into his manila envelope and stood up. "Do me a favor and stay put for a while. Order room service for your meals. I'm not exactly sure what those guys have in mind, but I think it's better that they not find you again."

"Okay," Josh agreed fervently. "I'm all for that. I have absolutely no desire to run into them again. I have a bunch of stuff to catch up on anyway, e-mails, updates to my reports, check in with Dr. Walsh. I'll be busy."

Hank left him in the hotel room. Waiting for the elevator, he pulled out his cell phone and called Karen.

"You free?"

"Yeah," she replied in a disgusted tone. "Bastards kept me waiting while they had some fuckin' meeting or other, then treated me like a droolin' imbecile for wasting time cuz I waited around for them. Bottom line, I'm done."

"Great. Come pick me up at the Ramada. We'll go talk to some people."

"Be there in ten."

"You're a jewel," Hank said, and closed his phone.

# 6

Peter Mah sat by himself at a small table in the back corner of the Bright Spot Restaurant near the swinging doors that led into the kitchen. It was a beat-up dump on Lexington Street in the heart of Chinatown that featured an old smoke-stained tin ceiling and booths with cracked red vinyl. A bar made of scrap wood and pieces of wall paneling ran down the middle of the seating area. The Bright Spot was owned by a numbered company controlled by Peter, and he used the entire top floor of the three-story building for his home and office. The second floor was split into a large apartment and several rooms. The apartment was used by the restaurant manager, Yi, and his family. The rooms were for other employees of Peter who needed a place to sleep while on call. Behind Peter was a staircase that led upstairs. There was also a fire escape in back. Security was not a problem, since Peter had installed state-of-the-art technology throughout the building that was backed up by a great deal of firepower in the hands of his employees.

A few old men sat at a table nearby amusing themselves with a game of fan tan, tea cups at their elbows and hand-rolled cigarettes dangling from their lips. Yi had emerged from the kitchen where Millie Lung, the cook, was overseeing preparations for the dinner rush. He sat on a stool at the bar reading a Chinese newspaper. The waiter, Yi's brother-in-law Wu, was behind the bar talking quietly on the telephone to his wife, Yi's older sister. The conversation was not going well. It was well known that Wu's wife kept him constantly in debt. She seemed to be asking him for money for something. There was little that Wu could do about it except say yes, since Yi was sitting there listening to every word he said.

Peter was glad he was single. It kept his options open. He was 31 years old and very good-looking, with boyish tousled long hair worn in a fashionable retro Beatles cut that was carefully maintained on a weekly basis by his personal hairdresser in the salon above the Golden Dragon. He wore a thousand-dollar black suit, a crisp white shirt and a pearl grey Hermès tie. He wore a diamond stud on each earlobe and sported a Breitling chronometer on his wrist. He also had a Glock 27 sub-compact .40 caliber hand gun in a holster on his belt under his jacket. He liked the gun because it was small and light. His fingers were delicate and slender, and the gun fit comfortably in his hand without the need of a grip extender. He was not sure if there was a license around somewhere for it. His cousin Stevie had given it to him a year ago and he kept it because he liked it as a possession, just as he also liked the Breitling or the iPhone sitting on the table in front of him, propped up on an angle against a thick white napkin. His eyes were currently focused on the screen, watching a horse race on which he had wagered ten grand. He was listening to a Cantonese feed through the wireless earbud in his right ear. He was going to

45

lose the ten grand. Whatever.

He started to think about ordering lunch. His personal chef, Daniel Chun, had said something this morning about fresh cantaloupes he'd just received and a recipe for *mut gua op sah lud*, roast duck and melon salad that he wanted to try. Peter thought it sounded good. He was looking forward to a quiet meal. However, it was not meant to be.

Footsteps across the floor of the dining area brought his eyes up as Billy Fung and Tang Lei slouched toward him. Billy had his hands shoved into the pockets of his plum-colored jacket. Tang's hands hung empty at his sides. They were alone. Sighing, Peter removed the earbud and dropped it into his jacket pocket.

"Imagine my disappointment when you did not return yesterday from the errand on which I sent you," Peter said.

They stood at the edge of the table. It was understood they were not allowed to sit down. Billy was seven years younger than Peter and anxious to please. Tang, on the other hand, was an older man, in his middle thirties. He was stolid and stupid. Unimaginative in his leather jacket and cowboy boots. Also quite sadistic, particularly with his hands and feet. They stood side by side, eyes lowered. Although much younger than Tang, Billy was the one who was required to answer Peter's question. He grimaced unhappily.

"We went to the hospital but he was already gone. So we went to the hotel to see if he was there, but the police showed up right away. In the room, just when we started to search it."

"Was the student there?"

"No. Just the cop. I have no idea why he was there. We ran out of the room. I fired a shot into the ceiling to slow him down when he tried to chase us. No one was hurt, though. Him and another cop, a girl, chased us around. When we got down to the car we didn't want them to follow us back here so we drove across the river and stayed at my cousin's place in Wilmingford last night until things died down."

"You couldn't call? Let me know what was going on? Send a text?"

"I was going to but my cell battery's dead. I can show you." He reached into his jacket pocket.

Peter shook his head sternly. "Was there anything in the room that would have been useful?"

"I think there was a laptop computer on the desk," Billy said, glancing sideways at Tang. "We were searching the desk when the cop came in. We didn't have a chance to grab the laptop."

"I see." Peter swallowed his disappointment and thought for a minute. "Who was the cop? Did you know him?"

Tang shook his head. "No."

Peter did not acknowledge Tang, whom he felt was a burden around his neck. The son-in-law of someone important in Hong Kong, Tang had been here for just over a year. He needed a place to stay in America while some kind of trouble back home died down, and Peter had agreed to keep him for a while.

Billy, on the other hand, had been with Peter for a very long time. Peter had recruited him into his street gang, the Biu Ji Boys, when Billy was still in grade school and Peter was a teenager making a name for himself. He brought him along slowly. When Peter accepted responsibilities from the society, leaving the Biu Ji gang behind for others to run, he brought Billy with him and gave him more important things to do than housebreaking and smashing store windows. He'd hoped that the young man was capable of living up to his expectations, but now Peter had serious doubts.

"I've seen him before," Billy said. "He's an older guy, brown fuzzy hair. Big guy. Can't remember his name. I'm pretty sure he's in homicide now but used to be in juvie. Been around a long time."

"Homicide," Peter repeated. He wasn't sure which cop it might be, so he made a mental note to ask his police insider. It didn't follow that a homicide detective would show up at the hotel room of the student just because of the beating. There must be a connection to Martin's murder. Perhaps Martin's case had been re-activated.

Beating up the student had been a mistake, and Peter had already chastised Billy for it. He understood that Billy had acted with Peter's welfare in mind, thinking the student belonged to the R Boyz gang and was looking to cause Peter trouble, but it was a mistake in judgment and Billy knew that now. Yesterday's errand had been an opportunity to recover face, to bring the student back to Peter for a conversation. The student needed to explain why Peter's name was written in the notebook taken from the knapsack, in addition to other things about his cousin Martin. The student also needed to explain his interest in Martin's murder. Instead of recovering face, however, Billy had made things worse. He'd evidently been seen by a police detective and had fired a shot, then didn't show up to explain to Peter what had happened. It was a fuck-up, and Peter was very unhappy about it.

Peter made a small gesture with his hand. The two men bowed and withdrew to the bar, where Yi shook out his newspaper and stared at them. They sat on stools and began to badger Wu for something to drink. Wu looked flustered and hung up the phone.

Peter looked at his iPhone. The race was over and an announcer was talking about something else. He touched the earbud in his pocket but did not take it out. He needed to think things through. His search for the killer of Martin Liu had been fruitless until last November, when his cousin's little boy had started talking about things he could not possibly know. The boy said two men had hurt him, and Peter had asked his police contact to follow up on the names for him. There had been nothing. Now, however, it appeared the police might have re-activated the investigation.

47

Peter had wasted time thinking that Martin had been killed during a power struggle between Lam Chun Sang, the current leader of the local Triad society, whose title was *Shan Chu*, or Dragon Head, and Philip Ling, a prominent member of the society who had opposed Lam. At the time, Peter was in the process of consolidating his position as *Hung Kwan*, or Red Pole, the enforcer of the society, and had assembled a very tough group around him. The brotherhood was in turmoil. The previous Dragon Head, Bernard Ho, was an ambitious but not especially bright man in his middle thirties who had become very rich smuggling counterfeit designer clothing and jewelry. Ho had spent a great deal of money getting himself elected Dragon Head. Unfortunately Ho had proven to be very weak and susceptible to influence, and his term had been marred by violence and infighting as several factions struggled for control.

The council that governed the business of the local society elected a new Dragon Head every two years. The Dragon Head functioned like a chairman of the council, overseeing the flow of business within the society, ensuring that the families of society brothers were taken care of, resolving disputes in a fair and appropriate way, even smoothing things over with law enforcement when necessary to minimize trouble for the brotherhood. The Dragon Head must not only be successful in his own right but also be someone who understood the traditional values of the society, values that included loyalty, integrity, trust and respect. Unfortunately Ho was more interested in money and popularity. His policies and decisions depended on whom he spoke to last, and often rival factions battled among themselves without realizing until it was too late that their conflict had been exacerbated by Ho's duplicity. The uncles, the elders of the society, struggled to maintain their temper until Ho's term stumbled to an end.

Once Ho was gotten rid of, the uncles insisted that one of them must step in to restore order to the brotherhood. Infighting was too bitter and deep-rooted to allow someone from one side to take control of the society to the detriment of their opponents. Lam Chun Sang agreed to come forward from among the uncles as a candidate. Known as Uncle Sang, he exerted a great deal of pressure on the brotherhood to fall into line behind him and ultimately won the election. Philip Ling was one of the most vocal of the dissenters among the brotherhood and refused to withdraw his own candidacy, but his supporters soon saw the wisdom in quietly acknowledging their loyalty to Uncle Sang. After Uncle Sang won the election, Peter's job as Red Pole was to bring the rest of the troublemakers into step. Philip posed the greatest challenge, as he continued to cause a great deal of trouble for Uncle Sang after his defeat, especially among the elders in Hong Kong. He refused to listen to reason, insisting that the election of an uncle as Dragon Head violated the traditions of the society. Ultimately it was judged necessary to eliminate him from the equation altogether.

First Peter had one of Philip's lieutenants killed as a warning that Philip should leave. The idea was that he should sell his business interests and his home, pack up his wife and children and whatever possessions he wanted to keep, and move away. It was a drastic step, as the brotherhood hated violence among themselves, but there seemed to be no alternative.

Unfortunately, Philip did not take the hint. Instead, he killed one of Uncle Sang's nephews in retaliation. Peter did not hesitate. He picked up Philip's security detail, a group of five men, and shot them all. Himself, personally, in a riverfront warehouse leased by one of Philip's businesses. He could have delegated it to his men, but his strong loyalty to Uncle Sang made him very angry at Philip's defiance, and the killing of the nephew was the last straw. Philip's home was burned and his wife and children were taken and bundled off to Hong Kong. Isolated, Philip lashed out, wounding one of Peter's men in a gun battle along the river. The next day Martin was found dead in the alley, and the dressing of the scene with heroin and syringes made Peter immediately think of Philip, since one of Philip's business interests was a distribution network for heroin.

Peter spread the word that Philip Ling's life was forfeit. Philip went into hiding and eventually surfaced in Hong Kong. Peter traveled there to find him. Philip disappeared again, perhaps to the Philippines, and Peter returned to the United States. Shortly thereafter Philip returned to America and made an attempt on Peter's life by hiring one of Peter's own men, Foo Yee, to kill him. Foo told Peter about it. Peter caught Philip by pretending to be Foo coming around to pick up his payment for the dirty deed. Peter worked very hard to force a confession from Philip that he was responsible for Martin's death. Philip denied it to the very end. His last words, forced through bloody lips, were: *I don't know who that is.*

Wasted time. While the real killers of Martin went free.

Now his cousin Grace's little boy was saying crazy things about having been Martin in his previous life. He knew things about Peter that he should not know. He was only three years old; how would he know these things? Grace swore she never talked to the child about Peter. Or about Martin, for that matter. What to think?

Peter was ready to believe what the child was saying. He had begun a search for Shawn and Gary, the two men the boy said had hurt him. He asked his police contact to run the names in the system, but there was nothing useful. Then the university student showed up. Peter wanted to know everything the student was finding out. However, now that the police were apparently involved again in the investigation of Martin's murder he was thinking it might be best if Grace and Taylor no longer dealt with them. He needed to find out the name of the cop. He also needed to talk to Grace, to tell her that little Taylor should be kept quiet. Grace should not talk to the police or the student, and Taylor should definitely not talk to them. He must go and see her right away.

49

He must make sure that she would stay quiet.

Peter chewed on his lower lip irritably. The renewal of the search for Martin's killers was taking time from his primary responsibilities. Uncle Sang had ordered him to investigate rumors that someone was doing business with outsiders in a way that was detrimental to the society. The fact that these rumors had come to the attention of the council via Hong Kong only made it worse. Dealing with outsiders was not forbidden *per se*, but if it was against the interests of the brotherhood it was a violation of the thirtieth oath and punishable by death. Diverting revenue that should benefit the families of the brotherhood was construed by the Dragon Head as just such a violation, and it was Peter's job as the Red Pole to enforce the oaths and punish violators. It was not up to him to make value judgments, merely to find the wrongdoers and deliver their punishment.

Peter had talked to a few people and everyone swore they knew nothing about anyone doing anything irregular. Idiots. But he had deliberately started with the individuals he had known to be fools, in order that word might spread throughout the society that Peter Mah was looking into things. Hopefully fear would make the guilty party careless and therefore easier to catch. However, even if the traitor were intelligent and brave, Peter would catch him anyway.

He was very good at his job.

Very good indeed.

# 7

"What's up with you and driving?" Karen glanced over as she changed lanes and accelerated into a hole in the heavy traffic ahead of them.

"Not sure what you mean," Hank said, watching the pedestrians along the street.

"Sure you do. You never want to do the driving."

"I prefer to be a passenger. Get to see more stuff."

"Do you even *have* a driver's license?"

"Of course I do."

Karen grunted. "Not that I care, mind, because I'd rather drive, but it gets me curious."

"Don't ask dumb questions."

"Okay, okay." She lifted a hand from the steering wheel in surrender. "Driving's a control issue and I wouldn't have thought you were the passive type."

"Control issue. Passive type."

She shrugged. "Guys in law enforcement are almost never passive types. Even Waverman makes a big deal about being in the driver's seat and who all sits where and who can roll down the window and who can't. He's got a control-oriented personality on top of being a wiener. But you ride everywhere. You scrounge rides or pay for a taxi. I don't get it."

"I like to look around," Hank said again. "Somebody else stares at the bumper ahead of us while I check out what's happening around me."

"Mmm." Karen lifted her eyes from the car ahead of them to glance right and left. Then she sighed. "So is Duncan completely nuts, or what?"

Hank filled her in on what Josh had told him. He described the video clips he had watched, he went over the family connections and he finished with Peter Mah.

"Nobody mentioned a Triad connection to the Liu killing," Karen said.

"Yeah, I know. It didn't come up. Joe didn't say anything about it, and I didn't see anything in the book about it."

"Well, no offense, Lou, but the investigation was a little superficial, don't you think?"

"It was a busy time," Hank said, "but I guess he was satisfied with the way it appeared. It looked like a drug deal gone bad."

"That how you saw it?"

Hank looked out the window. "No," he said finally, "not when I think back. I remember thinking that what I was seeing didn't jibe with the story. The drug stuff was supposed to suggest he'd been trying to work a sale and got beat up and shot for trespassing, but it was clear from the evidence he'd been shot somewhere else and transported there. Which made the drug sale narrative bogus."

"And so?"

Hank shrugged. "It was Joe's case, he had the lead. I was busy with other stuff. Then after he left it got sent to Cold Case along with his other open files. One of those things."

"So now we're driving all the way out to Springhill to check on the story of a concussed student who thinks some little kid knows about a murder that happened before he was born. This'll be good, huh?"

"I'm curious," Hank said, twisting in his seat to stare at her. "How does Sandy put up with your sarcasm and heavy attitude?"

"He thinks it's a major turn-on."

"Oh, wait, his mouth is just as trashy as yours, isn't it?"

"Not as. Feds have to have a little more polish than your average city cop." Karen's boyfriend, John "Sandy" Alexander, was a field agent with the FBI's local office. So far, the relationship had lasted for two years.

"Fung," Hank said suddenly.

"What's wrong?"

"Nothing," Hank said. "Fung. William Fung, a.k.a. Billy Boy. Fung."

"What about him?"

"That's who that was at the hotel. The guy in the purple jacket." Hank nodded. "I knew it'd come back to me. He's one of Peter Mah's employees. The other guy I don't know."

"And Peter Mah's Triad."

"Yeah. Mah ran his own gang as a juvenile fifteen years ago, the Biu Ji Boys. They were into typical street gang stuff, home invasions, extortion, distribution. His father, Jerome Mah, is said to have connections to the 14K Triad. The idea is that Peter grew up and joined the Big Leagues."

"Jerome Mah, the importer, is his father?"

"Yeah."

"Wow." Karen looked impressed. "He's big. Very big. And he's Triad, too?"

"I've been sitting here trying to remember. I don't get down into Chinatown very often. Yesterday morning, in fact, was the first time in months. As far as Jerome's concerned I'm not sure, but I've heard he's cooperative with them and is connected through his business to known Triad figures."

Karen accelerated up the ramp onto the expressway that would take them out to Springhill. "So the old man's not a Triad official, just an associate?"

"Could be. But Peter's said to be the Red Pole of the local society, responsible for enforcement, security, that sort of thing. He's got a bunch of guys working for him, including Fung."

"So riddle me this, Batman." Karen moved into the inside lane of the expressway and pushed the Crown Vic close to the speed of sound. "Why the hell is a Triad Red Pole leaning on a university grad student working a cock-and-bull reincarnation gig with a three-year-old kid? Why does this make perfect sense to the rest of the universe but not to me?"

Hank shrugged. "Maybe Peter Mah believes in reincarnation."

"Ha ha, very funny."

"Who knows? Maybe he does. Or maybe because it's his cousin and it's a family thing. Or maybe Martin Liu worked for the Triad and Peter screwed up the protection."

"And now he feels guilty and wants to find out who killed his cousin and whack their sorry ass."

"Could be. Maybe he's grasping at straws and thinks the kid'll say something that'll give him an idea of where to look. I don't know."

"Maybe somebody in OCU knows something," Karen said. "Who's the Asian specialist?"

Hank wasn't sure if Karen was kidding or not. The department's Organized Crime Unit was fairly small and spent most of its time liaising with the FBI or gathering and publishing statistics. During a budget crunch several years ago the original OCU had merged with the Anti-Gang Unit, a flashy, media-savvy outfit created during more prosperous times, and the resulting unit had been severely downsized. Most of the high-flying performers had jumped ship, and those left behind were generally viewed as a collection of computer jockeys and pencil pushers who were passive to the point that they might be mistaken for book-keepers at a suburban country club.

"It used to be Melton," he said. "I think he's still there." It had been a while since Hank had dealt with the Intelligence Division.

"Don't know him."

"He's been around for a long time."

"Yeah, well, so's the paper towel dispenser in the women's washroom," Karen said, "but I couldn't pick it out of a lineup if I had to."

"Ouch."

"Whatever. What the fuck's the address again?"

"It's 46 Parkland Crescent, same as it was fifteen minutes ago." Hank glanced at his watch. "Let's get something to eat first."

"Drive-through," Karen said.

"That's fine. It's my turn."

"Damn right it is."

Karen worked her way over to Ellison Avenue, the main commercial thoroughfare in Springhill, and drove past muffler shops, strip malls, hardware stores, electronics outlets and furniture shops before finding the fast food outlet she wanted. While they waited in line Hank reached into the back seat and dug out his show and tell file from the manila envelope. Karen pulled up to the microphone and gave their order: a grilled chicken Caesar salad and tea for her and a double burger with fries and a large root beer for him. Hank gave her the money when they reached the window and took the paper sack from her so that she could grab the beverages and stick them into the cup holders in the console between them. She drove the Crown Vic over to a spot at the far edge of the parking lot and shut off the engine. They dug into their food. Hank continued to look through the file.

"Check this out," Hank said, passing her an autopsy photograph.

"What am I looking at?" she said around a mouthful of salad.

"Bullet wound on Martin Liu. Inner left thigh, about three inches up from the knee."

"Yeah. So?" She swallowed. "Got one at the scene?"

Hank sorted through the file and pulled out another photo.

"Not much blood," she said, forking more salad into her mouth while she studied the photograph.

Hank didn't answer, being fully occupied with a mouthful of hamburger. Instead, he passed her one of the four-by-sixes that Josh had given him.

Karen studied it, frowning. "What the hell is this now?"

Hank swallowed, took a long drink of root beer, swallowed, touched his napkin to his lips and flicked the corner of the photo with his finger. "Josh Duncan tells me it's a pic of the Chan kid's leg. He has a birthmark in the same place as the Liu bullet wound."

"Bullshit." Karen propped the photo on the steering wheel and fumbled to get the autopsy photo back out from underneath the plastic salad container on her lap. She took the two photos in her hands and held them side by side. "Damned if they don't look the same. Gotta be a fake."

"We'll find out."

"Jesus," Karen said.

"I know, it's creepy. There's more."

"Why am I not surprised."

"The gunshot wound was a through and through. Kid has another birthmark on the back of his thigh."

"Jesus Christ." Karen held out her hand. "Let's see."

Hank juggled his half-eaten hamburger while he shuffled through the collection of autopsy photos. They were both completely oblivious to the graphic nature of the images. Hank occasionally wondered if it was a good thing to become that insensitive to such violent disruptions of the human body. He pulled out the photo of the back of Martin Liu's thigh and gave it to her.

"Here's the kid's other birthmark," he said, finding the second picture that Josh Duncan had printed out for him.

Karen held them side by side. "Is this for real?"

"Looks like."

54

Karen handed him the pictures and turned her attention back to her lunch. "Who gives a shit," she muttered, chewing. "We're not investigating a reincarnation hoax, we're investigating a murder. What we want is evidence that's admissible in court, not a bunch of paranormal bullshit off of late night TV. This stuff about the kid has zippo to do with Martin Liu."

Hank crumpled up his burger wrapper and shoved it in the paper sack with the empty cardboard sleeve that had held his french fries. He rammed the empty root beer cup on top and handed the bag to Karen.

"This kid's talking about the murder," Hank said, "coming up with names and details we haven't heard before. I don't believe in reincarnation any more than you do, and I don't believe this is the voice of Martin Liu talking through a three-year-old kid. Somebody around him must be talking about the murder and mentioning these names. I'd love to talk to these people to see if they know stuff they haven't bothered to tell us up to now."

"Sounds good to me," Karen said. She got out of the car and walked over to the nearest trash can, which was already overflowing with excess fast food packaging and other garbage. She shoved at the overflow, made a little space and crammed in their garbage with a mean expression on her face. As she walked back to the car her plastic salad container wormed back out of the trash can and fell on the ground. She got into the car and swore.

"You know, back home when I was a sophomore in high school I worked at one of these dumps and got stuck doing lot and lobby all summer. What I'd like to know is why these fuckin' idiots don't bother emptying out the trash bins anymore. Look at it. Goddamned disgrace."

She started the engine and gunned out of the parking lot into traffic. "What's the fuckin' address again?"

"Forty-six Parkland Crescent," Hank said, "same as it was ten minutes ago."

"I don't know why I put up with this bullshit from you." She glanced in her mirrors and switching lanes so violently that Hank was thrown against the door, sending a little shock of pain through his sore shoulder.

"Because you love me so much," Hank gritted.

"In your dreams, pal."

Fourteen minutes later Karen pulled up in front of an immaculate split level home on a quiet residential street with a grassy boulevard down the middle and mature maple trees lining both sidewalks. Hank studied the house for a moment, taking in the white siding and black trim, the green lawn and tidy gardens, the curtained windows and the big white front door with its large brass knocker.

"Nobody home."

"Looks like," Karen agreed.

They got out of the car and strolled up the front walk. On the left was a paved driveway leading to a double garage with big white doors. At the side of the garage was one of those big plastic bins that people put their garbage in to protect it from wandering dogs, raccoons and other prying vermin. Hank went straight for the bin while Karen went up the steps and pressed the door bell.

Hank lifted the lid and saw an aluminum garbage can and two recycling bins, one containing soda cans and empty bottles and the other holding paper waste. He took the lid off of the aluminum can and saw nothing promising. The smell of rotten fish assailed his nostrils and he put the lid back on. He moved on to the recycling bin with the paper. He was shuffling through advertising fliers when Karen came up behind him.

"Anything good?"

Hank pulled out a piece of paper. "Here we go." It was an internet printout of a real estate listing for a commercial property in South Shore West. There was a little picture of Grace Chan as the listing agent, along with the address and telephone number of the real estate office in Springhill where she worked.

Karen took it and folded it in half. "Anything else?"

"Naw." Hank rooted around a little more and saw one or two other property listings but nothing else of interest.

"Probably conscientious shredders," she said. "Takes all the fun out."

"Let's go before someone calls the cops."

Karen laughed.

They reached the real estate office twenty minutes later and swung into the small parking lot between it and a place that sold lawn mowers, chain saws and leaf blowers. Karen parked and they went inside. Although the outside was nothing special to look at, the inside was very sumptuously furnished. The receptionist sat at a glass desk with a discreet computer and telephone system on her right and a combined printer, copier and fax machine on her left. She wore clothing that might have come from the closet of a movie star. She was so beautiful it almost hurt the eyes to look at her directly. A small name plate on the desk declared that her name was Brandi Lemaire.

Karen rapped her knuckles on the glass desk. "Looking for Grace Chan."

Brandi Lemaire smiled. "Do you have an appointment?"

Karen badged her with a bored expression on her face.

"She's with a client, but they should be finished very soon."

"We'll wait."

Hank sat down in a leather-upholstered armchair and looked through a doorway into a little kitchenette. If they had been prospective clients Brandi would probably be offering them coffee and croissants right now, but since they were cops the best they could hope for was to be politely ignored.

After a few minutes a door opened down the hallway behind the re-

56

ception desk and three people came out. An older couple chatted briefly with a small Asian woman before shaking her hand and heading for the exit. Hank recognized Grace Chan. He stood up just as Brandi was pointing them out to her.

"Mrs. Chan?" he asked, stepping forward and showing his badge, "I'm Lieutenant Donaghue from Homicide and this is Detective Stainer. May we have a few minutes of your time?"

Grace Chan looked at them, flustered. "Homicide? I have another appointment in ten minutes."

"This won't take long," Hank said.

Grace Chan gestured behind her. "In my office." She led the way back down the hallway into a large office with a desk and computer, a meeting table with four chairs, and a row of filing cabinets. "Please, sit down," she said, indicating the meeting table.

They sat down and Hank looked at Karen. She looked back without expression. He turned to Grace Chan.

"We're investigating the murder of Martin Liu," Hank began. "I understand he was your cousin."

"Yes, that's correct," Grace said. "My mother, Anna Liu, and Martin's father, Stephen Liu, were brother and sister." She frowned. "But he died several years ago, and nothing has happened. Is the case being reopened?"

"We're taking another look at it," Hank said. "You and your husband have been consulting with Dr. Walsh from Thomas Gaines University in Memphis and a grad student of hers, Josh Duncan, with regard to your son, Taylor, is that correct?"

She nodded, reluctantly.

"Are you also related to a man named Peter Mah? Another cousin?"

"Yes, his mother was my mother's sister."

Karen leaned forward and gave Grace her cop scowl. "Josh Duncan was assaulted two days ago by a couple of men who work for Peter Mah. Any idea why your cousin would want to harm him?"

Grace looked shocked. "No! Assaulted? I don't understand. What happened?"

"Did you talk to Mah about Duncan?" Karen pressed. "Maybe suggest he was prying into family business that was better left secret?"

"No, of course not!"

"You didn't suggest that he lean on Duncan to get him to back off and leave your son alone?"

"I resent the direction of these questions!" Grace said, pushing away from the table. "Unless there's anything else—"

"Hold on a moment, Mrs. Chan," Hank said. "We understand your son Taylor has been making statements about the death of your cousin Martin. We'd like to ask you a few questions about those statements."

57

"They assured me their research would be discreet and confidential. So much for that."

"As I understand it, you and your husband signed a waiver permitting Dr. Walsh and Mr. Duncan to disclose information about Taylor to the authorities where criminal activity might be involved," Hank said. "Your cousin Martin was murdered, Josh Duncan was assaulted and they're both connected to statements your son's making, so the issue of confidentiality is moot at this point. However, we're prepared to be as discreet as possible in how we use information directly connected to your son. We're sensitive to the fact that he's only three years old and shouldn't be put in jeopardy by things he's saying in all innocence."

Off-balance, Grace opened her mouth and closed it again.

"How close were you to your cousin Martin, Mrs. Chan?" Karen asked.

"Not very. Our families got together once, maybe twice a year. Uncle Stephen and my mother were cordial, but a little distant."

"What about your other cousin, Peter Mah? Are you close to him?"

She shook her head. "No, when Aunt Mary married Jerome Mah the Liu family was very upset. The Mahs are very . . . traditional, and their business interests are, uh, well, my mother used to use the word 'unsavory' to describe them."

"But Peter comes around to visit you, just the same?"

"Only on Taylor's birthday. He visited me in the hospital when Taylor was born and was very kind to me. He brings Taylor a present every year."

"And you told him about the things Taylor was saying about Martin," Hank said.

"Yes. It was on Taylor's birthday last November. I was very upset and it just kind of came out."

"You told Peter that Taylor was claiming to be Martin Liu reincarnated."

"I know how insane it sounds. But I had just finished fooling around with the video camera, making sure it would work for later in the day, and Taylor said some things that were recorded. I played it for Peter and he wanted to talk to Taylor."

Hank nodded. "That was unusual for him, I take it? To stay and visit?"

"Yes, he normally just gives Taylor his present and leaves. Peter knows my husband disapproves of him very strongly, and Peter's considerate in that regard."

Karen snorted.

Grace looked at her. "He's a very considerate person, Detective. He's very polite and well-mannered. It comes from his traditional upbringing."

"So he stayed and talked to Taylor?" Hank asked.

58

"Yes. I showed him the video of Taylor saying he was Martin."

"What was Peter's reaction to that?"

Grace frowned. "I'm not sure. Whatever he was feeling, he hid it very well. But he became very interested in talking to Taylor, so I made some tea and Peter went into the living room with Taylor."

"And Taylor spoke to him about being Martin Liu reincarnated?"

Grace grimaced. "I suppose he did. He said something about some kind of game he'd kept secret from Peter or something like that. Then he said that two men hurt him, and Peter seemed very interested in their names."

"Shawn and Gary?" Karen asked.

"Yes, that's right."

"Did those names mean anything to you?"

"No, not at all. I have no idea where Taylor is getting these things."

"Would your husband know anyone named Shawn or Gary? Anyone that he might talk to you about around the house?"

She shook her head. "No, no. No one. Neither my husband nor I know anyone by those names who would've had any contact whatsoever with Taylor."

"Maybe something he watched on television?" Karen suggested. "Do any of his favorite programs have characters with those names?"

"No. I'm sorry, but my husband and I have wracked our brains and come up empty. We've questioned Taylor about this Shawn and Gary and he hasn't said anything more about them. It's very strange and upsetting. It's as though these memories, or whatever they are, come and go. He remembers them, speaks about them, and then seems to forget them again. You must understand how upsetting all this is for us."

"We do," Hank said. "I understand that Taylor has two birthmarks on his leg, is that correct?"

Grace nodded.

"Which leg is it, left or right?"

"His left leg."

"When did these marks appear, Mrs. Chan?"

"He was born with them," she replied. "That's the way it normally works with birthmarks, Lieutenant."

"Of course. We'd like to talk to Taylor, if that's all right with you."

"Absolutely not. I won't have him questioned by the police. He's only three and a half years old, for God's sake."

"It seems he must have overheard something about your cousin Martin," Karen said, "and it's very important we try to find out where he heard it. It may lead us to the person who killed Martin."

Grace sighed and stared at her hands, which were tightly clasped on the table in front of her. "I know. But he was already questioned by the people from the university. Can't you just talk to them?"

"With all due respect," Karen said, "they don't have the kind of training and experience the Lieutenant and I have. This isn't just a matter of some academic research, Mrs. Chan. It's a homicide, and anything Taylor may be able to tell us that'd put a killer behind bars would be extremely important."

"You'd put him in court. A little boy up on the witness stand being attacked by some defense lawyer." Tears began to form in her eyes.

"Not likely," Karen said. "The Assistant State's Attorney decides these things, of course, but I think it's fair to say that Taylor's statements, connected as they are to all this theory about reincarnation and so on, wouldn't play very well in court from a prosecutor's point of view. I've spent several years investigating crimes relating to children, Mrs. Chan, and I can tell you very bluntly that prosecutors don't like to see children give testimony if it can at all be avoided. If Taylor can point us in the right direction that'd be great, but the ASA would still expect us to establish reasonable grounds based on other sources separate from Taylor before she'd go anywhere near a courtroom with a charge of murder against someone. Do you understand what I mean?"

Grace nodded, brushing at a tear on her cheek. "I think so."

"We'd like to know why Taylor's saying these things," Karen said. "We'd like to hear it for ourselves, if possible."

"Please," Grace said, "let me talk to my husband about it first. He'll be against it."

"Lieutenant Donaghue and I can meet with you and Dr. Chan before talking to Taylor, if you like. We can set the ground rules beforehand so that y'all will be comfortable with what'll happen."

Grace closed her eyes. "Let me talk to him."

"All right." Karen stood up. "Here's my business card. Call any time."

Grace took the card from Karen and tried to smile.

They left the office and went back down the hallway into the reception area. A middle-aged man with a walrus mustache was sitting there, hands clasped between his knees. Grace Chan's next appointment, perhaps. Brandi was on the phone but Hank could feel her eyes drilling holes in his back all the way out the front door and down the steps to the parking lot.

They got into the car and Karen started the engine. "Where to now?"

Hank looked at her. "Nicely done."

"I was going to rough her up a little, but as soon as she started talking about her son I could see it was different. We need to find out where the kid's hearing this stuff."

"Yeah." Hank pushed his hand through his frizzy hair. "She pretty much corroborated what Josh Duncan was saying. Doesn't mean much, but it's a start."

"So what's next?"

"We need to backtrack on Martin Liu."

"Whatcha got in mind?"

Hank took out his notebook and flipped through the pages. "I want to talk to Martin's mother. See if we can nail down the connection to Peter Mah a little more firmly before we go have a word with him about this game the little boy was talking about."

"Okay. What's the address?"

"Don't you mean the fucking address?" When she just stared at him, Hank smiled. "She lives in Midtown but she's probably still at work, which is up in Granger Park."

Hank removed his cell phone and called the home phone number written in his notebook. After a few rings he heard the answering machine pick up, so he cut the connection and called her business number. After speaking briefly with Meredith Collier, he closed the phone and nodded at Karen. "Granger Park."

"Figures. What does she do for a living?"

"Receptionist in a chiropractor's office."

Karen backed out of the parking space and floored it, whipping onto the street into a gap in traffic that was more theoretical than actual.

As they raced out Hank caught a glimpse of a black sedan turning into the parking lot behind them. There was a heavy-set driver with Asian features in the front and a passenger in the back that Hank could not see. He looked behind him but in the split-second available was only able to get the last three digits of the license plate: 86H.

"What make of car was that?" Hank asked.

"What car?" Karen glanced in the rear view mirror and switched lanes abruptly.

"The black sedan that turned into the parking lot behind us."

"Lexus," Karen said. "New. Year old. Small limo."

"Catch the plate?"

"Nine-four-six something."

"Nine-four-six-eight-six H?"

Karen shrugged. "Could be."

"Catch the passenger's face?" Hank asked, reaching for the radio.

"In the back? No. Driver was Asian, though."

"Yeah." He thumbed the radio and gave the make and plate number to Dispatch. As Karen made her way to the ramp that would take them onto the northbound expressway, Dispatch told Hank that the car was registered to Dicam International Shipping, 11001 Industrial Boulevard in Wilmingford.

"Mean anything to you?" Karen asked, accelerating into the inside lane.

"Not at the moment."

"Wanna go back?"

"No."

"Good. Then you won't need a session with the chiropractor after we're done talking to his receptionist."

# 8

Another office in another strip mall. In contrast with the expensively-furnished real estate office they had just left, however, this one was cluttered and run down. The waiting room was small and cramped. A row of chairs sat along the wall inside the door beside a corner table covered with magazines and brochure racks. A potted geranium on the corner table was wilted and dust-covered. A plastic basket under the table was filled with toys, a few of which had escaped and lay forgotten under one of the chairs.

A muscular young man sat in the chair closest to the door reading a magazine, his bull neck, thick arms and shaved head suggesting a college football player. On the wall were framed photographs of underwater plant life and tropical fish. It seemed that Dr. Albert Delahunty, the chiropractor, was an avid scuba diver in his spare time.

As Hank walked up to the waist-high counter and made eye contact with the woman sitting there, he felt his pulse jump. Taking a breath, he showed his badge and smiled. "I'm looking for Meredith Collier."

"That would be me."

Hank nodded. "My name's Donaghue. We spoke on the phone."

He thought his voice sounded a little high-pitched and reedy. It was like finding a brand-new Maserati parked out front of a tenement building down near the docks and he was uncharacteristically flustered. She was 46 years old. She had wavy shoulder-length blond hair with a few stray threads of grey, a wide face with prominent cheekbones and a high forehead, blue eyes and impeccable white teeth that showed briefly between full lips as she forced a smile in acknowledgement. She picked up the telephone with a long-fingered, elegant hand and pressed a button.

"Mrs. Delahunty? My appointment's here. Thanks." She cradled the phone and stood up as a large African-American woman in a brightly-colored print dress entered the reception area and came around behind the counter.

"I appreciate this," Meredith said. "It won't take long."

"That's all right, hon, do what you have to do." Mrs. Delahunty settled down and looked up at Hank.

"Thank you," Hank said, trying out his most charming smile.

Mrs. Delahunty blinked back at him without expression.

"This way." Meredith Collier indicated a doorway on the left.

The room was small, cluttered with equipment and dominated in the center by a brown vinyl-covered padded examination table with a u-shaped cushion at one end. Hank had never been inside a chiropractor's office before and he imagined that patients were required to lie face down on the padded table with their head wedged into the u. He looked for straps to hold a person in place while their bones were being twisted out of joint, but saw none. The whole thing made him feel very uncomfortable. He sat down in a chair next to a tiny cluttered desk and looked at a calendar on the wall featuring a picture of an erupting volcano. He took out his notebook and opened it on his knee. Kåren sat on a little stool with wheels that presumably was used by Dr. Delahunty when he wasn't required to be on his feet for extra leverage. Meredith Collier leaned back against a green filing cabinet, folded her arms and crossed her ankles. Hank's pulse jumped again and he looked at Karen.

She rolled her eyes at him. She looked at Meredith, decided that she didn't like being below the eye level of the person she was interviewing, and stood up, sliding the little stool back out of the way with her foot.

"Thanks for taking the time to see us, Ms. Collier," she began. "We'll try not to take very long."

"What's this all about?" She looked at Hank. "You said on the phone you wanted to ask me questions about my late son."

"That's right," Karen said. "We have a couple of questions about your son's activities before his death."

"Why? I mean, why now? Has something happened? Has new information come to light?"

"We'll get to that in a moment," Karen said. "We understand you met with a student from Memphis named Josh Duncan, is that correct?"

"Duncan?" Meredith frowned. "Yes, that's right."

"When was that, Ms. Collier?"

"This Saturday just gone by."

"What did you talk to him about?"

"He explained the research he was doing, something related to reincarnation. He wanted to know how often I visited with my late husband's cousin Grace and her family, if I'd spent much time with their little boy, Taylor."

"And you said…."

"That I never see them. I've never seen the boy." She glanced at Hank. "I don't have anything at all to do with my late husband's family. The last time I saw Grace was at Stephen's funeral and that was for ten seconds while she expressed her condolences. The boy was at a babysitter's, so I didn't see him then. I was never very close to anyone in Stephen's family, and once he was gone there was nothing there. I sold the house and let all the former connections drop."

Hank tore his eyes from a large colorful illustration of the autonomic nervous system on the wall behind Meredith. "Do you ever go by the name Merry?"

"Only with family and very close friends."

*When I was Martin you didn't like my mama because her name was Merry and she had blue eyes. And I had green eyes.*

Hank looked into those blue eyes now and tried to smile. "What else did you and Josh talk about?"

"He asked me if I'd be willing to meet with the child. He said the child seemed to be recalling memories associated with Martin. There was something about him saying his name was Martin, and this Josh wanted me to meet with Taylor and see whether it would spark any other memories."

"What was your reaction to his request?"

"I refused." She spread her hand flat on her thigh and arched it so that she could look at her nails. "I found the whole thing rather absurd and unpleasant. Frankly, I'm surprised that Michael Chan would go along with it." She frowned at Hank. "Why are you interested in what I may or may not have said to this student?"

"He was assaulted in Chinatown on Monday," Karen said. "Someone else didn't like him poking around your son's murder. You talk to anyone about Duncan's visit afterwards? Maybe pass the word along that he was trying to stir things up?"

Hank watched Meredith look at Karen quizzically, as though not understanding the reason for her aggressive tone, before a different set of emotions passed across her face that Hank could see in the softening of her eyes, the parting of her lips and the gradual disappearance of the little frown lines across her forehead.

"My circle of friends is very small, Detective, and I don't discuss the past with them. No, I didn't talk to anyone about his visit. I thought it would be better to try to forget about it. I'm very sorry he was assaulted. Was he badly hurt?"

"Concussion," Karen said. "Some abrasions and contusions. He was kicked around by someone with cowboy boots."

Meredith winced. "That's awful."

"Was your son very close to his cousin, Peter Mah?" Hank asked.

Meredith sighed. "He liked to spend time with him, yes. For a while I tried to discourage it, but I really didn't have much say in what Martin did or didn't do."

"You're aware of Mah's Triad connections?" Karen asked.

Meredith nodded. "Stephen did his best to keep a distance between our family and his sister Mary. She was the oldest of the three children and when she married Jerome Mah it apparently created quite a controversy among the Lius. Stephen's younger sister Anna also put some distance between herself and the rest of the family after she married Warren Wong and had Grace. Everyone understood that Jerome Mah was powerfully connected and no one really wanted to have anything to do with that. And it was evident very early that Peter was heading down a road that was not very desirable. The stories began circulating when he was twelve or thirteen and got steadily worse as he grew older. We did everything we could, Stephen and I, to keep Martin away from it all."

"But it didn't work out that way," Karen said.

Meredith looked down at her shoes. "Martin was a typical teenager. He went through a rebellious stage where he wanted to experience things on his own terms rather than those of his parents. In high school he became very interested in his Chinese heritage. It was difficult for him, you understand," she glanced up at Hank and then looked away, "because he was only half Chinese. It upset him that his eyes were green, his hair was a little wavy, and his mother was Caucasian. He threw himself in the opposite direction and began to associate with Peter because of the traditional leanings of the Mah family. He wanted to learn everything he could about being Chinese."

"Including Triad business?" Karen asked.

Meredith shook her head. "No, I'm sure it never went that far. Certainly not the drugs and gangs and all that." She looked at Hank again. "There was never anything like that in Martin, not even after he started attending college at State. He was a boyish, good-tempered, kind and generous young man. Even though we argued and fought at times, there was never any meanness or hardness in him, never any sneakiness or lying or any of the other things that a parent recognizes in a child going bad. I know he was…" she paused for a moment to collect herself, "I know he was found with packets of heroin and that the police believe he was trying to sell drugs in the wrong neighborhood, but that's just not possible. He wasn't that kind of person."

"You'd be surprised the kind of person who ends up selling drugs," Karen said.

"No," Meredith shook her head. "You don't understand. He had a thing about drugs. He was against them. Prescription drugs, hard drugs, designer drugs, hash, ecstasy, you name it. All the stuff that swirls about our kids out there, he felt that it was wrong to get involved with them. He even refused to take pain relievers when he had a headache. He was very careful about what he ate or drank. No alcohol, no drugs, no nothing. Tea, rice, fish, vegetables, bottled water. He was very, very particular."

"So why would somebody kill him?" Karen asked. "Why would somebody shoot him and plant heroin on him to make it look like a botched drug sale?"

Meredith's eyes grew moist. "Don't you think I've asked myself the same question every night for the past four years? Don't you think I've gone over and over in my mind everything that he said or did before it happened? Searching for a clue, a hint of what might have caused it?" She brushed at her eyes and drew a deep breath, pulling herself together. "I'll tell you one thing: it had something to do with Peter Mah."

Hank picked up a box of tissues on the desk beside him and held it out to her. "Why do you say that, Ms. Collier?"

"Thank you." She took a tissue from the box and patted her eyes lightly, then balled it up in her fist. "He spent a lot of time with Peter in the months before it happened. He'd graduated from State the year before and his part time job at Dicam had become full time and permanent."

"Dicam," Karen repeated.

"Yes, Dicam International, or whatever they're called."

"What did he do there?"

"Computer programming. Martin was a genius with computers, he loved working with them. He earned a B.Sc. in Computer Science at State and while he was a student he worked part time at Dicam in their IT division. When he graduated they hired him on full time. Martin was thrilled." She rolled her eyes. "It was another tie to Peter, of course, since he'd helped Martin get in there to begin with."

"Oh?"

Meredith shrugged. "Well, the company's owned by the Mahs, of course."

Hank and Karen exchanged looks. Hank knew she hated it when someone knew something she was also supposed to know and didn't. He clasped his hands between his knees and leaned forward.

"You were saying he spent a lot of time with Peter before his death."

"That's right, Lieutenant Donaghue."

He bit his tongue just before telling her that she should call him Hank. Hank is fine, he was going to say. Instead, he said: "What sort of things did they do together?"

"Martin spent a lot of time just hanging around with him, like a cousins thing. Family's extremely important to Peter and he'd make time for Martin because they were cousins. They played pool in a billiards place downtown and Martin became addicted to the Chinese gambling games, pai gow in particular. He met Peter at a place called the Golden Dragon quite a lot. I mentioned that to Josh Duncan, actually. And also the restaurant, the Bright Spot, which is Peter's headquarters or whatever." She looked at Hank. "Martin told his father everything he did. He never hid anything; he was always very forthright with Stephen. He didn't tell me these things because I was becoming rather … marginalized in his life by this time, but he kept his father up to date. I think he was trying to appeal to his father to relax some of his restrictions against the Mahs, to come closer to them for the sake of family tradition."

"And what about his activities the last day or two?" Hank asked.

"Before he was murdered," she finished, as though it were important to her to say the words rather than tiptoe around them. "The day he was murdered I didn't see him. He had his own apartment, I guess you know that, and there were stretches of time when I didn't see him or speak to him. But the night before he was murdered he stopped by the house to see Stephen. He and his father watched a baseball game on television and talked for a while. I sat in the next room and read, because this is what Martin preferred me to do, but

I could hear their conversation."

"What did they talk about?" Hank asked.

"Martin talked about his job. He was very proud of it. He liked working at Dicam, the people were very nice to him and he liked what he was doing. They were apparently doing a major overhaul of their computer systems and Martin was very much involved in the programming end of it. He was also getting a chance to help design the systems architecture and he was excited about that." Meredith smiled. "I don't really know what that means, because I don't know much about computers, but it was very important to Martin."

"Anything else they talked about that might be relevant?"

"Yes. He was upset about one of his friends."

"Oh?"

"Yes, I heard him say to his father he thought this friend was in trouble and he didn't know what to do about it. He was asking his father for advice."

"What kind of advice?"

She shook her head. "It was four years ago now, and it's getting pretty muddled, but if I remember correctly he asked his father whether or not he should speak to Peter about it. I got the impression his friend was doing something Peter wouldn't like, and Martin was debating whether or not to intercede on his friend's behalf."

"What did your husband say to that?" Karen asked.

"I'm sorry, that's all I remember. Just Martin's concern about his friend."

"What was this friend's name?"

"That would be Tommy Leung. He and Martin were very close."

Hank wrote the name down. "What about girlfriends? Martin have anyone he was seeing on a regular basis?"

She nodded. "He had several female friends, but if it was a date then it was Susan Choi he went out with. Her married name is, oh dear, it escapes me. I saw her a couple of months ago in the Walmart. She's been married for two years now and is expecting her first. Damn, what did she say her husband's name was?"

"Her name was Susan Choi when Martin dated her?" Hank asked, writing it down.

"Yes." She pursed her lips. "Charles. That's it. Her husband's name is Charles. Charles Chong. Her married name is Susan Chong."

"Any idea where we'd find her?' Karen asked.

"Springhill somewhere, that's all I remember from the conversation. It was one of those two-minute things you do when you're shopping and you see someone that you used to know."

"All right," Karen said. "Have you spoken to Peter Mah lately?"

"No."

"Did Martin ever mention anyone named Shawn or Gary?"

68

Meredith shook her head. "No. The names aren't familiar."

"No one in the family, your husband's or yours, by that name?"

"Shawn or Gary? No."

"No one at work," Karen prompted, "no one that he hung around with, maybe neighbors or something?"

"No, Detective. I don't know anyone by either name."

"All right," Hank said. He stood up and put his notebook and pen in his jacket pocket. "Thanks very much for your time, Ms. Collier. We appreciate your patience. If you think of anything else you feel we should know, please give us a call." Hank handed her one of his business cards.

"I don't quite understand," Meredith said, taking the card and looking at it. "Why are the police re-opening Martin's case after all this time?"

"Well, it was never technically closed," Karen said, passing over one of her cards. "It was kept open and assigned to the Cold Case Unit, but in light of new information that's recently surfaced we've stepped in to investigate further."

"New information? What new information is that, Detective?"

"These two names, Shawn and Gary. That's why we were asking you whether they were familiar in any way. These names have recently been connected to your son's murder."

"Connected how?"

"That's what we'd like to find out." Karen nodded. "Call if you think of anything else."

"All right." Meredith held out her hand to Karen. Then she turned to Hank. "I hope you find them. It would be good to have it finally over."

Hank shook her hand. It was warm and soft, the grip firm and comfortable. "That's our objective, Ms. Collier. Thanks for your time."

In the parking lot Hank paused beside the car, looking around. Behind the mall were railroad tracks. A half a block to the west was an overpass where one of the main north-south arteries was elevated to avoid the tracks and the street. Across the street was a strip club set back from the street to allow for ample parking in front. There was only one car in the parking lot, a dusty blue Toyota with a dent in the fender and rust around the wheel wells. On this side of the street next to the mall was an empty lot with a rusted dumpster and tall weeds. Beyond that was a parking lot that ran all the way back to the tracks and a single-story building housing a thrift shop. In the parking lot next to the thrift shop, sitting among the telephone poles and tall weeds, was a police car. There were two officers inside. It looked like they were grabbing something to eat while they kept an eye on the strip club.

"Hey there," Karen slapped the roof of the Crown Vic to catch his attention. "What the hell was that, Lou, love at first sight?"

"Pardon me?"

Karen pointed with her chin in the direction of the chiropractor's office. "Went a little fuzzy on me there, didn't you?"

"I did not." Hank got into the car, slamming the door.

Karen got in, started the engine and grinned at him. "Christ, you went all glassy-eyed. She pressed your button, didn't she?"

"You're off base, Detective."

"Oops." Karen shifted into reverse, enjoying herself. Then she bit her lip and shifted back into park.

"Okay. Let's take a minute and walk through this. The kid worked for a company controlled by his cousin's family, doing computer stuff. The mother insists he was clean, stayed away from the drugs. You believe her on that? You think it could be true?"

"It's possible."

"It's possible." Karen rubbed her palm on the top of the steering wheel. "So let's say for the sake of argument it's true, that the vic didn't do drugs and that the drug-sale-gone-bad thing was bogus. We're leaning in that direction anyways. So say someone shot him somewhere else over something other than drugs, then dumped him in an alley in R Boyz territory and scattered a couple packets of horse to throw everyone off the trail. So why was he killed? Maybe the computer stuff he did for Dicam? Since the company belongs to the Mahs?"

Hank shrugged. "Could be. Maybe something will turn up out there."

"Another possibility is that he did something to piss off Mah. What did she just say? That his friend did something that Mah wouldn't like and he was trying to decide whether to stick his nose in? Maybe he interfered in Triad business and got killed for it. Maybe Mah offed his own cousin. Sounds like something a hood like that would do."

"Maybe, but not likely."

"Why not?"

"The family angle. Everyone says Peter Mah's a guy who places a high importance on family connections. Sounds like he was taking Martin under his wing, looking after him, bringing him into the circle where he'd prosper."

"Okay, yeah, I can buy that. So somebody other than Peter Mah kills Martin Liu somewhere, dumps him in an alley in R Boyz territory to make everyone think it's a gang killing, and they plant Triad-type drugs on him to make us think the Triad was trying to move into R Boyz territory with Triad product. It's enough to satisfy Joe Kalzowski, who's already thinking about where he's gonna go fishing on his first day of retirement or whatever, but now, looking back, it's lame and contrived. So let's go back to Martin Liu being worried about his friend doing something that Peter Mah wouldn't like. What would Tommy Leung be doing that Peter Mah wouldn't like?"

"Something contrary to Triad law, presumably," Hank said, "since

Peter is the Red Pole, responsible for punishing Triad wrongdoers."

"Like what? What are we looking for?"

Hank shrugged. "Could be anything. Betraying society secrets, betraying a Triad confederate, stealing from them, who knows? And we're assuming that Tommy Leung is Triad too."

"So we should find this Tommy Leung kid and ask him about it."

"He'd probably be relieved to get it off his chest."

Karen laughed dutifully. "Thing about Mah, though," she said, "is somebody killed his cousin right under his nose. That had to piss him off. He's the tough guy in charge of enforcement for his gang, the heavy duty bad ass dude, and somebody sneaks in a kidney punch when he's not looking. It's gotta really piss him off."

"Yeah, and it stands to reason he's been trying to find out who did it over the last four years. It's safe to assume he didn't succeed, given his apparent reaction when Taylor Chan started talking."

"Agreed. He breaks his routine with Grace, stays for tea, chats with Taylor, shows him his tats, the whole deal. He wants to hear more. Time has passed and he hasn't smacked the guy who dumped in his sandbox. He gets the two names and you can bet he's hunting them down like the dirty dogs they are."

"Then Josh Duncan shows up at the Golden Dragon," Hank said, "wanting to talk to Peter about Martin's murder."

Karen frowned. "Yeah, but they beat him up and rob him."

"There's some confusion there," Hank agreed. "But it's hired help, right? This Billy Fung isn't the sharpest knife in the drawer. So Fung thinks Josh is R Boyz and he rough-houses him thinking Peter will pat him on the head for it."

"But they go back for more the next day," Karen prompted.

"Yeah, and it struck me at the time that they were there on instructions from someone. Mah, obviously. Josh thought they were coming back to get him again, and maybe he was half-right. They weren't coming back to finish him off, but maybe to grab him and bring him around for a little chat with Peter."

Karen nodded. "They got his notebook and iPod and shit. Maybe Mah looked through it, saw what Josh was doing with the boy, and wanted to know everything that Josh had found out."

"Yeah. He's out front of us, beating the bushes for Martin's killer."

"Ha," Karen said, "check it out. We're being buzzed."

Hank glanced in the side mirror and saw a flash of black and white passing behind them. He looked behind Karen and saw the police cruiser slowly rolling back through the parking lot and behind the strip mall.

"Running our plates," Karen said.

"Who the hell else would be sitting in a Crown Vic Police Interceptor

71

flapping their gums after fifteen minutes in a chiropractor's office besides a couple of cops?" Hank complained. *"Christ."*

"Hey, lighten up, Lou. You remember the life. It'll brighten up their day a little."

Hank shook his head.

"Let's see if they come over or fuck off," Karen said. "A little IQ test."

They waited for a few moments and then the cruiser emerged from the far side of the strip mall. The two officers kept their eyes straight ahead as they left the parking lot and turned right, merging with traffic and disappearing down the street.

"Pass," Karen said.

"That was fun," Hank said, "but where were we?"

"Peter Mah trying to beat us to Martin Liu's killer."

"Yeah." Hank chewed on his lip for a moment. "He's going to want to know what the secret game was that Taylor's talking about. The boy apparently didn't tell him which friend, so we may actually be ahead of him after all."

"So we gotta talk to this Tommy Leung kid, shake the tree and see what falls out."

"I want to stop and talk to Melton in OCU first. He might know about something internal that the Triad dealt with four years ago. It'd help if we had an angle we could use when we question Leung."

"Okay, let's get our asses in gear." Karen threw the car into reverse and backed out of the parking spot. "Hey," she said, hurling out into traffic, "let's see if we can find that cruiser on the way and buzz them back."

"Christ," Hank said, shaking his head.

# 9

Detective Barry Melton's workstation was on the fifth floor, which was protected from casual traffic by a security door that could only be opened by fifth floor personnel who were issued a special swipe card for the purpose. This floor housed the Intelligence Division, including the Organized Crime Unit and all the security-related computer systems requiring specialized clearance. It was necessary for Hank to pick up the telephone on the wall outside the door and telephone Melton to come let them in. It was an annoyance to everyone except the staff who worked on the floor, since it effectively screened out casual traffic that might show up at one's desk from other floors to waste one's time with bureaucratic trivia.

Melton threw open the door and blinked up at Hank. "Come on in." He held the door open for them to pass through.

"Sorry to bother you," Hank said. "This shouldn't take long."

"No, no, that's all right," Melton said, leading the way. "All in a day's work. Over here."

This part of the floor was a warren of tiny work spaces with flimsy temporary walls and open doorways. Melton waved them into his workstation and began removing files, books and newspapers from the two chairs in front of his desk so that Hank and Karen could sit down. Hank watched him bustle about, adding files to piles of other files on the floor. Melton was very short, about five foot seven, and as stocky as a primate. He was bald except for a fringe of thick black hair that ran from ear to ear behind his head. His eyes were large and dark. His lips were thick and his cheeks were fleshy. His nose was flat, as though it had been broken several times. He looked like he might be at home down at the docks unloading cargo from a Liberian freighter, but his voice was very soft and cultured, with a faint British accent. He threw himself into the chair behind his desk and folded his hands in front of him.

"Now, what can I do for you?"

"We'd like some background on Asian OC in the city," Hank said, sitting down and opening his notebook on his knee, "with particular emphasis on Peter Mah."

"Mah?" Melton's thick black eyebrows crawled up over his forehead. "Peter Mah? Well, I'll see what I can do. What in particular would you like to know?"

"We're investigating the homicide of his cousin, Martin Liu," Hank said. "Four years ago. Was there anything big happening back then?"

"Triad-related?" Melton appeared to think for a minute. "Well, there was an internal struggle several years ago. I suppose that would qualify as something big."

"Tell us about it," Hank said.

"We don't really know much. The Triad picture is very murky, since they're secretive to a fault."

Karen was starting to get a little irritated. "Well what the fuck *do* you know?"

"Well," Melton leaned forward, "six years ago the local society elected a new Dragon Head. The Dragon Head is the leader of the local lodge. They call him the *Shan Chu*. Keep in mind that Triad organizations aren't as highly structured as most other organized crime groups. They don't have a widespread administrative structure, *per se*, with a headquarters-and-subsidiary type of mentality. They're more a network of localized units bound by personal relationships, history and loyalty. Local units have a specific internal organization with an hierarchy and clearly-defined roles and responsibilities, but laterally outside the unit there's no real power structure as such. The connections are more social and financial than anything else. And there's always a connection between here and Hong Kong."

Karen was supposed to be impressed but instead she radiated boredom, slumped in the chair next to Hank, staring at Melton. "So what about this election?"

Melton described the failed term of Bernard Ho and the resultant power struggle between Lam Chun Sang, the current Dragon Head, and Philip Ling that had occurred four years ago. The conflict ended with a gun battle along the river, Melton explained, "and the next day someone connected to Mah was found dead in an alley in South Shore East. The official line was that it was a drug sale gone bad, but those of us in OCU who keep track of these things figured it was connected to Philip Ling."

"The Martin Liu killing, right?" Hank said. "You're saying it was connected to this power struggle?"

"That's what we thought at the time."

"Is that what you still think?"

Melton stared thoughtfully at Hank for a moment as though considering how to answer the question. Then he shrugged. "Not really. More likely it was a personal thing unconnected to Triad business altogether. It's not of interest to us here."

"So what about Peter Mah?" Karen asked. "What kind of rap sheet has he got?"

"When you run it you'll find it's clean. No convictions. There were a couple of busts as a juvenile but those records are sealed. As an adult, he's as pure as the driven snow."

"I remember he ran a street gang at one time," Hank said.

Melton nodded. "Yeah, the Biu Ji Boys. Named after the third form of *ving tsun* kung fu. It means 'pointing finger.' It's a set of emergency techniques used by a *ving tsun* practitioner when he's in a very bad position and about to be overwhelmed by an enemy. Peter is said to have studied *ving tsun*

74

as a boy, although apparently he wasn't much good at it. Interesting choice of name. Anyway, I digress. The gang still exists, with a different leader of course, although they still look up to Peter as a type of figurehead. Nasty bunch."

"Home invasions?" Karen asked. "Leg breaking, that kind of thing?"

"No and yes," Melton replied, glancing sideways at her. "No, they don't really do many home invasions anymore; it's more the Vietnamese gangs who're the most active in that sort of thing now. Yes, they're very busy on the crimes against the person side of things. Assaults, murders, you name it. Also," he held up a hand and ticked off on his fingers, "heroin trafficking, illegal weapons, stolen goods, prostitution, pornography."

"Okay, so that's how he got his laughs when he was a kid," Karen said. "What's he into now that he's all grown up?"

"Peter's a businessman. He owns several properties in Chinatown, including the restaurant where he lives."

She snorted. "He's a businessman. Making his money selling chow mein and chicken balls, is that what you're saying?"

Melton frowned. "He's also a member of the society in our city that's affiliated with the 14K Triad. I've already explained that."

"What about Dicam International?" Karen asked.

"Dicam? Shipping, containers, freighters, trucking, even a fleet of cargo planes. Big operation." Melton turned to the computer on his desk and grabbed the mouse. "Here, give me a moment." He clicked, typed, and clicked, studied the screen, clicked and typed some more. The printer on the corner of his desk came to life. "Here's some basic info on Dicam from the *Lloyd's* database. FYI only, of course. It'll give you some basic background on the company. Corporate structure, Board of Directors, blah blah." He pulled the sheet from the printer and handed it to her.

"The CEO is Jerome Mah, as you can see. Peter's father. Homeland Security considers the company a bit of a risk for people smuggling, heroin and so on, but the seizure rate against them is surprisingly low."

"Really? And yet the old geezer is a Triad man. How does that figure?"

"Not really a Triad man. There's a fine line that's hard to explain. Lam sits on the board of Jerome's big import-export company, and Jerome sits on the board of one or two companies with a few other Triad members, so it's more accurate to describe him as an associate. Just the same, Jerome sits on the board of State University, as does your mother, Lieutenant, he's an active member of the Lions Club, he donates millions of dollars to our hospitals, and in every other respect is a shining member of our community."

"So Dicam's a Triad front?" Karen asked.

"No," Melton said. "I can't really go into detail on a lot of this stuff.

75

Ongoing investigation, you understand."

"What the hell does that mean?"

Melton crossed his arms across his barrel chest. "I'm not really sure you're cleared for this kind of discussion, Detective."

"You'll be cleared for takeoff right through the fuckin' window if you don't get with the program, buster." Karen pushed forward in her chair. "This is a fuckin' homicide investigation you're impeding here."

"Hey, hey," Melton protested. It was obvious that Karen was as mean as a snake. The normal civilized rules of office decorum meant nothing to her. She was liable to come right over the desk at him before anyone could do anything to stop her. Her confidence in her ability to cause him immediate physical harm was unmistakable.

Hank coughed. "Back up, Barry. We get it that some of your intelligence is Need to Know Only, we get that. Just the same, help us out a little."

Melton grumbled, looking around his little cubicle.

"We think Mah's been looking into Martin Liu's murder," Hank went on. "He got a couple of names last November and has been making inquiries. He had a kid beaten up on Monday, took his stuff, then went after him again. Heard anything about that?"

"No, I haven't."

"So run the names for us now," Hank said. "Shawn and Gary. Try S-h-a-w-n, S-e-a-n and S-h-a-u-n. Try both as a given name and a surname."

"Okay." Melton logged into the system, ran the queries and printed out the information on his LaserJet printer. He gathered up the sheets of paper and glanced through them.

"Four hits on Shawn," he said, "three for S-h-a-w-n and one for S-e-a-n. Eight hits on Gary, one as a surname." He handed the pages to Karen.

"What about Martin Liu?" Hank asked.

Melton shook his head. "The kid was clean. It was my understanding all along he had no connection to the Triad whatsoever except for the misfortune of being related to Peter Mah. No record at all."

"What about the fact that he worked at Dicam?" Karen asked.

"Peter got him the job," Melton replied, "but it was sheer nepotism and nothing else."

"Can you run a couple other names for us?" Hank asked.

Melton nodded, turning back to the keyboard. "Fire away."

"Charles Chong." Hank spelled it for him.

"D-O-B?"

"Sorry, I don't have anything other than the name," Hank said, "but he's likely in his mid- to late-twenties."

Melton ran it and then shook his head. "Nothing."

"Okay. Susan Choi, married name Chong, wife of the aforementioned Charles Chong, no date of birth but about the same age."

76

Melton ran it and shook his head again. "No."

"No problem. Tommy Leung." Hank spelled it for him. "About the same age."

Melton sat back. "I'm familiar with the name. I'm not going to run it."

"Why the fuck not?" Karen said.

Melton's eyes flickered. He was having obvious problems with Karen's aggressiveness. He turned to Hank. "Why are you asking about Tommy Leung? What's his connection to your case?"

"He was friends with Martin Liu," Hank said. "We want to talk to him. What's the problem?"

"The Leungs are part of an MAI. If I run a query on any one of them, I'll get a phone call within five minutes because our system's tied in with other agencies and they'll want me to explain my sudden interest."

An MAI was a Multi-Agency Investigation, which meant that the department was working with state and federal officials in an ongoing operation of some sort that involved the Leung family.

"Fair enough," Hank said. "Just explain to us where they fit in with Peter Mah."

"Edward Leung's a known Triad member. He's fifty-three years old, married, two sons and three daughters. Sole proprietor of Pagoda Home Electronics Corporation, a small chain of consumer outlets. Tommy's his oldest son and manages the warehouse operations on River Street. Edward, a.k.a. Eddie, is suspected of money laundering, fencing stolen electronics and credit card fraud but nothing's been proven. He has a DUI conviction on his record, plus an arrest for possession of stolen property but the charges were dropped."

"Does Tommy have a record?"

"No. He's clean, but the Feds probably have him under surveillance. They're looking at the entire society right now for a bunch of white collar stuff, counterfeiting, identity theft, credit card fraud."

Hank stood up. "All right, Barry, I appreciate what you've given us. If you hear anything else, let us know, all right?"

"Will do." Melton shook his hand, hesitated, then nodded at Karen.

At the elevators outside the secure door, Karen leaned against the wall. "Maybe I should have been nicer to him."

"I wouldn't want you to try to be something that you're not," Hank said.

The elevator arrived and they got on. They rode up to the ninth floor and walked to their desks.

"So," she said, sitting down, "we go squeeze Tommy Leung about what he was into four years ago that upset his friend Martin. According to doofus it didn't have anything to do with their turf war, so maybe it was something else connected to Triad stuff that Martin didn't like, seeing as he was so squeaky clean. Plus we can buzz the ex-girlfriend to see if she has anything useful to say."

"We also have the list of Shawns and Garys to run down," Hank said.

"That doesn't excite me so much. Coming from a three-year-old kid, I'd say it's a lot less interesting than this Leung angle."

"I'll ask Detective Waverman to run them down for us."

Karen grinned. "Right on."

"I'll also ask him if he can take a run out to Dicam International and talk to people out there. Get some more background on the victim from his co-workers."

"Sounds good to me." She sprang back out of her chair as though propelled by a giant spring. "So let's go look up Tommy Leung. Time's a'wastin'."

# 10

Peter Mah relaxed in the back seat of the black Lexus sedan and watched the familiar buildings of Chinatown pass as he was driven home to the Bright Spot restaurant. The conversation with his cousin Grace had gone well. She described the meeting with the two homicide detectives. When Peter suggested it was perhaps in Taylor's best interest that she not talk to the police any further, as they might put the child in jeopardy with their clumsy efforts to track a killer, she agreed. She understood that Peter was very protective of family, even though she herself didn't embrace the traditional Chinese value system from which this protectiveness sprang. She knew he'd do everything in his power to see that no harm came to them. He would atone for his failure to shield Martin from harm by serving as little Taylor's protector throughout his life. He explained to her that it was a *guanxi* obligation to him. If Taylor actually were Martin reincarnated, it would be especially important that Peter honor this commitment.

Peter made a mental note to call Martin's mother. He hadn't spoken to her since the funeral of Uncle Stephen because she'd removed herself from the family circle, which was the appropriate thing to do, given that she was a *seigweipor*, a Caucasian female, but he thought it would probably be best to talk to her for the same reason he'd talked to Grace. The police did not need any more information about Martin than they already had in their files. They'd had their chance to catch Martin's killer and had failed.

He studied the bald head of his driver, Benny Hu. Stocky and muscular, Hu had been with Peter for a number of years and was fanatically loyal. He'd twice been shot in altercations with enemies of the society where Peter had gone to deliver punishment for wrongdoings, and both times the guns had been aimed at Peter. Hu lived a very ascetic life and had never been arrested. Peter trusted him with his life. When Peter moved around in the city he often took someone with him in addition to Hu, for contingencies, but this afternoon it had not been necessary. It was only Grace, after all.

He removed his iPhone and speed-dialed a number. It rang twice and was answered.

"Organized Crime Unit, Melton speaking."

"You liked the names I gave you for the Phoc killing," Peter said.

"You read about the arrests, I take it."

"I did." Peter said. He'd given Melton the names of three members of the Fuk Wah gang who'd been responsible for the murder of a youth who recruited school children for a Vietnamese gang. The three had been arrested soon afterwards and arraigned on murder charges. Fuk Wah was a gang consisting of teenaged immigrants, almost all illegal, from the Fukian province of China. Fuk Wah's informal patron was William Chow, a snakehead who'd been a friend of Philip Ling but had quickly switched his allegiance to Lam after the election. Fuk Wah competed with Biu Ji for business on the streets of Chinatown and Peter had no love either for them or for their benefactor, Chow.

"You must be glad," Melton said. "Gets them out of your hair, I take it. Less competition on the streets for your boys."

"I'm glad as a concerned citizen who's alarmed at the rise of violent crime on our streets by uncontrolled mobs," Peter said.

"That's a laugh."

"They're no better than the Vietnamese gangsters they compete with," Peter said curtly. "They make the streets very dangerous and they invade innocent people's homes at random. They're like undisciplined dogs running around."

"Well, whatever. This'll keep their heads down for a little while, at least. Anyway, I was just about to call you."

"Oh?"

"Homicide's back on your cousin's murder, as you thought. Jointly with Cold Case. I just talked to Lieutenant Hank Donaghue and a Detective Stainer. Donaghue asked me to run a Susan Choi and her husband Charles Chong. He also asked about Tommy Leung. Apparently he was your cousin's friend. I told him none of them had a record on file. They're at the beginning, doing a basic background on the victim."

"All right," Peter said, disinterested. He'd already talked to Martin's old girlfriend a long time ago. She knew nothing of value. He'd also talked to Tommy right after Martin's murder, probing for a connection to Philip Ling. Tommy also had known nothing. "I appreciate the information."

"Yeah." A sardonic chuckle. "Meanwhile, you know I'm still looking for info on the credit card scams. If you hear anything about who's behind it, *I'd* appreciate it very much."

"Of course."

Peter ended the call. Immediately the phone rang again.

"*Wei?*"

"Mr. Mah, it's Henry Lee speaking." Henry was the *Cho Hai* or messenger of the society, referred to in English as the Straw Sandal. In addition, he was Peter's attorney and also represented Peter's employees whenever they needed a lawyer.

"Mr. Lee, how are you?"

"I'm well. I trust your day is progressing pleasantly."

"Yes, it is."

"I'm calling on behalf of the *Shan Chu*, who is on his way to your office and would like to speak to you."

"Thanks, Mr. Lee. I'm on my way there now."

"Very good. Uncle Sang will be gratified. He's having a difficult day,

Mr. Mah, and isn't in the best of moods."

"Good to know, Mr. Lee." Peter ended the call and looked out the window. He shifted slightly on the leather seat and felt the gun press against his hip in the leather holster on his belt. He made a mental note to make arrangements for a more disposable weapon after he met with Lam, a gun he didn't mind dropping into the river when he was done with it.

When he reached the top of the creaking, narrow staircase and emerged into the third floor hallway above the restaurant, he immediately sensed something in the air. Down the hallway on the left side were the doors leading to his private rooms. These doors were closed, as they should be. The doors on the right side of the hallway, which led into his private office and outer office, were also closed with exception to the door immediately in front of him opposite the stairs. This door, which opened into a vestibule contiguous to the outer office, was always left open, and so on first appearance everything seemed normal. However, Peter knew that it was not.

Benny Hu preceded him into the little vestibule. The room was decorated with red and gold leaf wallpaper, plaster columns with ornate carved dragons, antique furniture from Macau and painted tin ceilings. An enormous aquarium filled with tropical fish dominated the center of the room, and in front of the aquarium on a pedestal was a large bronze representation of Kwan Kung, the legendary Chinese general and god of war. Facing the door, Kwan Kung allegedly protected Peter's center of business from the intrusion of any evil spirit. Peter did not necessarily believe the superstition, but he definitely believed in the importance of Kwan Kung being seen by anyone who *did* believe the superstition.

This room, intended for visitors waiting to be shown through the outer office into Peter's inner sanctum, was empty. Peter followed Hu into the outer office, which was decorated in a style intended to remind one of British Hong Kong, with antique desks, a large metal-bladed ceiling fan, bamboo window shades and dark mahogany filing cabinets. Hu sat down at a desk he was permitted to use and took a newspaper out of the top drawer. Without a glance at Peter he began to read the paper.

Peter looked at the young woman sitting at the other desk in the outer office. Mikki Lung was his niece, his oldest sister's girl. She worked for him as an administrative assistant, answering Peter's telephone, screening his e-mail, and so on. Sitting on the corner of her desk was Jimmy Yung. Jimmy liked to hang around the office talking to Mikki. One look at both of their faces told Peter that Lam was indeed waiting for him in his inner office.

He opened the door and walked in. Leaning back in Peter's large leather chair was the *Shan Chu*.

"Hello, Uncle Sang," Peter said in Cantonese. "How are you?"

"I am unwell, thank you," Lam Chun Sang replied. "My feet hurt and my back is sore this morning. Thanks for asking." Lam weighed nearly three

81

hundred pounds, rather heavy for a man in his seventies, but he was addicted to pastries and chocolate and it was hopeless even to think of losing weight. He wore a rumpled grey jacket and a white shirt open at the neck, grey trousers a shade darker than the jacket, and expensive Italian shoes. Lam ran a hand over his bald head.

"You have this place looking like something out of nineteenth-century San Francisco," he said, waving his hand at the office around them. "Why don't you move uptown into one of my high-rises and enjoy more modern conveniences?"

"I like it here, Uncle," Peter said, disappointed that Lam did not appreciate the atmosphere he wished to create.

"This is Lester Ping," Lam said, pointing to a little man sitting in one of the two wingback chairs arranged before Peter's large teak desk. "You may already know him."

"Yes," Peter said, "we've met before. How are you, Mr. Ping?"

"I'm well, thank you," Ping said with a nervous smile.

"Sit down, Peter," Lam directed. "You can dispense with the hospitality, I'm bloated with all the tea I've had today. We're both busy men and I won't waste your time."

"You never waste my time, Uncle," Peter said. He sat down and composed himself, folding his hands neatly in his lap. He smiled politely. Calmness was essential. Calmness, respect, loyalty, obedience. These were the traits that endeared Peter to Lam.

Lam turned his gaze on Lester Ping. "I like this little man, I find him very interesting. His wife's sister is married to a good friend of mine back home, did you know that?"

"No," Peter said.

"Lester here is the baby of the family and I promised to keep an eye on him while he's away from home. Right, Lester? Keep you out of mischief?"

"Yes, Uncle Sang," Lester answered nervously. In his middle forties, he wore a grey suit that was as neat as a pin, accented by a black tie, black over-the-calf socks and black shoes. He did not look like anyone's baby as far as Peter could see.

"Lester, here, has been in this country for two years now. He's an artist, a genius. His work is without parallel."

"I agree," Peter said. "I myself have one of his documents and it's been very useful to me."

Lester Ping was a counterfeiter who specialized in passports. In an age where technology had endowed personal identification documents with everything from holograms and machine-readable code to embedded chips, Lester was a master whose work was undistinguishable from the real thing. He was on loan to Lam in payment for services rendered to the elders in Hong

Kong, and his original assignment had been to train counterfeiters working in a shop owned by Eddie Leung. However, the talent pool had proven to be disappointingly shallow and Lester was doing much of the important work himself.

The arrangement was that Lester worked for Eddie and was paid by him. Eddie in turn sold the finished product and pocketed the profits, on the understanding that his society brothers had priority when a document was required on short notice. Eddie was also required, along with the other members of the society, to donate generously to a charitable fund that was used to assist the less fortunate in the Chinese community in accordance with one of the thirty-six oaths each member had sworn to obey when joining the brotherhood. It was an arrangement that worked very well, even in the case of an idiot like Eddie Leung who was currently on bad terms with the society, but Peter suspected that something had gone wrong. Otherwise, the Dragon Head would not have brought Lester Ping to Peter's office for this meeting.

"Lester's been telling me an interesting story," Lam said. "I wanted you to hear it."

Peter looked at Lester Ping and made a conscious effort to relax his expression. "Please speak freely, Mr. Ping. I'm very interested in anything you may wish to tell me."

Lester Ping nodded, folding his hands in his lap. "Mr. Leung has been very good to me. He pays me very well for my work and treats me with respect."

"Of course," Peter said.

In addition to his big box electronics outlets located in Chinatowns in a number of large American cities, Eddie Leung also ran a profitable business out of the back door in pirated DVDs, stolen goods, wholesale pornographic movies and other such commodities. A cluster of warehouses along the riverfront were managed for Eddie by his son, Tommy. When the time had come to set up a full-scale counterfeiting operation, the Dragon Head and White Paper Fan of the day had deliberated long and hard before deciding that Eddie was the appropriate choice to operate the business. Although not well-respected, he had a knack for making money and his electronics stores provided an ideal distribution system. Help came to Eddie from all sides. Once the business was in operation everyone was pleased. At the center was identity theft, where personal information was illegally obtained from the public and used in a variety of ways, including phony bank loans and mortgages, false tax returns, theft from bank accounts and a variety of counterfeiting activities including fake credit cards, birth certificates and passports. It was very profitable for Eddie right from the beginning.

However, the internal war between Lam and Philip Ling had spoiled Eddie's position within the society. He'd been friends with Philip before all hell broke loose and although he publicly disapproved of Philip's rebellion against the will of the society he privately sympathized with his friend. At first he quietly helped Philip behind the scenes but when the killing began he told his friend he would no longer be involved. A coward, he was deeply afraid of Peter. He made a great deal of noise about sitting on the fence and not taking sides in the dispute, but this position was as unpopular with his brothers as his earlier sympathy for Philip. Loyalty and fidelity to the society were of paramount importance, and since Lam was now the Dragon Head once again everyone was obligated to provide unconditional support to him, not sit on the fence and strike a phony pose that no one believed. It cost Eddie a great deal of face, and as a result he was marginalized within the society. No one interfered with his businesses or family and he was still expected to meet all his society obligations, but among his brothers his status and influence were greatly diminished.

"You're aware," Lester Ping said to Peter, "that I work in one of the warehouses on River Street used by Mr. Leung for his electronics business."

Peter nodded.

"Young Mr. Leung, the son, is in the next building. He has a large office upstairs, nicely furnished, very comfortable. Last week was the first time I ever saw the inside of this building, as I always mind my own business and stay where I'm told to stay."

"I understand, Mr. Ping," Peter said. Ping was excusing himself for not having reported before whatever it was that he was reporting now.

"Last week, however," Ping went on, "I delivered a bundle of credit cards to young Mr. Leung's office as a favor for one of the others. The man in question had to rush off unexpectedly, as his wife was giving birth. Mr. Leung was expecting the cards within the hour and I agreed to finish the job and take them over. Inside the other building I had to ask the way to Mr. Leung's office. It was necessary to hand-deliver the cards directly to Mr. Leung, you see. So I was shown upstairs and into Mr. Leung's office. I gave the cards directly to Mr. Leung."

Ping paused.

Peter suppressed a wave of impatience. "And?"

"I left as soon as he took the bundle of credit cards from my hand. They were very good work, incidentally. We pay ten dollars each for the holograms and have developed a technique to embed them into the plastic of the card rather than affix them to the surface where they can be felt by someone with a sensitive touch."

"I know," Peter said, "I've seen them."

"In any event," Ping went on, "when Mr. Leung's office door was opened for me by his secretary he was showing two men out another door at the back."

"I see," Peter said.

"I only saw them for a second, but I saw them again a few days later."

"The same two men?"

"They were unmistakable. It was mid-afternoon and I had walked around the back for a cigarette. Mr. Leung was talking to them in the parking lot behind his building. One man was a *gwailo* and the other a large black man. He shook hands with them, patted the black man on the back and they got into their car and drove away."

Lam stirred. "Lester told me about this immediately."

Peter raised his eyebrows. "Interesting. Well done, Mr. Ping. Can you describe them in more detail?"

"The Caucasian was perhaps five-ten and weighed about 180 pounds. He was maybe 40 years old. Straight dark hair. The black man was very big, maybe six-three or six-four, two hundred and forty pounds, shaved head. Black golf shirt, baggy chinos, big white sneakers. Obviously a muscle man."

"I see," Peter said.

"They drove away in a black sport utility vehicle."

"Did you happen to notice the license plate number?"

Ping recited the number.

"I've heard from Hong Kong," Lam said, "that something's wrong here. The whispers say that someone has been revealing *Hung* secrets to outsiders and stealing money that should be coming to the brotherhood. Obviously these violations of the sworn oaths must be corrected immediately. Perhaps Eddie Leung can help you find the culprit."

"Leave it with me," Peter said.


Within an hour he was walking unannounced into the flagship store of the Pagoda Home Electronics chain on Lancaster Road with Jimmy Yung, Donald Sheng and Foo Yee. Benny Hu remained in the car outside the front door.

Donald Sheng was a stocky, taciturn fighter who'd come to Peter from his father's dockyards many years ago. Foo Yee was a slender, wiry man from Hong Kong who'd been with Peter for four years. He was a master in multiple martial arts and an expert in firearms.

Peter led the way past displays of widescreen televisions, iPods, home theater systems and digital cameras to a staircase in the back corner leading upstairs to the main offices. At the foot of the stairs his way was blocked by a chunky Asian woman in black trousers, a yellow golf shirt with the Pagoda Home Electronics logo on the front and a name tag that said "Annie" and "Assistant Manager."

"May I ask where you think you're going, young man?" she said, fists on her hips.

Peter gazed at her in surprise. Behind him, Jimmy Yung grunted but

Peter made a quick, unobtrusive signal with his hand to negate any action. A man dressed identically to Annie came hurrying over to defuse the situation. His name tag said "Ken" and "Manager."

"I'm very, very sorry, Mr. Mah, please forgive her. She's new, from the store in Wilmingford." His face filled with alarm and fear, he moved Annie away from the staircase.

"That's quite all right," Peter said. "No harm done."

"Thank you, Mr. Mah, thank you." Ken herded Annie toward an aisle of printer cartridges, hissing in her ear, "Don't you know who that *is*?"

Peter went up the stairs and down a long, well-lighted corridor to a reception area. A man sitting in a chair reading a newspaper hastily got rid of the paper and began to stand up. Jimmy stepped over and put a hand on his shoulder, forcing him back down into the chair. A secretary behind a large desk half-rose from her place but sank down again when Foo pointed a warning finger at her. Peter opened a large oak door and walked into Eddie Leung's expansive office. Jimmy followed him in, closing the door behind them, while Foo and Sheng remained in the outer office to ensure there would be no interruptions.

Eddie was on the telephone with his back to the room, staring out the large window behind his desk. He turned around, frowning, and abruptly hung up the phone without saying goodbye. He made a quick movement with his hand that Peter answered, ritualistic gestures that acknowledged their mutual membership in the society and also indicated an understanding of their relative status within the society, authority on Peter's part and deference on Eddie Leung's part.

He reached for the telephone again. "Please, let me call for refreshments. Will you have tea?"

"No."

Eddie quickly replaced the phone and put his hands flat on the desk in front of him where they would stay out of trouble. "I'm honored by your visit. What can I do for you?"

Peter sat down in a comfortable armchair positioned at a corner of Eddie's desk and crossed his legs. He steepled his fingers and tipped them toward Eddie.

"You manage to keep informed about various events that affect your brothers?"

Eddie glanced nervously at Jimmy Yung, lounging against the closed door. It was a difficult question for him to answer, because it implied an acknowledgment that Eddie was a leper within the society, avoided by most members. He wasn't sure if he would be betraying someone by admitting that he had talked to them. Finally he swallowed and nodded.

"Yes, I manage to pick up things here and there. I have lunch now and then with Harry Chung. He fills me in on what's happening."

86

Peter nodded. Harry Chung was a chinless weakling who operated a fleet of tour buses. When called upon, he transported family members who had illegally entered the country to their loved ones in other cities in the region.

"Maybe you've heard rumors from Hong Kong about someone causing trouble."

Eddie shook his head wordlessly.

Peter slowly stood up. He withdrew a Mont Blanc pen from his inside jacket pocket and, reaching out, gently took hold of Eddie's left wrist. Pulling it to him, he brushed open Eddie's hand and drew the symbols for the number 25 on Eddie's moist palm. It signified "traitor." Then he gently folded Eddie's hand into a fist and put it down on the desk.

"I'm looking for that person," Peter said, resuming his seat and crossing his legs again. "I expect all brothers to help me in this search."

"I don't really know anyone, uh, like this."

"Business is going well?"

Eddie blinked, confused by the change of subject. "Not bad. Can't complain. Actually, it could be a lot better. The economy being what it is these days."

Peter made a face. "I don't mean this," waving a hand over his shoulder toward the electronics store, "I mean the business on River Street."

"Oh. Oh!" Eddie leaned back in his big leather chair. "That! Yes, going very well. You should see the credit cards we're turning out these days. Absolutely perfect!"

"I've seen them," Peter said. "Your son looks after things down there."

"Tommy? Yes, he does."

"Has he reported any problems I should look into for you?"

Eddie shook his head vigorously. "No, no. Nothing at all. Everything's fine."

"No outsiders trying to shake him down or move him out?"

"No, that's all fine. I have security people down there to look after that sort of thing if it happens but it hasn't, believe me."

"No inquiries from the police?"

Eddie looked shocked. "Not at all. It's very quiet."

"No outsiders bothering him?"

"Not at all."

"You're confident he's passing on to you everything that's coming in?"

Eddie looked blank for a moment until he understood what Peter was driving at. Horror swept across his face. "Yes, of course, absolutely! Tommy's a wonderful boy, completely trustworthy."

"I'm going down there this afternoon. Will he be there?"

"Uh," Eddie looked at his watch, "he should be."

Peter moved his thumb fractionally in the direction of the telephone on Eddie's desk. "Call him and tell him to wait for me. I want to make sure everything's all right."

"He'll be there," Eddie promised. "And thank you. Tommy will be glad to know you're keeping an eye on things to make sure no one tries to fuck with us."

Peter raised an eyebrow and stood up. Either Eddie Leung was a complete fool, or he had a reserve of courage somewhere inside that would prompt him to say such a thing in the face of complete disaster. As it was, Eddie's son Tommy had two choices before him. He could run, in which case Eddie's businesses would be taken away from him and given to someone else and Eddie would end up in several plastic bags at the municipal dump. Alternatively Tommy could stay and deal with Peter, in which case Tommy might end up in several garbage bags. Either way, the Leung family was in deep, deep trouble.

# 11

The warehouse complex owned by Eddie Leung was surrounded by high chain link fences. Karen pulled up at the gate and lowered her window. After a moment the sash slid back in the guard booth and a face stared down at them.

"This place closed to all visitors," the guard said in a heavy accent. "Leave immediately."

Karen held up her badge. "We're here to see Tommy Leung."

"Mr. Leung not here. Leave now."

"Funny man." Karen clipped the badge back on her belt. "Open the gate and we'll have a look for ourselves."

"Not without warrant. This private property."

Karen glanced over at Hank. "They're well trained, anyway." She turned back to the guard. "Call Leung and tell him we're here to see him."

"Mr. Leung not here."

Hank got out of the car and walked up to the little window in the booth. He noticed a security camera perched above the booth and assumed it was real. He stared at the man sitting inside and then nodded.

"I know you. I've seen your face before. You're wanted on a federal warrant. Step out of the booth right now."

"You fucking nuts."

"What's your name?" Hank challenged, moving his jacket to one side to expose his gun.

"Got no name. Get lost."

Hank turned his head slightly. "Detective, call it in. We've got the fugitive William Lee Fung here. Call for backup and call the Feds. Might as well call the TV station to send a truck down here, we'll get on the ten o'clock news for sure with this one. This is big."

"Right, Lieutenant," Karen said, reaching for the radio.

The man in the booth couldn't see past Hank to know for certain whether or not Karen was actually calling it in. "TV?"

"You bet. This warehouse will be seen on every TV from here to Canada. The Leungs are going to be really pissed."

Panic flickered across his face. "Wait, you wrong. Not William Fung. Got green card right here."

He started to reach for his wallet but Hank stopped him with a raised hand. "Hold it. No fast moves."

"No calling."

"Get Tommy Leung down here right now."

"Okay, tell her no calling."

"Wait for a moment, Detective," Hank said over his shoulder.

"All right, Lieutenant," Karen sang out dutifully.

Hank pointed. "Get him down here. Now."

The guard picked up a push-to-talk mobile phone and spoke briefly in Cantonese. There was a reply and the guard nodded to Hank. "Be here soon."

"He better be. I hate waiting."

"Be here soon," the guard repeated.

The mobile phone flared and the guard replied before nodding to Hank. "Coming now."

"Great."

Karen shut off the engine and got out of the car.

A few moments later a small entourage arrived on the other side of the gate. Words were exchanged in Cantonese and a narrow door opened in the fence between the guard house and the large gate blocking the driveway. A young man stepped out, followed by two others who stationed themselves behind him.

"I'm Tommy Leung," he said. He was fairly tall and a little heavy in the torso and hips. He wore a plain white shirt with the collar open and the sleeves turned up on his forearms, black denim jeans and black wingtip shoes. His glasses had thick black frames and his watch was large and expensive. The two men behind him were muscle. They stared at Hank and Karen, arms folded on their chests.

"I'm Lieutenant Donaghue," Hank said, showing his badge, "and this is Detective Stainer. We have a few questions for you. Why don't we go inside to your office and sit down for a few minutes?"

Tommy Leung shook his head. "We can talk here. I don't have a great deal of time, Lieutenant. What's this about?"

"How old are you, Tommy?" Karen asked.

"Twenty-eight. Why?"

"Where'd you go to school? State?"

"Yeah, that's right."

"You graduated five years ago and started working for your father right away, did you?"

"Yeah, but I don't understand—"

"Did you work for him while you were still a student?"

Tommy frowned. "Yes, part time."

Sensing Tommy's discomfort, the smaller man behind Tommy took a step forward. Karen smiled at the little group. "Why don't y'all run along and chew on a dog biscuit somewhere before somebody gets hurt?"

"Tommy," Hank said, "we understand that you were friends with Martin Liu when you were both students at State."

"Martin?" Tommy's eyebrows went up. "Yeah, sure. We were friends. Is that what this is about?"

"Any idea who shot him, Tommy?" Karen snapped. "Maybe one

90

of these mongrels?" Before Tommy could answer she looked at Hank. "No need to wait on backup, Lieutenant. Let's take them all downtown right now. They'll be pissing down their legs inside of two minutes."

Tommy turned and barked orders in Cantonese. The men bowed quickly and disappeared back inside the fence. "I apologize for any misunderstanding. There's a lot of crime in this neighborhood and one can't be too careful."

"Yeah, I'll bet," Karen said. "What about the question? Any idea who shot your friend four years ago?"

Tommy made a face. "No, not at all. It was very upsetting. We were good friends. Whoever did it deserved to be caught and punished, but the police never found the person responsible." He looked from Karen to Hank. "Have you reopened his case?"

At that moment the guard stuck his head out the little window and said something in Cantonese to Tommy, who frowned and replied impatiently.

"I'm sorry," he said, "there's a call for me from my father. I said to tell him I'll call him back."

"What do you do for your father around here?" Hank asked.

"I'm the manager of warehouse operations."

"So you run this place?"

"Yes. This facility supplies all of the stores in the Pagoda chain along the eastern seaboard."

"Is that what you did four years ago?"

"Yes."

"Were you looking after your father's side interests back then as well?"

"I don't know what you mean."

"Sure you do, Tommy," Karen said. "Fencing stolen property, laundering bags of cash, that sort of thing. Were you taking care of that for your dad back then, too?"

"This is a legitimate business operation and I resent the racial slurs implied in your accusations. I'm going to speak to our attorney about it and file a complaint of racial harassment."

"Help yourself, Tommy," Hank said. "We'd be happy to get all this on the record."

"You'll both be writing parking tickets in Granger Park in a week."

Hank looked pained. "See, that's a real mistake, Tommy, to try to lean on us like that, because we're both stress addicts and we love to take on little arsewipes like you. It spices up an otherwise bland day, but I understand you might not know that about us. You might be thinking we're self-conscious civil servants with pensions to protect and publicity to be afraid of, but nothing could be farther from the truth. We're nothing like that. We're really har-

91

dassed sonsabitches who love to mix it up, and the way I see it you've got two choices. Either stand here and answer our questions like a good little boy or else call those meatheads back and we'll take all of you downtown like Detective Stainer here suggested. I'm beginning to think she's right that you had something to do with Martin Liu's murder. It's time to find out."

Tommy held up a hand. "No. Look. That's wrong. It's not like that."

"Not like what, Tommy?" Karen pressed. "You saying you didn't kill Martin Liu or have one of those shitheads do it for you?"

"No, no, of course not! Marty was my friend, I really loved that guy! I can't believe you think I had something to do with it."

"Then set us straight," she said, crossing her arms. "Any idea who did kill him?"

"No, not at all."

At that point a whirring sound started up in Tommy's pocket. He grimaced and removed his BlackBerry to look at the display. "My father," he said, slipping the device back into his pocket.

"We understand Martin was upset the day before he was killed," Hank said. "Know anything about that?"

"No, I don't. I didn't see him that day."

"When was the last time you saw him?" Karen snapped.

"I don't know, I can't remember. It was a couple of days before he died, we spent the night barhopping. He seemed all right to me."

"He wasn't upset with you about anything?" Hank asked.

"No, not at all."

"He wasn't pissed because you were running stolen property out of your daddy's warehouse?" Karen asked. "He didn't try to talk you into going straight?"

"No, nothing like that happened. Where are you getting all this from?"

"Was Martin running drugs?"

Tommy looked shocked. "Of course not! He was as straight as an arrow." Understanding dawned in his face. "That's right, he was found with heroin on him. But there's no way he was selling."

"Wasn't branching into a little side business for you, was he, Tommy? Did you set him up with a little merchandise and send him off to start up his own little enterprise?"

"Of course not! I'm not involved with drugs. I'm not stupid."

"No," Karen agreed, "somebody else handles that piece of the pie while you look after the stolen property and the cash. Just a part of the big machine."

"It's not like that."

Karen sighed. "It's exactly like that. We're not stupid either, Tommy. Look, it's a lot of fun playing whack-a-mole with you, kid, but all we're inter-

92

ested in is who killed Martin Liu. I don't think there's much doubt you know something that could lead us to your friend's killer."

"I agree," Hank said. "I'm just not sure why he'd want to let the guy get away with it. He mustn't have been much of a friend. We must have that part wrong."

Tommy looked pained, but he shook his head stubbornly. "I'm sorry; I just don't know anything that will help."

Karen took out a business card and stuffed it into Tommy's shirt pocket. "Sure you do. And we'll be back to talk about it again real soon, but if you change your mind before then just give me a call and we'll come back for another chat."

They got into the Crown Vic, slamming the doors loudly. As Karen reversed out of the driveway and accelerated down the street Hank looked back at Tommy Leung, who stood where they had left him, arms folded defensively across his chest. Moving his eyes to the side mirror, he saw Tommy take out his BlackBerry and put it to his ear.

"That was pretty juvenile," Karen remarked, running a stop sign at the corner and turning left onto Haymarket Street.

"You mean with the guard and the ten o'clock news?"

She looked at him.

He smiled out the window.

# 12

It was late. After Karen dropped him off at his apartment building Hank showered and changed his clothes. He put on black trousers, a navy t-shirt, a black windbreaker and black sneakers. He put his wallet, badge, cell phone and gun into various pockets. He put a carton of cigarettes into a plastic bag. He put an envelope containing two hundred dollars in twenties into the pages of a large hardcover book and put the book into the bag with the cigarettes. He called a cab and went out for dinner at a restaurant that he liked down in South Shore West. After a few drinks at a bar he took a taxi across the river to a rat trap in South Shore East called the Turbo Club. When the taxi pulled away from the curb he turned his back on the Turbo Club and began to walk. Twelve blocks and three turns later it became quieter around him. Car traffic dropped to next to nothing and the sidewalks were empty. He doubled back for a block, took an alley to a side street and walked another six blocks. When he was satisfied no one was following him he changed course again and walked four blocks to the entrance of another alley.

One hand near his gun and the other holding the plastic bag, Hank turned into the darkened alley and paused for a moment to allow his eyes to adjust to the gloom. He began to make out the vague shapes of the dumpsters, the piles of cardboard cartons and torn garbage bags. Claws scuttled on the pavement and scraped on the metal dumpster lids as he moved forward. He smelled rotting garbage, old vomit, urine. He reached the end of the alley where it debouched into a back laneway. He turned right and started down the laneway, moving slowly and quietly.

After about half a block he came to an eight-foot high brick wall that enclosed a small yard behind one of the buildings. The building itself had once contained an appliance repair business and three floors of rat-infested apartments above it, but it was now abandoned and derelict, like most of the buildings in this neighborhood. He stopped at a solid wooden door that he knew was heavily barred from the inside.

He took a step back and cleared his throat. He took the cigarettes out of the plastic bag and tossed them over the wall. The carton thumped quietly on the ground on the other side. He waited patiently, glancing up and down the laneway. The immediate area was quiet. In the distance he could hear the incessant throb of traffic on the expressway and the sound of a ship's horn on the river.

A faint scraping sound told him the bars were being lifted away. In a moment the door cracked open and an indistinct figure showed in the darkened space.

"Evening, Smoke," Hank said quietly.

The door opened the rest of the way, revealing a tiny, elderly African-

American man wearing stained overalls, rubber boots and a dark shirt. The carton of cigarettes was shoved into one of the big pockets of the overalls. Smoke stepped aside and Hank went through the door. The old man barred the door behind him and led the way through a narrow trail between piles of scrap metal, broken appliances, bundled newspapers, computer monitors and other scavenged refuse. They reached the back door of a ten-by-eight clapboard enclosure that had served at one time as a back shed to the main structure. The walls had been crudely insulated with scavenged pink batting and covered with scraps of clear plastic serving as a makeshift vapor barrier. The floor, originally unpainted wood covered with thin, aged linoleum, was now a patchwork of industrial carpet scraps of various colors that had been painstakingly fitted together into a surprisingly neat and attractive surface. What could be seen of it, of course, for the shed was as crammed with stuff as the yard outside.

There was a neatly made cot, an armchair that tilted slightly to the right, a rocking chair, one rocker of which was held together with grey duct tape, a kitchen table and chair, a cluttered counter and sink, a toilet curtained off by an old sheet, and a small kerosene stove for cooking. A kerosene lamp gave the room its only light from an upturned wooden box next to Smoke's rocker. The rest of the room consisted of pile after pile of books, for Smoke was an avid reader.

"Thanks for the cigarettes." Smoke motioned to the armchair.

Hank sat down. "No problem."

Smoke settled gingerly into the rocking chair and began to rock. "You weren't seen, were you?"

"No."

Smoke shrugged as though he did not necessarily believe in Hank's ability to avoid being followed but was willing to suspend disbelief temporarily.

"How're you feeling?" Hank asked.

"Oh, not bad, not bad. Better than when we spoke last." The last time had been early January, during a snow storm, and Smoke had been very sick with a chest cold that Hank suspected was bronchitis. He had brought the old man a parka from an army surplus store. He could see the parka hanging on a nail in the corner.

Smoke's real name was Warren Archer. He was 67 years old, stood five feet six inches and weighed 137 pounds. His white hair was bound behind his neck in a long pony tail and his white beard was neatly trimmed. He wore glasses with heavy black rims and thick lenses. The glasses were mended at both hinges with black electrical tape.

A former high school history teacher, Warren had been accused of sexually assaulting a female student in 1975. He was fired by the school board when charges were laid, but when it went to trial the student admitted that her

95

accusations were false. She and her boyfriend, whom her parents disliked, had concocted the story to hide their own relationship and her pregnancy. It was too late for Warren to salvage his life, however. His wife had already filed for divorce, forcing him from their home, and his friends had turned their backs on him in distaste. Although he was innocent, the whiff of scandal stained him and Warren found himself without a job, a family or a home. He lived in his car while he hunted for work but soon discovered that the publicity surrounding the case had rendered him unemployable. He sold the car for a few hundred dollars in cash to buy food. He fell into the street life because it was the path of least resistance and he'd been there ever since.

He became known as Smoke because he liked to ask passersby for a smoke before following up with a request for spare change. Alcohol kept him warm at night and became a problem for a while, which was how Hank first met him. Drunk one summer night, Smoke was beaten up by teenagers and robbed of the few dollars in his pockets. Someone called it in and Hank, a patrol officer at that time, responded. He checked on the old man while he was in hospital and after Smoke was discharged made it his business to visit him whenever he could. When Hank became a detective, Smoke began to furnish useful information about what was happening on the street. Being in South Shore East and well inside R Boyz territory, the old man saw a great deal.

"What's happening around?" Hank asked. It was understood that Smoke wouldn't offer him any hospitality such as tea or coffee. He wouldn't be staying long.

"Oh, this and that." Smoke removed one of the packs of cigarettes from the carton and peeled off the cellophane.

"I'm looking into the shooting of a Chinese kid off 121st Street four years ago."

"Long time ago." Smoke freed a cigarette from the pack and lit it with a match from a book of paper matches that advertised a restaurant not far from here. Hank knew that the cook gave Smoke a meal once in a while from the back door in exchange for taking out the garbage and performing other simple chores.

"Yeah. His name was Martin Liu. He was found in the alley next to the Biltmore Arms."

"Not many Chinese come into this 'hood." Smoke tipped his head back and exhaled, looking at the rafters above him. "I 'member, vaguely. Kid had horse or something he shouldn't have. How come you asking questions 'bout it now?"

"New information," Hank said. "A couple of names, Shawn and Gary. Shawn's a black guy and Gary's a white guy. May have had something to do with it."

"Shawn," Smoke repeated softly, rubbing his thumbnail across his lower lip. "Shawn and Gary." He shook his head and dragged on the cigarette.

"Nobody jumps right out." He smoked for a few moments. "Gary means nothing to me," he said finally.

"That's all right. What about Shawn?"

Smoke shrugged. "Only person come to mind is ShonDale."

"ShonDale. Who's that?"

"ShonDale Gregg. Works at a place owned by RaVonn Pease."

"R Boyz, that's what you're saying?"

"Yep."

"This ShonDale Gregg's some kind of tough guy?"

"Like to think he is," Smoke said, making a face. "Big sonofabitch, that's for sure, and like to throw his weight around. Quick with the fists. Bouncer at the En-R-G Club or whatever they call it, and extra security shit for the man."

ShonDale. Hank thought about the way in which a three-year-old boy might have difficulty saying the name and considered it a possibility.

"Arrogant sonofabitch too," Smoke went on. "One time I was looking for bottles behind the club and he come after me, like to kick my hairy ass into next week. If it weren't for Pease yelling at him to get in the car I'd've ended up in the hospital for sure. Arrogant bastard."

"Can you think of any reason why ShonDale would want to kill an Asian kid and dump him in R Boyz territory and fake a drug sale?"

Smoke stared into the shadows. The breath whistled through his nostrils. "Nope," he finally said. "Strange dude, though. Heard he moved out of the 'hood a while back, stopped hanging with the homies and got himself a crib down on the waterfront. Expensive digs, so I heard."

"When was this?"

Smoke pursed his lips. "Couple years back now. Still shows up at the door of Pease's club time to time, twisting arms and such. But putting on airs, like he's got a better gig and is just coming back to the slums for old time's sake."

"He been seen hanging out with Asians at all?"

"Nope," Smoke said, then frowned. "No, I'm wrong. Now you mention it, I heard tell a buncha Chinese been coming round to that club the last while. Damned strange, it being an R Boyz club and all." He looked at Hank. "They wouldn't get through the door less somebody let them, never mind live through the experience to come back for more. Heard it was Gregg watching out for them. Forgot that."

"That's very unusual."

"Tellin' me. Pudgy rich-lookin' Chinese kid and a couple tough guys, the way I heard it. And a white dude, too. Imagine that."

Somewhere in the alley a tin can rattled across the cracked pavement. Smoke butted out his cigarette and turned down the light from the kerosene lamp. As they sat in shadows, they could hear the sound of voices coming up

97

the alley.

Hank held his breath, listening. It was a couple of kids, young teen-agers from the sound of it. Hank listened as the voices grew loud and then faded as the kids moved away down the alley. When they were gone, he stirred in his chair.

"I better go."

"Thinking the same." Smoke cautiously turned the light up enough that Hank could see to leave.

Hank handed Smoke the plastic bag. "Thought you'd like this."

Smoke took the bag and removed the hardcover book that was inside. He held it under the lamp, studying the paper jacket. "*Team of Rivals*," he read aloud, "'*The Political Genius of Abraham Lincoln*, by Doris Kearns Goodwin. Winner of the Pulitzer Prize.' Well, now." He hefted the book and looked at Hank. "You read this?"

Hank nodded. "Last summer, while I was on vacation."

Hank was famous for his vacations, in which he took three weeks in September, rented a car and drove somewhere with the back seat full of books. It was the only time he drove a car himself. He picked a destination on the map and headed out, stopping whenever he felt like it to read and soak in his surroundings.

"This is very nice of you," Smoke said, leafing through the book. He saw the envelope containing the cash and kept on leafing.

"I think you'll like it. I know it's a period that interests you. It covers Lincoln's campaign to become President and the other Republican candidates who went on to form his cabinet after he was elected."

"I'll let you know what I think." Smoke set the book down carefully. "Lincoln was the greatest American of the nineteenth century."

Hank rose and began to make his way out of the cluttered shed. At the heavy wooden door, he paused. "Be safe."

"Always."

Back in the street after a slow negotiation of the laneway and alley, Hank walked six blocks to an all-night convenience store. He took out his cell phone and called a taxi. While he was waiting for it to arrive, he thought about the alley in which Martin Liu had died. He thought about the little boy who claimed he had been Martin Liu in another life. Maybe Karen was right, maybe it was all bullshit. Hank shivered, knowing that he wanted to hear the claims himself, coming from the boy's mouth.

# *13*

"Let's get married," Sandy Alexander said, propping himself up on an elbow to reach for his glass of beer on the nightstand beside the bed.

"No." Karen rolled over onto her side and stared at the folds in the drawn curtains hanging in her bedroom window.

"I was thinking maybe the last week of September. We can both book it off, get married, fly down to Jamaica, have a little vacation and honeymoon at the same time. It'd be nice."

"No," Karen repeated.

Sandy put the glass back on the nightstand. "Yeah, you're right. We could wait until November. That would be better."

"I ain't the marryin' kind," Karen drawled.

"Of course you're not," Sandy shot back. "Neither am I, but why should we let that stop us?"

Karen looked at the clock next to her bed and saw that it was 11:46 p.m. "When was the last time you went to church, Sandy?"

"A church wedding would be fine. Small, though. Nothing big."

Karen rolled over on her back and closed her eyes. "No, seriously. When was the last time you went to church? Voluntarily, I mean."

"Seriously?" Sandy slowly exhaled. "Voluntarily? I'd have to say when I was 17 years old. Don't forget, I'm from small-town Virginia. Church-going was serious social business for most families. I went every Sunday with my parents until I left home to go to college." Sandy was a graduate of the University of Virginia, where he majored in criminology, wrote music reviews for the university newspaper and deejayed late at night on the university radio station. He considered his small-town upbringing a tiny blip in the rear-view mirror that was steadily fading away in the distance behind him.

"We weren't church-goers at all. My parents sent me to Sunday School one summer when I was twelve," Karen said. "I beat up a kid, broke his nose, and there was a hell of a fuss. My father got the idea that maybe Sunday School'd make me a better little girl. It wasn't much of an experiment."

Sandy rolled over and rubbed her shoulder. "You never told me this before."

"What, going to Sunday School?"

"No, Christ. Beating up a kid when you were twelve and breaking his nose. How old was the kid?"

"Fifteen. He was picking on my brother. Brad was only ten."

"That's hot, Stains. So, how many guys have you beaten up over the years?"

"That's not what I'm talking about and you know it. I'm talking about church and religion. Believing in God. Be serious for a minute."

99

He patted her shoulder. "All right, you mean-assed ballbreaker."

She sighed.

"Okay. I haven't been to church just for the fun of it for ages. It's just not something that comes to mind as a thing to do when I get up on Sunday morning, know what I mean?"

"Do you believe in God?"

He thought about it for a moment. "Yeah, sure, I guess."

"And Heaven and Hell and all that?"

"I suppose. It's all part of the deal, isn't it?"

"Do you believe in reincarnation?"

"Reincarnation?"

"Yeah, you know, coming back after this life to live another life."

"You mean, like, if I'm a total prick in this life I could come back in the next life as a roach or an ostrich or something?"

"You're gonna come back as bacteria if you keep this up."

Sandy smiled in the darkness. "No, I'd have to honestly say I don't buy into that one. I mean, think about it. It would drive you crazy if you believed that stuff. Every time you swat a fly, you could be killing your great grandfather or something. It's too far-fetched for me. I figure you've got one shot. You make it good, you go to heaven. You screw it up, you go to hell. Simple as that."

"Yeah. I guess."

"Why do you ask?"

"No reason. Just wondering." Karen threw off the sheets and got out of bed. They had a hard and fast rule: no talking about their respective cases in the bedroom or any other place where they happened to be naked. Cases were professional and sex was personal and the two did not mix. The only time they allowed themselves to talk business was in an office or some other neutral setting where they might collaborate the way any two law enforcement officers might collaborate on business of mutual interest. As far as anyone was able to collaborate with the FBI, of course.

She walked over to the closet and took out a white terry towel robe. Behind her, Sandy switched on the lamp on the nightstand so that he could watch her.

"Let's get married, Stains."

"No." She tied the sash around her waist and walked barefoot out the bedroom door. "Maybe."

"Did I hear *maybe*? *Maybe*? She said *maybe*!"

Karen went to the bathroom and then on into the study to turn on the computer. While it was booting up she got herself a bottle of beer from the refrigerator in the kitchen. She uncapped it and took it back into the study. She logged onto the internet and ran a Google search on Thomas Gaines University. She found their website, tracked down the Division of Supplementary

100

Studies and found Dr. Maddy Walsh. As she browsed through the website she heard Sandy get up and go into the bathroom. The shower started and he began to sing off-key. *Hell*, she thought, *I'm gonna have to think about it. Goddamn him anyway, the cute little bastard.*

She found a series of links to articles published by Dr. Walsh on reincarnation, childhood memories of previous lives, near-death experiences and other things that they researched in Memphis. She began to read them, one by one, and was barely aware of Sandy coming in, kissing her on the top of her head, telling her he'd call tomorrow, and letting himself out of her apartment.

She needed to read.

She needed to understand this reincarnation stuff.

# *14*

The next day was busy. When Hank finally found time to run Shon-Dale Gregg in the system in the afternoon he turned up the usual rap sheet for a muscle man with gang connections. It featured a number of arrests and a couple of convictions, one for assault. He'd done a short stint in prison. It was a typical record for a gang member known for intimidation.

Karen sat down at her desk and shook her head. "Nothing from Liu's ex-girl friend. According to her, they weren't that close and he didn't talk a lot about himself. Didn't talk at all about Mah."

Karen and Waverman had gone out to Springhill to interview Susan Chong, Martin's girl friend before his murder.

"Waverman doesn't like the way I drive," Karen said. "Control issue, I guess."

Hank laughed as his cell phone rang. He took it out, looked at the call display, didn't recognize the number, and thumbed the button.

"Donaghue."

"Hello, Lieutenant Donaghue? This is Michael Chan speaking."

"Dr. Chan, how are you?" Hank looked at Karen, who stopped what she was doing to listen.

"Fine, thank you," Michael replied. "Uh, listen, I wonder if I could talk to you about this whole thing with my son, Taylor."

"That would be fine, Dr. Chan."

"Please, just call me Michael."

"All right, Michael. What would you like to discuss?"

"Frankly, some of the things my son is saying have me concerned. I understand you and another detective met with my wife yesterday."

"That's correct. Detective Karen Stainer."

"Right. You mentioned to Grace that the student, Josh Duncan, was hurt by associates of my wife's cousin, Peter Mah. Anyway, I kept the business card you gave her, although I didn't think there'd be any point in talking to you."

"But you've changed your mind, I take it."

Michael sighed. "Taylor said some things this morning in the car that upset me. Things about this Martin Liu and who killed him. I called Grace about it and said we should reconsider talking to you. She seemed a little strange and then admitted her cousin Peter asked her not to involve the police any further, that it wouldn't be in Taylor's best interests. I'm not at all comfortable with that."

"I see," Hank said.

"I know where Grace is coming from, Lieutenant. You have to understand that Peter Mah has a very forceful personality and Grace is intimidated by him. But I'm not, and I won't have him dictating to me what's in the best interests of my son."

Karen was writing something on a scrap of paper. She slid it over.

"All right, Michael. What would you like to do?" Hank looked down at the scrap of paper.

*Talk to the kid.*

"I'm calling from my office right now," Michael said. "Could you come out here to State and meet with me before the end of the day?"

"We can be there in about forty minutes."

"Half an hour," Karen said.

"That would be fine," Michael said, sounding relieved.

"We'd like to talk to your son," Hank said.

"Okay. He's in daycare right here on campus. I drop him off in the mornings and pick him up at the end of the day." There was a pause. "I don't think that would be a problem. If you want to meet me here in my office we could talk together before you see Taylor and then we could go over to the daycare."

"Sounds like a plan," Hank said. "Detective Stainer and I will see you there."

"Thank you very much, Lieutenant."

"Our pleasure."

They went downstairs and piled into the Crown Vic. Karen ripped out of the parking garage onto the street. On the expressway she relaxed her grip on the steering wheel and glanced over at him. "I'd really like to talk to this kid. I've been reading up on this stuff, Hank. It's very weird."

"You've been reading up?" Hank repeated incredulously.

"Stuff it, Lou. There are kids all over the world like this Chan kid. They start reading at two years old all by themselves, for cryin' out loud, and they can describe places in other cities they couldn't possibly have seen before. They can sometimes even speak a language nobody else around them speaks. You know, a little four-year-old kid spouting Turkish or Punjabi or some goddamn thing. It's freaky."

"You *have* been doing your homework."

"Yeah, well, I like kids." She frowned and tapped the bottom of the steering wheel with her thumbs. "But this is so far out in left field. I hate not understanding something right in front of me. These guys, this Dr. Walsh and the rest of them at the university who're studying this stuff, they have a shit-load of information on the internet. It's pretty scientific. I mean, it's not that New Age crap you see about inner enlightenment and great spirits or whatever the hell those idiots go on about all the time."

Hank smiled.

"They're very scientific," she repeated. "I admit it, it hooks you. I really wanna see those birthmarks." She sighed. "It's not something we can

103

just up and ask him to show us out of the blue. The kid has a right to privacy and we can't just tell his dad to pull down the kid's drawers so we can take a look. I tell you, though, Hank, I really wanna see those birthmarks with my own eyes."

"I hear you."

They reached the campus of State University and found their way to the building in which Michael had his office. Karen parked in the lot outside and, disdaining the meter on the sidewalk, tossed the police placard on the dashboard of the Crown Vic before following Hank inside.

They took the stairs up to the second floor and passed several class-rooms before turning a corner and heading down a corridor lined with offices. Passing students flicked glances at them before looking away. They might as well have had *COP* tattooed on their foreheads.

"What's the office number again?" Karen asked, looking around.

"You mean the fucking office number? Two-twenty six."

She shook her head at him. "Don't be so juvenile."

Hank stopped at an open door and knocked.

"Come in."

Michael Chan rose from his chair and came around the edge of his desk toward them. It was a small, narrow office lined with bookshelves on both sides. There were two wooden chairs waiting for them in front of the desk.

"Lieutenant Donaghue? I'm Michael Chan. Thanks for coming."

"Professor Chan." Hank held up his badge and shook his hand. "This is Detective Karen Stainer."

"Detective." Michael reached past Hank to shake Karen's hand. She was holding up her badge but Michael didn't seem to notice it. "Please," he said, "sit down. I really appreciate you taking the time to see me. You can understand this has been very difficult for all of us."

Hank and Karen sat down. Hank took out his notebook and pen. "I can imagine. You mentioned on the phone your son was saying some things to you that we should hear?"

Michael sat down and clasped his hands together on the desk in front of him. "That's correct. We were driving in this morning." He paused. "It was just before the off-ramp for Youland Boulevard, on the expressway. A black limo passed us. Taylor saw it and thought it was Peter."

"He thought it was Peter Mah's limo?"

"That's right. He pointed to it and said, 'Peter.'"

"Does Peter Mah travel in a limo like the one you saw?"

"To be honest with you, Lieutenant, I don't know."

"Would Taylor have seen him in a limo like it?"

"Again, I don't know. We don't have anything to do with Peter Mah, and when he does come around to our house, which is almost never, it's always when I'm not home because he knows I don't like him. So I've never seen what car he drives. Or is driven in, however it works with *them*."

Hank heard the distaste in Michael's voice. "Okay. Go ahead."

"Well, Taylor said he used to go for rides in that limo when he was Martin. And no, I don't know if he's ever ridden around with Peter, but I seriously doubt it. I can't see Grace letting things go that far. Anyway, he went on to talk about going to parties with Peter in the limo and it having a bar and food in it and so on."

"Maybe he went for a little ride in it," Karen said, "and Mrs. Chan hasn't mentioned it because she knows how you would feel about it."

Michael looked at her, compressing his lips in a visible attempt to control a surge of frustration. "Perhaps, Detective, but I doubt it. And from there it just got farther and farther afield. He started talking about one of his friends, someone named Johnny. No, Tommy."

"Tommy?" Hank said, writing it down. "He mention a last name?"

"No, just Tommy. He said something about going to school with this Tommy, who was his best friend. I asked around at the daycare and there's one boy named Thomas and the parents insist he be called that, Thomas, and Taylor doesn't play with him at all, anyway." Michael looked from Hank to Karen. "He doesn't have any friends named Tommy. He takes swimming lessons with a kid named Timmy, but there's no Tommy."

"Anything else?"

"Yes. He talked about this Tommy being scared of Peter, that Peter sometimes hurts people and that Tommy was scared of him."

"Really." Karen leaned forward.

"I started taking notice at this point," Michael told her, "because Taylor's never shown any signs of being afraid of Peter before. Of course he's not an approved topic of conversation around our dinner table, but just the same in the few times he's spoken of Peter in my hearing there was never any negative emotion at all. This was quite unexpected."

"And it wasn't that *he* was afraid of Peter," Karen said, "it was that this Tommy was afraid of him."

"Correct. Peter was mad at him, or was going to be mad at him, or something. Then it got really bizarre. He said he knew what this Tommy was afraid of, and that he, meaning himself, should have told Peter about it. He said, 'I should have told Peter about it because he trusted me.'"

Hank said nothing, writing. Karen waited for the rest of it.

"You don't seem to understand," Michael said. "Taylor's only three and a half. Trust is a concept we haven't really discussed with him yet. It's implicit in what we've told him about his caregivers, you know, if someone bothers him he should tell us about it right away, and so on, but we haven't really used that word very much with him yet, especially in this context. That Peter would trust him, as in *rely* on him or *expect* him to speak up about something that someone else was doing."

"Maybe it's something they've talked to the kids about at daycare," Hank suggested. "You know, if someone comes along and bothers you, go right away to someone you trust and tell them about it."

"Maybe. I don't know. But then he went on to say his other daddy, his real daddy, used to say to him that Peter was a criminal who should be put in jail. *Then* he said that I shouldn't worry, Peter would never hurt him. *Then*, on top of everything else, he said this Tommy knows who murdered him when he was Martin."

"Oh?" Karen raised her eyebrows.

Michael spread his hands. "You see, Detective, each one of these things can have a simple explanation. Occam's Razor, right? The simplest explanation that fits the known facts is usually the correct one. But put them all together, back to back like that, and then cap it off by saying we should tell the police that Tommy knows some guy named Shawn killed him when he was Martin, then I start to get a little bit upset."

"That's understandable," Hank said.

"Having said that," Michael went on, "the last thing I want to do is expose my son to a police investigation."

"We understand, Dr. Chan," Karen said, "but the things your son's apparently saying, and the fact that Josh Duncan was assaulted by associates of Peter Mah on Monday because of his research into your son's case, are things we can't completely ignore."

"I know." Michael looked grim. "Can you tell me something? About your investigation?"

"That depends on what it is," Karen replied.

"I never really knew Martin Liu at all, to speak of. He attended our wedding and I think I spoke to him once briefly at some gathering after that. Did he have a friend named Tommy?"

Karen glanced at Hank. "Yes he did, as a matter of fact."

Michael bit his lower lip and looked away. He leaned back and closed his eyes for a moment. Hank and Karen watched him struggle to maintain his composure. Finally he took a deep breath, opened his eyes and turned back to them.

"When ... Taylor says things like 'my before daddy' or 'my other daddy,' I feel as though I haven't been a proper father to him, as though he has to invent some other father who was much better than I am. It kind of ... rips me apart, know what I mean?"

"Yeah," Karen said.

"My initial reaction, on the surface, is always that he's just making these things up. He has an active imagination and like any kid, he hears stuff on television he's not supposed to hear and then repeats it out of context. But when Taylor says these things my skin starts to crawl. I don't quite know how

106

to deal with it. And now you're telling me that there really was a Tommy." He paused and searched Karen's face. "*Is* a Tommy?"

She nodded. "We've talked to him about Martin. He doesn't have anything useful to say at this point."

"He won't want to talk to Taylor, will he?" Panic crackled across his face. "Will he come around looking for Taylor? Will he hear about these things Taylor's saying about him?"

"Not from us, he won't," Karen said firmly. "Like I said to your wife the other day, we don't consider Taylor a source of evidence in this case. If he can tell us something that'll point us in the right direction, great, but the Assistant State's Attorney'll expect us to build our case with more, uh, traditional evidence as a foundation. We'll do everything we can to insulate y'all from our investigation in every way possible." She stood up. "It'd be great if we could see Taylor now."

"Of course." Michael glanced at his watch. He stood up and grabbed his briefcase. "Are you parked in the lot downstairs?"

"In front of this building, yeah." Karen moved aside as Hank stood up and Michael bustled forward, fishing his keys from his pocket.

"My car's in the faculty lot behind. I'll drive around to the front and you can follow me from there. The campus is a bit of a rabbit's warren."

"I'm a State grad," Karen said. "I remember my way around pretty well, although there wasn't a daycare back then."

"Really? What was your major?"

"Criminal justice."

"Of course. Well, the daycare is right at the back of C quad. Do you remember where that is?"

"Yep."

"Fine, let's go."

They went out into the corridor and Michael locked his office door behind him. The man's emotions were all over the place, no doubt because of the stress under which his son's experiences were placing him. Is this what it's like having a kid? Karen watched Michael's shoulders hunch up involuntarily as they followed him down the hallway. It was a question she'd already asked herself a hundred times before in her career as she watched a parent trying to deal with crisis after crisis. She knew she'd been hard on her own father, but that had been nothing compared to what she'd seen since becoming a cop. She was hardnosed and tough, but she wasn't sure if she was hardnosed and tough enough to be a parent.

Down in the car she started the engine and looked at Hank. "I reserve the right to change my opinion as more information comes to light, Lieutenant. That's all I'm saying."

Hank looked sideways at her. "What?"

"I know what I said before, you know, about paranormal bullshit off of late night TV and all. I'm just saying it should be okay to be a little flexible here. You got a problem with that?"

Hank shook his head. "Nope."

Michael pulled up behind them and tooted his horn. Karen shifted into reverse and, as Michael drove away, she swung out of the parking space and followed him.

The daycare center turned out to be on the other side of the campus from the building in which Michael Chan had his office. It was pick-up time for many of the parents and the parking lot was busy with cars pulling in and backing out. Karen started to pull into an empty space but stopped, finding it blocked by a mother who was putting her child into a car seat in the back of a blue hatchback. Hank glanced at Karen, expecting her to be gritting her teeth in frustration, and was surprised to see a benign smile on her face as she waited patiently for the mother to secure the child, close the rear door, wave apologetically at them and slip into the driver's seat. Karen slid into the empty spot and killed the engine.

"It's possible the kid won't have anything to say right now," she said. "Apparently it's something that can come and go with them."

Hank unbuckled his seat belt. "We'll take our chances, I guess."

They followed Michael to the entrance of the daycare where he turned around and held up a hand.

"I'll go in and get him. You can talk to him out here."

"All right."

They killed time for a few minutes outside the front door, watching the parents and children come and go.

"Ever wish you had kids, Lou?"

"Yes and no."

Karen chuckled. "My sentiments exactly."

"Here we go," Michael said, coming out the door.

Taylor walked slowly in front of him. He wore dark blue jeans with the cuffs turned up above his sneakers and a blue and green knitted sweater. There was a small knapsack on his back featuring television cartoon characters. He looked up at Hank, who was standing closest to the door. The boy's eyes were wide and his mouth was slightly open.

"Hello, Taylor," Hank said.

"These are the police officers I told you about, Taylor," Michael said. "Let's go over here and we can talk to them for a minute." He led the way away from the front entrance across the paved courtyard to a spot that was free from the traffic of parents and children leaving the center.

Hank bent down so that his eyes were on a level with the boy's. "My name's Hank. Your name's Taylor, right?"

Taylor pressed himself back against his father's legs, staring at Hank.

"We were talking to your daddy," Hank went on, "and he said you wanted to talk to us about some things you remembered."

The boy said nothing, staring at him, his eyes traveling from Hank's frizzy brown hair to the white teeth in his smiling mouth.

"About Martin Liu. Do you remember Martin Liu?"

The boy turned and buried his face into his father's leg.

"Jesus, Lou," Karen muttered. Standing behind Hank, she unclipped her holster and reattached it to her belt behind her back, under her jacket, where the boy wouldn't see it. She tapped Hank on the shoulder. "Come on, back off. Leave this to me."

Hank stood up and looked at her.

"You're just too big and scary looking," Karen said. "Stand aside."

Hank moved out of the way.

"Just take a walk back to the car, will you? You're spooking the shit out of him."

Hank began to walk back toward the parking lot.

"Hey there, Taylor, my name's Karen. Do you have a nickname, like Tay, or Tikki or something, or do you like to be called Taylor?"

Taylor took his face out of his father's pant leg. "Just Taylor."

"Well, that's fine. My nickname's Tex, on account I'm from Texas. You can call me Tex if you like, or just Karen."

"Karen's better," Taylor said quietly. "Tex is a boy's name."

"Yeah, sometimes, I guess. Hey, are those swings over there?" She pointed at the play area not far from where they were standing.

"Yeah."

"You think they'd let me go on the swings for a minute? I love to swing."

Taylor looked at her. "You're not too big. I think it's okay."

"Great. Wanna swing with me? If your daddy says it's okay?"

"Go ahead, Taylor, if you want to," Michael said.

"Okay."

She took him by the hand and led him off toward the swings. "Do you have one that's your favorite?"

"No."

Michael started to follow them, hesitated, slowed down, and then drifted back toward Hank, who had reached the edge of the parking lot.

"The kids are all going home now," Karen said, "so we can have whatever swing we want." She sat down in the middle swing and pushed back and forth experimentally while Taylor watched her. "Come on," she said, "don't just stand there." She pushed at the swing next to her. "This one's calling your name. It's saying, 'Taaay-lor, swing on me, man.'"

Taylor rolled his eyes. "No, it's not." He sat down on the swing.

"Can you swing high?" She began to swing back and forth, looking at him. "Come on, swing!"

She began to put a little effort into it, swinging higher and higher. "Come on!"

Taylor began to swing. In a few moments he was grinning at Karen when they passed each other in their individual arcs. Finally Karen began to slow down, lightly scuffing her shoes on the dirt each time she reached the bottom of an arc until she was barely moving back and forth. Taylor soon realized that she was stopping and he did the same. When they were motionless he looked into her eyes.

"Are you really a cop?"

"Yep." Karen unclipped her gold shield and handed it to him. "Check it out."

He took it and examined it closely, running his fingertips across its surface. "Wow."

"I say the same thing every morning when I put it on, Taylor. It's pretty cool."

"Yeah."

Karen took her shield back. "There was something you wanted to talk to me about."

Taylor glanced over his shoulder, looking for his father.

Karen pointed. "He's over there with Lieutenant Donaghue."

Taylor searched, found his father standing next to Hank, arms folded, trying not to watch them. "He doesn't like Uncle Peter."

"Yeah, that's what he said. Do you like Uncle Peter, Taylor?"

"Yeah. He brings me presents and he teaches me Chinese words."

"That's cool," Karen said.

"Yeah."

There was silence for several moments. Karen waited patiently.

"My friend Tommy's scared of Uncle Peter."

"How come?"

"'Cause he did something Uncle Peter doesn't like. He was friends with other men and shared his money with them. Not Chinese men."

"You mean somebody stole Tommy's money?"

"No, he shared it with them. It was like a game. Tommy took people's money and he shared it with a *gwailo* instead of his daddy. If Uncle Peter found out, he'd hurt Tommy."

"What kind of word was that, Taylor?"

"*Gwailo*. It means a white man. Not Chinese. Uncle Peter taught me that when I was Martin."

"Did you like Uncle Peter when you were Martin?"

"Yeah, I always like Uncle Peter."

"Did he ever hurt you when you were Martin?"

"No!" Taylor looked at her sharply. "He never hurt me! I don't know

110

why Daddy, my now Daddy, doesn't like him. He's really nice to me."

"That's all right, Taylor. I understand. But Shawn and Gary hurt you, did they?"

Taylor shut his mouth tightly and looked away.

"I know it's scary," Karen said. "We don't have to talk about it if you don't want to."

Taylor said nothing.

"Did you like Josh? The man who came to your house to talk to you about when you were Martin?"

Taylor nodded his head.

"Yeah, he seems nice," Karen said. "He told me he likes you, too."

Taylor said nothing, watching a bird fly across the yard.

"Josh told me that you said Shawn looked like him. Like Josh, I mean."

Taylor shook his head. "He looked different, but he had dark black skin like him."

"Shawn looked different."

"Yeah."

"How did he look different, Taylor?"

Taylor said nothing.

"Was he bigger than Josh?"

Taylor nodded.

Karen waited.

"He had a bald head and a picture on the side of his neck," Taylor said quietly.

"A picture? You mean a tattoo?"

Taylor nodded. "Uncle Peter has pictures too. I watch them on TV do them."

"Oh, sure, I've seen that show too. *Miami Ink.* Cool stuff." Karen paused. "What tat did Shawn have on his neck, Taylor? What'd it look like?"

Taylor shrugged. "It looked like writing on a wall."

"You mean graffiti?"

"I think it was an R."

"An R? You know your letters already?"

"Sure, I learned them already."

"Wow, that's pretty impressive, Taylor." Karen paused. "What about Gary, who was he?"

Taylor shrugged. "I don't know. I didn't know those men before. I heard the other man call him Gary, that's all."

"You heard Shawn call him Gary?"

"No, the other man."

"There was another man there besides Shawn and Gary?"

"Yes."

111

"Do you know what his name was?"

Taylor shook his head.

"That's all right. What'd he look like?"

"Mean," Taylor said. "White, like you."

"Okay, good. So what did Gary look like?"

"Not so big."

"Not as big as Shawn, you mean."

"Yeah. And his skin was white, too."

"What color was his hair?"

"Not like yours," Taylor said. "Black, like mine."

"Okay. What else do you remember about Gary?"

"Nothing." He paused. "He was crazy."

"Crazy? What do you mean?"

"He kept yelling at me. I was crying and he kept yelling at me to tell him who I told and I kept saying 'I didn't tell anybody' and he kept yelling 'you're a fucking liar, who did you tell?' and I just kept crying and saying I didn't tell nobody."

Karen shivered. She gripped the ropes of the swing tightly. Taylor had lowered his voice to imitate the man and the effect was chilling. Tears slipped down the boy's plump cheeks. She slid off the swing, took a tissue out of her pocket and knelt beside the boy, dabbing at his tears.

"That's all right, Taylor. It's all right now."

"Shawn kept hitting me, and he hit me with his gun, and he kept hitting me with the gun and it went off."

"The gun went off while he was hitting you with it."

The boy sobbed. "He hurt my leg! Gary yelled at him 'you stupid asshole!' and Shawn said 'I'm sorry, I'm sorry, I didn't mean to, it was a accident' but my leg hurt bad and the blood was coming out and it was awful!"

He came out of the swing and threw himself into her arms, sobbing.

"Shh!" Karen whispered into his ear, rubbing his shoulder. "There there, Taylor, it's all right, we don't have to talk about it any more."

Behind her she heard the footsteps of Michael and Hank as they came toward them.

Michael took Taylor from her and swung him up into his arms. "That's enough, Detective. That's quite enough."

Karen looked at Hank wordlessly.

Michael turned and began to walk toward the parking lot, swinging Taylor around onto his right hip. Taylor pulled his head up from his father's shoulder and took hold of his ear.

"Wait, Daddy, wait. I didn't tell her about Tommy!"

"I think we've had enough of this for one day, Taylor."

"No, wait!" The boy twisted in his father's arm, looking for Karen.

She moved around beside Michael so that Taylor could see her.

112

"What is it, Taylor?"

Taylor let go of his father's ear and wiped his tears. "Tommy saw."

"You mean Tommy saw them hurt you? He was there?"

The boy nodded. "Tommy told them to."

Karen nodded. "Thanks, Taylor, for telling me all this stuff."

"Okay."

"Time to go home now," Michael said.

"Okay, Daddy."

Hank and Karen watched them walk between the parked cars and down the row to their car.

"Sounds like he talked to you," Hank said.

Karen exhaled noisily. "Sweet Jesus, Lou." She looked at him. Her face was pale and her eyes were wide. "I never heard anything like it before in my life. The kid's only three and a half."

"What did he say?"

She shook her head. "In the car. I gotta sit down."

They walked to the car and got in. Karen put the keys in the ignition but didn't start the engine. She stared sightlessly out the windshield at the swings. Hank waited patiently.

"Okay," Karen said finally, "okay. He repeated the story to me, the one you saw in the video from Duncan or whatever. These guys picked him up and took him some place and started working him over. This Shawn character and Gary. Gary's all crazy and yelling at him to spill what he knows, and this Shawn is pistol-whipping him until the gun goes off and shoots him in the leg."

"Did he say where this happened?"

Karen shook her head. "We didn't get that far. He was getting real upset, and then Chan came over and it was time to let it go."

"All right," Hank said.

"There was another guy there, white, some guy whose name Martin, Taylor, whatever, didn't know. And that fuckin' Tommy Leung was there, god-dammit. He told them to work Martin over." She paused. "Listen to me. Jesus. I sound like I believe all this stuff."

Hank looked at her.

"There's no way," she said flatly, cutting the air with the edge of her hand, "no fuckin' way this kid's reciting lines somebody's taught him. No fuckin' way. It's something else." She looked at him with a challenge in her eyes. "I don't care what you say, that kid genuinely thinks he remembers this stuff. Either the kid's a complete psychotic lunatic at the age of three and a half, or else. . . ."

She didn't really want to finish the sentence.

"Did you try him on the full name, ShonDale Gregg?"

She shook her head. "These things are kinda linear with kids. If you

113

change gears too fast you lose them."

"I understand, that's all right."

She started the engine. "He said this Shawn character had a tat on the side of his neck, like a gang tat, with an R in it."

"R Boyz?"

"Could be," she said. She threw the car into reverse and backed out of the parking spot. Most of the parents had already left with their children, and the lot was much quieter than when they had arrived. She accelerated down to the end of the row, swung left, and headed for the exit.

"Anything else?"

"How the hell do you get out of this place again? Oh, yeah." She turned right and gunned away, ignoring the signpost begging her to limit her speed to 20 miles per hour. Hank realized he had forgotten to put on his seat belt and hastily secured it around him.

"The kid said Tommy was playing some kind of game where he stole people's money," Karen said, gripping the steering wheel with both hands, "only he shared it with other people instead of his father. He used some kind of Chinese word, I forget what it was, meaning white people. Sounds like Tommy was thumbing his nose at the Triad, probably using outside help like ShonDale and this white guy Gary and some other white guy to run some kind of business. Gambling, maybe? Hard to say. Except Uncle Peter was going to be pissed off when he found out."

"According to Chan," Hank said, "Taylor said that Peter would have trusted him to tell him about something like that, and he didn't."

"And from what the kid just told me, Tommy and these guys grabbed him and pounded on him because they thought he *did* tell someone. One thing led to another, Martin got shot, started to bleed out, and they took him to the alley and dumped him. Some fuckin' friend Tommy was."

"So Tommy's running some kind of business behind the Triad's back," Hank said. "My CI told me Asians have been showing up at the En-R-G Club, where ShonDale still works from time to time. Could be Tommy and his muscle."

"So we got ShonDale, a white guy named Gary, Tommy and another white guy." She reached the main gates of the campus and accelerated around the corner onto Youland Boulevard. "I say we go with this. I say the kid's connecting some dots for us and we go with this, Lou."

"You sure?" Hank asked. "You comfortable with that?"

"No, I'm not fuckin' comfortable," she retorted, "not by a long shot. But it's making that funny sound, know what I mean? The sound of pieces fitting together."

"Yeah," Hank sighed, "I think it is. It wouldn't hurt to follow up."

"All right, then." Karen said. "Let's go have another palaver with that goddamned Tommy Leung."

114

# 15

Tommy, however, was nowhere to be found. They went back to the warehouse but were told by the floor supervisor that he'd left abruptly after their visit yesterday and hadn't been seen since. When pressed, the man led them to Tommy's reserved parking space. It was empty.

"He usually calls me if he's not coming in," he said. "He always has a list of stuff he wants me to do before he gets here. He didn't call. No list."

"Has he done this before?" Karen asked.

The man shook his head. "He's a workaholic. And a fanatic about efficiency. Very, very focused."

They went to his condominium and pounded on the door, but there was no answer. They convinced the building superintendent to let them in, but there was no sign of Tommy. It was a beautiful condo, expensively furnished, and nothing looked out of place. Nothing seemed missing from the bathroom and there were no empty hangers in the closet to suggest that Tommy had packed for a trip somewhere.

It was getting late so they went to The Brass Pump, where Karen had arranged to meet Sandy before dinner. They ordered beer and took a booth near the back.

"D'you think Mah's old man is connected to this?" Karen asked.

"Jerome Mah?" Hank shrugged. "Can't see how."

"Well, you just never know with these organized crime dudes."

"I met him once," Hank said.

"Who, Jerome Mah?"

Hank nodded. "When I was working in the Chief's office, I attended a charity event and met him there."

"Oh yeah, I heard you were a golden boy at one time. On your way to becoming Chief until you stepped on the wrong toes."

"You heard wrong," Hank said.

Karen scoffed. "That's probably why I like you so much. The toe-steppin' part, I mean."

Hank said nothing.

"What's old man Mah like?"

"He's nice enough. Modest, polite."

"And yet there he is, with a punk for a son."

"Who's a punk?" Sandy Alexander asked, sitting down at their table.

"Hey, baby," Karen said, leaning forward to kiss him. "How was your day? Bust any asses?"

"Nah, not today," Sandy said. "Sorry I'm late. How're you doing, Hank?"

Hank shook his hand. "Not bad, thanks."

"Who's a punk?" Sandy repeated, looking from Hank to Karen.

"Peter Mah," Karen said.

Sandy's eyebrows shot up. "You guys looking at him for something?" He snapped his mouth shut as the server approached to take his order. When she had brought him a beer and left again, he held up a hand. "Don't answer that question. But if you want a Bureau perspective on the local Triad, you could call Marie Louise Roubidoux or Will Martin."

"Sleaze," Karen muttered.

Sandy grinned at Hank. "We had a Christmas thing at the Four Seasons last year. "Will was new in town. He tried to pick her up before he knew she was already spoken for."

"Spoken for, ferfucksakes."

"She broke one of his fingers before I could get over there to straighten it out," Sandy said. "He's still scared to death of her."

Hank laughed.

"Yuk it up, funny boy," Karen snapped. "He was reaching straight for my 36 Cs."

"He was reaching past her to get his drink off the bar," Sandy explained, "and she misinterpreted the gesture."

Hank's cell phone rang. He took it out. "Donaghue."

"Oh, hello, Lieutenant Donaghue, it's Meredith Collier."

"Hello, Ms. Collier," Hank said, "how are you this evening?"

"Am I calling at a bad time? I can hear that you're out somewhere."

"No, it's fine," Hank said. "Is there a problem?"

"I just got a call from Peter Mah and I thought I should let you know about it."

"Did he threaten you?"

Karen leaned over to Sandy. "The Lou's new sweetie."

"No, but I should discuss it with you," Meredith Collier replied. "I can hear you're with someone; perhaps I should call back another time."

"No, that's all right, it's just Detective Stainer." Hank looked at Karen, who made a face.

*Just Detective Stainer*, she silently mocked.

"If you like we could meet and you could tell me about it."

"Did you want me to come downtown?" Meredith asked.

"I can come up there right now if you like."

"There's no emergency or anything," she said.

"Whatever you think is appropriate."

"All right then, if you could stop by I'd appreciate it."

"What's the address?" He took out his pen and notebook as she recited it. "I'll be there shortly." When he put the phone away, Karen grinned.

"Got a date, Lou?"

"For Christ's sake, it's not a date. She got a call from Peter Mah. Are you coming with me?"

"No thanks."

Hank stood up, putting the notebook and pen in his pocket.

"Don't do anything I wouldn't do," Karen said.

"That gives me a lot of latitude."

Sandy laughed.

Hank stopped at the bar. He caught the attention of the server and put two twenty-dollar bills on the bar. "That should cover the table," he said, nodding toward Karen and Sandy. "I don't think they'll stay long. Put the rest in the kitty."

"Thanks, Lieutenant. Take care."

"I will. Could you call a taxi for me?"

"No problem."

As she reached for the telephone, Hank went out onto the sidewalk and inhaled the night air. When the taxi arrived Hank got in and gave the driver Meredith Collier's address.

The taxi took twenty minutes to make its way through the heavy Midtown traffic. Hank paid the driver and stepped out in front of a high rise apartment complex on the harbor front. This neighborhood had been the subject of a recent multi-billion dollar development project to inject new life into the waterfront. There were four identical apartment towers in a row, glittering steel and glass monoliths affording a spectacular view of the river from the back and a panoramic cityscape from the front. Meredith lived in the second tower from the left. Hank walked through the large double glass doors into the lobby, found her number on the intercom panel and pressed the button below it.

"Yes?"

"Lieutenant Donaghue, Ms. Collier."

"Come on up."

The door clicked and he went in, admiring the newness of the place. The building was no more than five years old and it seemed that no expense had been spared. The floors were laid with immaculate ceramic tile, the walls were clean and hung with works of art, and the light fixtures in the ceiling were tasteful and discreet. He walked over to the bank of elevators and pressed a button. The nearest elevator opened with a soft chime. He stepped in and pressed the button for the twenty-eighth floor. The doors closed gently and he felt the elevator begin to rise.

At the twenty-eighth floor the doors opened and Hank found Meredith Collier waiting for him at a door at the end of the corridor. She wore a discreet knee-length black dress, comfortable black shoes and a string of pearls.

"Thank you for coming, Lieutenant," she said, holding out her hand.

117

"I'm very sorry to drag you away from your evening."

"Not at all," Hank said, shaking her hand. He felt a jolt of electricity that he tried to ignore.

"I appreciate it," she said, closing the door and leading him through an open concept area down a hallway into a large living room with a spectacular view of the river.

"Very nice place," Hank said.

"Thank you." Meredith led the way to a seating area near a bar. "Please, sit down. Can I get you a drink?"

"No thanks," he said automatically, easing down into a leather armchair, his eyes moving to the lights along the river.

"You're off duty, aren't you, Lieutenant?" she smiled at him. "I'm going to have a beer. Why don't you have one with me?"

"A beer would be fine, then, thanks," Hank said.

She went behind the bar and opened a refrigerator. "Domestic or imported? I'm having a Bass."

"That's fine."

"Glass?"

"Just the bottle, thanks."

Meredith brought over two bottles of Bass beer and handed him one. She sat down in a love seat across from Hank and looked at him seriously. "I wanted to talk to you about Peter."

Hank set his beer aside and slipped his notebook and pen from his pocket. "When did he call?"

"Late this afternoon, a few minutes after I got home from work."

"What did he say?"

"He said he'd been meaning to call me earlier but had regrettably not found the time."

"Was that a veiled threat?"

"No, not at all." Meredith slipped off her shoes tucked her legs underneath her on the love seat. "You have to understand that Peter had a very traditional Chinese upbringing and adheres very closely to traditional cultural values. Family is very important to him, and the fact I was his cousin's mother includes me in his family, however peripherally. So he'd feel it inappropriate to threaten me in any way. The purpose of his call was simply to suggest that I didn't need to see Grace's boy or have anything to do with the student's research into these so-called memories of Martin."

"I see," Hank said evenly.

Meredith raised her hand. "Indulge me for a moment. I should explain this in the context of the traditional cultural values Peter follows so closely. It may help you understand him a little better."

Hank set his notepad and pen aside and picked up his beer. "Take your time."

"Thanks." She took a deep breath before continuing. "I'm originally from California. I went to UCLA. I took courses in Asian culture and studied Cantonese. After I graduated I got a job teaching English as a second language in Hong Kong and spent a year there. I loved it. I met a man from here, Asian, who was in Hong Kong visiting relatives, and we started a casual relationship. When my contract was up, I moved back here with him. It didn't last, but I met a friend of his, Stephen Liu, and I knew I'd found someone special. Stephen and I married, and Martin was our only child. We were very happy. Stephen had had a very non-traditional upbringing, and in fact his Cantonese was very poor, but none of that mattered. We were just very happy.

"I mentioned before that his older sister was married to Jerome Mah, which was a source of considerable tension within the Liu family. We stayed away from the Mahs as much as we could, and so did Stephen's younger sister Anna, who married a man named Warren Wong. Their daughter Grace, of course, was Martin's cousin."

Hank nodded, watching her thick blond hair slip over her left eye as she talked.

Meredith drained the bottle of beer and set it aside, flicking her hair back with a toss of her head. "Stephen considered himself American first and foremost, and we raised Martin the same way, but I want you to understand that I have a very sound appreciation of the traditional cultural values that are so important to Peter. I studied them closely in school and while I was in Hong Kong. I was something of an intellectual back then, I guess, and I took my work very seriously. I immersed myself in the culture, improved my grasp of the language, and applied what I learned to my teaching methods."

"So you speak Cantonese?"

She nodded. "It's a little rusty now. I also speak some Mandarin and I even know a little Shanghainese, the dialect of Wu that's also heard in Hong Kong. Anyway, I want you to understand Peter's point of view. It may help your investigation because I'm convinced Peter was connected to Martin's murder. If you understand Peter, it may help you manipulate him into revealing the truth."

"You said Peter wasn't threatening when he told you to stay away from Taylor Chan."

"Correct. He was very polite."

"I see."

"Perhaps not fully, Lieutenant." She moved her hair back with her fingertips and looked at him. "Politeness is a strategy that traditional Chinese use to preserve face in situations which may be complicated. It's a signal to someone that says, 'I know what I'm about to ask may potentially cause us both to lose face, but I'll try to proceed in such a way as to minimize that risk.' Everything he said after that was geared to minimize causing negative face for either of us." She laughed lightly. "He was a little uncomfortable because

119

these strategies are used between males much more so than between a male and female."

"So he asked you politely to stay away from Taylor Chan."

Meredith looked at him, amusement in her eyes. "You're just teasing me, Lieutenant, but that's all right, I don't mind. As I've been trying to explain, he didn't ask me politely to stay away from Taylor Chan. He said that Taylor was a very fine young boy who had a great future ahead of him. He said Grace was a very fine mother to the boy and that Michael was an excellent provider who would ensure that Taylor would lack for nothing as he grew up. He expressed regret that Michael didn't embrace his own heritage and said he himself would always be available to the boy, should he wish to learn the traditional Chinese ways when he became older. He said Taylor seemed to like him and that he'd always be looking out for the boy. He then went on to say that with the police asking people questions about Martin and examining possible connections between Martin and Taylor, it was natural I might become concerned about the welfare of Taylor and feel a need to take some kind of future action involving the boy. He said this would not be necessary, that he, Peter, would ensure no harm would come to the boy as a result of these activities of the police. I could rest easy in the knowledge that no action whatsoever would be necessary on my part."

"Well," Hank said, "that's a very indirect way of telling someone to butt out."

Meredith laughed. "Since I want nothing whatsoever to do with this student or Grace or the boy, it was pretty easy to respond to Peter's roundabout request. I told him I appreciated his interest in Taylor. I said he had far greater means than I to assist Grace in looking after the boy's best interests, and that I had no wish to worry him further that any action of mine might cause Taylor distress or discomfort. I told him I'd explained to the student I couldn't help him in his research and that I considered the matter closed. It was a way of responding to Peter's request that didn't cause any negative face for him, and it also signaled to him that his request did not cause any negative face for me."

"That's a pretty complicated dance," Hank remarked.

"Face is a pretty complicated concept," she replied, "and it's extremely important to Peter Mah."

"I see," Hank said.

"There are actually two kinds of face in Chinese culture," she went on, "*mianzi* and *lian*. *Mianzi* relates to a person's social status as they become rich and powerful. The more successful business transactions they achieve, for example, the greater their *mianzi*. Failures, on the other hand, may lower it. We would say gaining face or losing face. So Peter is very conscious of his status within his network of friends and associates, and he's very careful to maintain a high level of *mianzi*.

"The other type of face, *lian*, has more to do with a person's moral

120

reputation. A person of much *lian* is known to be reliable and trustworthy. He'll fulfill his obligations to his network regardless of the cost, he can always be depended on to do what's expected of him, and he'll always be seen to behave properly. If he has a particular role within his network and is known to have failed to act in that role when needed, for example, it'll cause him to lose considerable *lian*. On the other hand, if he were to perform these actions unfailingly, particularly at some sacrifice to himself, he'd gain *lian* in the eyes of others."

"I like the way you use the word *network*," Hank smiled. "That's very good."

Meredith's face clouded over and she turned away to look out the window. "Network, Triad, whatever."

"I'm sorry," Hank said hastily, "I didn't mean to sound sarcastic."

"Never mind." She put her feet back down on the floor and slipped them into her shoes. "I'm just trying to help you understand Peter Mah and his motivations."

"I understand that. I'm sorry. Why did Mah show so much interest in Martin? You said before you thought he was helping Martin regain his cultural heritage?"

She folded her hands on her lap. "Yes."

Hank slid forward in the chair and raised his hand. "Look, I offended you and I'm very sorry. It's my cop sense of humor, I guess. You're being a big help to me here and I really appreciate it. Feel free to hit me over the head any time you like."

"It's tempting," she said, looking away.

Hank thought he saw a smile playing around the corners of her mouth and his heart stopped pounding. He reached for his notebook and pen. "How did the conversation end?"

"Peter said that should I ever wish to call him back, at any time or for any reason, I should feel completely free to do so."

"What did he mean by that?"

Meredith tossed her hair back. "That I should understand there was a relationship between us, that I should consider myself part of his *network*, that he appreciated my willingness to do nothing related to Taylor and that the relationship between us could be beneficial to me in the future."

Hank winced a little at the force with which she used the word "network" and at the sharpness of her tone. "Is this as crude as just saying he would make it worth your while to keep your nose out of this business?"

"No, it's not that crude." Meredith folded her hands in her lap. "Look, although you had your fun with me suggesting that I was using 'network' as a euphemism for 'Triad,' the fact of the matter is that I wasn't. The concept is referred to as *guanxi*, which translates as 'personal connections' and has to do with the complex relationships between a person and their family, their

121

friends and their business associates. Peter was making it clear he felt there was *guanxi* between us he'd previously neglected and was now prepared to acknowledge, particularly given that I understood what he was driving at and was willing to cooperate.

"Traditional Chinese place an enormous value on interpersonal relationships. No doubt you twitch when you hear the word *tong*, thinking of murderous street gangs running drugs and all the rest, but the word simply means 'common,' as in a group of people who have common interests. While some of the people who belong to Chinese Tongs are criminals, many others aren't. A Tong is like any other businessman's association, sharing favors and helping one another get ahead.

"In the same way, the Triad society to which Peter belongs," she smiled at him ironically, "and I don't see the point in using euphemisms in this context, is constructed around the same principle of *guanxi* among associates. Key to this network of relationships is the idea of *renqing*, which is like the glue holding a *guanxi* network together. *Renqing* implies an emotional commitment to a *guanxi* relationship, first of all. For example, Peter felt genuine affection toward Martin, and he no doubt feels genuine loyalty toward other members of his Triad. But *renqing* also refers to the exchange of favors or financial considerations that bind a relationship together. Peter developed his *guanxi* with Martin through a process of *renqing* that included helping him get the job at Dicam, bringing him down to the Golden Dragon and introducing him around, and generally watching out for him. Martin would then have been expected to reciprocate in his own way. That's what really bothers me about all this, Lieutenant. What exactly was Martin's *renqing*? Did he do something for Peter that got him killed?"

"I'm not sure yet," Hank said, making a note of the terms she was teaching him. It occurred to him that perhaps it was because Martin failed to uphold his *renqing* obligation to Peter that he ended up dead.

"I'm not trying to minimize the criminal nature of Peter's business," Meredith said, shifting forward. "You understand that, don't you? I'm not romanticizing this by any means. While people like Peter are polite, loyal, self-effacing and all the rest of it, they're still a bunch of criminals for whom murder is just another negotiating tactic." She made a fist. "We tried so hard to keep Martin away from it all, to keep the wall intact between our family and the Mahs. But Peter was too persuasive. Martin couldn't resist the lure of discovering his cultural heritage. There was nothing Stephen and I could offer that was a greater attraction. It was a battle we were doomed to lose."

"I can understand how hard it must have been," Hank said. "If it's any consolation, we've reached the conclusion that the drug angle was phony. We're still looking into the connections between Martin and Peter Mah, but we don't see any evidence of criminal involvement on Martin's part. There was something else."

"Thanks for saying that." She smiled faintly. "It means a lot."

"How well did you know Martin's friend Tommy Leung?"

"Not well. They graduated together. Martin liked to go over to Tommy's place a lot. Tommy almost never came over to our house." She thought for a moment. "He worked for his father. They have some kind of big electronics store."

"And you don't have any idea what kind of trouble Martin thought Tommy was in?"

"No. Sorry."

"Not a problem." Hank closed his notebook and put it away. "Thanks. I really appreciate your help in all this."

"You're welcome, Lieutenant," she said, rising. "You'll find Peter to be quite charming. You'll find him open to developing some sort of a relationship with you based on an exchange of information or whatever. He's probably already done that with other policemen; it's the way he works. Just don't make the mistake of believing he's acting as an individual with an individual's motivations. Peter is ambitious, *very* ambitious, but bear in mind you'll have a very hard time predicting which way he'll jump if you think that money and power are the only things he cares about. Remember, as Jerome's only son he stands to inherit enormous money and power when the old man's gone. That's a great deal of *mianzi* for him right there, following in his father's footsteps, but he's chosen a different path for his life. The ancient calling of the Triad is very powerful to him, and he'd rather die than betray the *guanxi* he finds there."

They walked back down the corridor from the living room into the open concept area where he had first entered the apartment. She opened the door and walked with him down the corridor to the elevator.

"Be very careful," she said. "He's very intelligent and not a person to take lightly."

"I understand."

"I appreciate your coming to see me," Meredith said, patting his arm. "I hope I wasn't too grouchy with you."

He looked at her in surprise. "No, that's fine, I understand. It was my fault. I should have known better."

"Let me know if I can be of any further help."

"I wouldn't want to put you in a bad spot with Peter Mah."

She laughed lightly. "Peter won't bother me. Give me a call, any time." She walked back down to her apartment and closed the door.

As he rode the elevator back down to the lobby he could still feel her touch, as though her fingers still rested on his arm.

# 16

It was a few minutes before 11:00 p.m. As he stepped out into the street behind Jimmy Yung, Peter Mah slipped on a pair of Persol sunglasses with brown frames and burnt orange lenses that had cost him only £150 during a recent trip to London. He favored the glasses for night wear because they provided him with the elegant appearance he sought without unduly compromising his vision. He was wearing a black sports jacket that he did not particularly like, blue jeans, and a light blue shirt open at the neck. Jimmy looked to the left and the right as they approached the vehicle at the curb but Peter looked only straight ahead, staring at Jimmy's back.

The vehicle was a sleek black 2001 Mercedes-Benz S Class Pullman limousine, the W220 model with six doors and seating for seven. It was not as big as a stretch limousine, which Peter appreciated because it did not draw undue attention to itself, but it allowed five people to sit comfortably in the back, two in the rear on either side of the center console and three in the middle, facing back, when the center console was folded up. However, the limo was not for luxury travel but was a working vehicle, an alternative to the Lexus when Peter required a number of people to ride with him. It was beautiful, just the same, with active ventilated leather seats, privacy windows, burled walnut root trim, a laptop docking station, small tables and computer monitors that folded up out of the rear center console, and other amenities. The leather upholstery, however, was not the original. In fact, the interior had been re-upholstered twice since Peter had begun to use it. It too, like the Lexus, was registered to Dicam International but was reserved for Peter's exclusive use.

Benny Hu was driving and Billy Fung rode in the front passenger seat. Jimmy opened the rear door and Peter got in, seating himself opposite Donald Sheng, who lowered his eyes as Peter settled in. Also in the seat opposite Peter, on the far side, was Foo Yee. Between Sheng and Foo sat a tall, heavy-set African-American whose wrists and ankles were bound with plastic locking straps. He was in his late twenties with a shaven head and a large graffiti-style tattoo on the right side of his neck. He wore a baggy cotton shirt with pineapples printed on it, baggy blue jeans, and large white sneakers. A flashy watch glittered on his wrist and four large rings, two on each hand, caught the overhead lights as Jimmy got into the rear seat beside Peter on the other side. The prisoner's eyes settled on Peter.

"Yo, wha' the fuck's up wit' all this, man?"

Foo moved faster than the eye could see, his elbow catching the prisoner on the side of the neck. The man gasped, eyes rolling, and he slumped sideways into Sheng, who pushed him back upright.

"You were told to remain silent," Sheng said quietly. "You won't be told again."

124

The limo pulled away from the curb and made its way slowly through the streets of Chinatown. Peter looked at their prisoner with grim satisfaction. ShonDale Gregg. A friend in the Department of Motor Vehicles had run the license plate number Lester Ping had supplied and it had led to this man. Peter felt certain he'd found one of the men with whom Tommy Leung was breaking his society oaths. He should be able to resolve this matter very quickly. Uncle Sang would be pleased.

After a few moments ShonDale's eyes refocused and his breathing evened out. After trying in vain to follow their progress through the narrow side streets of Chinatown, he began to stare at Peter, perhaps hoping to impress him with a show of machismo. Sheng noticed it, however, and lightly cuffed ShonDale across the mouth.

"Lower your eyes, dog."

ShonDale raised his arms to wipe his sleeve across the corner of his mouth where it had started to bleed. He drew breath to say something but Foo stirred beside him and he thought better of it. He let his hands drop between his knees and stared at the plastic locking strap around his wrists. It was amazing how strong something that thin could be. It was also not lost on him that both men sitting beside him wore latex gloves. Not a good sign.

Before long the limo pulled up underneath one of the massive bridges spanning the river into South Shore East. Waiting for them was a nondescript Ford Escort. Lounging against the front fender of the Escort was Stevie Mah, Peter's cousin. Stevie had stolen the car from the other side of the river and had driven it here for the rendezvous.

Benny Hu turned the limo so that the immediate area was illuminated in its headlights. Peter got out and walked over. "Stevie, how are you doing?" He held out his hand.

Stevie lowered his head respectfully and then shook his cousin's hand. "I'm very well, Peter. And yourself? Feeling fit?"

"Feeling very well tonight, very well." Peter released Stevie's hand and glanced at the car. "I appreciate your help with this."

"It's nothing," Stevie said. "It's what I do."

It was true. Stevie Mah was one of the best car thieves Peter knew. Peter stepped aside as Sheng and Foo muscled ShonDale Gregg past them into the shadows underneath the concrete pilings of the bridge. The plastic locking strap around his ankles had been cut to allow him to walk, but the one around his wrists was still in place. Billy Fung followed them. Peter removed his sunglasses and gave them to Benny Hu, who handed Peter a thick envelope in return and went back to the limo.

Peter gave Stevie the envelope. "Get in the limo. We'll take you home shortly. This won't take too long."

Stevie slipped the envelope inside his jacket. "Thanks, Peter." He lowered his head again and followed Hu to the limo.

125

Peter turned and walked over to the group under the concrete pilings. ShonDale had been forced to his knees by Sheng and Foo, who stood on either side of him. There was enough illumination from the car headlights that Peter could see their faces.

Billy was waving a gun under ShonDale's nose.

Peter confronted him. "Go back to the limo."

The arrogance slowly drained from Billy's expression, replaced by fear as he saw the contempt in Peter's face. He put the gun away and hurried back to the limo.

Peter stood in front of the remaining trio.

"You're ShonDale Gregg."

ShonDale said nothing, head down. Sheng roughly pushed on the back of his neck. "Answer the *Hung Kwan's* questions, dog."

"Yeah," ShonDale muttered, 'yeah, thass me."

"You belong to the R Boyz?"

"Thass what the tat says, so ah'm guessin' it be true."

"How do you know Tommy Leung?"

"Leung? Who the fuck dat be, man?" ShonDale started to raise his head to look at Peter, but Sheng roughly struck it back down.

"Answer the *Hung Kwan's* questions. You won't be told again."

"Why have you been seen with Tommy Leung?" Peter asked. "Is your gang doing some kind of business with him?"

"Doan' know what you be talking about, man."

Peter made a quick gesture and Foo struck ShonDale across the back of the neck. ShonDale hit the ground hard, rolling into a fetal position, grinding his cheek into the dirt that covered the hard paved surface, lips scooping particles into his gasping mouth.

"Tommy Leung," Peter said, leaning down.

"Yeah, yeah, man, all right. Tommy and me used to be like homies, man. Like bros. We chilled together now and then, back in the day."

"I'm tired of the ghetto talk," Peter said, gesturing once again to Foo.

Foo proceeded to give ShonDale a beating that was quick and efficient but required them to wait a while afterwards for ShonDale to recover sufficiently to speak again. Foo took a little walk toward the river, shaking his hand as though he'd hurt it. When ShonDale's eyes finally opened and focused, Peter leaned down until they were almost nose to nose.

"Speak properly or he'll beat you again."

"All right," ShonDale mumbled.

"What are you doing with Tommy Leung?"

"Went to ... school together, man. State U. Friends."

"You went to State University with Tommy Leung, that's what you're saying? You were friends?"

126

ShonDale nodded, coughing.

"I find it hard to believe he'd be friends with someone like you."

"You mean a nigrah like me. Well, it's so. Go way back, Tommy an' me."

"What about now? Are you and Tommy in business together or something?"

"Fuck, man," ShonDale croaked, "don't mean nothing. Just a little action. Don't mean no harm."

"What kind of action?"

"Just a little skimming, man. That's all."

"Credit card skimming?"

"Yeah, man."

Credit card skimming involved the use of a small device, often hidden under the counter at a convenience store or gas bar. The cashier would swipe an unsuspecting person's card twice, once in the business's device and a second time in the skimmer, thereby capturing data that could be used to make counterfeit cards. The data was stored in a laptop hidden nearby. The laptops were routinely collected and the data downloaded to be used in the making of counterfeit credit cards. Peter knew that Eddie Leung was supposed to be in charge of skimming in addition to his counterfeiting businesses. Eddie had apparently entrusted it to his son, who was also a sworn member of the brotherhood, but Tommy had diverted the operation to include his outsider friends and was likely withholding revenue from his father and by extension his community.

"Who else is involved with this? Is your gang in this, or just you?"

"Gang?" ShonDale sounded a little confused.

"The R Boyz, you idiot. Is the R Boyz gang connected to this, or are you on your own?"

ShonDale shook his head. "Just me, man. RaVonn would hand me my ass in a plastic bag if he knew about it."

"Who else, then, beside yourself?"

"Just me and Tommy, Gary, and Tommy's partner. That's all, man."

"No one else?"

"No, man. Gary and me, we drop off the laptops and pick them up, and we pay the drones along the string who do the skimming. Tommy takes the laptops and does his thing."

Peter's focus had shifted as ShonDale talked. He stared at the ground for a moment, thinking hard. Gary. ShonDale. Shawn and Gary.

"How long?" he asked. "How long have you been doing this with Tommy Leung?"

"Few years now, man."

"How many years?" Peter demanded sharply.

"I don't know, man. Three, four. Something like that."

"Four years?"

"Yeah, I guess."

"Four years ago you and this Gary killed a young Chinese named Martin Liu, isn't that right?"

"Liu?" ShonDale rocked back and forth. "Name don't mean anything to me, man."

Peter stood up and moved back, signaling once more to Foo, who proceeded to give ShonDale another brutal beating. Peter walked aimlessly beneath the overpass, looking at the lights reflecting on the black river. Could it be that the two things were actually connected?

When Foo was finished Peter stood over ShonDale, who lay on his side gasping for air. "Who shot Martin? You? Gary? Tommy Leung?"

ShonDale began to struggle, trying to get up. Suddenly he vomited. Peter moved out of the way and turned his back. He heard Sheng and Foo drag ShonDale aside and haul him up on his knees. They waited patiently and then asked ShonDale if he was done. There was silence, and they asked again. Finally ShonDale answered that he was all right. Peter turned back.

"Who's this Gary?"

"Thatcher," ShonDale managed.

"Tell me about him."

"Prick," ShonDale mumbled. "Knew him at State. Tommy liked him. Brought him into our thing. Got a place downtown. Thatcher Enterprises, some fuckin' thing. Stuff with the city."

"The city?"

"Yeah, man. Fixing contracts for big bucks, like that."

"Did Tommy Leung shoot Martin Liu?"

ShonDale shook his head.

"Gary Thatcher?"

ShonDale shook his head again.

"You shot him, didn't you?" Peter felt the adrenaline surge through him.

ShonDale began to cry.

"Why did you shoot Martin? Because he found out about the skimming?"

"An accident, man. Wasn't supposed to go off. Just pistol-whippin'."

"An accident," Peter repeated.

ShonDale cried raggedly.

"Stop that," Peter commanded. "Act like a man."

ShonDale sobbed, looking up at Peter. "I didn't mean ... for it to happen, didn't mean it. I hit him a few times with the gun, trying to get him to talk, to answer the fucking *questions*, man. It went off by accident. Didn't mean to shoot him."

128

"So you took him to 121ˢᵗ Street and dumped him in an alley to die."

ShonDale sobbed. "Sorry, man, so fucking sorry, so sorry, so sorry."

"Where's Tommy Leung now?"

"I don't know, haven't seen him for a while."

"What about the skimming? Surely you saw him to pick up your latest cut."

ShonDale shook his head. "Tommy and his partner shut it down. Said somebody was sniffing around. Might get caught."

Peter frowned. "Who was sniffing around?"

"He was scared it was Triad, man. Rolled everything right up."

"Who's his partner?"

"Don't know. Only saw him once, when we, when the Liu guy, when…."

"Describe him."

"Dunno, man. White dude. Older guy. Going bald."

"What else?"

"That's all I remember, man. I'd tell you more if I could."

Peter held out his hand and Foo produced a pair of latex gloves. Peter noticed a small cut on the middle knuckle of Foo's right hand. As he took the gloves and put them on, he frowned at Foo.

"You're cut," he said in Cantonese. "Put on fresh gloves."

Foo obediently took Sheng's spare pair and put them on, balling up the damaged pair and shoving them into his pocket.

When Peter had put on his gloves, Sheng took out a handgun that was inside a plastic zip-lock bag. It was ShonDale's own gun, a Beretta M92 nine millimeter, taken from him when they picked him up. Peter removed the gun and gave the bag back to Sheng.

Sheng and Foo bent down and held ShonDale in place on the ground. Peter stooped and touched the muzzle of the gun to ShonDale's left thigh.

"This was where you shot Martin."

"Fuck, I'm so sorry, man."

Sheng grabbed him by the throat and squeezed. "Shut up."

Peter fired the gun, sending a bullet through ShonDale's leg in almost the same spot that Martin had been shot four years ago. ShonDale twisted and howled in agony through Sheng's grip on his throat.

Peter straightened and motioned with the gun for Sheng to move aside.

"Blood for blood," he said, and fired twice more.

# 17

Hank was sitting in a lounge having a drink. Across the table from him was a woman with fair hair who smiled and told him about flowers she grew on the roof of the apartment building where she lived. He was very fond of this woman. She leaned forward as she told him about the flowers because she wanted to be near him. A timer began to ring at a table just behind Hank and the woman excused herself to see to it. The ringing continued until Hank woke up and grabbed the portable telephone beside his bed.

"Donaghue."

"Woke you up, did I?" Karen asked.

"No," Hank mumbled, "I was reading a book."

"Right. We got a call. I'll be there in fifteen."

"All right." He disconnected and dropped the phone back into its base, looking at the red numerals on the face of the clock next to the phone. It was 3:24 a.m. Wednesday night. Or Thursday morning, depending on your perspective.

He showered quickly, then looked in the mirror and decided not to shave. He got dressed, grabbing a black suit from the back of his closet that he didn't particularly like and tended to save for working a crime scene. The memory of the woman in the dream lingered as he moved around his bedroom, getting ready. He was out the door, into the elevator and down to the lobby in time to see headlights pulling up in front of his building. He went outside and got into the car.

Karen had turned in the Crown Vic for servicing and was driving her personally-owned vehicle, a 1979 Pontiac Firebird Esprit, the Redbird edition. An older brother, Delbert, was an auto mechanic in Houston and had bought the car in 1999 for three thousand dollars from a regular customer who found himself short of cash. Delbert put a thousand dollars' worth of work into it and sold it to Karen for four thousand dollars. She drove it back from Texas and drove it every summer since, putting it in storage each winter and switching to a beat-up pick-up truck.

She had clipped a dual strobe light to the passenger sun visor and plugged it into the cigarette lighter, and Hank watched the blue and red lights flicker across the big red hood with the yellow pinstripe down the middle as they raced insanely through the quiet streets. He listened to the throaty roar of the four-barrel V-8, 301 cubic inch engine and wished, not for the first time, that the damned car had cup holders because he was desperate for a cup of coffee.

As Karen gunned through a red light Hank ran his hands through his frizzy hair and tried to shake a nagging headache that had started in the shower. "We gotta stop for coffee."

130

"No problem, Lou, we'll hit a drive-through on the way to the expressway. So what happened, lose your razor?"

Hank fingered his cheeks self-consciously. "Just trying something different."

"Looks hot. The Widow Liu's gonna flip when she sees it."

Hank shook his head. "So what's the call?"

"You're not gonna like it."

"It's four o'clock in the fucking morning," he complained. "I already don't like it."

"It's ShonDale Gregg."

"Damn."

They stopped at a 24-hour fast food restaurant and bought two jumbo coffees. Hank held Karen's for her, burning his mouth with hasty gulps of his own as she accelerated up the empty ramp and hit the expressway as though trying to blast out of the earth's atmosphere. Traffic was light and she settled into the inside lane, reaching for the cup of coffee.

"Byrne has the scene right now," she said, steering with her left hand as she raised the cup of coffee to her lips. Senior CSI Tim Byrne was a crime scene investigation team leader who worked the night shift. Formerly a detective in the Arson Unit, he'd successfully competed for an investigative position in the Criminalistics Section when the CSI Unit's budget had expanded and technology had begun to make crime scene investigation much more intensive and rewarding. He was a short, stocky man in his mid-forties, with neat red hair, small pig-eyes, a florid complexion and a square, jutting jaw. Intelligent and well-read, he had the personality of a porcupine and Hank didn't particularly like him, but he appreciated working a case in which Byrne had the crime scene, for he knew that every scrap of evidence available would be gleaned from the scene, literally down to the molecular level where necessary.

"Found him in an alley off 121$^{st}$ in South Shore East," Karen said. "Multiple gunshot wounds. That's all I got from Jarvis. He's gonna be there."

Bill Jarvis was the supervisory lieutenant for the Homicide Unit. He went out to homicide crime scenes when Ann Martinez was not available.

"121$^{st}$?" Hank repeated. "Near the place where Martin Liu was found?"

"I don't know," she said, glancing over. "Guess we'll find out."

Hank watched her thumb tap a rhythm on the bottom of the steering wheel and knew that the adrenaline was stoking her up. They flew over the bridge into South Shore East and worked their way over to 121$^{st}$ Street. They saw the flashing lights of the emergency vehicles and police cruisers as soon as they turned onto 121$^{st}$ and in a matter of moments they were getting out of the Firebird and tossing away their coffee cups into a trash barrel at the first set of barricades at the end of the block.

They passed through the curious onlookers gathered at the barriers,

131

avoiding reporters who looked as tired and grouchy as Hank felt, and showed their identification to a uniformed officer who moved a wooden barrier aside for them to pass. As they walked up the street toward the inner barrier that enclosed the crime scene, Hank knew it was the same place, the same alley in which Martin Liu had been left for dead four years ago.

They stopped at the secondary barrier of crime scene tape and nodded to the uniformed officer with the clipboard who was controlling access to the primary scene. Karen went through first. When it was Hank's turn he gave the officer his ID. As his name and badge number were being written down on the clipboard, Hank looked at the officer's face. He was a muscular young cop who looked fresh out of school. He glanced at the man's name tag, which said *Shanks.*

Hank signed the clipboard and took back his ID. "Any relation to Detective Shanks, used to work in Auto Theft?"

Officer Shanks looked at Hank without expression. "My uncle, sir."

Hank smiled. "I spent quite a few long night shifts with your Uncle Jerry. Taught me everything you'd ever want to know about stealing cars. How's he like retirement?"

"Hates it," Officer Shanks said.

Hank nodded and slipped his ID back onto his belt.

"Please walk to the right of the green markers, Lieutenant," Officer Shanks said.

Hank saw that a trail of luminous green versa-cones had been laid out to mark a safe route into the crime scene. He followed them toward the entrance of the alley. On his left was a dusty Ford Escort parked at the curb beneath a street lamp about fifteen yards from the alley. Evidence technicians were busy processing the car, around which they had set up a series of 600-watt lamps on tripods. On his right, along the far side of the street, were two long rows of barricades to prevent anyone from coming out of the buildings into the scene. There were only a few stray bystanders there, and Hank suspected that the buildings along that side were all abandoned. Most of this neighborhood, well inside R Boyz territory, was economically depressed.

A small area had been set up near the front of the Biltmore Arms apartment building as a command post. Karen was talking to Byrne, Lieutenant Jarvis and a uniformed officer wearing sergeant's stripes.

"—first put the tape across the front of the alleyway," the sergeant was saying, "then when they realized the car was part of the scene they moved the tape back to where you see it now." He nodded to Hank and turned his attention back to Karen. "The ME has been here for a while."

"Identification was made how?" Karen asked.

"Vic's wallet was conveniently left open next to the body so the driver's license was visible," replied the sergeant. He was squat and muscular, with a fringe of short grey hair on his head. "You'll see when you go in. The responding officers left everything just like they found it, touched nothing. The scene's clean."

"Eye witnesses?" Karen asked.

"Not that we know of so far. We've started going floor by floor in the apartment building," nodding at the Biltmore Arms, "and we're checking it out across the street in case there's some squatters who might have seen something. The buildings are mostly empty around here."

"Anybody talk to the media yet?" Hank asked.

"I'll have a quick word with them before I leave," Jarvis said, turning to Karen. His hand moved reflexively across his cheeks as though to assure himself that he had in fact shaved before coming down to the crime scene. "If you want to give them anything later I'll leave that up to you. For now I'll give them a basic rundown of the situation."

"All right," Karen said.

"Light on the details, Bill," Hank cautioned. "No mention of any connection to the cold case."

"Thank you, *Lieutenant*," Jarvis retorted, eyes flashing. "I'll take that under advisement."

"ME says come on in," a crime scene technician called over to them.

Karen glanced at Hank, caught his nod, and went. They would take turns approaching the scene in order to get their own first impression. Byrne gave her a head start and then followed.

"I've got to get back," Jarvis said to the sergeant. He looked at Hank. "It's Stainer's case, Donaghue. Don't get in her way."

"Okay, I'll try not to screw it up."

"Asshole." Jarvis strode quickly away down the street toward the media. Hank knew he was looking forward to seeing himself on breakfast television in a few hours.

"I'm Donaghue," he said, holding his hand out to the sergeant.

"Yeah, I know, Lieutenant," the sergeant replied, shaking hands with a crushing grip. "Daravicius. Honored to meet you."

Hank frowned and put his right hand behind his back before flexing his fingers to ease the pain.

"I was a year behind you coming out of the academy," Daravicius explained. "I was still a newbie in Riverfront District when you cracked the Post kidnapping."

Hank nodded.

"Jarvis I never met before. He's charming."

Hank chuckled. "How do you like South Shore East?"

"S-S-D-D." Same shit, different day.

"I hear you."

"Jarvis said this might connect to something else you're already

133

working."

"Could be," Hank said. "It was a 911 call?"

"Yeah. Anonymous. We were on the scene within six minutes."

Hank turned away, his mind already roving into the alley toward the body that waited for him.

Daravicius lifted his radio and called his officers inside the Biltmore Arms for an update.

Hank took out his penlight and slowly walked into the entrance of the alley. Along the wall of the building on the left was a collection of overflowing garbage cans and a pile of garbage bags being examined by one of Byrne's technicians under the light of several 600-watt lamps. On the right was a dumpster that emitted a bad smell. Hank slowly walked down the middle of the alley, shining his penlight from side to side. He glanced at a yellow versa-cone with the numeral 8 and saw next to it a packet of white powder. He took two more paces and knelt down beside cone 9, which marked a syringe that looked new and unused. He straightened and walked to the dumpster, shining his light inside. The smell drove him back.

"Bad, huh?" The technician grinned at him. "Four plastic grocery bags filled with rotting fish heads."

"Lovely."

Hank moved on, past the other dumpster along the wall on the left, past the pile of garbage bags, to where the body waited for him. The medical examiner and a crime scene technician were crouched by the body and Karen stood nearby, talking to Byrne, so Hank hung back for a moment. He took out his notebook and started writing.

When Karen caught his eye he made his approach, pausing to look at the footprints marked with versa-cones 10 through 14. Two types of shoe, one that looked like a smooth-soled dress shoe and the other like a crepe sole with a stucco-like pattern. He reached the body and bent down.

"Jim," he said, nodding to Dr. Jim Easton, who was crouched on the other side of the body. Easton still wore the large gold wire-frame glasses and the trademark blond caterpillar moustache across his upper lip, and he still looked as though he were fresh out of college, but he had moved up the ladder in the four years since they had last met in this particular alley over the body of Martin Liu.

The Office of the Chief Medical Examiner employed death investigators at several levels within its hierarchy. At the lowest level were Forensic Investigators, who were contract workers paid on a per diem basis. They were often recruited from hospitals where they had gained experience in death investigation or trauma care. At the next level were Assistant Medical Examiners, employees of the city who had probably started out as Forensic Investigators. Above the AMEs were Medical Examiners, who were experienced forensic pathologists, and finally the Chief Medical Examiner, who had migrated from the realm of forensic pathology to the far different world of administration and politics. Four years ago Easton had been a newly-minted Assistant Medical Examiner, on the city payroll for only a short time after six months as a Forensic Investigator, and now he was a Medical Examiner who, rumor had it, was thinking seriously about the Office of the Chief Medical Examiner in the not-too-distant future. Hank figured he was still a little too young to understand the consequences of coveting the CME's job. Or maybe he did understand and was anxious to escape the exhausting, stressful responsibilities of a forensic pathologist for the brave new world of administrative power and political influence.

"Good morning, Hank," Easton said. "Ringing any bells for you?"

"Yeah." Hank noted the rumpled clothing with indentations where someone had obviously gripped hard while carrying the body. He saw the large bloodstain on the left leg just above the knee and two neatly drilled holes above the bridge of the nose, but there was virtually no blood at all on the ground beneath the body. ShonDale was lying on his back, legs slightly bent, hands bound together by a plastic locking strap, eyes open. Paper bags had been placed on his hands and feet in order to preserve trace evidence.

He stared at ShonDale's bald head and at the tattoo on the side of his neck. It was a stylized letter R designed to resemble the graffiti markings of the R Boyz that everyone had seen on walls, mailboxes and overpasses in this part of the city. He caught Karen's eye and pointed. She nodded grimly.

Just as Taylor Chan had described it. *He had a bald head and a picture on the side of his neck. It looked like writing on a wall. I think it was an R.*

Crime scene technician Butternut Allenson worked silently next to Easton, using tweezers to remove hairs from the shoulder of ShonDale's pineapple-print shirt. She dropped them into paper trace evidence folds, sealed the folds and labeled them. She worked methodically, with a patience Hank admired. Thirty-four years old, she was married to a carpenter and had twin ten-year-old daughters. She was fairly tall, at five feet eight inches, wide-hipped, and her mouth and eyes were large. Her thick shoulder-length hair was the color of butternut wood, between blond and brown, hence the nickname her husband had given her. Hank had worked with her before and had never heard anyone call her by her given name, June.

"You remember the Martin Liu case, do you?" Hank asked Easton, bending forward to look closely at ShonDale's hands.

"Not until your colleague reminded me," Easton said, glancing at Karen. "Once she mentioned it, it came back. Same alley, same gunshot wound in the left leg, obvious dump job, drugs left at the scene."

"But this is different," Hank said, pointing to the plastic locking strap that bound ShonDale's wrists together, "and so is this," indicating the two bullet holes in ShonDale's forehead.

Easton nodded. "Double tap to the head, execution style."

"Would I be right in guessing that he was shot in the leg first, then in the head?"

"Could be. A lot of blood soaked into his pant leg, so that probably came first." Easton shifted position, still on his haunches. "The face was pounded up something like this in the other case, too, wasn't it?" It was a statement, rather than a question, as the details of the Martin Liu homicide were coming back to him.

"Yeah."

"I'll pull the file when I get back and look it over," Easton said. "Time of death was approximately four to five hours ago, so we're looking at..." he glanced at his watch, "Christ, it's after four in the morning. So, eleven p.m. to midnight, give or take."

"Can we turn him over?"

Butternut nodded, making a note on a sealed packet. "I'm done with this side, actually. Give me a second to put this away, because I'll want to photograph him as he's turned."

Byrne stepped forward and bent down next to Hank. "Excuse me, Lieutenant, and I'll help Dr. Easton turn the body."

Hank straightened and moved out of the way to give them room. When Butternut was ready with her camera, they rolled ShonDale over onto his stomach. Butternut worked quickly, documenting the change in position.

"What's on his ass?" Karen asked, pointing to stains on the seat of ShonDale's pants.

Butternut took out a swab from her kit and wiped at the stain. "There's more on his leg," she noted. She held the swab to her nose and sniffed. "There was power steering fluid spilled in the trunk of the car, so I expect that's what it is."

"A lot of dirt and shit on his clothes," Karen said.

"Yeah," Butternut agreed, "and on the soles of his shoes as well. There's a bit in the trunk, but we figure it was transferred there from the primary scene."

"Transferred from him to the trunk while he was being transported."

"That'd be my guess," Butternut said.

"If he was beat up at the primary scene before being shot," Hank said, "he probably picked it up while rolling around on the ground."

"At least he won't have to face the dry cleaning bill," Byrne said.

Karen crouched down for a closer look. "Exit wound," she said, pointing to the back of ShonDale's thigh. "Through and through."

Hank nodded. "Like Martin Liu."

"But we've got these two waiting for us," Easton said, pointing at the head.

"Nine mil, no doubt, from the Beretta over there." Karen glanced at the gun that had been left next to the victim's wallet. "Anything on his hands? Under the nails?"

"I looked before we bagged them, but it's not hopeful," Butternut said. "He's wearing a Rolex and some nice rings, so robbery would seem to be out."

"Maybe we'll find something under his nails during the post," Easton said, "but I doubt it. Logically, if his hands were bound while he was being held at gunpoint, which you'd figure, given how big he is, there'd be no chance for him to defend himself while he was being tossed around. So I doubt we'll find anything under his nails to connect him to the perpetrator."

"What'd he have with him?" Hank asked.

"Key ring with four keys in his front left trousers pocket," Byrne recited, "a tissue, front right trousers pocket, package of spearmint chewing gum, front right trousers pocket, two pieces of gum missing. The watch. The rings. Two twenty-six in the wallet, plus four credit cards."

"No electronics?" Hank looked at Karen. "No cell phone? No iPod?"

She shook her head. "Nope."

Byrne said, "Maybe taken by the killer." He began to examine the flip side of ShonDale's corpse.

Hank looked up. "I wonder what they have on the ownership of the car."

"Let's go ask." Karen led the way along the path of green versacones to the car where Sergeant Daravicius stood watching the crime scene technicians finish processing it.

"Funny you should ask," Daravicius said when Karen put the question to him, "I just got the update. Car is registered to a Victor Peter Danati, 1476 Juniper Lane, DOB six-twelve-sixty. Works as a night maintenance man at the Eastbank Mall across the bridge in Strathton. We called the home phone number and got his wife out of bed, said her husband took the car to work. Got the work number and spoke to Danati, who said he punched in at ten p.m. and had no idea the car was gone from the parking lot. Thought it was a practical joke at first."

"So we're looking at a professional job," Karen said. "Steal a car, whack the guy somewhere quiet, transport the body over here and dump it, leave the gun and drugs, leave the car, bug out."

Hank looked at the abandoned building in front of which the car had been parked. The windows were boarded up with plywood on every story up to the roof. He took a step back, looked into the alley at the windows of the Biltmore Arms and saw that several lights were on. Had anyone been awake at the time of the murder?

"Who were the responding officers, Sergeant?"

"Johnson and Whitefish."

137

"They see any lights on in the apartment building when they arrived?"

"You mean lights on the side facing the alley?"

"Yeah."

"Good question. I don't know." He lifted his radio. "Johnson, you copy?"

"Yeah, Sarge," the radio buzzed.

"Come here a sec, will ya?"

A police officer detached himself from a small knot of officers interviewing bystanders at the barricade and walked over to them. He was a slight African-American in his late thirties who walked like a cop and gave Hank and Karen the once-over like a cop, slowly, thoroughly and dispassionately.

"Johnson, this is Lieutenant Donaghue and Detective Stainer," Daravicius said. "They've got a few questions for you."

Johnson nodded. He appeared to be waiting for the sort of nit-picking, condescending criticism that responding officers occasionally received from investigating detectives.

"When you and your partner arrived and secured the scene," Hank said, "did you notice any lights on in any of the windows on the alley side of the apartment building?"

Johnson's eye's involuntarily flicked up to the building. "Yeah, there was one."

"Where was it?"

"Between the two dumpsters," Johnson replied, "five or six floors up. Hang on, I wrote it in my notebook." He took it out and flipped it open. The pages already used were held together with an elastic band so he could immediately open the notebook to the first blank page available for that day. He flipped forward a page. "Here it is. Sixth floor."

Hank wrote it in his notebook. Then he remembered there had been eyewitnesses four years ago, an old woman and her grandson. They'd seen the body from their bathroom window, hadn't they? He turned back a few pages to look through the notes he'd made while re-reading the Liu murder book. Yeah, there it was. Mrs. Ethel Williams and her 14-year-old grandson, Millard. She'd seen the body from her bathroom window in apartment 605 and sent Millard down to take a look. Was it possible they'd seen something again this time? It was the same floor.

"You said your officers are going door to door in the Biltmore right now, Sergeant. Anybody covered the sixth floor yet?"

Daravicius checked on his radio and then shook his head. "Not yet. We've covered the basement to the third so far."

"That's the same floor as the old woman who was a Liu witness four years ago," Hank said to Karen. "How about I take a walk while you continue down here?"

138

"Sounds good," Karen said.

"Can I borrow Officer Johnson?" Hank asked.

The sergeant glanced over at the far barrier and saw that the other patrol officers had pretty much finished questioning the spectators who stood there watching the scene. "Be my guest," he said.

"This way, Officer," Hank said to Johnson. He led the way past the alley entrance and through the heavy walnut front door of the Biltmore Arms. On his right was a long row of mailboxes. Only a few had names written in different colors of ink on pieces of paper or cardboard. There were three names over boxes numbered in the six hundreds, and none of them was Williams. He pushed through the inner door and went over to the elevator. A handwritten sign said that it was out of order. Sighing, Hank started up the stairs. The air stank of mildew, urine, curry, burned toast, stale vomit, and a medley of other smells that Hank tried to block out. He turned back over his shoulder.

"What's your first name, Officer Johnson?"

"Robert."

"Like the blues man."

"Yeah."

"You like the blues?"

Johnson shook his head. "Country music."

Hank continued up the stairs. After an eternity they reached the sixth floor.

"So it'll be about half way down," Hank said. "Apartment 605."

He reached the door and knocked as Johnson took up a position on the other side of the doorframe and casually unholstered his weapon.

The door abruptly opened. A short, slight African-American man in his early twenties stood there with his hand on his hip, glaring at them. He wore a purple robe and his feet were bare. He had short hair and a trimmed beard. A lit cigarette jutted from the corner of his mouth and he was squinting against the smoke that curled from its glowing end.

"What the hell's going on around here tonight, anyway?" he demanded before Hank could open his mouth.

"Police, sir," Hank said, holding up his badge. "Sorry to disturb you. Have you been awake for a while tonight?"

"Hell, yeah," the man replied. "Goddamned insomnia. Why? What's going on?"

"Is there a Mrs. Ethel Williams or a Millard Williams who lives in this apartment?"

"Don't know no Williams, there's just me. Been here four months now and damned if I'm going to stay. I might as well try to sleep in a damn bus station as sleep around this damn place."

"What's your name, sir?"

"Harden. Marcus Harden. Why?"

139

"Did you happen to see or hear anything outside in the alley tonight, Mr. Harden? Maybe around midnight or so?"

"Looked out and saw you dickin' around down there," he said to Officer Johnson, "then saw when the other guys came and set up all the goddamned lights and shit, clacking and banging like they were getting ready for a party or something."

"Anything before that? Before the police arrived?"

"No, I was reading in bed until you guys started crashing around."

"Reading," Hank said. "What were you reading?"

"Fuck you care?"

"Humor me," Hank said.

Harden left the door and came back a moment later with a large text book in his hand, which he held up so that Hank could see the title on the front cover: *Tietz Textbook of Clinical Chemistry and Molecular Diagnostics*. "I'm half-way through the section right now on analytes," he said in a condescending tone. "Porphyrins and disorders of porphyrin metabolism." He looked at Johnson and back at Hank. "Not that you'd know what a porphyrin is, but we're talking about organic compounds that provide the basis for hemoglobin, chlorophyll and some enzymes."

"You're a student?"

"Uh huh. So what the hell's going on out there?"

"There's been a death," Hank said. "We need to question everyone in the building."

"Like I said, man, I didn't see or hear nothing until you folks started raising hell."

"Well, we're sorry to have bothered you, Mr. Harden," Hank said. "Another officer will be by shortly to take your statement in more detail. Sorry for the disturbance."

"What-fuckin-ever." Harden closed the door abruptly.

"We're supposed to believe he's still got insomnia after reading that book?" Johnson said.

Hank started to turn back the way they had come when he noticed the door to the next apartment down the hallway was open a crack. He caught Johnson's eye and pointed, then slowly made his way down to apartment 607. Hank stopped in front of the door and saw a pair of eyes staring out at him.

"Hello there," he said, "police. Can we talk to you for a minute?"

The door opened slightly to reveal a tiny, wizened old man wearing pajamas, a black silk robe and red plaid carpet slippers. His skin was the color of dark chocolate, his hair was snow white, and the hand holding the door was small and delicate. "I didn't hear anything."

"Hello, sir," Hank said, holding up his badge. "Could you open the door all the way, please? We'd like to talk to you for a second."

"All right." The door opened fully and the old man stepped back.

140

"Would you like to come in?"

"Just for a moment," Hank said, crossing the threshold into a cluttered living room. He looked over his shoulder and nodded to Johnson that he could return his gun to its holster. "My name is Lieutenant Donaghue and this is Officer Johnson. What's your name, sir?"

The old man looked at Johnson and nodded, then met Hank's gaze. "Randolph Jenkins. What's going on, Lieutenant?"

"A body was found in the alley," Hank said. "Did you hear or see anything tonight, perhaps around midnight or so?"

Jenkins gravely shook his head. "As I said before, I didn't hear anything."

"How long have you lived here, Mr. Jenkins?"

The old man looked down, pursing his lips. "Oh, now, I suppose about eighteen years, it would be. I'm seventy-eight, I came here after I retired at the age of sixty, so, yes, that would be about right. I was a librarian. I dabble in used books now."

"You remember Mrs. Ethel Williams, used to live next door?"

"Oh yes, lovely woman. She moved out at the end of last November, went to live with a cousin in Baltimore. Did you need to get in touch with her, is that it?"

Hank shook his head. "No, she was a witness to a homicide four years ago in the alley outside. Do you remember that?"

Jenkins nodded gravely. "I do. Very sad. Unfortunately I didn't see anything that time, either."

"What about Mrs. Williams's grandson, Millard. Is he still around?"

"No," Jenkins sighed. "He was shot to death coming home from school. That's why Ethel decided to move away. She just couldn't bear to be around here any more with all the bad memories."

"I see. That's too bad." Hank paused. "You live alone, Mr. Jenkins?"

The old man hesitated.

"Mr. Jenkins?"

He put his hands into the pockets of his silk robe and looked at the floor. "My son Charley lives with me. But he didn't hear anything, either."

Hank let his eyes wander around the apartment. "He here now?"

"No, sir, he's upstairs."

Hank frowned. "Upstairs?"

"On the roof." Jenkins pointed at the ceiling. "He spends most of his time up there, even sleeps there when the weather's good. He has a little garden up there where he grows things."

"He's been up there how long tonight?"

"Since seven o'clock or so. I fixed supper and he took a plate up with him and I haven't seen him since. He has an old rocking chair that he likes to

141

sit in, just rocking and listening to the sounds of the city." Jenkins looked at Hank with a serious expression on his face. "He's not quite right in the head, you understand. My wife and I were older when we had him, in our forties, which was late. He was our only child. My wife died giving birth to him and I raised him myself from a baby. But he has a learning disability. He's a little slow."

"I'm sorry to hear that, Mr. Jenkins."

"He's a very nice boy," Jenkins added quickly, "don't worry about that. He's very kind and gentle, a quiet boy with very deep feelings. He just never developed intellectually. The doctors said mentally he'd always be ten years old. If you could be careful not to frighten him, I'd be very much obliged. He's never talked to the police before."

"I'll do my best," Hank said. He and Johnson left the apartment and went back into the stairwell. "How many floors does this building have, any-way?" Hank wondered aloud.

"Ten," Johnson replied.

They plodded up the stairs until they found themselves before a metal door with the word *ROOF* stenciled on it in faded red paint. Hank glanced at Johnson and drew his weapon. He removed his penlight and held it in a sword grip beneath his gun so that the index finger was able to turn the light on and the bottom three fingers enclosed the gripping fingers of his weapon hand.

Johnson nodded and drew his gun, adding his larger patrol officer's flashlight in a Marine Corps grip, his hands pressed together and the rim of the flashlight pressed against the tips of the fingers holding his weapon. "If it's a grow op, he may be a little protective. He might not be the nice boy the old man thinks he is."

"My thoughts exactly."

Hank put his hip into the crash bar and pushed the door open. He moved his gun and penlight around, saw nothing threatening, and stepped out onto the roof. They stood beneath a trellis and arbor arrangement that was covered with plants on both sides and across the top. It looked as though it had been made with scrap two-by-fours and softwood strapping. He took several steps forward and Johnson followed, letting the door ease quietly closed behind him. Their feet crunched softly in the grit that covered the roof. They cleared the arbor. Hank took the left, Johnson the right. There were plants everywhere, growing in salvaged containers of all shapes and sizes. Hank looked at staked tomatoes, carrots, snow peas and many other vegetables, plus other plants that looked like herbs. It was hard to tell for certain in the darkness, but none of the plants appeared to be illegal. Hank marveled at all the work involved in putting the arbor together, collecting the material and containers, and hauling the soil up to the roof.

A slight crunching sound brought Hank's hands around. His penlight moved across a figure sitting in a rocking chair and came back just as Johnson's flashlight found it from the right. They stared at a dark figure with wild hair and a thick woolly beard. He wore a black t-shirt, stained khaki trousers and rubber boots. He held a hand up to his eyes to shield them from the flashlight.

"Stand up slowly, sir," Hank ordered, "with your hands out in front of you where we can see them."

The man sat still, unable or unwilling to move.

"Sir,' Hank repeated, softening his voice a little, "I'd like for you to stand up now and show us both your hands. Can you do that for me?"

"Uh huh," the man said, bringing his other hand up in front of his face.

"Okay, now stand up slowly."

"Uh huh." The man stood up, hands dropping to his sides.

"Slowly now," Hank warned, "and keep your hands up where I can see them."

"Sorry, I forgot," the man said, abruptly thrusting his hands high over his head like a stage coach holdup victim in an old western movie.

Officer Johnson moved in and quickly gave him a pat down as Hank covered him with the gun and penlight. Johnson nodded and stepped back.

"Are you Charley Jenkins?" Hank asked.

The man nodded vigorously. "That's me. Charley."

"Okay, well, you can put your hands down, Charley, it's all right." Hank holstered his weapon. The man's intellectual disability was immediately evident, as was his desire to please. "We just want to talk to you for a few minutes, if that's all right."

"Okay," Charley said. "You want me to turn on the lights?"

"You have lights up here?"

"Yeah."

"Okay, that might be good."

Charley shuffled down a row of garden beds and plugged an extension cord into another cord jutting from a ventilation shaft, turning on a series of white Christmas tree bulbs tied to the arbor. It was enough light to see around this part of the roof. Hank smiled. It was almost festive.

"You have a nice garden up here, Charley."

"Thanks."

"You wouldn't be growing any weed up here now, would you?" Johnson asked.

"No sir, I pulled up all the weeds, but I don't get very many way up here. Not like people do on the ground."

"I was thinking more of marijuana," Johnson said.

Charley's eyes grew wide. "Oh no, sir, that's bad. Mr. Washington wanted me to grow that for him, he's the super, but Papa said no, it's bad, so I don't grow it."

"Something happened in the alley tonight, Charley," Hank said, thinking that Officer Johnson would probably have a word or two with Mr. Washington later on. "Did you see or hear anything?"

Charley lowered his head and nodded.

"What did you see, Charley?"

"A lot of men. They put up lights and started cleaning up the alley. There's a lot of garbage and stuff down there. Somebody's got to clean it all up."

"Those are people from the police department, like we are," Hank said. "Someone died in the alley tonight and we're trying to find out who killed him."

"Oh."

"Did you see who came here, Charley, and left the man in the alley?"

Charley nodded again.

"Tell me what you saw."

Charley glanced at Johnson, hesitating. The uniform seemed to be making him nervous.

"I forgot to introduce us, Charley," Hank said. "This is Officer Johnson, and my name's Hank. Officer Johnson here was telling me when we were coming upstairs that he likes music. Do you like music, Charley?"

Charley nodded. "I got a tape player up here I listen to sometimes. I like Marvin Gaye."

"Hey, so do I," Johnson said, playing along.

"I like Wilson Pickett, too. I got his tape, you want to hear it?"

"Maybe another time," Hank said.

"Okay."

"It would really help me out, and Officer Johnson, too, if you could tell us about what you saw earlier tonight before the police arrived."

"I saw two men and they was carrying another man."

"Tell us what you remember."

"They came in a car. I heard the car stop, but I didn't get up to see because I was looking at the stars and I didn't want to move. I like sitting in my chair looking at the stars. Papa taught me the names of some of the stars."

"What happened after you heard the car stop?"

"I heard the car thump. Two times, then another thump later. Then I heard their voices."

"What did they say?"

Charley brought his gaze down from the stars and looked at Hank. "I dunno, it was funny talk."

"Funny talk?"

"Yeah," Charley said, "not like the way we talk. They didn't look like us. Not black like us," he glanced at Johnson, "and not white like you. They

144

was China men."

"You saw them? You know what they look like?"

Charley shrugged. "I just saw they was China men. It was far away and it was only when they was near the sidewalk and the street light was shining on them I could see them. I went over and looked down when I heard their voices because I wanted to know who was talking funny. I never heard that kind of talk around here before."

"Show us where you were standing," Hank suggested.

Charley led the way to the edge of the roof. Hank looked down into the alley and saw that ShonDale's transportation had arrived and the body was in the process of being taken away. Karen stood at the end of the alley talking to Byrne.

"What did the men do, Charley?"

Charley stood beside him and pointed. "They carried the man into the alley and put him down there. One man had a plastic bag with stuff in it. He took stuff out of the bag and put it on the ground. Then they left."

"Which way did they go, Charley?"

He pointed up the street past the abandoned building on the other side of the alley.

"Did you hear the car again?"

"No, I just heard them walk away. But I did hear a car a little later."

Someone coming to pick up the two men, Hank thought. "Do you know what time it was?"

Charley shook his head. "I don't know how to tell time. Papa tells me when it's time to do stuff."

"That's all right." It wasn't much, but it was something. They had an eyewitness who confirmed that the body was dumped. Two Asian men left the body, the gun, the drug packet and the syringe. It was a start.

"Anything else, Charley?"

He thought about it for a moment. "Nothing else happened until the policemen came." He looked at Johnson, standing on the other side of him. "Was that you?"

Johnson nodded.

"I thought it was you. I saw you."

"I didn't see you, though."

Charley smiled. "I know. Nobody sees me if I don't want them to."

"Do you see the woman standing on the sidewalk?" Hank asked, pointing.

"Yeah."

"Her name's Detective Stainer. I'm helping her try to catch the men who did this. Do you think you could come downstairs with me and tell her what you saw, just like you told me and Officer Johnson?"

"I don't know," Charley said, taking a few hesitant steps backward.

145

"She's very nice," Hank lied, "and you'd be a really big help to her. It's wrong to kill someone. She wants to find the men who did this and punish them."

"Do I have to?"

"Would you like your father to come down with you? Would that help?"

"Papa? Is he in trouble, too?"

"No, Charley," Hank said, "he's not in trouble, and neither are you."

"Police is here," Charley said, looking at Johnson's uniform. "Police want me to go with them. That's trouble."

"Well, I'm the police too, Charley, and I'm telling you you're not in trouble. I didn't show you my badge." Hank unclipped his badge from his belt and held it up. "See? Officer Johnson has his on his shirt, and I keep mine on my belt, on this leather holder."

Charley took a hesitant step closer to stare at the badge.

Hank held out the badge. "Let's take it down and show it to your papa. You can carry it, if you like. Then we'll go down and talk to Detective Stainer."

Charley took Hank's badge. He looked it all over, gently running the tips of his fingers over the surface. "Gold."

"Yes, it is."

Charley looked at Johnson. "Yours ain't gold."

Johnson chuckled. "No, it's silver, but some day I'll have me a gold one like that."

Charley looked at Hank. "I'm gonna show it to Papa."

"If you promise to talk to Detective Stainer."

"Okay."

They walked back under the arbor and through the door into the stairwell, Hank leading the way, Charley behind him and Johnson bringing up the rear. Suddenly Hank remembered the dream he'd been dreaming when Karen's phone call woke him up, a dream of a woman who grew flowers on the roof of her apartment building. In his mind the woman was Meredith Collier, he realized. Here he was now in a rooftop garden, surrounded by plants, thinking about Meredith Collier.

What was that called again? Meaningful coincidence? Synchronicity?

They went down to the sixth floor and knocked on the door of the Jenkins apartment. Randolph Jenkins had dressed in a clean white shirt, brown trousers and brown oxfords. Hank explained that he wanted Charley to go downstairs to give his story to the investigating detective. Jenkins got his keys from a bowl on a shelf inside the door and stepped out into the hall, locking his apartment door behind him.

"Look at the badge," Charley said, holding it out.

"Very nice," Jenkins said. "Where'd you get it, Charley?"

"Him." He pointed at Hank.

"It's very nice, Charley. You should give it back to the policeman now because he'll need it."

"Okay, Papa."

Hank took it back and clipped it onto his belt, noting the contrast between father and son as they stood together in the hallway. Charley was tall and thick where his father was small and slight. Charley looked as though he'd wandered in from a farm with his rubber boots, uncut hair and thick beard while his father looked as though he could walk into a library and resume putting books on a shelf without missing a beat.

The intellectual difference between them was just as obvious. It must have been difficult for Jenkins to raise the boy entirely by himself while coping with his disability. It must have been very lonely for such an intellectual man not to have been able to share his learning and his interests with his only son. But the love between father and son was as plain as day.

Hank led the way down the hall past the elevator to the stairwell. "How long's the elevator been out?"

"Several months," Jenkins replied. "It fell. Mrs. Candelaria broke her hip. She's suing the landlord, but I don't think she'll have much luck. She weighs three hundred and fifty pounds and they'll use it against her."

"Probably a better idea to use the stairs anyway, then," Johnson said, holding the door for them.

# 18

Karen started the Firebird and closed her eyes. "Christ, I'm beat."

Dawn had arrived unnoticed, and with it a fine mist had begun to fall. She opened her eyes and flicked on the windshield wipers before looking over at Hank. "I need a big-assed cup of coffee right about now. And a steak sandwich. And about ten hours sleep."

"Sounds good to me."

They drove back across the bridge and found an all-night place that was gearing up for the morning rush. They took a booth at the back. Once Karen had her coffee and steak sandwich and Hank had his coffee and cheeseburger with French fries, they were ready to compare notes.

Karen swallowed coffee. "Connected to the Liu killing."

"Yeah. Not an exact copy. The body was positioned differently, the gun was left, there was the double-tap, things like that, but it was obviously staged in the alley to make us think of Martin Liu."

"Yeah. Packet of heroin, syringe, through-and-through in the left thigh, same alley." She bit hungrily and then had something else to say. Hank waited for her to swallow. "Mm. ShonDale worked security for the R Boyz, right?"

Hank nodded, eating.

"Your CI say whether he was known to have offed anyone?"

Hank shook his head, swallowing.

Karen slurped at her coffee. "Let's say our man ShonDale was there when Liu was killed four years ago. So maybe Mah decided it's time for payback." She slurped again. "Got no evidence to connect the two killings other than they look alike. We got little Taylor saying he's Martin Liu and that some bad guy named Shawn, a.k.a. ShonDale, shot him in the leg, and we got a scene that looks like the Liu scene, but other than that, there's zippo. I like it anyways."

"It's a place to start," Hank agreed. "The staging's difficult. There's the hassle of stealing the car, grabbing some heroin to plant, transporting the body from the primary scene, dumping it and getting away without being seen, but Mah would have gone to the trouble. Annoying as hell that ShonDale's popped within twenty-four hours of us getting his name."

"Maybe your CI told someone you were interested in him."

"Not a chance. The guy lives like he's behind enemy lines. Talk like that could cost him his life, and he's far too careful. Besides, he doesn't have any interaction with Asians where he is. How does word get to Asians that fast?"

"Asians are going to that gangsta club where ShonDale worked," Karen shrugged.

"Yeah, but that sounds more like Tommy Leung and his fun boys than Peter Mah."

Karen drained her coffee and looked at the bottom of the cup in disgust. "Christ, that didn't last five seconds." She stood up. "Want another one?"

Hank shook his head. She went up to the front and returned a few minutes later with another cup of coffee and a breakfast muffin.

She sat down and began to peel the paper off the bottom of the muffin. "So if this is Shawn, who's Gary?"

Hank looked at her. "You think there was a Gary?"

She destroyed half of her muffin in vicious bites before answering. "Am I buying into the kid's talk? Yes, I am. Call me insane if you want, but this was Shawn, and somewhere there's a Gary who's next on Mah's shopping list."

"We'd better find him."

"You're tellin' me." She made the rest of the muffin disappear and took out her notebook. "All right. We're looking for two Asians who either shot ShonDale Gregg or helped clean it up. Easton said he'll be doing the autopsy this afternoon, so there's that. They've already run the gun and it belonged to Gregg. We need to take a look at his crib, check into family, all that stuff. You said he did a little time. I'll contact his parole officer and see what I can get." She began to jot things down in her notebook.

"I'll get a list of Peter Mah's known employees and we'll start bringing them in," Hank said, taking out his own notebook. "Check out their alibis. I'll check out Gregg's residence and see what I can find."

Karen tapped her pen on the table top. "We'll see if the lab comes up with anything interesting from the scene. Maybe the car will have something good. You know what'd be cool?" She pointed her pen at Hank. "Some rock-hard *evidence*. That'd be cool."

"Evidence would be cool," Hank agreed.

# 19

"Glad you could join us, Detective," Dr. Jim Easton said, glancing up from his laptop. "We've already finished the external examination. Mr. Shaniwatru will give you a rundown while I catch up on my notes."

"Yeah, sorry." Karen's unfastened surgical gown billowing around her as she hurried into the autopsy theater. She was running late because Charley Jenkins had shown up downtown with his father to look through a set of photo arrays of Asian men, including eight who worked for Peter Mah. He hadn't recognized anyone, unfortunately. It had been too far away for him to have seen their faces clearly.

"Please tie your gown," Easton said, "and finish your coffee over there before you come any closer." He pointed at the corner of the theater.

Karen drained her coffee in three long gulps and threw the cup into a waste receptacle in the corner before tying her gown and heading back toward the table on which lay the body of ShonDale Gregg.

The Forensic Medical Center was only three years old and still felt brand new to the detectives who had to drive across town to get there. The old building had been right downtown but had been a nightmare for the Medical Examiner's Office in their struggle to maintain its national accreditation. Refrigeration units were prone to failure, storage space was very limited, and the ventilation system occasionally stopped working, resulting in a stink that filled the entire facility for days. Additionally, there was virtually no parking for visitors. This new building, however, had ample parking, the HVAC system kept the air as fresh as possible, and the corpses stayed at the proper temperature, which meant that Karen had to listen to fewer complaints when she showed up for an autopsy. The longer drive was a fair exchange.

"Good afternoon, Detective Stainer," said Harry Shaniwatru, a tiny man of Thai descent in his mid-twenties who worked for the Medical Examiner's Office as a contract forensic investigator while completing his MD at State University. He usually worked the midnight shift, and it was rumored that he got by on only three hours of sleep each day. He also boxed professionally as a flyweight to help pay the bills, with a record of 16 wins and two losses. He was a serious-minded and extremely tough little son of a bitch, and Karen liked him.

"Hi, Harry. I didn't expect to see you up so late."

"I'm pulling a double. Fall tuition's coming up."

"So bring me up to speed."

"The deceased is ShonDale Gregg," Harry said. "He weighed 111.58 kilograms, or 246 pounds and measured 1.98 meters or six feet, six inches tall."

"Taking notes, Detective?" Easton asked, still typing.

"Should I? Are you going to be leaving this kind of stuff out of your report?"

Silence.

Harry waited, knowing that Easton liked to bait some detectives in the autopsy theater. When it was apparent that the exchange was finished, he went on. "We've already washed him, Detective, but I'll take you through what there was. We removed the bags from his hands and the plastic strap from his wrists and sent them to Byrne's lab for trace analysis. I scraped under the fingernails and there was a bit of dirt but nothing hopeful in terms of DNA sources that I could see. There were bags on the feet and I removed these, along with the shoes, and sent them to Byrne as well. There were a lot of particles of various types on the soles of the shoes that should keep them busy for a while. Clothing was removed and bagged. Blood was swabbed from the bullet holes front and back in the leg of the pants and from other places on the body. Everything was photographed."

"All right."

"Features of interest," Harry went on, his voice rising in a sing-song imitation of a tour guide, "include this gang tattoo on the right side of his neck, an R in a graffiti-style script, and this old scar on the left pectoral, likely a knife wound. As you can see the victim was circumcised. Here's the entrance of the through-and-through in the left thigh. Looks like the gun was held about six inches away when it was fired. Here you can see the exit wound; these are very old scars on both kneecaps, probably from childhood accidents. These abrasions on the knees were ante-mortem; I expect he was kneeling on grit-covered pavement. This scar on the back of the right calf is quite old and possibly from a piece of glass. Moving back up here on the left shoulder we have a nice tat of a heart and the word 'Candie,' perhaps a girlfriend, and here below it another one of a horse's head, I think it is, and another name, 'Patty,' and the numeral nine. A few old scars on each forearm, burns and cuts and what not. These–" he pointed at a cluster of knotted white scars on ShonDale's left wrist "–look like old dog bites. These narrow contusions on both wrists are ante-mortem, from the plastic locking strap. Of particular interest are his hands. Both left and right hands show extensive damage, broken knuckles, scars, left little finger broken and healed badly; see how crooked it is? Obviously a fighter who liked to swing at the face of his victim where it would make the biggest splash, so to speak."

"Career bouncer and tough guy," Karen said.

"Makes sense. I recognize the tattoo on the neck. R Boyz. He also had two broken toes on his right foot, maybe a year or so ago. Might have kicked something hard without proper footwear."

"Probably some loser's ass," Karen said.

"Anyhow, so much for that." Harry moved back up to the top of ShonDale's body. "He sustained a fair bit of damage ante-mortem, as you can see. Contusion on the left side of the neck from a sharp blow from something round and blunt. Maybe an elbow. Then we have this collection of abrasions, contusions and lacerations on his face, scalp and neck from the beating that he took, the aforementioned scrapes on the knees, and also contusions on the torso, groin area, backs of both legs, I'd say from being kicked."

"Okay," Karen said, "I got it. Had the snot beaten out of him, got shot in the leg and then a double tap to the head."

"In a nutshell," Harry agreed. "We took swabs of all the blood, as I said, in case someone else might have donated to the cause. Of particular interest are the particles I gathered, Detective. Stuck to his scalp, cheeks and clothing and especially inside his mouth. Abrasions inside his lips and on his gums suggest his face was being ground against the pavement during the beating, and he picked up a fair collection of particles that stayed inside his mouth for us to examine. The lab has them now."

Easton abandoned his laptop and moved over to the table. "All right, time for the main event."

"Yes, Dr. Easton," Harry said, reaching for a scalpel. "Shall I begin?"

"Please do." Easton looked at Karen. "Detective, a little elbow room, please?"

"Uh, yeah, sure, Doc," Karen said, stepping back. "Be my guest."

She hated autopsies because they were long and boring. Even the thrill of discovery was sucked out of the experience for her because Easton was extremely observant and never missed a thing. If there was anything to learn from the body, Easton would find it first and then dangle it in front of her like a dog toy that she was expected to jump and snap at like an excited terrier. The bastard. Hopefully this wouldn't kill the rest of the day. She didn't want Hank to have all the fun, for chrissakes.


Hank rode over to ShonDale Gregg's condominium with Butternut Allenson. He gave a copy of their search warrant to Anwar Boublil, the building's live-in concierge, who invited them into his condo while flipping through the documentation. They stepped into a tastefully decorated living room that featured a fireplace and large curtained windows.

"Please, sit down. Can I get either of you a cup of coffee?"

Butternut shook her head.

"No, thanks," Hank said. He looked around the room at the antiques on the fireplace mantel and side tables. "Are you a collector?"

"Yes, I specialize in bisque figures."

"How long did Mr. Gregg live here?"

"Just over three years now."

"Did the place come furnished or did he move in with his own

152

stuff?"

"All our condominiums are unfurnished," Boublil replied. "Our clients are not interested in other people's leftovers. Of course, Mr. Gregg didn't have very many things when he first moved in, but he'd been adding to his collection since then. I loaned him a few books on antiques to help him out, and he asked my advice a few times."

Boublil described ShonDale as a serious-minded and polite young man who obviously came from humble means but was doing everything he could to better himself. He spoke well, lapsing into ghetto slang only for humorous effect, often wore expensive tailored suits, and had to be reminded only once that when he entertained he was expected to keep the noise down and observe decent hours.

"What type of tenants do you generally get around here?" Hank asked.

"Our *clientele*, Lieutenant, represent a cross-section of the more successful members of our community. All races and religions are welcome. I'm a Jewish Moroccan, we have Muslim-Americans, Anglo-Saxon Christians, you name it. If you're asking whether Mr. Gregg stood out here because he was African-American, the answer is no."

"He have any friends in the building?"

"No."

"Do you know if he ever associated with anyone named Gary?"

"I have no clue who he associated with, let alone their names."

"Did you see anyone unusual come in yesterday or last evening, or see Gregg go out with anyone unusual?"

Boublil shook his head. "No, sorry."

"Maybe the people across the hall saw or heard something."

"Mrs. Weems isn't home," Boublil said. "She's been in Indiana for a month visiting her daughter."

Okay, so much for that. "I noticed a surveillance camera downstairs in the lobby. Is it real?"

Boublil scoffed. "Of course."

"Any chance I could see the tape covering the past twenty-four hours?"

"There are no tapes anymore, Lieutenant. Our system's connected to a computer with a video capture card using MPEG-4 compression. The data's stored on a digital video recorder. I noticed the search warrant mentioned surveillance video. It's no problem to make you a copy on DVD."

"That'd be nice," Hank said.

"Would you like the video from the hallway on Mr. Gregg's floor as well?"

"There's a camera in the hallway?"

Boublil smiled. "It's in the head of the fire sprinkler in the ceiling."

"I'll take it."

"No problem. I'll copy that as well and have them ready for you when you leave."

Boublil rode up with them in the elevator and opened Gregg's door. Hank took the key, thanked him and shooed him back downstairs.

As soon as they stepped inside the door of the condo they made their first discovery. The foyer was about fifteen feet long and six feet wide. A doorway on the left at the end led into the rest of the condo. The floor was covered with expensive carpeting. At the end of the hall was a table. On the table was a vase in the center and a figurine on the right. There was nothing on the left. Hank saw the missing figurine lying on the floor beneath the table, broken in several pieces.

"Slowly," he said to Butternut, pointing.

She approached cautiously, examining the carpet before her. "Fragments." She unslung her SLR digital camera from over her shoulder. "A piece that was stepped on and crushed."

After a careful search to ensure there was no one in the condo, Hank returned to the front entry where Butternut crouched before the pieces of the figurine ground into the carpet. "There's probably fragments in someone's shoe."

"Gregg's?"

"There was a bunch of stuff on the soles of his shoes," she recalled. "We'll see." She pointed. "The table is a card table, Regency. Really nice rosewood cross-banding, see? From about 1810 or so, worth about four grand. The top of the table swivels open so you can keep visitors' cards in it. People gave them out when they came calling. Cartes de visite and so on. That's why they were called card tables. We'll see if ShonDale kept anything inside it." She picked up her camera. "The vase is Staffordshire, about fifty years older than the table, and worth about five grand. The figurines are Royal Dux, a shepherd and shepherdess, about 1880. Probably paid two grand for the pair." She shrugged. "Antiques are a hobby of mine."

"Eleven thousand dollars just to decorate the hallway," Hank said.

"Look, Lieutenant, we need to cover our bases here. I called Tim and he's sending me some help, but we'll need to do the front entrance and both elevators before anything else. The intercom button," she held up a hand to count off on her fingers, "door frames, door handles, mailbox, the entire inside of each elevator."

"I understand," Hank said.

"I'll go back down and look at the video first," she said. "If I can spot them coming and going, it'll narrow down the surfaces we need to cover."

After she left, Hank stepped across the hall and knocked loudly on the door of the condo belonging to Mrs. Weems. There was no answer. There were two other condos on the floor, farther down the hall. The one on the same side of the building as ShonDale was occupied by a man named George Claddy. A widower with a bad leg, he was lonely enough to be starved for company and kept Hank for twenty minutes, although he had nothing of value to offer as far as his next-door neighbor was concerned.

"Seen him in the elevator once or twice, that's all. Big bastard. Scared the hell out of me, but he was polite enough. Not the kind you'd borrow a cup of sugar from, though."

The other condo belonged to a married couple. The wife, Janice Townsend, was sick in bed with the flu. The door was opened by the house-keeper, who explained that Mr. Townsend was away on business in Atlanta and had been gone for three days, leaving his ill wife to fend for herself. Hank talked his way inside and briefly questioned Mrs. Townsend, who assured him that she had taken a flu remedy last evening that had knocked her out from nine o'clock onward. She hadn't heard a thing.

By the time he came back out into the hallway Butternut had returned from downstairs. Help had arrived and someone was processing the south elevator in which, according to the security video, two men had ridden up to ShonDale's floor and ridden back down with ShonDale between them. Butternut had already finished the hallway and had moved into the kitchen.

"Half-finished glass of orange juice," she said, pointing, "half-eaten sandwich, looks like ham, cheese and tomato. He was interrupted while eating a late snack and forcibly taken out." She watched him remove a pair of latex gloves from his jacket pocket. "We've photographed the living room, master bathroom and master bedroom."

Hank wandered into the living room, unzipping his portfolio to re-move his notebook and a copy of the documents Karen had received from ShonDale's parole officer. ShonDale was 27 years old, six feet, six inches and two hundred and forty-five pounds. Two years at State University, majoring in business administration and starting defensive end on the football team as a sophomore before he dropped out because of academic problems. Priors included marijuana possession, disorderly conduct, careless driving and the conviction for assault.

RaVonn Pease was the only employer listed in ShonDale's jacket. It mentioned his part-time job at the En-R-G Club but nothing else. Hank mulled it over. A typical street punk with gang connections who got noticed for his size and aggression, began working his way up in the R Boyz and then started associating with Asian gangsters on the side. The two years at State didn't seem to fit until it occurred to him that Tommy would have gone to State at the same time as ShonDale. They must have known each other.

According to the file, ShonDale's mother died six years ago from lung cancer and his father's whereabouts were unknown. He had four sisters: Cynthia, age 30, now living in Phoenix; Marissa, age 28, whereabouts un-known; Candie, born in 1986 and deceased in 1996, shot to death in the street

155

by a playmate; and Patti, born in 1987 and deceased in 1997 from a staph infection. A note from the Parole Officer said that he had no contact with his sister in Phoenix. There was no steady girl friend. "He says he's still playing the field," the PO had handwritten in the margin for Karen's attention.

Butternut appeared in the doorway holding up two kitchen canisters decorated with chickens. "Test indicates coke," she said, dipping the canister in her left hand. "About 200 grams." She lowered the other can. "Right next to it, a little kitchen protection. HK45. Another canister has a spare magazine and loose ammunition."

Hank put the file and notebook back into his portfolio. He wandered around the room. There was artwork hanging on the walls, tastefully selected stuff that no doubt would have pleased Boublil, if he'd been consulted, but Hank could see nothing personal in the room. No framed photos on the wall, no photo albums. He walked over to a cabinet that contained a sound system and looked at the compact discs on the shelves. He saw rap and hip hop, some names that he recognized and many that he did not. There was also a small collection of classical music, including Berlioz, Tchaikovsky and Grieg, next to Lionel Ritchie, Earth Wind and Fire and Kenny G. Easy listening for the ladies of the field with whom he was playing, classical music for people he wanted to impress, and street music when he was alone and wanted to be himself.

He walked into the master bathroom and opened the medicine cabinet. He looked at the usual assortment of pain relievers, deodorant, hemorrhoid ointment, shaving cream, razor blades, razor, adhesive bandages, condoms, toothpaste, toothbrush and mouth wash. There was a bottle of diuretics and a box of prescription medication for the reduction of cholesterol. Hank saw another drugstore label and used his pen to move aside a bottle of ibuprofen for a better look. It was migraine medication, the kind taken once a day.

He made a note of the pharmacy and the prescribing doctor. ShonDale suffered from migraines and apparently had also come under fire from his doctor for his excessive weight. Hank could imagine the blood tests coming back with high cholesterol levels and the ensuing lecture about heart disease. ShonDale had filled the prescription almost three months ago but the bottle looked virtually untouched, so he'd gone through the motions and then shoved the medication in here, forgetting about it. The migraine medication had been filled at the same time but was about half-empty; ShonDale apparently took his headaches more seriously than the condition of his arteries.

Hank went on into the master bedroom and looked at the king-sized bed, which had been inexpertly made up, the bedspread showing a few bumps and wrinkles where the bedclothes underneath had not been completely straightened. The pillows were tossed into place at the head of the bed but were a little crooked. The rest of the room looked spotless. Hank took a quick walk back to the bathroom, looking at the shower and toilet. Everything was clean. He came back up the hallway and checked the top of the picture frames on each wall. No dust. Must have had a housekeeper who came in a few times a week. He re-entered the bedroom and looked again at the bed. Apparently he possessed enough self-discipline to attempt the basics himself and was self-conscious enough that he didn't want the housekeeper to think he was a slob. No way, though, that he would do his own dusting and keep his toilet that spotless. If he did everything himself, the bed would look like something in an army barracks.

On the left of the bed was a night table holding a lamp and nothing else, while on the right was a matching night table that held a matching lamp, an open can of Budweiser that sounded empty when Hank tapped it with his pen, and the base of a portable phone. The phone was gone. Curious, Hank pressed the button labeled "Locate Handset" with the end of his pen and nearly jumped out of his skin when the handset began to wail underneath one of the pillows on the bed. He lifted the pillow carefully, pressed the red button on the phone with his pen to shut it off and lowered the pillow over it again. He heard voices behind him and left the bedroom.

Talking to Butternut in the kitchen was CSI Jon Beverley, a 53-year-old former patrol officer with a degree in chemistry who'd been shot in the arm while on duty just after the expansion of Criminalistics and had decided that a switch in career path might be in his best interest. He was short, stocky and balding, and he had a grouchy, negative disposition that had earned him the nickname "Mini-Byrne" behind his back. He grinned at Hank, showing long yellow teeth.

"Screwing up my scene back there, Lieutenant?"

"Trying not to. Have you been out on the terrace?"

"Just came from there."

Hank went out onto the terrace to look around while Beverley went back into the master bedroom. There was nothing of interest on the terrace other than a deck set that included a table and four chairs. The view of the river was spectacular.

ShonDale Gregg lived like a prince while working only part-time at a club. Obviously what he made at the En-R-G Club wouldn't pay for the lifestyle he was maintaining here. Smoke thought Gregg might be looking out for Asians who were slumming at the En-R-G Club. Maybe he spent a lot of his time with his old college friend Tommy and his gang, making extra money on the side.

Beverley called him in and showed him a gun he'd found in the drawer of the nightstand.

"Kel-Tec," he said, holding it up by the end of the stock with his right thumb and index finger. "P-3AT, three-eighty. I have my laptop with me, so I can run the serial number if you're interested."

"I'm interested." Hank thought about it for a moment. Gun in the kitchen, gun in the master bedroom. Gun in every room?

157

He walked back out into the living room and began to search. After a few minutes he was down on his knees, staring at a dark shape underneath the sofa.

"Bev! Can you give me hand for a minute? In the living room."

Beverley came in muttering under his breath.

"Something under here," Hank said, straightening up. "Can you help me tip it up?"

"It better not be a cat," Beverley groused, setting his camera aside. "I got scratched by a cat that had been shut in a closet at a scene last week. Lucky I didn't get infected."

Hank took one end of the sofa and Beverley the other, and together they tipped it back onto its rear legs. Beverley released his end and kneeled down.

"Nice one, Lieutenant."

A holster had been affixed to the underside of the sofa. Beverley snapped a couple of photographs before putting down his camera and gently removing the revolver. "Nice. Smith and Wesson 686." He knelt on the floor, examining it. "Well kept. Better than the Kel-Tec in the bedroom." He opened the cylinder. "Fully loaded." He tipped the rounds out into his hand.

"Bev?"

"Three-fifty-seven magnum," he murmured, looking at the rounds in his palm.

"Bev?"

"Hmm?" Beverley slowly looked up.

"Can I put the sofa down now?"

"Oh, uh, sure, Lieutenant." Beverley moved out of the way, allowing Hank to lower the sofa back down onto the floor.

"I take it you'd like me to run this one, too."

Hank nodded. "And the one Butternut found in the kitchen." He looked around, musing. "Master bedroom, kitchen, living room. Let's take a look in the master bathroom."

They found a Glock 31 loaded with .357 SIG cartridges at the bottom of the laundry hamper. Unlike the Smith and Wesson 686 in the living room, it had seen rough handling during its day. Hank shook his head at the bipolar nature of the victim and his living space: expensive, upscale decor and furnishings mixed with coke in the kitchen and a gun in every room. And the capper? Somehow, with all this firepower distributed around the place, someone had gotten the drop on ShonDale while he was sitting in his kitchen eating a bedtime snack.

Beverley told him that although the Smith and Wesson revolver from the living room was registered to ShonDale, the Kel-Tec from the master bedroom was registered to a Roderick Allan Borden of Washington, D.C., and had been reported lost a year ago last January. A search of Mr. Borden's record

showed that he was a small-time dealer with several convictions for possession and trafficking. Similarly, the Glock 31 from the laundry hamper had most
recently belonged to a Terence Dean Milligan of Manchester, about a hundred
miles upstate. Milligan had a conviction for possession of marijuana.

"Where the hell is he getting these guns?" Beverley frowned at the
screen.

"He was a bouncer and security guy. Maybe he took them from losers
trying to get into the En-R-G Club and then just kept them."

"Could be. I'll test fire them when I get back and see if we get any
IBIS hits. You never know." The Integrated Ballistics Identification System
provided law enforcement agencies with a database of projectile and shell cas-
ing evidence for comparison to evidence recovered at crime scenes.

"His computer's in the guest bedroom," Hank said. "Check his
e-mail, Facebook account, Twitter, whatever the hell you can find. I want to
know about his connections."

"Aye aye, sir."

Hank's cell phone vibrated. It was Karen.

"I'm downstairs. Are you just about done up there?"

"I can be. What's up?"

"They've started bringing in Mah's worker bees. We need to get
started on them."

"Sounds good. I'll be right down."

As he punched the button to summon the elevator he thought about
what they'd found in ShonDale's apartment and shook his head. How the hell
had they gotten the drop on the guy?

# 20

They used three interview rooms to interview Peter Mah's employees. Hank took one, Karen another, and Waverman reluctantly worked the third room with Tim Byrne. Additionally, a patrol officer named Buddy Hum came in on short notice from Midtown District to act as an interpreter as required while Captain Martinez and Lieutenant Jarvis listened in from the observation rooms.


Hank began with Yi Chin.

"Mr. Yi, you're the manager of the Bright Spot Restaurant?"

"Already said that."

"Were you at the restaurant yesterday evening?"

"Already said that, too. Until closing time."

"When did the restaurant close?"

"Sunday nights close at eight o'clock. Very slow."

"What did you do afterwards?"

"Went upstairs to watch baseball game, have dinner."

"You went upstairs to your apartment above the restaurant? Can anyone corroborate that?"

"Wife. She at market now. You miss." Yi grinned at him.

"Yeah, okay. We'll have a word with her. Did you go out at any time after that?"

"No, fell asleep. Boring game. Nobody score. How win bets with nobody scoring runs? You tell me that."

Hank showed him a photograph of ShonDale Gregg. "Ever seen this guy?"

"No. Who he?"

"Peter Mah ever talk about a guy named ShonDale?"

"I no listen to Mr. Mah when he talk, unless he talk to me," Yi said gravely. "When he talk to somebody else, bad for health to listen."

"Peter Mah ask you to do a special favor for him? Take this guy for a ride and put a few bullets in him?"

"You crazy? Mr. Mah never ask me to do anything like that. Mr. Mah give me shit for slow food, lazy waiter, ask Daniel to fix dinner. Don't have nothing to do with these other things you talk about."

"Anyone unusual stop by the restaurant last evening?"

"Unusual? No."

"Was Peter Mah there?"

"In restaurant, you mean? He come downstairs for dinner at seven, like always. Go back upstairs at eight."

160

"Anyone meet with him during dinner?"

Yi shook his head vigorously. "No way. Nobody ever bother Mr. Mah during mealtime, I make sure. Bad for health. Mr. Mah get very upset."

"Bad things happen when Mah gets upset?"

Yi shrugged. "Mr. Mah don't like indigestion. Do you?"


Meanwhile, Waverman and Byrne were questioning Daniel Chun.

"Where were you yesterday, Mr. Chun?"

"At home," Daniel replied. "It was my day off."

"What about last night?"

"At home, I said."

"Can anyone corroborate that for you?"

"Of course. My wife, for starters."

"You work for Peter Mah, Mr. Chun?"

"Yes."

"You're the cook at the Bright Spot Restaurant, are you?"

"No," Daniel replied shortly.

Waverman looked at Byrne, confused. "Tim, isn't this supposed to be the cook?"

"Explain it to him, Chun," Byrne said.

Daniel sighed. "I'm a chef, you cretin."

Waverman blinked. "Chef? Oh, uh, right. Like a cordon bleu chef, something like that?"

"Something like that," Daniel said sarcastically.

"You have to forgive the detective, Chun," Byrne said. "He's a little confused as to why someone who claims to be a trained chef would be working in a dump like the Bright Spot deep frying chicken balls and steaming bean sprouts."

"I'm employed by Mr. Mah to prepare his meals for him. I also oversee the preparation of the restaurant food, but we have a *cook* who's directly responsible for that."

"Who's that, Mr. Chun?" Waverman asked.

"The cook? I believe her name's Millie."

Waverman shuffled through papers in his file. "Millie? Uh, Millie Lung? Would that be her?"

"Could be."

"It says here you live at 547 Jackson Court, Unit 2301, Mr. Chun. That's a long way from Chinatown. How do you get to work in the morning?"

"Mr. Mah sends a car for me."

"Someone picks you up? Who's that?"

"I don't know their names, for godsakes. Sometimes it's the big bald

161

guy and sometimes it's the punk with the scar or the muscular guy with the long nose."

"But you don't know their names?"

"Why on earth should I? They're drivers."

Byrne placed a photograph of ShonDale Gregg on the table in front of Daniel. "What about this guy, know his name?"

Daniel glanced at the photograph. "Of course not."

"Ever see him around the restaurant?" Byrne pressed. "Maybe talking to Mah or one of his flunkies?"

"No. We don't get people like that in the restaurant."

Byrne leaned forward. "Maybe you saw him in the trunk of a stolen car with a couple of bullet holes in his forehead?"

"That's not very funny. I have a sensitive stomach."

"I take it that's a no?" Byrne said. "You didn't see him with a couple of bullet holes in his head?"

"No, no, of course not!"

"Ever heard your boss talk about Jim Brown?"

"No."

"ShonDale Gregg?"

"No."

"Virgil Trucks?"

"No."

"Someone named Gary?"

"No, no, no. I pay absolutely no attention to what goes on in Mr. Mah's business. He pays me phenomenally well to prepare his meals for him and to ensure that Millie, or whatever her name is, doesn't poison the customers. Other than that, I mind my own business."

"But what about between times?" Waverman insisted. "Between meals? Surely you're interacting with the restaurant staff and overhearing things. Maybe one of those names came up and you heard some talk."

Daniel stared at him. "Are you out of your mind? I told you I mind my own business. Between meals I sit at a table in the back room, I drink coffee I make myself from my own private stock and I read."

"You read?" Waverman repeated incredulously.

"Yes, Detective. I read. You know, books, magazines. Perhaps you've heard of them?"

"I don't believe it. You're telling me that Peter Mah pays you phenomenally well, as you put it, to sit there and read?"

"No, Detective," Daniel replied, his voice heavy with contempt. "He pays me phenomenally well to prepare for him the most exquisite food he's ever tasted. Not something you'd know anything about, I suspect, at your pay scale."

Waverman looked at Byrne. "I'm done here. This guy's no help to

162

us at all."

"That'll be all, Mr. Chun," Byrne chuckled. "You're free to go. Have a nice evening."

Waverman rubbed his forehead as Daniel walked out the door. "What an asshole."


Karen, meanwhile, was in the third interview room with Wu Tan, the waiter at the Bright Spot. She showed him a photograph of ShonDale Gregg. "Do you know this man, Mr. Wu?"

"Never seen before," Wu replied.

"Heard anyone talking about a guy named ShonDale Gregg around the restaurant?"

"Nope."

"What about a guy named Gary?"

"Nope."

"Where were you last night, Wu?"

"Work."

"At the restaurant? How late did you work?"

"Eight."

"Then what?"

"Went home."

Karen pretended to be surprised. "Right home? Without going anywhere else?"

"Yeah, sure. Right home."

"Bullshit you did. Unbelievable. What the fuck are you lying for, Wu?"

"Not lying."

"Sure you are, and as soon as we talk to your wife we'll have the truth, now won't we? Patrol just brought her in. We'll find out you were off somewhere putting a bullet in this guy's brain." She tapped the photograph of ShonDale Gregg with a finger.

"Wife? You brought wife here?"

"Sure. Why, what's the problem?"

Wu pointed at the one-way mirror. "She there? Listening now?"

"No, no," Karen replied impatiently, "they've got her down the hall in another room, talking to her."

"Sure?"

"Of course I'm sure."

"All right," Wu said, "Look, I tell you. Went to girlfriend's place. Wife gone to club with friends, I told her I be home right after work but went to girlfriend's place."

"What's this girlfriend's name?"

163

"Amy Chang, 11463 Carton Boulevard, apartment 1278."

"How'd you get there from work?"

"Take bus."

"How long did you stay?"

"Late. Left about two in morning."

"What about your wife? Weren't you scared she'd come home and find you were out?"

Wu shook his head vigorously. "When she go to club with friends, stay out all night. Come back next morning hung over as hell."

Karen chuckled. "Did you go straight home?"

"Yes. Had to walk long way for bus. Should be more buses during night. Don't they know some people stay up late?"

"What bus did you ride?"

"Forty-seven. Only bus running in whole fucking town."

"Anybody see you when you got home?"

"Hope not."

Karen shrugged. "We'll see if the girlfriend'll back up your story."

"For godsake don't bring her here if wife here! She find out about girlfriend, they kill me!"

Karen looked at him. "Who'll kill you, Wu?"

"You stupid or something? Wife and goddamned brother Yi, that's who!"

Karen laughed and waved him away. "Beat it, loser."


Hank sat down across the table from Mikki Lung.

"What's your relationship with Peter Mah, Ms. Lung?"

"Uh, he's my uncle," Mikki replied. "My mother's his sister."

"I see. And you work for him, is that right?"

"What's this all about? Has somebody done something wrong? You're scaring me half to death."

"Just answer the questions, Ms. Lung, and everything will be fine. Do you work for Mah?"

"Yes, I'm his administrative assistant. I work in his office upstairs, above the restaurant, I mean."

"How long have you worked for him?"

"Well, let's see, I guess it'll be two years next month."

"What does your job involve?"

"Oh, I answer the phone, I look after the e-mail and the regular mail, I look after Uncle Peter's files, I run errands, that sort of thing."

"What kind of errands?"

"Like going to the bank, picking up his dry cleaning, whatever he asks me to do."

"Who else works in the office with you?"

"Nobody, just me. I'm kind of a one-woman show there."

Hank frowned. "Oh? No one else at all who works upstairs for Mah?"

Mikki laughed nervously. "Oh, I see what you mean. Well, there's Uncle Peter's driver, Mr. Hu. There's Mr. Goenda, the bookkeeper, but he actually has his own office across town. There's Jimmy Yung and Donald Sheng."

"What do they do for Mah, Ms. Lung?"

"Donald does deliveries and Jimmy's like a personal assistant to Uncle Peter." She smiled. "I think Uncle Peter really likes Jimmy and is grooming him for bigger things."

"Oh, what kind of bigger things?"

"I think some day he'll take over the restaurant for Uncle Peter. When Mr. Yi retires, of course."

"I see. Anybody else work upstairs for Mah?"

"Uh, let's see. I said Benny, Jimmy, Donald. Oh yes, Mr. Foo. He helps Donald with delivery. And Billy Fung." She made a face. "He doesn't do very much."

"You don't like Billy Fung?"

"He's pretty useless. And oh yes, some guy from Hong Kong who goes around with Billy. Tang Lei. He makes me nervous."

Hank put a photograph of ShonDale Gregg down on the table in front of her. "Have you ever seen this man, Ms. Lung?"

"No, I sure haven't. Who is he, Lieutenant?"

"We believe it's someone your boss wanted to meet. His name was ShonDale Gregg. Did you ever hear Mah mention that name?"

"Gregg? What was the first name again?"

"ShonDale."

Mikki shook her head. "No, sorry, Lieutenant. I never heard that name before."

"What about someone named Gary?"

"Um, I don't think so."

"What about Mah's cousin, Martin Liu? Ever hear him talk about him?"

"Martin? Oh, you mean the boy that was killed? I remember that. I was a sophomore in high school. My parents talked about it when it happened. My mother was upset because Uncle Peter was upset. We went to the funeral. His poor mother was just devastated. I wonder what happened to her. I haven't seen her for years now. Not since it happened."

"What about Mah, Ms. Lung? Has he been talking lately about Martin?"

Mikki shrugged. "I suppose so. I heard him say once to Jimmy that

165

he really wanted to find out who shot that boy. He..." she hesitated, "didn't think the police did a very good job finding out who did it."

"What about the last week or so? He say anything in the last week about Martin?"

"This past week? Let me think. Um, not that I can recall. He doesn't talk about personal things very much in the office, Lieutenant."

"You didn't hear him talking to one of his men about this ShonDale guy, suggesting that he may have had something to do with Martin's death?"

Mikki's jaw dropped. "Wow, he did? I mean, is that true? Did he kill Martin? Uncle Peter would sure like to know about that if it's true."

"Just answer the question. Did Mah talk to any of his men about this ShonDale Gregg?"

"If he did, it's news to me."

"All right, thanks, Ms. Lung."


Interviews were also conducted with Millie Lung, Mikki Lung's older sister, who had completed a college program in food preparation and worked at the Bright Spot as the daytime cook, Tom Wong, an elderly man who was the busboy, and two other waitresses. No one recognized the photograph of ShonDale Gregg or had heard his name mentioned around the restaurant, and no one knew anything about what their boss had been doing late last night. Everyone agreed that he came downstairs for dinner at seven and went back upstairs at eight, and no one remembered seeing him after that. They were all sent home as their interviews were completed.

Missing from the roster were Jimmy Yung, Billy Fung, Tang Lei, Benny Hu the driver and Peter Mah himself. After her interview, Mikki Lung called her boss. Peter then called Henry Lee and gave him his instructions. Henry hurried downtown and inserted himself into the process, arriving as Hank was interrogating Foo Yee. The attorney was a short, stout, middle-aged man who was well-dressed without being obvious about it. His dark suit looked expensive but had a few wrinkles from being carelessly crammed into the closet between wears. His watch was understated and the wedding ring on his left hand was a plain gold band. His thinning black hair was shot with grey strands. It was too long and slightly mussed, as though he had driven to the station with his car window down. Hank could detect the odor of cigarette smoke coming from his clothes, and he guessed that Henry was a smoker. He was given a few minutes to confer in private with his client before the questioning resumed.

"Counselor," Hank said, sitting down across from Foo, "this is Officer Buddy Hum from Midtown District. He's been kind enough to lend his services where English might be a problem."

"I believe we've met before," Lee said in Cantonese to the uniformed

166

officer who sat down in the chair across from him. "Your mother is the sister of Anthony Wong, is she not?"

"No," Hum replied in the same language, "she's his cousin on her father's side. My mother has no brothers, only sisters."

"My apologies, Mr. Hum. Mr. Wong is a client of mine."

"I didn't know that." Hum turned to Hank, switching to English. "Mr. Lee was inquiring about my family. One of my mother's cousins, Anthony Wong, is a client of Mr. Lee's."

"Are you satisfied with Officer Hum's competence in Cantonese?" Hank asked Lee.

"Yes, of course."

"Fine. We've reached a bit of an impasse with your client here, but it has less to do with language than his inability to remember where he was Wednesday night. Now that you're here, maybe he can tell us what we need to know.

Lee turned to Foo and said in Cantonese, "Go ahead and answer their questions. Where were you last night?"

"I had a few drinks and went to a few places."

"He says he had a few drinks and went to a few places," Hum translated, then turned to Foo. "Where did you go?"

"I don't know. Around."

"I asked him what places," Hum said to Hank, "and he said he doesn't know. Around."

"Who were you with?" Hank asked.

Foo listened to Hum's translation and shrugged. "Sheng."

"Who's that?" Hank asked.

"He's referring to Donald Sheng," Henry Lee supplied. "He's another of Mr. Mah's employees."

"Were you with anyone else?" Hank asked.

Foo listened to the translation and made a face. "Guys came and went."

"He says that people came and went," Hum told Hank.

"What about between eleven and midnight last night?" Hank asked, leaning forward. "Where were you?"

"A club," Foo replied when Hum had translated the question. "Don't know for sure which one. Maybe Sheng remembers."

When Hum had translated, Hank slid a photograph across the table. "Seen this car before?"

Foo stared at the photograph and said something to Lee, who replied with impatience. Foo sat in silence. Hank looked at Hum.

"Mr. Foo said, 'why do they ask me about this piece of shit?' and Mr. Lee replied, 'I don't know. If you haven't seen the car before, just tell them that.'"

167

Hank tapped the photograph. "So, Foo, have you seen it before or not?"

Without waiting for a translation, Foo snapped in Cantonese, "I haven't seen this piece of shit before. Don't waste my time with shit like this."

"He said—"Hum began.

Hank raised a hand. "I got the general drift." He stood up and walked around the table until he was behind Foo. Leaning down over his shoulder, he said, "here's the thing, Foo. This car was stolen Wednesday night and used to transport a murder victim to a dump site in South Shore East. We're going over it right now and I'm betting that we're going to find evidence that proves you were in it. Why not just tell us about it and save yourself a lot of trouble later?"

"He says that we are examining the car and expect to prove that you were in it last night," Hum told Foo in Cantonese. "He says it would be better to tell them about it now."

"Like fuck. He can fuck his neighbor's dog for all I care."

"He says you can fuck your neighbor's dog," Hum said.

"My neighbor doesn't have a dog, smartass." Hank went back to his chair and sat down. "Counselor, if your client wants to be treated like a har-dassed gangster we can do that. No problem."

"Give me a moment," Lee said. To Foo he said in Cantonese, "I told you before what was expected of you. Mr. Mah's instructions are quite clear. Cooperate and give whatever answers you can. Otherwise, keep your mouth shut. Do you understand?"

Foo sighed. "I understand." He looked at Hum. "Tell the dog's asshole I haven't seen the car before."

"He says he hasn't seen the car before," Hum said.

Hank slid another photograph across the table. "What about this guy? Seen him before? Maybe Wednesday night?"

Foo looked at the photograph and turned to Henry Lee. "I haven't seen this piece of shit before. Can I go now?"

"He says he hasn't seen him before," Hum translated.

"Know anything about a man named Gary?"

Foo listened to the translation and shook his head.

"Can I see the bottoms of your shoes?"

After a moment's silence, Hum said, "show him the bottoms of your shoes."

"Like fuck I will."

Henry Lee stirred impatiently. "Foo, you idiot, show the man your shoes."

"These people are fools." Foo lifted up his left leg and draped it over the corner of the table.

168

Hank got up and looked at the sole of Foo's left shoe. "Now the other one."

"The other one," Hum translated. "Show him the bottom of your other shoe now."

"Why not?" Foo draped his right leg over the corner of the table next to his left leg, smiling.

"These shoes are brand new," Hank said. "When did you get them?"

"This morning," Foo replied affably after listening to the translation. "Doesn't everyone put shoes on when they get dressed in the morning?"

"He says he put them on this morning," Hum said.

"What happened to the shoes you wore Wednesday night? Where are they?"

Foo cackled something and grinned at Hank.

"He says he got tired of them and threw them out," Hum said.

Hank stood up and walked around the end of the table. "Tell him to hold up his hands."

"Hold up your hands," Hum said to Foo. "Lieutenant Donaghue wants to look at them."

"Fuck that."

"Show him your hands, Foo!" Henry Lee snapped.

Foo reluctantly held out his hands, palms down. Hank bent down for a close look. "This small cut here looks sore," he said, pointing at the middle knuckle of the right hand. "A bit of infection starting. Mostly you used the edges of your hands but here you must have gotten a little angry and punched Gregg in the mouth so that his tooth cut you." He straightened and looked at Henry Lee. "We'll swab the cut and his hands and I'd also like a DNA sample."

Henry Lee turned to Foo. "Put your hands down. He's going to swab your mouth for your DNA and also swab your hand. Tell him you'll permit it."

"What the fuck does he want to do that for? I'm not letting him touch me."

"You'll do what you're told, you idiot."

"Counselor?" Hank prompted.

"He says he'll allow it."

Hank looked at Hum. "Is that what he said?"

"Not yet, sir."

"Tell him to say the words, Mr. Lee."

Lee glared at Foo. "Tell them you'll permit the samples. Mr. Mah expects you to do what you're told."

Foo shrugged. "All right. They can do it."

Hum translated.

Hank patted Hum on the shoulder. "Wait here for a moment. I'll have

169

a technician come in."

The last person to be interviewed was Donald Sheng. Hank and Karen grilled him together without generating anything of interest. Afterwards they walked down to the hall toward the bullpen area, tired and frustrated.

"It's like the Great fucking Wall of China around here," Karen groused. "Nobody's going to give up Peter Mah."

Hank was forced to agree. "Nor could we get anything solid on Gary. We have to find him before Mah does."

Tim Byrne and Dennis Waverman were waiting for them. "We've got some lab results," Byrne said.

They went into Martinez's office and closed the door. "The shoe prints in the alley," Byrne began, "unfortunately get us nowhere. They don't match the shoes of anyone interviewed today. The shoes worn when the vic was killed are probably on their way to a landfill site as we speak. The particles found on the vic's body and clothes are more interesting."

"Do they point to a location of the primary scene?" Martinez asked.

"I'd say so. First of all we found particles of asphalt, so it was a paved area. There were grains of sand typical of what might be blown inland from the shore of the river. Most interesting, though, were the particles of dried bird droppings that point to *Phalacrocorax auritus*, the double-breasted cormorant, which nest under the overpasses and bridges. I think it's fair to say he was taken down under a bridge along the river and worked over there."

"So we need to search those paved areas under the bridges," Martinez said.

"There are six bridges," Hank said.

"Twice that amount if you count the inland forks," Waverman said.

Byrne shook his head. "The cormorants tend not to nest that far into the city. I think we're safe to stick to the six main bridges. We're already out checking them."

"Good, excellent," Martinez said. "I really want to find that primary scene. What else do you have? Anything to tie one of these characters to the vic?"

"Yes, but just to finish with the particles, we found more samples in the trunk of the Danati car, transferred from vic, but also in the front on the floor, both driver and passenger sides, from the missing shoes. Plus, traces in the footprints at the scene. So there's continuity there between the primary and secondary scenes. As well, mixed in with the particles on the vic's shoes and on the passenger side were particles of ceramics and glaze that match the broken figurine we found in the hallway of the vic's condo. This establishes another connection between the kidnapping and the stolen car."

"What about the video?" Hank prompted.

170

"Right. The digital feed from the surveillance system of the building where the vic lived that shows us two perps. We see them in the front foyer where they were buzzed up to the vic's condo, and we actually have audio for that as well. They have a pretty good system in there. You can hear the vic answer the buzzer. He asks, 'what do you want?' and then one of the perps leans forward and says, 'Tommy sent us. We have something for you.' The vic says, 'What is it?' and the perp says, 'money.' That was good enough for the vic to buzz them in."

"Nice one," Karen remarked. "Way to go, ShonDale."

Hank shook his head. Now he understood how ShonDale had allowed his attackers to get the drop on him.

"Can we identify anyone from the video?" Martinez asked.

"Not directly, Byrne replied. "They wore masks. A clown face and a dog mask. We also have footage of them approaching the vic's condo down the hallway, forcing their way inside when he opens the door, then shortly after, marching him down the hall onto the elevator. We've been able to determine that one of them was five foot ten, one hundred and sixty to one-sixty-five and the other was five foot eight, one hundred and forty to one-forty-five. Donald Sheng and Foo Yee fit the bill. We're matching samples of their voices to the audio to see if either of them was the speaker."

"Probably Sheng," Hank said. "I don't think Foo speaks English."

"I like our chances," Karen said.

"So do I," Byrne agreed. "But we don't have anything that puts the victim's gun in their hand. It was definitely the murder weapon. Ballistics confirms that the two rounds taken from his head were fired from his own gun, but we don't have either of those two goofballs pulling the trigger. The packet of heroin and the syringe were clean. The gun was clean and both Sheng and Foo tested negative for GSR. Oh, and did I mention that we took a hair from the car that's a match to Foo Yee?"

"You didn't mention that," Karen grinned.

"So we have them as accessories at a minimum," Martinez said.

"Yes. And we're waiting for the blood swabs taken at the autopsy to be processed. I'm willing to bet we'll find that Foo donated a sample when he cut his knuckle on the vic's teeth."

"So let's process them," Martinez said. "Then we'll pressure them to give us Mah as the shooter."

"I should mention," Byrne went on, turning to Dennis Waverman, "that I have something for you too, Detective."

"Me?" Waverman looked confused.

"I had them process your evidence on the Liu cold case because of the possible connection. It's amazing the advances that have been made in forensic technology in only four years. For example–"

"The point being?" Martinez interrupted.

"The point being that we found a workable print on one of the packets of heroin found at the scene of the Liu homicide four years ago that matches our current vic."

"You mean ShonDale Gregg's print was on one of the bags of heroin used to stage the Liu secondary crime scene?" Hank said.

"That's what I'm saying, Lieutenant. He obviously helped dress the alley scene four years ago. Your theory of a revenge killing is getting a lot stronger."

Martinez stood up. "Tim, I'm sure you understand how important the voice comparison analysis and the autopsy blood samples are to making our case right now in the Gregg homicide."

Byrne nodded. "We'll get on it right away."

"The computer from Gregg's condo," Hank said. "We need to know if there's a Gary in there somewhere. A Facebook friend, e-mail. Something. We have to find this guy before Peter Mah does."

"I understand," Byrne said.

"Thanks, Tim, we appreciate it." Martinez looked at Hank. "I want to squeeze those two jackasses, Foo and Sheng, until they give up Mah. Understand?"

"Absolutely," Hank said. He turned to Karen. "Let's go knock them off the goddamned wall."

# 21

Peter Mah walked through the lobby of the office complex in Midtown with Jimmy Yung on his left and Billy Fung on his right. Benny Hu and Tang Lei waited outside in the limo.

Consisting of two towers joined by a mall and concourse that covered half a block of prime downtown real estate, the complex was busy throughout the day and Peter had to wait for an elevator at the bottom of the north tower. He didn't mind, however. He felt calm and relaxed.

He stepped into the elevator and Jimmy pressed the button for the twentieth floor. The elevator car quickly filled, but Peter didn't mind that it was crowded. No one paid him the slightest attention. As far as the people around him were concerned, he was just another anonymous businessman in a building crammed with anonymous businessmen.

When they reached their floor, Peter left the elevator and went through a set of glass doors into the office space leased by Thatcher Enterprises. The reception area was very well-appointed, featuring a lot of dark wood and burgundy-colored walls, and the women working behind the crescent-shaped counter were very beautiful. The atmosphere was one of success, wealth and importance.

Billy stepped forward and caught the attention of a blond woman who might have been a former Playmate of the Year. The gold sign in front of her said that her name was Ms. Davis.

"Mr. Mah is here to see Gary Thatcher."

Ms. Davis smiled and frowned at the same time. "Mr. Mah?" She checked the computer in front of her. "Do you have an appointment?"

"No appointment," Billy said, "but Thatcher will see Mr. Mah."

Ms. Davis studied the computer for another moment as the smile faded. "I'm sorry, but Mr. Thatcher isn't here right now and his calendar doesn't show anything."

"We'll take a look around to be sure," Jimmy said, walking around the desk toward another set of glass doors that led back to where the main offices were located.

"You can't go back there," Ms. Davis said.

Another woman stepped up, raising a hand. "Just a minute, sir, you can't go back there. If you don't have an appointment I'll have to ask you to leave." She was shorter and older, with grey hair. The name plate on her desk identified her as Mrs. Forrest.

Billy stepped between Jimmy and Mrs. Forrest. "Move back and don't interfere with Mr. Mah's business."

"Interfere?" Mrs. Forrest glared at Jimmy. "Just who does Mr. Mah think he is, anyway?"

Billy chuckled. "That's not Mr. Mah. *He's* Mr. Mah."

Mrs. Forrest followed the direction of Billy's nod and locked eyes with Peter. She saw the flat, cold, passionless gaze of a killer and decided to cooperate.

"I'm calling security," Ms. Davis called out.

"No." Mrs. Forrest raised a hand. "That won't be necessary."

"Smart woman," Billy murmured.

She stepped up to Peter. "Mr. Thatcher's out of the office, but I'll show you around the suite if you like so you can see for yourself."

"Thank you," Peter said.

"This way." She walked around Jimmy with a look and opened the glass doors, leading them into a short corridor. She stopped at the first door on the right. "Washroom."

Billy opened the door and turned on the light. The washroom was empty.

Mrs. Forrest stared at him with a disdainful expression, then glanced at Peter and continued down the hall. The next door, on the left, was actually a set of double doors that led into a boardroom. Dominated by a large oval table and leather chairs, it was also empty, as was the next room on the right, a break-off room with a square table and six chairs.

They passed through another set of glass doors into an inner reception area. Mrs. Forrest pointed to the right. "Down there are our administrative and research people."

"How many people?" Peter asked.

"Twelve. I think everyone's in today."

Peter nodded at Billy, who set off to check out the offices down there. He turned to the left. "And here?"

"The offices of our senior executives, Mr. Payne, Ms. Lerner, Ms. Foley and, of course, Mr. Thatcher."

Peter raised an eyebrow, looking around. "What do you people do here?"

"Government contracting," Mrs. Forrest replied. "Mostly city contracts. Waste disposal, recycling, demolition, site clean-ups. Mr. Thatcher used to work for the city."

Peter smiled faintly.

Billy returned, shaking his head. Peter set off toward the offices on the left.

Mrs. Forrest quickly got out in front of him. "This is Mr. Payne's office."

The door was open. Peter ignored a young man sitting at a desk outside Payne's door and looked within, where a middle-aged man was talking on the telephone. Jimmy walked into the office. Payne's eyes focused on them for the first time and a scowl began to form. Jimmy took the telephone out of

174

his hand and hung it up, then sat on the edge of Payne's desk.

"Hey, what the hell–"

"Shut up," Jimmy said, leaning forward and raising his voice just a little.

"Are you Thatcher?" Peter asked.

"Who the hell are you? You can't come barging in like this! Margaret, have you called security?"

Jimmy leaned across the desk and slapped Payne hard across the face. "Answer his question."

Payne rocked back in his chair, shocked.

"Are you Thatcher?" Peter repeated.

"No, hell, I'm David Payne. Gary's not here right now."

Peter turned away and headed for the next office. Behind him, Jimmy leaned forward, patted Payne's red cheek in an almost friendly gesture, and got up to follow his boss.

Billy remained in Payne's doorway as Peter walked past the next office, in which a woman sat reading something on her computer, and the next office, which was empty. He went on to the final office and looked at a name plate on the wall that said "Gary Thatcher, President."

A red-haired secretary rose from her desk. "You can't—"

Peter ignored her and walked into Thatcher's office. Behind him, Mrs. Forrest spoke quietly to the redhead, who sat down again. Jimmy turned around so that he could see everything, all the way back to where Billy stood at Payne's office.

Peter surveyed the empty office. Again, no expense had been spared, and the view from the enormous windows was spectacular. Perhaps, he thought, Uncle Sang had a point when he said that Peter should abandon his quaint headquarters above the Bright Spot and move into one of these office towers downtown. It certainly made a very strong impression on visitors.

He walked out of the office and looked at the redhead.

"Where is he?"

"Um, um." She glanced at Mrs. Forrest, who was staring at her. "He went out."

"Where?"

"He didn't say."

Behind him Jimmy stirred, but Peter made a small signal with his hand and Jimmy relented. Peter sat down on the corner of the redhead's desk and picked up her name plate.

"This is you? Gloria Ferguson?"

"Yes."

"You're Thatcher's private secretary, Gloria?"

"Yes."

Peter put the name plate down and smiled at her. "How long have you

175

worked for him, Gloria?"

"Two, um, three years."

"Long enough to get to know him fairly well, I'd say."

Gloria nodded.

"So where'd he go?"

Her jaw quivered and she closed her eyes for a moment as she swallowed. It was amazing, Peter reflected, how people knew instinctively when they were in physical danger, like animals in the wild who understood that a predator was about to catch them. Our species is still not very far from its natural origins, he mused.

"Out, for something personal."

"How long ago?"

"Maybe an hour and a half ago?"

"When do you expect him back?"

"I'm not sure."

Peter frowned.

"There's nothing in his calendar for the rest of the day," Gloria said hastily. "Sometimes he takes the rest of the day off and doesn't tell me. I guess he's taking care of something personal. He's kind of in and out that way. Did I say that already? I'm sorry."

"Call him."

She bit her lip. "He doesn't really like it when I do that."

Peter's right hand, which was at his side, made a quick small movement and Jimmy stepped over beside Mrs. Forrest, invading her personal space. She involuntarily began to step back but Jimmy took hold of her elbow and drew her close to him. He turned to look impassively at Gloria, who watched with wide, fearful eyes.

"Call him," Peter said again. "Tell him Mr. Johnson is here for his appointment."

Gloria snatched at the telephone and punched in the number of Gary Thatcher's cell phone. When Thatcher answered she told him that Mr. Johnson was here.

"I know, I'm very sorry, Mr. Thatcher, but for some reason it wasn't in the book. Well, I can ask him but I don't think he wants to reschedule, he's rather insistent."

She listened and then covered the receiver to look at Peter. "He's asking me what it's about."

"Tell him it's about office space," Peter said. "A series of contracts. Tell him we can meet somewhere else if he likes."

She repeated this into the phone and listened. "He wants to know what you have in mind."

Peter held out his hand for the phone. She gave it to him wordlessly.

"I'm listening," Peter said.

"I'm in a meeting at city hall right now," Gary Thatcher said. "Tell you what, though. I'll meet you in Governor's Park at nine o'clock this evening. I'll be waiting for you on one of the benches in front of the fountain. That way we can discuss your situation in private."

"That might be all right," Peter said. He heard a dull background noise over the phone. It took him a moment to identify it as the sound of a jet taking off. Gary was not at city hall, he was at the airport.

"You do a lot of business at city hall, do you?"

"Yes, I do. Look, I have to go." A flight announcement began in the background, completing the exposure of his lie. "See you in the park at nine."

The line went dead. Peter handed the phone back to Gloria and turned to Jimmy just as his iPhone began to vibrate. "Listen carefully to me, both of you," Peter said to the two women. "Don't interfere, don't call anyone about this, don't become involved. Your boss wouldn't want our negotiations to be ruined by thoughtless interference from support staff. Am I making myself clear?"

Gloria nodded as though her head were on a string. Mrs. Forrest opened her mouth to say something, then thought better of it and pressed her lips tightly together.

Peter took out his iPhone. "*Wei?*"

"Uncle Peter, it's me," Mikki Lung babbled in his ear. "Where are you? Never mind, don't answer that. We've all been taken down to police headquarters for questioning. I've never been so frightened in my life."

Peter stepped into Thatcher's office and closed the door.

"Slow down, Mikki. What are you talking about? Who's been taken to police headquarters for questioning?"

"Me! Everyone. Yi, Wu, even Daniel. They asked me all kinds of questions about my job and who else works for you and what they do. And they showed me a picture of some big black guy, Greg or somebody, and asked me what I knew about him. I was scared half to death!"

"What did you tell them?" Peter asked, a little sharply.

"Nothing, Uncle Peter! I don't know what everybody really does for you, so I told them they do deliveries and stuff."

"What did you say about the black man, Gregg?"

"I never heard of him before."

Peter willed himself to calm down. "All right, very good, Mikki. You did well. You say they brought the restaurant staff down?"

"Yes, and I saw Mr. Sheng and Mr. Foo here, too."

Peter's pulse jumped again and he knew that somehow the police had made the connection between him and the murder of ShonDale Gregg. Time was now an issue and it would be important to act quickly.

"Thank you for calling me, Mikki. I'll send someone to pick you up and take you home."

"No, it's okay Uncle Peter. I called my dad and he's coming to get me."

Peter ended the call and immediately speed-dialed Henry Lee. He gave the attorney his instructions and then made another call to have his restaurant staff picked up and brought back to the Bright Spot. He started to call Sheng's cell phone and then realized it would be a mistake. Let Henry Lee handle it. He had to get to the airport immediately before Gary Thatcher got away.

He put away his iPhone and looked around the office. Predictably, there were numerous photographs of the same man hung in groups on the wall, a short, dark-haired individual posing with local politicians and athletes. Some of the photographs were autographed "To Gary, best wishes" and so on. Obviously, this was Gary Thatcher. Peter took an 8-by-10 glossy of Thatcher with Mayor Watt from its frame and folded it in half. Slipping it into his jacket pocket, he strode out of the office, snapping his fingers for Jimmy to follow.

# 22

They were back in the interview room, this time with Donald Sheng again on the hot seat.

"You should know, Mr. Lee," Hank said, "we have a voice analysis matching a sample of your client's voice and the voice speaking into the intercom at the victim's apartment building. With that and analysis of the video footage we can prove Mr. Sheng here was one of two men who abducted ShonDale Gregg from his condo and took him to what ended up being his death. As we speak, a warrant to search Mr. Sheng's residence is being executed, and anything further we find will just be icing on the cake."

"You're looking at accessory to murder for starters," Karen snarled at Sheng, who stared back at her impassively.

"Detective Stainer's right," Hank said. "The time to negotiate a deal to mitigate the impact of our evidence on the rest of your life, such as it is, would be right now."

In the observation booth, Assistant State's Attorney Leanne DiOrio turned to Ann Martinez. "The only way we're going to get Mah is if one of these guys gives him up." She was a short, heavy-set woman who wore a black skirt and jacket that matched her short, straight black hair and the heavy dark circles under her eyes. "We're a long way from getting the complete story on this thing," she complained, filling the small room with her aggressive personality.

Henry Lee spoke quietly to Sheng in Cantonese, who stared into space.

"What's the verdict, Sheng?" Karen demanded. "Are you gonna give us Peter Mah or are you gonna be roasted on a spit over a slow fire?"

Sheng tucked in his chin and rattled off several angry sentences to his attorney.

"Where's that cop?" DiOrio demanded, glaring at Martinez. "The one who speaks Chinese? What are these guys saying to each other?"

"My client is willing to answer your questions," Lee said unexpectedly.

Hank leaned forward and stared at Sheng. "Did Peter Mah kill ShonDale Gregg, or did he order you to do it?"

"No." Sheng replied impassively.

"No, what?" Karen demanded. "That's one answer for two questions. Let's take them one at a time, smart guy. Did Peter Mah shoot ShonDale Gregg?"

"No."

"Did you shoot ShonDale Gregg?"

"Yes."

In the observation booth, DiOrio dropped her BlackBerry on the floor. "Did he say yes?" she asked, hurriedly picking it up.

Karen sat back. "What'd you shoot him for?"

"Didn't like him."

Hank scoffed. "You didn't like him? So you shot him?"

Sheng looked at Hank with absolutely no expression on his face. "Didn't mean to shoot him. Gun went off by accident."

"Take us through it," Karen demanded. "Tell us how it went down."

"Big drug guy. Heard he wanted to bring coke into Chinatown, sell it to our kids. We don't like that shit, so I took him for a ride. It got rough."

Karen eyed him. "You look okay. It must have gotten rough one way, fella."

Sheng said nothing.

"Where'd you shoot him? Where'd it happen?"

"Down at the river. Under a bridge."

"Where?"

"Who notices street names?" Sheng shrugged. "Off Baywater somewhere."

"How'd you get him there?"

"Stole a car. Picked him up."

"You stole a car, drove it to his apartment building, picked him up, took him down to the river somewhere off Baywater Street, roughed him up and shot him, then loaded him in the trunk of the car and drove him across the river to 121$^{st}$ and dumped him in the alley? That what you're saying?"

"Yes."

"Where'd you steal the car?"

Sheng said nothing.

"Can't tell me where you got the car? Where you stole it from?"

"Who notices street names?" Sheng said again.

"Why that alley in particular? Why drive from the river all the way over to that alley just to dump him? Why didn't you just throw him in the river?"

Sheng said nothing.

"Can't think up something fast enough for that one, can you, shithead?" Karen snarled at him. "Mah told you to take him there, didn't he? After *he* shot him. Right? Am I right?"

"No," Sheng said. "Wrong. I shot him."

"So why the big-assed drive all the way over to that alley with Shon-Dale deader than road kill in the trunk?"

"Throw you off the trail. Make you think gangsters shot him."

"Oh, bullshit." Karen stood up and walked around the table until she was standing next to Sheng. "That's just bullshit, Sheng, and you know it. That's the same fucking alley, the *same fucking alley* that Peter Mah's cousin

180

was found in with the same *fucking* gunshot wound in the thigh with the same *fucking* bag of horse and the same *fucking* needle, so don't give me that *fucking* bullshit because I know this is Peter Mah's doing and you're going to give him to me *right now* or I'm going to personally make sure they strap you to a chair and put you down like the fucking *dog* that you are!"

By this time Karen was leaning down, close to shouting, her nose about six inches from Sheng's.

Sheng leaned slowly back and stared at her with absolutely no expression.

"Mah shot Gregg," Karen said, very quietly. "Right?"

"Nooo," Sheng replied, drawing out the word sarcastically.

Karen straightened, looked at Hank, raised her eyebrows and sat down on the corner of the table. "Who stole the damned car, Sheng?"

Silence.

"What car did you and that moron Foo take to pick up Gregg at his condo?"

Sheng said nothing.

"Why the hell did you shoot him in the leg first?"

Sheng said nothing.

"Where'd you get the heroin you planted next to him?"

Sheng said nothing.

"Are you guys going to shoot Gary next? Huh? Is he next?"

Sheng said nothing.

Henry Lee stirred and folded his hands before him on the table. "My client, unfortunately, has admitted that he shot Mr. Gregg, and he has explained his reasons for doing so. He has explained he didn't mean to shoot the man and was just beating him up when the gun went off. That's all there is, I'm afraid."

181

# 23

That evening Hank stopped by the mansion in Granger Park to see his mother. They sat in her newsroom, a large, high-ceilinged chamber on the ground floor with French doors leading out to the side garden. A computer with multiple screens maintained constant access to several internet news sites and a bank of flat panel plasma televisions were tuned to news, weather and business channels, including CNN, Bloomberg News and Fox News. A newscast was underway when he arrived and they watched it together, sipping Maker's Mark over ice.

Anna Haynes Donaghue was 83 years old but still in very good health. She was slender and still somewhat tall, despite having lost several inches in old age, and her hair, carefully styled, was pure white. It had thinned somewhat, but Anna went to a salon every Tuesday morning where they treated her scalp with something that was supposed to preserve the follicles. She explained it once to Hank but he'd forgotten exactly what it was.

She saw her doctor every three months, practiced Tai Chi, took long walks and swam every morning in the pool. She was probably in better shape than Hank. She wore a cream-colored dress with a discreet flowered pattern, comfortable Italian shoes, a five thousand dollar watch, her wedding and engagement rings and a simple gold chain with a small cross at her neck. The veins on the backs of her hands were large and purple, and there were liver spots on the skin. Her blue eyes sparkled at him behind her glasses.

"Forget to shave?"

Hank rubbed his cheek. "No, just trying something different."

Anna smiled tolerantly. She'd always been closest to Hank, the youngest of her four children. A former State's Attorney for Glendale City, she was still active in the upper echelons of the Republican Party. Her late father, Charles Goodwin Haynes, was a former Governor and her grandfather, Edward Willis Haynes, had enjoyed a prominent career as a long-serving justice of the state supreme court.

Hank got up to freshen their drinks at the bar in the corner of the room, his eye straying to the framed photographs on the wall. He smiled inwardly at a picture of his late father hanging onto a rope on someone's sailboat at sea somewhere. Taken about twenty years ago, it betrayed Robert's nervousness around anything deeper than a mud puddle. Born and raised in Alliance, Ohio, Robert Vernon Donaghue was the son of a physician and the grandson of a watchmaker. A graduate of Case Western Reserve University, where he attended one of the oldest law schools in the country, he moved to Maryland during the Korean War and established himself in Glendale as an up-and-coming criminal defense attorney.

He and Anna met on opposite sides of the courtroom when he defended a man accused of murdering his mistress and her young son. At that time an experienced Assistant State's Attorney, Anna had the advantage of overwhelming circumstantial evidence and a judge who had himself been a prosecutor earlier in his career, but Robert somehow managed to obtain an acquittal despite overwhelming odds. Proud and fierce, Anna discovered she was less angry in defeat than she ought to be; she was smitten by the calm, persistent, left-leaning – and oh, yes, handsome – man who'd systematically dismantled her carefully prepared case. They were married four months later.

Beside the photograph of his seasick father was the high school graduation portrait of Hank's oldest brother, Tom, who had left home shortly after sitting for it and never returned. He was the only Donaghue who'd ever demonstrated a talent for music. According to Anna, her maternal grandfather Charley Peach had played the cornet in a band, which was viewed by the Haynses as an eccentricity forgivable only because Charley was insanely rich as a result of his coal business, but neither she nor Robert could as much as carry a tune, let alone play a musical instrument. Tom, however, showed an aptitude and an interest from a very early age, and by the time he was five years old he was spending three to four hours a day at the decorative Steinway grand piano in the music room that no one else touched. He pestered his parents for lessons, quickly began to absorb the classics and started to compose his own little pieces. In high school he formed his own band that played weddings, dances and whatever else they could get. When he graduated he put off going to college, instead taking the bus to New York to look for work as a musician. It was a decision that changed the entire course of his life.

His number was called and he was shipped over to Viet Nam. Frightened to death, he took advantage of the ubiquity of drugs to hide from the horrors around him, ultimately becoming a heroin addict. His tour became a long, indistinct haze that ended in hospital after a speedball nearly killed him. He returned stateside and was discharged as an addict and a nervous wreck. It took him several years to get back on his feet. He played for money when he could and waited on tables and cleaned offices when he couldn't, moving from city to city, New York to Chicago to Detroit to Los Angeles, then Denver, Minneapolis, St. Louis and Buffalo. Estranged from the family, he occasionally appeared in Glendale to play at one of the small clubs downtown. Hank never missed a performance, but they never spoke and Tom refused to have any contact with Anna.

Beneath a photograph of Anna and Mayor Darrien Watts was a studio portrait of Hank's sister Jane with her husband and three children. Temperamentally Jane was a carbon copy of her mother, coldly rational, unforgiving of others and quick to anger. She was so like her mother, in fact, that they fought constantly, like worst enemies, perpetually at each other's throats, neither one willing to give ground or compromise. The day that Hank watched Jane pack her things into the back of her boyfriend's van and drive off to Columbus,

Ohio to enroll at Ohio State University he'd felt more relief than anything else. There would be one less person for his mother to fight with, one less reason for the house to be filled with turmoil and anger. When Jane became a doctor Hank was initially concerned about her bedside manner with prospective patients, but when he learned that she'd chosen pathology as her career path he knew with faint relief that it was the right decision. Jane now lived in San Francisco with her family and spoke to Anna twice a year on the telephone, on her birthday and at Christmas.

As Hank screwed the cap back onto the bottle of bourbon and picked up the two tumblers from the bar, he glanced at a photograph of Robert Junior, next in age between Jane and Hank. Robert's arm was thrown around a former Mayor of Miami-Dade County. Hank had never been any closer to Robert than he'd been to Tom or Jane. As a boy Robert had always run with his own group of friends and was seldom at home. When Hank was eight, Grandfather Haynes passed away and a sizeable chunk of his legacy went into trust funds for each of the grandchildren. It meant they were child millionaires, a concept lost on young Hank but not Robert, who'd been saving his allowance and money from odd jobs since he was ten. Robert got a part-time job as an office gofer at Grandfather Haynes's law firm. He hung around a few of the junior partners, asking questions and listening to them talk about their cases, he spent his lunch breaks in the firm library reading law reports and made copious notes in a notebook he carried everywhere. Laconic and aggressive, he earned a law degree at Harvard and was recruited by several prominent law firms but chose to spend his first few years in practice in Grandfather Haynes's former firm, after which he accepted a partnership in a firm in Miami that virtually controlled corporate law in that city. He was worth many millions of dollars, he'd divorced three times and had four children whom he seldom saw, he owned a yacht and a private jet and, like Jane and Tom, was a virtual stranger to Hank.

"I wouldn't mind a cigar," Anna said. "Help yourself"

Hank delivered the drinks and went back for two cigars from a humidor at the end of the bar. They were Upmann lonsdales with a 42 ring size, Anna's preferred gauge. He clipped the ends and gave one to Anna with a box of wooden matches. She struck a match and ignited the end of her cigar before putting it in her mouth. Hank lit his and settled back down in his chair, aware that his mother was watching him through a veil of smoke.

"How's work?"

"The same," Hank replied. "The hours suck, the pay is worse and all my clients are dead."

"I've heard there's some turbulence in Chinatown right now."

"Where'd you hear that?" Hank asked, unsurprised.

"Oh, I'm still connected." She sampled her bourbon. "Be careful."

"Always." Hank examined his cigar tip. His mother was stiff-necked, conservative, self-righteous and always right, but she'd never hidden her affection for her youngest.

As a boy Hank showed the quick intelligence that ran through the family, entering primary school early and achieving such high marks that he was accelerated twice in elementary school, reaching junior high at the age of nine. In his disposition he was very much like his father, quiet and patient, and as a result he was occasionally tested in the schoolyard by bullies who thought he would be easy pickings. However, he'd also inherited his father's size and his brother Robert's athleticism, and after a few fights the older kids decided to leave him alone. He threw himself into his studies and continued to excel, enrolling at State University as a 15-year-old freshman.

When he was sixteen his father passed away from a massive heart attack. He felt the loss deeply and buried himself in his studies. He was majoring in Criminology and Criminal Justice at his mother's insistence. The program was new to State and largely the result of Anna's aggressive campaigning as a member of the Board of Governors. He studied criminal law, criminal investigation, sociology, profiling, victimology, corrections and other related subjects. He completed a Bachelor's degree and went back for a Master's. The completion of a law degree was a logical progression and at the age of 22 Hank passed his bar exams and accepted a job in the State's Attorney's office. He worked for a year as an Assistant State's Attorney, getting a feel for the job, experiencing the stresses and tensions associated with heavy case loads, noisy, distracted court rooms and exhausted, unpredictable judges. He and Marla Hennerton, another ASA, got married in a quietly-arranged civil ceremony.

He slowly gravitated toward the police officers who gathered the evidence and made the arrests in the cases he was prosecuting. He got to know them over a glass of beer after hours, asked questions about their methods and procedures and became fascinated by the job. A conversation with his mother on the subject degenerated into an argument which ended when she condescendingly told him that he sounded like his father, who could always be counted on to take the opposite of any opinion she might have on a given subject. Hank walked out of the mansion in Granger Park and applied for admission to the police academy that same day. It was a rash move, like joining the navy, and he knew it would cost him dearly in terms of career standing over the long run. But he had a strong gut feeling it was the right thing for him to do. Plus, he wanted to prove his mother wrong about a few things.

He and Marla quietly divorced not long afterward.

He passed through the Academy with flying colors. After graduation he put in his eight weeks of field training and received his permanent assignment as a beat cop. Not long after finishing his probationary period he had the kind of break for which most law enforcement officers wait their entire career in vain, the break that transformed him into the Hero Cop, splashing his name and picture across front pages throughout the state.

185

At that time, city council was dominated by Adolphus Post, the African-American politician who was widely touted as the next mayor on the Democratic ticket. Less than a week before he was to toss his hat into the ring, his only child, fourteen-year-old Cedric, was kidnapped and held for ransom. Thirty-four hours into the crisis Hank was checking doors down by the river when he came upon a black unmarked van parked at the loading dock of an empty warehouse. Suddenly the back door of the warehouse opened and two men emerged, holding the Post boy between them. Hank took them without incident.

Thereafter the glow surrounding Hank's career persisted. He earned a promotion to detective less than a year later, working in Auto Theft and Homicide, followed by another promotion to sergeant. He spent three years as a supervisory sergeant in Juvenile Crime before writing the next set of exams to earn a promotion to lieutenant. By this time Adolphus Post was Mayor and Gerald White was his hand-picked chief of police. Hank spent a year in the Chief's office as media spokesperson, representing the Chief at special events and cleaning out the ashtrays, figuratively speaking, whenever they needed it. He stepped on a few toes and made a few enemies, including Myron Heidigger, who was at that time captain of Major Crimes. Heidigger was part of the old guard who believed they should be allowed to manage their own little fiefdoms as they saw fit without interference from above and away from the public eye. Chief White, on the other hand, was a new broom who was sweeping clean, and he firmly believed that the public would trust the police and be more cooperative if they better understood police methods and motives. To this end, he used press releases and statements to the media as tools to create a sense of increased openness. With his high media profile as the Hero Cop, Hank was one of his means toward this end. Unfortunately, Hank's active support of Chief White's agenda earned him the everlasting enmity of many senior cops, including Heidigger, who bitterly despised him.

Despite this animosity, Hank eventually requested and received a transfer back to Homicide as supervisory lieutenant. This move put him under Heidigger's direct supervision, but as long as White occupied the Chief's office there was an angel on Hank's shoulder and Heidigger was forced to watch his step. However, when Mayor Post's term ended and conservative candidate Darrius Watts was elected to replace him, Chief White was forced to step aside in favor of Orvell Jenkins. A ripple effect was felt throughout the department. Hank became the subject of several investigations by Internal Affairs, all groundless, but with the result that he was transferred out of Major Crimes to Public Affairs, where he spent the next few years writing responses to complaint letters from the public. The sudden death of Chief Jenkins from a heart attack, however, brought another new broom in the form of Wilson Bennett, who parachuted in from the FBI as the new Chief along with Douglas Barkley and several other senior people. Eventually Hank returned to Homicide for a third stint, although not as a supervisory lieutenant this time, as Bill Jarvis already occupied that position. Ann Martinez found a way to squeeze him into her budget and assigned him to work with whichever detective was currently without a partner. He worked with Joe Kalzowski, a detective named Beckert who moved on to Missing Persons, and then Karen Stainer.

As Hank and Anna watched an update on the stock market his cell phone vibrated. He took it out, checked the caller ID and answered it.

"Donaghue."

"Lou, what's your twenty?" Car horns honked in the background as Karen cursed under her breath.

Hank recited the address. "What's going on?"

"They found a stiff at the airport. Might be our Gary."

"Okay. Don't run anyone down before you get here."

"Don't tempt me."

Hank disconnected and put the phone away. "I have to leave. Detective Stainer's picking me up."

"I understand. Finish your drink first. You have a few minutes."

Hank drained his glass, took a long draw on the cigar and reluctantly set it down in the ash tray to burn out.

"How's she doing?" Anna asked.

"Karen? She's doing well. Adjusting."

"Don't forget she has a ceiling, given her history and personality. The best you can do is help her reach it."

"I know." Hank frowned. "We've had this conversation before."

"Just the same."

"Not everything is about vertical movement, Mother. She won't rise any higher than Detective but she has a chance to be a difference maker as a homicide investigator. She has a relentlessness you have to admire, and she's fearless. Good qualities that the department needs."

"Sounds like someone I know."

Silence fell as Anna exhaled a thick cloud of smoke. Did she still harbor disappointment over his ultimate career choice? If so, she kept it well hidden.

"The department's changed," Anna mused, looking at the television screen. "It's much softer than it was in my day. Back then a cop wasn't afraid to break a few heads if it meant cracking a case."

"Society changes," Hank said, "cops change, the world keeps turning."

Anna smiled fondly at him. "My son, the philosopher."

# 24

It took a while to piece together what had happened to Gary Thatcher. His body was found early Thursday evening in the tunnel connecting the short-term parking garage to the lower level of the airport terminal. Maryland Transportation Authority police on site cordoned off the area and called in Homeland Security and the FBI. Marie Louise Roubidoux and Will Martin from the local FBI field office caught the case and telephoned Captain Martinez as a courtesy. When Roubidoux mentioned the name Gary Thatcher Martinez beckoned to Karen, who was passing her office door.

"There's a body at the airport, Gary Thatcher. Might be your guy."

Karen put her hands on her hips. "What happened?"

"Knifed on his way to the lower parking garage."

"On his way out? Not on his way in?"

"Go check it out. Get Donaghue."

Hank was waiting for her outside the mansion gate when Karen pulled up to the curb. He barely got the door closed before she floored the accelerator, the resultant g-force slamming him back into his seat and creating a vacuum where his stomach used to be.

"Sad," she said, running a stop sign, "that you had to grow up in a log cabin with a dirt floor like that. Explains a few quirks in your personality, though."

"Quirks? Funny."

At the airport Karen examined the body as Hank listened to an update from Roubidoux. A tiny middle-aged woman with short black hair and small, sharp features, she slipped on a pair of cheaters and frowned at her notebook.

"We have a witness who was getting on this elevator when it happened," she said, pointing with her pen. Hank looked at the middle of three elevators on this side of the tunnel. It was apparent that the victim had made an unsuccessful attempt to get on the elevator while the doors were closing. He'd been grabbed from behind, wrestled around, stabbed in the abdomen, then stabbed several more times while he lay on the floor in a pool of his own blood.

"The witness saw him pull away from two men walking on each side of him," Roubidoux went on. "He saw the one guy grab him before the doors closed. At that point he thought it was only a fight, and wasn't going to bother reporting it until he saw an MDTA cop in the washroom upstairs and mentioned it. The cop called it in, they checked and here we all are."

The victim was a short, stocky Caucasian in his early thirties. He was well-dressed and well-groomed. His driver's license listed an address in Granger Park. In the inside pocket of his jacket was a one-way ticket to Miami. It went without saying that he'd missed his flight.

"One-way ticket," Karen remarked, joining them. "He must have been bugging out."

"What do you mean?" Roubidoux asked.

Hank explained their theory that the victim might have participated in the murder of Martin Liu four years ago. He went over their investigation of the ShonDale Gregg homicide, touched on the Shawn and Gary names provided by a "confidential informant" and speculated that Thatcher might have been using Miami as a staging area to switch identities and disappear into the Caribbean.

"The guy who stabbed him was some mad," Karen noted. "Looks like a whole mess of wounds. Any ideas on who did it?"

"Will's upstairs with Homeland and the MDTA people looking through the video. Are you going to want this one?"

Hank said, "If he's connected to the Liu case, we'll want it."

"We'll have to see." Roubidoux put away her notebook. "Will and I are swamped, so it won't break my heart. Anyway, let's go upstairs."

Before long they were sitting on folding chairs in a crowded security office while an MDTA technician retrieved video footage from the tunnel during the time period when Thatcher was thought to have been killed. After some fast-forwarding they saw their witness, an elderly man, enter the tunnel from the parking garage. He was pulling a small suitcase on wheels. He pushed the button for the elevators and waited for a few moments before the middle elevator door opened. He disappeared inside just as the far door from the lower level of the terminal opened and three men appeared in the tunnel. Suddenly the man in the middle shoved the man on his right and bolted for the closing elevator door. The man he'd shoved recovered his balance and grabbed the victim before he made it into the elevator. The elevator door closed; the witness was now gone. The assailant wrestled the victim to the floor. They saw his right arm arc up and down. His accomplice grabbed at him and tried to pull him off the victim. The assailant shoved the other man away, turned back and stabbed the victim repeatedly. It was fast and brutal. The MDTA technician swore under his breath and closed his eyes as the two men left the body and strode out of the tunnel into the parking garage.

Hank stood up and moved close to the monitor. "Stop it there and run it again."

The technician didn't move until Will Martin tapped him on the shoulder. "Dave? We need to see it again."

Reluctantly the technician complied. Hank watched until the man who'd been on the victim's left glanced briefly in the direction of the camera before running through the door. "There," Hank said. "Stop it for a moment."

Hank looked at the face and then turned to Karen. "It's Billy Fung. The other guy, the killer, I don't know his name for sure, but it seems to me Mikki Lung said his name's Tang, something like that."

189

"You know them?" Roubidoux asked.

"Yeah. They're wanted for assault on a young guy connected to the Liu case," Hank said. "We also want to talk to them about the Gregg homicide. They work for Peter Mah."

"Ah ha." Will Martin raised his eyebrows.

"I'm getting mighty sick of cleaning up after that goddamned guy," Karen said.

"He finds Gary and takes him out within a day." Hank rubbed his forehead. "Gregg must have told him who he was and how to find him."

"Yeah, somewhere between the pummeling and the double tap to the skull."

Hank turned to Roubidoux. "We need to run with this. It fits with the other two we're working. It'll give us additional leverage when we pick up those two damned punks and start squeezing them dry."

Roubidoux nodded. "Then we'd better start making our phone calls."

# 25

They lost Friday trying to convince a judge to approve warrants to search the Bright Spot restaurant, to arrest Peter Mah on a charge of conspiracy to commit murder, and to seize the Mercedes limousine that entered the short-term parking garage at the airport shortly before Gary Thatcher was murdered. Assistant State's Attorney Leanne DiOrio fumed and foamed as Karen wrote and rewrote the applications, but in the end the judge was unconvinced. True, Peter Mah was found on video at the airport after a long and exhaustive search, but he turned up only in the international arrivals area, where he apparently waited in vain to meet someone disembarking from a flight from San Francisco. In the absence of evidence demonstrating that Peter had ordered his employees to find Gary Thatcher and bring him down to the parking garage, a warrant to arrest Peter was denied, as were the warrants to search his restaurant and limo. The limo proved particularly frustrating. Although the camera at the parking garage entrance caught it arriving and departing, the limo parked in a blind spot inside the garage and there was no way to see who actually got in and out of it.

The video did, however, ultimately show them everything they needed to see connecting Billy Fung and Tang Lei to Thatcher's murder. The pair first appeared in the tunnel from the parking garage, walking alone. Billy Fung was seen passing something to Tang that looked like a photograph. Tang studied the photograph as they reached the far end of the tunnel and went through the door into the lower level. Surveillance cameras inside the terminal picked them up as they crossed the lower level, skirting the food court, weaving their way through the crowd. Tang gave the photograph back to Billy, who put it in his pocket. They rode the escalator up to the upper level and turned right, heading for Concourse B. When they reached the security barriers to enter Concourse B, Billy turned and said something to Tang, who wandered off to buy a magazine from a nearby vendor as Billy took an airline ticket from his jacket pocket and passed through security. He wandered around the concourse, obviously in search of Thatcher, and disappeared from view for several minutes as he checked the men's' washroom. Finally he left the area and headed off toward Concourse A, Tang falling in behind him, where the same routine was repeated with a different airline ticket. This time Billy had better luck. He emerged from the washroom with Gary Thatcher. The two left the concourse, joined by Tang, and rode the escalator back down to the lower level. Thatcher balked near the food court, stopping short and engaging Billy in a brief argument. However, the camera showed Tang stepping very close to Thatcher, who looked down, presumably at something in Tang's hand. Billy grabbed Thatcher's elbow, pulling him, and the three walked the rest of the way across the level to the door leading through the tunnel to the parking garage, where

191

Tang knifed Thatcher and they left him to bleed to death as they hurried back into the parking garage.

Interesting to note was the fact that a comparison of cameras showed that the limousine left the garage while Tang was wiping his knife on Thatcher's jacket after having killed him. If Billy and Tang had been hoping for a ride home they were out of luck.

This one puzzled Hank for a while and sent him back through the video once more. Eventually he found footage that showed another Asian male, not Peter Mah but perhaps another of his employees, entering the lower level from the parking garage about ninety seconds after Billy and Tang. This man also ascended the escalators to the upper level, but turned left and walked down to Concourses C and D, which included international departures. The man passed through security, circulated through the area as though searching for someone, then rode the crowded escalator back down to the lower level only sixty seconds behind Billy, Tang and Thatcher. As the trio stopped to argue, this man passed them without a glance. He preceded them through the door into the tunnel by about thirty seconds. He walked down the tunnel and through the door into the garage. Hank took a closer look at the video of the murder and thought he saw the far door open again briefly as Tang was stabbing Thatcher.

Mulling it over, Hank decided that this third man must have come back to see why Billy and Tang hadn't come through the door with Thatcher. He'd seen Tang stab Thatcher and had hurried out to the limo to get Peter out of the garage before he could be connected to the murder. Unlike Billy, however, this third Asian was better at keeping his face averted from the surveillance cameras and they weren't able to find a single frame that would allow them to make an identification.

On Saturday morning, while Karen continued her efforts to get a last known address on Billy Fung, Hank caught a ride into Chinatown with Horvath and Peralta, who were making another attempt to locate and interview John Li, son-in-law of the murdered grocery store owner. Li had disappeared under very suspicious circumstances and Horvath and Peralta were running into a frustrating series of blank walls.

Hank got out in front of the Bright Spot restaurant, tapping on the hood of the Crown Vic as Horvath tooled away from the curb. It was warm and Hank wore a spring suit in a grey worsted with a robin's-egg blue tie and black oxford lace-ups. He checked his watch and saw that it was just past 10:30. The place looked like a dump, and as he opened the door and walked inside he saw that it was virtually deserted. Yi, the manager, glanced at him from a stool at the end of the bar before returning to the newspaper he was reading. An old man sitting alone at a table near the front window watched him with the absorption of a bird watching a cat. As Hank removed his sunglasses and slipped them into his jacket pocket the old man got up and left the restaurant.

A man sat at a table in the back talking on a cell phone. The remains of his morning meal lay scattered on the table in front of him. As Hank approached he ended his call and put away the phone, rising from the table and coming around to meet him.

"My name's Peter Mah," he said, extending his hand.

Hank shook his hand while taking out the folder containing his badge and identification. "Lieutenant Hank Donaghue." He opened the folder and held it up. "Got a few questions for you."

Peter's grip was soft and he released Hank's hand quickly. He didn't bother to glance at Hank's badge. "An honor to finally meet you, Lieutenant. Won't you sit down?" He indicated an empty table next to the one at which he had been sitting.

As Hank drew out a chair and sat down, Peter snapped his fingers at Yi and gave a curt order. Yi hurried over and began to clear away the dishes from Peter's table.

Peter sat down across from Hank, his back to the wall. "Yi will serve us tea. Or would you prefer coffee, Lieutenant?"

"Tea's fine."

"I was speaking to Mr. Lee when you came in," Peter said. "He'll be here shortly. I hope you don't mind a slight wait before I answer your questions."

"You think you need a lawyer present in order to talk to me, Mr. Mah?"

"Please, call me Peter. I don't want to appear uncooperative, but I prefer Mr. Lee to be here. I hope you understand."

Yi returned from the kitchen with a tea service which he left for Peter before returning to his stool at the end of the bar. Peter poured tea into two small cups and placed one in front of Hank. He drank from his own cup, flipped the remnants into a bowl next to the tea pot and put the cup down. "You've been with the police department for quite a while, Lieutenant."

"That's right."

"I understand you were a prosecutor before that."

"In a previous life."

"Your mother was State's Attorney, I believe."

Hank drank tea, emptied the rest into the bowl and put the cup down. "You've done your homework."

"Although we haven't met before," Peter said, pouring more tea into their cups, "I made a point of learning what I could about you. I have an interest in the people who police our city. I think you're all to be commended for your bravery and your dedication to the safety of the people of this city."

Hank made a noise at the back of his throat.

Peter looked hurt, but said nothing more. The front door opened and Henry Lee bustled in, looking as disheveled and harried as ever.

193

"Mr. Mah," he said, giving a slight bow, "Sorry for being late."

"Nonsense," Peter said, indicating the chair to his right. "Please, sit down." He took a third cup from the tea service and poured for Henry. "Have some tea. Lieutenant Donaghue and I were just exchanging pleasantries, but I think he has a few more serious things to discuss."

Hank shook Henry's hand as he sat down. "Counselor, nice to see you again."

"Lieutenant." Henry nodded. "What did you want to question my client about?"

Hank looked at Peter. "I wanted to talk to you on Thursday when we had your employees downtown, but we couldn't seem to find you. Same thing yesterday. Where've you been?"

Peter smiled politely. "Upstate. A little trip to see some people."

"Upstate. To see some people." Hank looked skeptical. "This trip was spur of the moment, was it?"

Peter shook his head. "Not really. I have friends in Aberdeen who've been asking me for a while to come visit them. I decided to go on Thursday night because it was my friend's birthday yesterday. I stayed overnight and came back late last night. It was nice."

"I'm glad. You'll provide names and addresses, I take it?"

Peter looked at Henry, who nodded. "Of course, Lieutenant."

"Very nice." Hank folded his hands. "So. What about earlier on Thursday. What were you doing then?"

"This and that. I went to the airport late in the afternoon."

"Oh? What for?"

"To meet a flight."

"Which flight was that?"

"The United Airlines flight from San Francisco. I don't remember the flight number, sorry."

"Why'd you want to meet that flight?"

"I was told my Aunt Rose had arrived from Hong Kong and was flying in to visit us. But it seems she missed the connecting flight and will come east another time."

"Aunt Rose." Hank stared at Peter. "You have an Aunt Rose?"

"Apparently her grandmother was Irish."

Hank chuckled. "All right. Aunt Rose. So what did you do when she didn't show?"

"I left the airport."

"Who was with you?"

"My driver, of course."

"Who's that?"

"Benny Hu."

"Any one else with you?"

194

"No, because after the flight came in I had Benny drive me to Aberdeen."

"You didn't go up to the airport with Billy Fung and two other guys that work for you? Looking for someone trying to leave town?"

"I went to the airport to meet my aunt, who didn't show up," Peter said.

"Maybe I don't understand the situation," Hank said. "Billy Fung and this Tang guy, they work for you, don't they?"

"Billy works for me. Tang doesn't. He's a visitor. Hopefully he'll leave soon."

"Oh? Don't like him?"

Peter said nothing.

"Where are they?"

"I don't know, Lieutenant."

Hank pretended to be shocked. "Don't your employees have a schedule? Is he AWOL?"

"There's no formal schedule," Peter replied, "except for the restaurant staff. That schedule's kept by Yi."

"But Billy doesn't work in the restaurant deep-frying chicken balls, does he? He breaks legs for you, isn't that right?"

"Lieutenant," Henry broke in, looking distressed. "Please try to respect Mr. Mah's dignity in his own residence and place of business. He's trying to answer your questions as best he can."

Hank sat back. "You're right, Mr. Lee. I apologize, Mr. Mah. What does Billy Fung do for you?"

"He runs errands," Peter said. "He makes deliveries for the restaurant and every now and again he takes some of our customers home."

"He takes customers home? I don't understand."

Peter shrugged. "It's Chinatown, Lieutenant. The elders in our neighborhood like to get out and socialize. We have a little circle that gathers at the Bright Spot pretty much every night. They stay until we close. Old men, some of them in their eighties. We keep a few tables on the far side for their use. They eat and drink, gossip, enjoy themselves. Sometimes when it's late I get Billy to drive some of them home. Make sure they get home okay."

Hank frowned.

"It's a matter of respect, Lieutenant," Henry Lee said. "Mr. Mah has a great respect for the elders of our community."

Hank opened his mouth and closed it again, remembering Meredith's frustration when he'd joked with her about traditional networks.

Watching Hank's expression closely, Peter's eyes sparkled with amusement.

"All right, fine." Hank shifted gears. "What about earlier on Thursday? Were they with you earlier in the day?"

195

"Yes," Peter nodded.

"Oh?"

"Billy was with me when I went to pay a visit to a man downtown."

"A man named Gary Thatcher, isn't that right?"

"Yes," Peter replied. "That's right."

"Why were you looking for Thatcher?"

"Someone gave me his name as a man with connections," Peter said. "I've been considering a move downtown for my business, and someone told me Thatcher was a man with excellent connections at city hall and in the local construction industry. I have some capital to invest and figured Thatcher could put me in touch with the right people in one of the new office towers that will be built downtown."

"I heard your boys threw their weight around. Scared Thatcher's staff half to death."

Peter grimaced. "I'm sorry about that. I was eager to find the man. At the same time, I wanted his people to understand that secrecy was important. To get in on the ground floor, these things often have to be done clandestinely and I understood that was how Thatcher worked. I'm very sorry, though, if it came off the wrong way."

"Did you order Fung and Tang to find Thatcher at the airport and kill him?"

Peter shook his head. "Why would I do such a thing?"

Hank leaned forward and rapped the table with his knuckle. "Maybe because you found out Thatcher was involved in Martin Liu's murder. You wanted revenge. Eye for an eye."

"Can you confirm that, Lieutenant? Do you have evidence that connects this Thatcher to Martin's death?"

"Come on, Mah. Don't bullshit me. You've heard what your cousin's little boy has been saying about Shawn and Gary. Now we've got a dead ShonDale and a dead Gary, both killed by Asians who work for you. Do you really expect me to believe you didn't order both these murders to take care of unfinished business?"

"Lieutenant," Henry Lee protested, "if you have a reasonable question to ask my client then ask it, but throwing around wild accusations will do no one any good."

"Did you kill ShonDale Gregg?"

"I understand that Donald Sheng confessed to this murder," Peter replied. "It seems like a waste of time to ask me about a murder someone else has already told you they committed."

"Did you order Donald Sheng and Foo Yee to kill ShonDale Gregg?

"Absolutely not."

"Did you order Billy Fung and Tang Whatever to kill Gary Thatcher?"

"Absolutely not."

"Lieutenant," Henry Lee interjected, "Mr. Mah has now answered these questions. Unless there's anything else...."

"Do you know where Billy Fung and Tang are right now?"

"No." Peter shook his head firmly.

"Where does Fung live?"

Peter shrugged. "He used to live with his mother on Crescent Street, but she threw him out a few months ago. I didn't hear where he ended up."

"We'd like to talk to Tommy Leung," Hank said, shifting gears again. "Any idea where he is?"

"No," Peter said. "I'd like to talk to him myself."

"I bet you would. It might be better, though, if you left Tommy Leung to us. Unless you've already eliminated him, too. Have you?"

"Lieutenant!" Henry Lee said sharply.

Peter held up a hand. "It's all right, Mr. Lee. No, I haven't eliminated Tommy Leung. May I ask you a question now?"

Hank leaned back. "Sure. Why not? Ask away."

"You mentioned my cousin's little boy, Taylor." Peter dropped his eyes to his hands for a moment before raising them again. "Can you assure me that the police will stop poking and prodding him like some kind of specimen?"

Hank reached for his tea. "Our interest in him is minimal." Hank shot Peter a quick look. "You've heard the things he's saying. Hard to believe, aren't they?"

Peter said nothing.

"The boy has zero for us in terms of hard evidence," Hank went on. "Nothing we'd take to court. Detective Stainer explained to the boy's mother that children generally don't help us very much on the witness stand in homicide cases. Certainly not unless the child witnessed the murder, and even then their testimony is viewed as a desperate last resort. It's debatable whether Taylor actually witnessed a murder or not. He's pointed us in a direction, and that's pretty much it."

Peter's eyes met Hank's and held them steadily. Then he seemed to relax slightly. "May I ask another question?"

"Sure."

"Do you believe ShonDale Gregg killed Martin four years ago?"

"Yeah, I'd say so."

"What about this Gary Thatcher? Are you saying he was one of Martin's killers?"

"It's possible," Hank replied.

"Tommy Leung was there," Peter said, "and apparently also a fourth man, if Taylor's telling the truth. Will you continue your investigation until Tommy and this fourth person are brought to justice?"

197

Hank shrugged. "That's the general idea."

"Do you know who the fourth man is?"

"Sorry, that's one question too many." Hank said.

Peter shot his cuff, looked at his watch, massaged his right forearm with his left palm, folded his hands together and opened them up, thumbs outstretched, to look at his upturned palms.

"You're a man of the world, Lieutenant" he said finally. "You deal with hard, concrete facts. Do you believe the things Taylor says? I'm curious. Are you just using him as a tool or do you actually think he's remembering things only Martin would know?"

"That's quite a question."

Peter stared at him. "You seem to be an honest man who says what's on his mind. Myself, I'm just not sure. I'm not a very religious person, not really. Up until now I wouldn't have given a second thought to something like reincarnation. But now I have to say I'm reconsidering what I believe. What about you? What do you think about what he's saying?"

"It doesn't matter what I think," Hank said. "All I care about is evidence that's admissible in court." He stood up, pushed in his chair and held his hand out to Henry Lee. "Counselor, good to see you again."

"Likewise, Lieutenant," Henry Lee replied, getting to his feet to shake hands.

Peter walked him to the door. "Martin was a very nice guy. He was very serious and very smart, but a very friendly guy who just wanted to be liked."

Hank stopped at the door, waiting for the rest.

"He looked up to me," Peter went on. "He had absolutely no interest in business but he was very interested in our culture. Our heritage. I ... let him down. His parents never forgave me. I don't blame them. Their son didn't deserve to die."

"Nobody deserves to die," Hank said.

Peter shook his head. "I don't believe that, Lieutenant. That's not part of my personal philosophy and frankly, I don't think it's really part of yours, either. Given what you've chosen to do with your life."

Hank stared at him for a long moment before walking out.

198

# 26

Hank and Karen stood on either side of the scarred and battered door of a basement apartment on King Street in Chinatown a few minutes before nine o'clock that evening, weapons drawn and ready. Their clothes were damp and they had left wet shoeprints on the concrete floor behind them. The rain had put Karen into a foul mood. Hank ran the sleeve of his jacket quickly over his face to remove clinging droplets of water.

The uniformed officers they had brought with them eased into position. Jim Polenti, short and wiry, 38 years old, a 16-year veteran of the department, stood behind Karen. His job was to remain outside and cover the corridor. Polenti had two teenaged boys, ages 16 and 15, and a nine-year-old girl. The girl was already a stand-out in gymnastics and her picture had been in the newspapers twice. Polenti's wife, Janice, was a dental hygienist and the family lived in a four-bedroom house in Bering Heights. The other officer was Susan Cameron, a 25-year-old African-American who stood behind Hank, ready to follow him into the apartment. Susan had two little girls, ages four and two, and her husband Steve owned a coffee shop uptown. She was tall and athletic, like a professional tennis player. The family lived in a small apartment above the coffee shop. All their money had been poured into the business downstairs.

Their backup, Officers Breyer and Lewis, were outside in the rain, watching the front and rear entrances of the building in case Billy made a break for it.

There were only two apartments in the basement, the one in which Billy Fung lived, according to the text message Karen had received an hour ago, and the other directly across the hall which was said to be vacant.

When everyone was ready, Hank nodded and pounded on the door with his fist. "William Fung! This is the police! We have a warrant for your arrest! Open the door now!"

Silence.

"This is the police!" Hank pounded again. "Open the door!"

Someone stirred inside the apartment. The chain lock was removed. Hank and Karen both took a step back and leveled their guns at the door.

It opened and a young Asian female peeked out. "Nobody home," she said in a heavily accented voice.

"Step back and raise your hands where we can see them," Hank commanded, putting his hip into the door and forcing it open. He stepped inside and moved to the left. Karen followed and moved to the right.

"No one here but me," the girl repeated, frightened, as Cameron and Karen began a room by room search of the apartment. In a few moments they were back, shaking their heads. There was no one else in the apartment.

"Where's Billy Fung?" Hank demanded.

"Not here," the girl said. She clasped a thin silk robe to herself nervously. She was very small and looked no older than eighteen or nineteen.

"Yeah, but where?"

The girl's eyes involuntarily flicked to the apartment door across the hall before dropping again. "Don't know."

Karen moved first, striding out into the hallway, her eyes on the door of the other apartment. She motioned to Polenti to take up a position on the right side of the door while she approached it from the left.

"Watch the girl," Hank said to Cameron.

At that moment the door of the apartment across the hall exploded into splinters as a shotgun was discharged through it.

Reacting to some kind of sixth sense, Karen managed to dodge back and avoid the blast. Polenti was not quite as agile, and his feet tangled as he recoiled from the explosion. He fell heavily backwards and his head smacked the floor, his gun skittering away from him. He grunted and rolled over, eyes fluttering.

"Police, fucker!" Karen shouted, adrenaline surging. She delivered a punishing kick to what was left of the door, bursting it open, and dodged back as the shotgun discharged again out into the hallway.

Hank was still crouching inside the door of Billy's apartment. He glanced over his shoulder and saw that Cameron had dragged the girl out of the line of fire and was handcuffing her to a pipe that ran from the floor to the ceiling in the corner of the living room. He threw himself into the hallway and crashed into the far wall on the right side of the ruined door next to Polenti, who had gotten himself onto his hands and knees. Karen bounced to her feet.

"Okay?" he called out to her.

"Son of a bitch!" she answered. She swiveled around the door jamb, weapon fully extended, both elbows locked, and saw a man in a leather jacket and cowboy boots standing in the middle of the floor fumbling with the shotgun, trying to thumb more shells into the breech. "Freeze, asshole!"

Tang Lei lifted the shotgun and Karen shot him twice between the eyes.

Hank threw himself into the room, crouching low, and saw Billy Fung standing toward the back of the empty room, weapon held loosely in his hand, not pointing at anyone. "Drop it, Billy! It's not worth it!"

Karen entered the room on Hank's left and crouched, weapon leveled at Billy. "C'mon, asshole!"

Cameron moved into position at the edge of the door, her gun also pointed at Billy.

"It's over," Hank said. "Put the gun down slowly on the floor and kneel down with your hands behind your head. Now!"

Billy hesitated, his eyes flicking to the still form of Tang on the floor in front of him. Then he slowly raised his hands, showing his palms, and bent down to place the gun on the floor. He knelt and put his hands behind his head.

Karen rushed forward, swept Billy's gun away with her foot and swiftly handcuffed him.

"You're under arrest for the murder of Gary Thatcher," she told him, then gave him his Miranda warning and shoved him toward the door.

Hank kicked the shotgun to one side and cautiously knelt beside the body of Tang, feeling the neck for a pulse. Nothing. He looked briefly into the lifeless eyes that stared back at him. Then he stood up and began to search the rest of the apartment. Polenti, now back on his feet and moving a little uncertainly, secured the shotgun.

Hank looked in the bathroom and saw a few toiletry items but nothing else. He looked in the bedroom and saw a small cot with tangled bedclothes, a wooden chair, discarded fast food wrappers, empty beer cans, an open suitcase with a few items of clothing and an array of firepower in the corner, including an assortment of assault rifles, several handguns and boxes of ammunition. Apparently Tang had been flopping here, despite the information they'd received that the apartment was empty.

He followed Karen and Billy out into the hallway as Breyer and Lewis came in, rain spraying from their uniform and boots as they hurried forward.

"Fun's over," Cameron told them, emerging from Billy's apartment with the handcuffed girl.

"This pinhead would like a ride downtown," Karen said, passing Billy over to Lewis. Breyer took the girl and the two officers walked their prisoners out to their cruiser.

"I want my lawyer!" Billy called out over his shoulder.

Karen looked at Hank. "Asshole."

# 27

The call came as Peter was in the middle of Sunday brunch. He was listening to a local newscast on his iPhone in which the arrest of Billy Fung for the murder of local businessman Gary Thatcher was being given headline treatment. He muted the news audio and answered the incoming call.

"*Wei?*"

"I apologize profusely for interrupting the *Hung Kwan* during his meal time," Henry Lee said in Cantonese, "but the *Shan Chu* required the *Hung Kwan's* presence immediately."

"No problem, Henry," Peter said, hiding his concern. "Where'll I go?"

Henry explained that Lam was where he usually preferred to spend his Saturday afternoons. Peter called for Benny Hu and took a last few bites, but the food tasted like sawdust and he gave it up as a lost cause.

Hu drove him in the Lexus. As he stared out the window, Peter made a call that would set in motion the final silencing of Billy Fung, who would shortly be found hanged to death in his jail cell. When Peter put his iPhone away he felt depressed. It should never have come to this. He should have taken care of Billy before now, but he'd allowed his preoccupation with Martin's revived case to have a negative effect on his focus. It was time to snap out of it.

Hu pulled up in front of a busy Chinese grocery store. The parking space immediately in front of the store was always vacant, despite the heavy traffic on the street and the popularity of the store. The neighborhood knew that important people used this parking space at unpredictable times and it was always left free. Anyone not from the area who made the mistake of parking in this spot was quickly told to move their vehicle. Arguments about whether or not to comply were never very long.

Peter walked through the grocery store, opened a door at the rear and stepped out into a small courtyard. An old woman looked up at him as she sorted fruit into two crates, one for good fruit and one for spoiled. Peter did not acknowledge her presence. He walked quickly through the courtyard. Finches chirped in a bamboo cage suspended from a tree branch nearby. He opened a gate that led into another courtyard and entered a garden containing a wide range of perennials and herbs, potted bulbs and ceramic ornaments spouting water. A little white dog skipped forward to meet him.

"Lucky!" a hoarse voice called out in Cantonese. "Don't be a bother!"

They were sitting at a table in the shade with tea, bowls of salted nuts and plates of half-consumed sweet rice cakes. Peter bowed to Lam and to Tu Pang Pong, the owner of this place. Another former Dragon Head, Uncle Pong controlled most of the heroin traffic in the state and was extremely powerful. A small, bald man, he wore a starched white shirt under a brown sweater vest, navy trousers, and brown leather slippers. The old dog, Lucky, belonged to him, and it now curled up obediently at his feet beneath the table. Uncle Pong was fearsome, but he was reasonable and slow to anger. Peter understood the importance of providing good answers to Uncle Pong's questions.

Peter nodded at the third man at the table. William Chow wore a navy pinstripe suit over a white shirt open at the collar with no tie. He watched Peter approach the table with eyes that were like two black stones. He was a *shetou*, a snakehead, a people smuggler. He moved females for the sex trade, he moved family members for Chinese here in America, and he moved workers and soldiers back and forth. Many of the people he moved were illegal immigrants from Fukian province in China. He managed two pipelines. One traveled from Hong Kong to Thailand to Mexico and San Diego, then across the country in rickety buses owned and operated by small-timers who considered themselves lucky to be a part of his organization. The other pipeline traveled west from Bangkok and ended up off the coast of Massachusetts, where Chow's men brought them ashore and piled them into trucks for the final leg of their journey. Passage was expensive, commonly costing as much as $80,000 per person, and the flow of people passing through his network was steady. Chow had been the snakehead in this community for ten years, having wiped out the competition in the early going, and had become extremely wealthy. He lived in a mansion in Granger Park, was married to a woman from another powerful family in Hong Kong, and had three children, a twelve-year-old boy, an eight-year old boy and a five-year-old girl. He was tall and slender, and he kept himself in shape, exercising regularly, watching his diet and limiting his intake of alcohol. Cigarettes were his only vice.

Uncle Pong gestured to an empty chair. As Peter sat down a young woman came forward and poured tea for him, arranging an assortment of pastries close to his hand. He willed his breathing to remain normal. As she withdrew Uncle Pong cleared his throat and smiled.

"You look well, Peter, but a little tired." It was odd, hearing a guttural voice emerge from such a small body. It was rumored that Uncle Pong had some kind of throat problem, perhaps even cancer, and listening to the odd growl Peter thought that it must be true.

"You've been working hard." Uncle Pong watched Peter sip his tea. "You need to rest. The council wouldn't like to have your father mad at us because we're overworking his son."

"Rest comes once the work is done," Peter replied, knowing that Uncle Pong mentioned his father not only as a gesture of respect but also to remind Chow that Peter was not a hired hand but rather the son of an important pillar of society. The dynamics of the moment seemed to be arranged such that Lam was generally supportive of Peter, Uncle Pong was neutral but concerned, and William Chow was antagonistic. Peter knew that Chow was anxious to go on the attack. Uncle Pong was signaling that he was willing to help Peter, but only so far.

"Tell us what you found out," Lam prompted.

"Our sworn brother Tommy Leung has violated his oaths," Peter said. "He has a partner, a *gwailo*. Enlisting the help of two other men, a black gang member and another *gwailo*, he and his partner took the skimming business and ran it for themselves. He cheated his father of the money, and since his father could not pay the families of his brothers according to his obligations, he cheated the brotherhood as well."

Uncle Pong sighed. "Eddie's such a fucking idiot." He picked at the nuts in the bowl in front of him but did not take one.

Peter waited.

"These deaths," Uncle Pong eventually said, "the black and the *gwailo*. They're the outsiders you mentioned?"

"Yes," Peter said.

"And you felt it appropriate to enforce *Hung* justice on them as well?"

Here was the trap. He could either lie and step into it, or tell the truth and avoid it.

"There was a personal matter, Uncle, involving these men. A matter of face. Otherwise they wouldn't have needed to die."

"Oh?" Uncle Pong pushed out his lips.

"I need a glass of that rice wine of yours, Pong," Lam said. "It'll probably put me to sleep, but I need something a little stronger than this tea."

Uncle Pong snapped his fingers without turning around. Instantly the young woman was at the table distributing wine glasses and pouring rice wine for Lam and Uncle Pong. Chow moved his glass aside and Peter politely shook his head.

Lam drank most of his wine in one long swallow. "This kind of business can upset the nerves. It goes back to our problems with Philip Ling. Peter's young cousin, uh, what was his name again?"

"Martin Liu, Uncle Sang."

"Yes, that's it. Martin." He set down his glass and looked at Uncle Pong. "A young man who worked in one of Jerome's businesses. Unfortunately got himself killed during all the trouble with Ling." Lam looked at Peter. "But I thought Ling's men had done it. Why all this fuss now?"

"Ling didn't do it," Peter said.

"Tsk," said Chow, folding his arms across his chest. "Are you saying this rash of killings is because you've been looking after some kind of personal problem?"

Peter did not respond.

"Don't you realize the trouble you've caused us with all this attention

204

from the police?" Chow continued. "It's not just your own people who're being hauled in and questioned, don't you realize that? The entire community's been disturbed. I thought it was connected to this business with the traitor, but now you tell us it's because of a *personal* matter?"

Uncle Pong frowned. "Our community is also in turbulence because someone insists on killing grocers when they cannot pay their debts. Perhaps it would have been simpler, Chow, just to send the man's daughter and son-in-law back to China so that we wouldn't have regular visits from the police because of that problem, as well."

A silence followed that Chow, chastened, wisely did not interrupt.

"I'm sorry if I've caused problems," Peter said finally, addressing his words to Uncle Pong, "These men killed my cousin to stop him from coming to me about Tommy Leung's violations of his oaths. It was a matter of honor, retribution for murdering someone under my personal protection, but it also involved the honor of the society. Defiance of the *Hung Kwan* speaks of contempt for the society itself."

"We'd like to be reassured that peace and calm will return to our community," Uncle Pong said.

"It will, Uncle," Peter said.

"However," Chow spoke up, "there's still Eddie Leung and his son. Shouldn't the council discuss what has to be done with them?"

"The council's aware of the situation," Lam replied.

"The price for violating their oaths—"

"Is death," Lam finished, "I know, Chow. You're not telling me anything new." He looked at Peter. "Take care of the two of them, will you? Chow will make arrangements for Eddie's wife to go back to Hong Kong. Then it'll be all over and done with."

"The Leung family businesses should be passed over to steady hands," Chow said.

"So you said before," Lam said.

Uncle Pong frowned. "Are you talking about yourself, Chow?"

"No. But I know someone very trustworthy. For a fifty percent take he will do an excellent job, and the brothers can split the rest."

"This is a conversation for another day, Chow," Uncle Pong said.

"Yes, Uncle. Of course."

"All I care about," Lam groused, "is that things quiet down again."

A speckled bird landed on the courtyard wall and began to cackle. Lucky stirred between Uncle Pong's feet and the bird flew away. "There's one more person I still need to find," Peter said.

Chow groaned. "Uncles, please. The *Hung Kwan* can't continue to disrupt everything because of personal business."

"Hear me out," Peter said. "Tommy Leung had a partner, another *gwailo*, as I said. This person would have been made privy to *Hung* secrets

205

that an outsider should not know."

"We can't have more killing of outsiders," Uncle Pong said. "We need less attention from the police, not more."

"I need to find out who this man is," Peter said, "and he has to be dealt with, but I give you my word I won't cause any more trouble for the brotherhood."

"More killing means more trouble," Uncle Pong said.

"I won't kill this man. I give you my word."

Uncle Pong glanced at Lam and said, "I don't need to tell you what'll happen if you break your word."

"No," Peter replied. "You don't."

# 28

They found Ann Martinez sitting on a high stool at a table for one along the far wall of Phil's Deli, a cubbyhole one block from headquarters that usually catered to the lunch-time crowd. Since it was nearly 8:30 on a Sunday evening the place was deserted except for Martinez and a young woman at the front counter who leaned on her elbows staring out the front window while listening to music through the earbuds of her iPod.

Hank pulled over a stool from the next table and sat down across from Martinez, his back to the front door. Karen grabbed another stool and sat on Martinez's right, blocking the aisle. The captain wore an elegant black evening dress with a black lace shawl and high-heeled shoes. A small black evening bag lay on the table next to the remnants of a smoked meat sandwich and a half-finished cup of coffee.

"My husband and I had dinner reservations and tickets for the theater," Martinez said, sipping her coffee, "but Barkley's working late tonight and so's the Chief, so here we are."

Hank put his shoes up on the bottom rung of the stool and unbuttoned his jacket. "What's up?"

"Couple of things." Martinez set the china coffee cup down on the saucer with an audible clack that betrayed her frustration. "Barkley puts me on the spot by asking for confirmation that the Gregg and Thatcher homicides are connected and that they're both connected to the Liu cold case. So I tell the Chief they are. So the Chief gives me shit for not tracking down Thatcher faster than the Triad. I don't know what to say, I mean, it was only 24 hours between the two murders, right? Mah must have gotten Thatcher's identity from Gregg before he died."

"That's the going theory," Hank agreed. "He got to Thatcher before we could."

"Yeah, well, that's the thing. Barkley asked me to confirm that you'd gotten a line on Gregg while he was still alive, but you didn't bother looking him up before Mah nailed him."

"You gotta be kiddin' me," Karen snapped.

Martinez held up a finger, looking at Hank.

"Uh huh," Hank said. "And so?"

"Barkley said he'd received information you'd queried ShonDale Gregg in the system the afternoon before he was murdered. So the question was, why didn't you bring the guy in for questioning right away instead of leaving him out there for Mah to get?"

"Duh, maybe because we were busy," Karen said. "Maybe because we were down in Springhill interviewing the kid who seems to know more about the case than anybody else at this point."

"Yeah." Martinez rubbed her forehead. "Our famous CI. A three-year-old kid who claims he was the victim in a previous life."

"He's been right on the money so far," Karen said defensively.

Martinez stared at Hank. "When the Chief wanted me to confirm that our confidential informant was a little kid with psychological problems who was leading my investigators down the garden path when they should have been out in the street where they belonged, I had to blow smoke like a fifty-year-old Volkswagen hippie van. *Then* I had to confirm there were still two more suspects out there."

"I don't understand. Where are they getting their information?"

"A damned good question. But it gets better. Billy Fung was found hanging in his cell at 4:30 this afternoon. Amazingly, there's nothing what-soever on how it happened. No video, no prints, no nothing. Apparently he committed suicide by hanging himself with his underwear out of remorse for his wrongdoings."

Hank sighed. "Which leaves us empty-handed if we try to connect Thatcher's murder to Peter Mah."

"Unless we can do the impossible and identify the third Asian guy who was at the airport when Frick and Frack killed Thatcher." Martinez shook her head. "MDTA has been canvassing airport employees for us to see if any-one remembers him, but there's nada. He's a blank. We're out of luck. So Fung's dead, Tang's dead, and Mah's looking bullet-proof on this one, too."

"I'm sorry," Hank said. "You shouldn't be taking the flak on this."

"Of course I should," Martinez contradicted, "it's my job to take it. That's how this works. You know that."

Hank said nothing.

"Tommy Leung's target number three, correct?"

Hank nodded. "I'd say so."

"Well, get out there and find him before Mah gets us all fired."

"We've been trying to," Karen said. "He's gone into a black hole."

"Find the goddamned black hole and pull him out of it. And find the fourth guy who was mixed up in this. Let's close this damned thing and get rid of it for good."

"All right." Hank stood up and returned his stool to the next table. "Sorry your evening out with your husband got messed up."

"Don't worry about it. I love these sandwiches, and Ken left my tick-et at the box office window." She glanced at her wristwatch. "I'll probably get there by half time."

Hank smiled. "Intermission."

"Whatever. I'd much rather go to a Ravens game, but Ken has this thing for plays. Me, I prefer playoffs."

Karen headed off to the front door but Hank stopped when Martinez put a hand on his arm.

"Just a minute, Hank. Before you go."

At the front door, Karen turned around to look at him.

"Be right there," Hank told her.

Karen nodded and went outside.

"IAD has another file going on you," Martinez said, glancing at the young woman at the front counter, who was staring at Karen out on the sidewalk. "I got the word from a trusted source I bumped into in the washroom."

"I understand," Hank said.

"The story is, someone's getting too cozy with Chinatown, leaking information to the Triad. The Chief wanted to know if I was comfortable with you staying on this case. I said yessir, I am. It was either that or tell him to fuck off. Which was on the tip of my tongue, believe me."

"Either way," Hank said, "you're putting your ass on the line for me. I appreciate that."

Martinez tried to smile. "We've been here before, haven't we?"

He nodded. A decade before he'd been the subject of several IAD investigations. One had arisen from suspicion that he was accepting bribes from known criminal elements. The impetus of this investigation was a photograph showing Hank exchanging money with an elderly Asian man. In fact, it was a photo of Hank paying for a container of noodles (not in the picture) at an outdoor stand on Lexington Street during Chinese New Year celebrations. For more than six months he was followed, photographed, wiretapped and otherwise spied upon before it ran out of steam and was shelved.

However, it was another investigation a few months later that Hank knew Martinez had in mind. He was the supervisory lieutenant in Homicide at the time and still relatively fresh from his stint in the chief's office, still the Hero Cop who'd saved the son of Mayor Post from his kidnappers. Still feeling aggrieved by Hank's actions while working in the chief's office, Myron Heidigger was determined to bring Hank down. Searching for leverage, he fastened on a series of glowing performance assessments Hank had written for a young detective just emerging as a rising star in the department.

Ann Martinez was a young hotshot at the time with a nose for evidence and a knack for closing cases. She was self-confident, brash and relentless, and Hank began to steer the higher-profile investigations her way. The media caught on and her face time shot through the roof. Heidigger and his circle resented the attention a minority female was receiving at the expense of what they considered to be more deserving senior investigators and they decided Hank must have an ulterior motive.

Thinking it was the leverage against Hank that he'd been searching for, Heidigger goaded his contacts in Internal Affairs into launching an exhaustive investigation of Hank's personal life. His friends reported strange phone calls, high-pressure interviews and veiled threats that included possible charges of obstruction of justice and lying to police during the course of an investigation. Hank was questioned on multiple occasions by an investigator named Bloom, who turned up in washrooms, on street corners and in elevators to ask pointed, intrusive questions that led nowhere.

They had enough sense to avoid his mother entirely.

For her part, Martinez was engaged to be married and her fiancé became so upset that he broke off their relationship and took back his ring, not because of what the investigation turned up but because he didn't like the scrutiny. It wasn't what he'd signed up for when he'd asked Martinez to marry him.

Shortly afterward an interim report mysteriously landed on the desk of the Chief. He read it with dismay and ordered IAD to discontinue the investigation, worried about the negative publicity nightmare that might arise if the media heard the department was investigating two of its highest-profile personalities.

A year later, Martinez wrote her exams for sergeant and never looked back. For his part, Hank found himself exiled to Public Affairs as the political pendulum swung him out of favor. However, one of the first things Martinez did after becoming captain of Major Crimes was to engineer Hank's transfer back to Homicide. She already had Jarvis as her supervisory lieutenant but found a way to fit Hank into her budget as a lieutenant assisting unpartnered detectives with their investigations.

"This thing worries me," she told Hank, picking up her purse. "Heidigger's like a bad smell, he never goes away."

He patted her on the shoulder. "Don't sweat the small stuff, Ann."

"It's not small stuff. Heidigger's a relentless bastard. I wonder if he's getting his information from Waverman."

"Not his style," Hank shook his head. "He doesn't use rookies."

Martinez touched his arm. "Watch your back, for godsakes."

He winked at her. "Always."

# 29

On Monday morning a black Lexus rolled into the parking lot of the campus day care center. There were no available parking spots and so it carelessly stopped behind two parked cars. Benny Hu shifted into Park and killed the engine.

Peter turned to Grace Chan and tried to smile. "Just bring him out for a few minutes and then he can go back and rejoin his little friends. I just need to ask him a few questions."

"Michael won't like it," she said, upset.

Peter patted her wrist. "You know I want what's best for him. I don't want him agitated by all this business, but he may be able to tell me something that'll end it for good. Then everything will be fine after that, I promise you."

Grace hesitated, then nodded. "You want me to bring him out here?"

"Yes. Then he can go back inside."

"All right."

Grace got out of the car and went into the day care center. She was not as well known there as Michael, and so the manager of the center, Mrs. Miller, was called out. Grace explained that she needed to talk to her son privately for a minute about some important family business. They would be in the parking lot and she'd bring Taylor back in as soon as they were done. Mrs. Miller asked for identification, which Grace provided. When everyone's resistance to this break from normal routine had been worn down, Grace was allowed to take Taylor outside. Mrs. Miller watched from the window as mother and son walked out to the parking lot and got into the back seat of the Lexus.

"Hello, chum," Peter said jovially as Taylor settled down on the seat between his uncle and his mother. "How are you today?"

"Pretty good, Uncle Peter."

Peter spent a few minutes chatting with the boy to set him at ease, and then got down to it. "Do you remember when you were Martin, Taylor?"

The boy lowered his eyes. "Mama doesn't like me talking about it."

Peter glanced at Grace, who was looking out the window. "I understand, Taylor. You have a new life to live now, and that's what's most important. But I need you to remember back to when you were Martin for just a moment. Can you do that for me?"

Taylor nodded.

"Good boy," Peter said, turning in his seat to face Taylor. "When you were Martin we took many rides in cars like this. Do you remember?"

Taylor nodded again, his face lighting up. "We went to the show, once. The Park Show."

"You mean Park's Theater?"

"Yes, we saw shadow plays. With puppets."

Peter felt a chill go through his body. It was uncanny. This was indeed the spirit of his cousin Martin sitting next to him. About a year before Martin's death they had gone down to Park's Theater with a friend of Peter's father, Ling Ting So, who was a professor of Asian Studies at State University. They watched a series of modern one-act plays based on stories from the Song Dynasty. Martin had devoured the performance and had asked Professor Ling a thousand questions. Peter suddenly felt very nervous. He felt a strong impulse to drop everything, to hurry the child out of his car, drive quickly away and never bother the boy again.

He remembered Ling Ting So explaining to them that puppets from the shadow plays were the source of much superstition among the players in ancient times. The heads of the puppets were kept separate from the bodies when not in use, so that the puppets would not come to life at night. Peter remembered the story now with dread. Was Taylor a puppet suddenly come back to life next to him, Martin's head stuck onto a little boy's body?

"That was fun," Taylor said.

"Huh?" Peter was a little disoriented for a moment before he realized Taylor was saying that their night at the theater had been fun. "Yes. Yes, it was."

"Can we go again some time, Uncle Peter?"

"We'll see, Taylor. I want you to remember something else for me now."

"What is it, Uncle Peter?"

"The men who hurt you. The men who sent your spirit out of your body as Martin and into this body as Taylor. The men who shot you and left you in the alley."

The boy said nothing now, staring down at his hands.

"I know it upsets you, Taylor. Just this once, and then I'll never ask you about it again. I promise."

The boy remained quiet.

"I've found two of them. Shawn and Gary. One was ShonDale Gregg, the big black man. He's dead now. The other was Gary Thatcher. He's dead now, too."

Grace exclaimed softly and began to cry.

"I know Tommy was there. Your friend Tommy. He betrayed you, Martin, just as he betrayed all his *Hung* brothers. But you told the police there was another person. Another *gwailo* besides Gary. Who was he? Who was the fourth man?"

"Please don't," Grace murmured, crying.

Taylor began to cry as well, not only because he was afraid of the question but also because his mother was crying.

Peter felt exasperation fill his chest and threaten to cut off his breath.

212

"Think!" he hissed. "Who was Tommy's partner?"

"I don't know!" Taylor bubbled through his tears.

"Do you remember the alley? Do you remember where they left you to die?"

Taylor nodded.

"Peter, please." Grace pleaded.

"But what about the other place? Where they first hurt you? Where the other man was?"

Taylor shook his head.

"Damn!" Peter slammed his fist on the armrest.

"Peter," Grace begged, "let us go. You're frightening him!"

"Remember, Taylor! You must remember!"

Taylor buried his head in the crook of his mother's arm and cried.

Peter was desperate. This wasn't working, and he knew he would not get another chance with the boy. It was now or never. On impulse he thumped the back of Benny Hu's seat.

"Drive!"

# 30

Hank's cell phone rang as he was handing Karen a cup of coffee at her desk in the Homicide detectives' bullpen. He put down his own cup, took out the phone, looked at the display and thumbed the green button.

"Donaghue."

"Hello, Lieutenant Donaghue, it's Meredith Collier. I hope I'm not interrupting something."

"Not at all, Ms. Collier," Hank said. "What can I do for you? Did Peter Mah contact you again?"

She laughed with embarrassment. "No, no, nothing like that. Ah, um, actually I'm calling just on impulse. Now I feel a little silly."

"Not at all," Hank said.

"Let me get on with it so I won't keep you from your work. I was planning a dinner here this evening with a girlfriend of mine and she just cancelled. I have a very nice piece of fresh salmon I was going to grill, and I was wondering if you'd be willing to stand in for her. If you have nothing else planned, I mean."

It took Hank a moment to react. Meredith stepped into the silence with a nervous laugh. "I thought of you right away because I've been feeling guilty for the way I treated you the other night. I was a little grouchy, and you must have thought I wasn't very nice. I'd like to repay you for having been patient with me and for not having gotten grouchy back."

"Sure," Hank said, touched by the nervousness in her voice. "What time?"

"Would eight o'clock be all right?"

"That'd be fine."

"You do like salmon, don't you?"

"Absolutely."

"Fine, I'll see you then."

Hank put his phone away and lightly rubbed his chin.

Karen grinned at him. "I told you she's got a thing for you, Lou. When's your date? Tonight?"

"It's not a date," Hank said.

His phone rang again and he answered it without looking. "Hi again," he said, thinking that Meredith was calling back to ask him to bring something.

"Lieutenant Donaghue, this is Michael Chan."

"Professor Chan, what can I do for you?"

Karen guffawed.

"Peter Mah's taken Taylor from day care, along with my wife. He's taking them somewhere, I'm pretty sure against my wife's will."

214

"Are you sure? That doesn't sound like him."

"The day care called me, Lieutenant. Grace showed up unexpectedly, asking for Taylor. She took him out to a car and got in the back and then the car drove away. They called me because she'd said she'd bring him right back inside."

"I see. Where are you right now?"

"I'm following them. We're on Youland right now. I think he's heading for the expressway."

"Slow down, Professor Chan. Who exactly are you following?" Out of the corner of his eye Hank saw Karen put down her coffee and lean forward, listening.

"It's a black Lexus, with Maryland license plates." He recited the plate number. "I know it's Peter. He's kidnapped them."

"If you believe that's the case, you should call 911 and report it."

"No!" Michael exclaimed. "If a police car shows up and chases them, Taylor and Grace could be hurt!"

"You need to tell the police what's happening," Hank insisted.

"I am, dammit! I called you! You're the police! Do something!"

Hank paused for a moment. "Where are you now?"

"At a red light, on Youland at Brockton. They're two cars ahead of me."

"Stay on the line. Detective Stainer and I are on our way. Don't take any unnecessary risks, and pay attention to your driving. If they get away, they get away. I'm sure Peter won't hurt them."

"All right! Just hurry!"

"We'll be there as soon as we can."


Karen hit the expressway at top speed, dash lights flashing, and once she reached the inside lane Hank began to breathe again. Using a USB connector that was kept in the glove compartment he had plugged his cell phone into the audio system of the Crown Vic, which Karen had reclaimed from the garage, and now they had Michael Chan on speaker as he continued to follow the black Lexus.

"We're still on the expressway heading south," Michael said, his voice sounding a little muffled through the speakers.

"Probably not going far," Karen remarked.

Hank pushed the Mute button and looked at her. "I know where he's going."

"South Shore East."

Hank nodded. "One-twenty-first Street."

"But what the hell for? What's the point?"

"Probably to jog the boy's memory, either to find Tommy Leung or to

215

get the identity of the fourth man."

"We can't tell Chan we know what's going on," Karen warned. "He'll try to stop him."

Nodding, Hank punched the Mute button. "Michael, are you still with him?"

"Yes, but they're slowing. It looks like they're taking the next exit."

"Which one?" Karen asked.

"Kenney Avenue-McPhail Road."

"South Shore East," Karen remarked. "Look, Professor Chan, we're about five minutes behind you and closing. Stay within sight if you can but don't take any chances whatsoever. Okay? We'll be right behind you before you know it."

"Do you know where they're going? Do you know where he's taking them?"

"Could be any number of places, Professor Chan," Karen said, "but the best thing is to let this happen. He won't hurt them, they're his family."

"They're *my* family!" Michael retorted angrily.

"I understand," Karen soothed, "but I'm just saying, family's right there at the top of Mah's value system. His protectiveness of family members will come into play here, you'll see."

"I hope you're right," Michael gritted.

"I am, you'll see. The best way for us to play it is not to be confrontational but just to find out what he wants from them and get them the hell on out of there again."

"All right, Detective."

They reached the Kenney Avenue-McPhail Road off ramp two minutes behind Michael. Karen swung right at the first set of traffic lights onto Kenney heading east. Three intersections later they stopped at the back of a long line of traffic waiting for a red light.

"I'm at Kenney and Jarvis," Michael said. "I'm right behind them."

"Then we're right behind you," Karen said. "How close to the intersection are you?"

"The Lexus is first and I'm second."

"Okay," Karen nodded. "We're too far back for a visual but close enough for rock and roll. At the next intersection make a right and let us move into position."

"No way. I'm staying with them."

"Professor Chan, let us do our job, will you? You called us in because you wanted our help, well, this is us helping. Get the hell out of the way."

"Not a chance. I'm sticking right with them."

Karen sighed. The light had turned green and traffic was slowly starting to move. "Look, tell you what. Make that right and circle around the block if you want, come up behind us. All I'm saying is, let us get right behind him

216

so we can handle this."

"But you may lose him if you can't get through the intersection in time."

"I won't lose him," Karen said firmly.

"But you can't be sure."

"Professor Chan, I do this shit for a living. I *won't* lose him. Now do what I'm asking while I'm still in a good mood, huh?"

"Okay. All right. Okay. I'm changing lanes. Couple of cars are changing lanes behind me; looks like you'll be able to move up several places."

"See?" Karen said sweetly. "A lotta traffic goes north-south on 125th. I'm moving up. There you go, we see you turning, we're through 125th and I've got a visual on the Lexus. Piece of cake."

They heard Michael sigh loudly. "Thank God. I'm still going to come around, though. Will you tell me where you go?"

"If you promise to behave."

"Detective! This is no laughing matter!"

"Relax, Professor," Karen said. "Come back onto Kenney and go east until you reach 121st. Hang a left and you'll see us in a couple of blocks."

"You *do* know where he's taking them!"

"It's just a little show and tell," Karen said. "When we get there we'll separate them and have a little chat with Mah about what he wants to know. It'll go fine, just stay calm when you get there and follow our lead, okay?"

"All right, Detective."

A few minutes later Chan told them there had been an accident on Kenney between 125th and 124th and he was having trouble getting around it.

"It must have happened right after you went through there," he said.

"Just be careful and don't take any risks," Karen urged him. "We've got it under control here. Trust us."

When they reached the alley on 121st Peter Mah was already there with Taylor and Grace. Karen parked behind the Lexus. Hank got out and walked up the driver's side of the Lexus as Karen trotted across the street.

Hank rapped on the driver's window with a knuckle. It slid down and Hank showed his badge to the chunky, bald Asian behind the wheel.

"Do me a favor and stay put while we talk to your boss," Hank said. "Anyone else in the vehicle besides yourself?"

The driver shook his head.

"No cause for alarm, just need to find out what he wants with the boy. Put your hands on top of the steering wheel and keep this window down, okay?"

The driver nodded, sliding his hands up to the top of the steering wheel.

"Thanks, appreciate it," Hank said. "Are you Benny Hu?"

The driver nodded again, staring at Hank with glittering, reptilian

217

eyes.

"Thought so. We missed you when we were talking to the rest of Peter's staff. My name's Donaghue. Been with Peter for long?"

"Few years."

Hank nodded as though this were fascinating information. "This is a nice vehicle. You also drive him around in a Mercedes, though, don't you? Where's it at right now?"

Benny Hu shrugged. "They tell me drive this, I drive."

"Yeah, but what happened to the Mercedes?"

"Company sold it, I guess. I don't know."

"Okay." Hank smiled and patted the door. "Look, I'm going across to chat with your boss. Remember what I said about keeping your hands on the steering wheel, okay?"

Benny Hu stared at him.

"Nice to meet you, Benny."

Hank trotted across the street. Karen had already moved Grace Chan back out of the alley onto the sidewalk and was quietly talking to Peter Mah and Taylor. Hank walked up to Grace and put his hand on her arm.

"Come with me, Mrs. Chan." He started to move her across the street.

"What are you doing? Where are you taking me? I'm not leaving Taylor here!"

"It's all right, Mrs. Chan," Hank soothed, "I just want you to sit in our car for a minute while Detective Stainer and I talk to Peter and Taylor. We've got everything under control and nothing will happen to Taylor."

"He's already upset! I don't understand why Peter's doing this. He's got Taylor scared to death!"

Hank opened the rear passenger door of the Crown Vic for her. "Detective Stainer has a great deal of experience in family-related investigations and she knows exactly what she's doing. Taylor will be fine, you'll see. Let her do her thing."

He coaxed her into the back seat and crouched down so that he was on eye level with her.

"I don't understand what he's doing," she said again.

"He wants Taylor to remember something connected to Martin Liu, right?" Hank said. "He won't hurt Taylor, he loves him very much."

"Yes, that's what he's been asking Taylor about but Taylor can't remember what he wants to know. Taylor's just a little boy. This isn't right."

"I know," Hank said. "Just wait here for us, please. We'll bring Taylor right over to you."

He closed the door of the Crown Vic and walked back across the street, figuring they still had a few minutes before Michael Chan reached the scene. Karen was crouched next to Taylor, looking up at Peter. By lowering

218

herself to the boy's level she was lessening the threat that she posed to Peter while aligning herself with Taylor to support the boy's emotional state. Hank stood next to Peter, a head taller, balancing the equation back out again so Peter would not feel in control.

"He must remember!" Peter was insisting. "He must tell me who else was there when Martin was killed!"

"But I told you, Uncle Peter!" Taylor said through his tears. "Shawn kept hitting me and Gary was yelling and Tommy was yelling and the other man was yelling too!"

"Who *was* the other man?" Peter demanded.

"I don't *know*!" Taylor whined. "I never sawed him before!"

"What did he look like?"

"He was a *gwailo*, Uncle Peter. He looked like a big monkey with no hair on the front of his head."

"No hair?"

"The rest of his hair was on the back of his head. I don't *know* him!"

"That's enough," Hank said. "Let the boy go back with his mother now. He can't help you."

Peter stared into Hank's eyes and then nodded. He dropped to a knee and looked at Taylor. "I'm sorry, little one. I needed to know."

Taylor sniffled. "Are you mad at me, Uncle Peter?"

"Mad?" Peter looked surprised. "No, of course not!"

"You won't hurt me?"

"Oh, my god, I'd never hurt you." Peter held out his hand. "I'm very, very sorry I upset you."

"You scared Mama," Taylor said, looking at Peter's hand.

"You're right. I need to tell her I'm sorry."

"You never scared my other Mama," Taylor said quietly.

"Pardon me?" Peter frowned.

"My other Mama, Merry." Taylor sniffled. "She's not scared of you."

"Martin," Peter whispered, his throat constricting, "I'm so sorry I wasn't there when you needed me."

"It's okay," Taylor said.

Peter drew the boy to him, his eyes closed, heedless of the filth that stained the knees of his expensive suit as he held him tightly.

Hank turned at the sound of a vehicle behind them. Michael Chan had arrived.

Karen stood up. "That's his father," she said to Peter. "Let me take the boy now so there won't be any trouble."

Peter released him and slowly stood up.

"Come on, Taylor," Karen said, taking his hand. "Let's go home."

"All right, Tex."

Chuckling, Karen led Taylor out of the alley as Michael Chan flew out of his car and started across the street.

"Stay right there!" Karen ordered, holding up her hand like a traffic cop. "We'll come across to you."

She led Taylor across the street.

"I needed to know who Leung's partner was," Peter said to Hank.

"Let Detective Stainer defuse the situation," Hank said. "We don't want any unnecessary trouble. Just stay still and don't say anything."

"Who the hell do you think you are?" Michael Chan shouted at Peter. "You stay the hell away from my family, do you hear!"

"Quiet!" Hank growled at Peter.

"Do you hear me, you thug? Stay away from us from now on!"

Hank and Peter watched as Karen herded Michael Chan back to his car. While he was securing Taylor in his child support in the back seat, Karen released Grace Chan from the Crown Vic and ushered her to her own car. When Michael closed the door on Taylor he walked past Karen, staring into the alley, and was about to shout at Peter again when Karen cut him off.

"Do you want to press charges here, Professor Chan? You want we should bust his ass?"

Grace rolled down her window and spoke before Michael could reply. "No! Michael, just let it go! It's not worth the trouble!"

Michael whirled on her. "Are you serious? He kidnapped you and our son! He should be in prison with the rest of his kind!"

"He's my cousin!" she cried. "My family! I can't do that to him! Just let it go."

"Yes or no, Professor," Karen said.

Michael worked his jaw, eyes flashing between the alley and his wife. Then without a word he threw himself around the front of his car, got in behind the wheel, slammed the door and drove away.

As he reached the intersection and slowed to turn, he was forced to swerve to avoid a large black Hummer swinging aggressively around the corner in front of him. Karen watched the Hummer rush toward her, then turned at the sound of another vehicle behind her. It was an identical black Hummer that threw itself sideways across the street to block passage. The Hummer in front of her did the same, and the doors began to open.

"Oh fuck," Karen said.

All hell was about to break loose.

# 31

"Police!" Karen shouted, holding her badge high above her head. "Stand down!"

Three Asians tumbled out of the Hummer in front of the Lexus. As Karen waved her badge she saw they were pointing Colt M4 Commando short-barreled rifles her. A quick glance told her that three more men had emerged from the other Hummer, weapons trained on Hank and Peter in the alley.

She threw herself back across the sidewalk into a doorway as the trio in front of her opened fire. Rounds punched into the Lexus and the Crown Vic, sounding like hail rattling on a tin roof. As she crouched in the doorway of the abandoned building, pressing back against the sheet of plywood nailed across the heavy walnut door, Benny Hu tumbled in beside her, crashing against the barricade in a heap. The doorway was only about eight feet deep, which didn't give them much room. If their assailants advanced to the point where they could get a flash-bang or other grenade inside, Karen knew they were toast.

"Stay down!" she shouted at Benny Hu, drawing her weapon. She quick peeked and saw one of the men edging between the Lexus and the Crown Vic in a slight crouch, looking through the windshield of the Crown Vic to see if anyone was inside. She fired twice and threw herself back down against the barricaded door, aware that the other two, still concealed behind the Lexus, would now know her position.

Gunfire was being directed into the alley by the assailants who had emerged from the other Hummer on her left. She could hear Hank returning fire sporadically.

"Switch sides!" she said to Benny Hu, who nodded and rolled to the left side of the doorway, allowing Karen to press against the bricks on the right side. She saw that Hu had drawn a gun but wasn't about to quibble with him right at the moment. She popped up and looked over the roof of the Crown Vic. Three men were firing into the alley at Hank. She squeezed off four quick shots and then threw herself down as the top half of the doorway exploded in a hail of bullets.

"Switch sides!" she shouted again, and once more Hu rolled out of her way as she moved across the doorway. She stayed flat on the ground and thrust her weapon clear of the corner on the right, butt against the sidewalk. She fired three shots before pulling back. Her shots punched into the side of the Lexus, as she knew they would, but the intent was merely to drive her two remaining assailants back into cover. She was down to three rounds and although she had only one backup magazine in her jacket pocket she swapped anyway. She still had her little Kel-Tec strapped to her ankle in reserve, if it came to that. Crouching back into the back corner of the doorway, she fumbled for her cell phone to call it in.

In the alley Peter had just turned to Hank, about to say something, when they heard the arrival of the two Hummers.

"Police!" Karen shouted. "Stand down!"

From where they were standing, next to the dumpsters against the wall of the Biltmore Arms apartment building, Hank could see the nose of the Hummer that had fishtailed into position behind the Crown Vic. He saw three Asian men appear in the street, weapons leveled, and as they opened fire into the alley he pushed Peter behind the dumpster against the wall of the abandoned building on the other side of the alley and fell on top of him.

"Stay down!" he hissed into Peter's ear. "Don't move!"

He drew his gun but held his fire, not knowing where Karen was and not wanting to hit her by mistake. "Police!" he shouted. "Hold your fire and put down your weapons!"

Bullets rattled down the alley in response.

He got into a crouch, pressed his hand down on Peter's arm to remind him not to move, and threw himself across the alley in a brief lull in the firing. Rounds hammered the dumpster in front of him, syncopated by the sound of Karen's gun from across the street. Knowing she had made it to cover, Hank took a few breaths, listened to another burst of four rounds from Karen, then popped up above the rim of the dumpster.

He saw one of the men drop like a marionette whose strings had been cut. Hank recognized him as one of the security men who'd been with Tommy Leung outside the fence last Tuesday. Hank opened fire on the man closest to the entrance of the alley. The man sagged to one knee as Hank ducked back again.

"Are you all right?" he called across to Peter.

"Yes!" Peter replied. He had taken out his little Glock 27.

Hank shook his head. "No! Put it away!"

Peter merely looked at him.

Hank moved around the edge of the dumpster. The man Hank had shot was back on his feet and was being supported by Tommy Leung.

"Abort!" Tommy shouted. "Let's get the fuck out of here!"

"Police! Freeze!" Hank called out. "Drop your weapons, now!"

The wounded man raised his weapon and fired a short burst in Hank's direction before Tommy hauled him back toward the safety of the Hummer.

The rounds flew wildly above Hank's head except one, which passed completely through his right shoulder, spinning him around with the impact. Hank fell with enough awareness to strain his head forward, trying to minimize the blow when he hit the pavement, but the back of his head struck the filthy surface of the alley with enough force to cause him to black out.

222

When he opened his eyes he saw Peter Mah crouching over him, checking his shoulder.

"Get to cover," Hank managed.

Peter shook his head. "They're gone. You've been hit but it doesn't look too bad. Don't worry, I called 911 already."

"I won't," Hank mumbled, meaning that he wouldn't worry; he had complete confidence in Peter's ability as a diagnostician. If he said it didn't look too bad, then it wasn't. He felt fuzzy. He heard footsteps somewhere down below him and the sound of Karen's voice.

"Officer down! Officer down! Get the fucking EMS here pronto!"

"I'm okay," Hank said.

"Shut the fuck up, Lou," Karen said, kneeling beside him.

Peter had removed a white handkerchief from his jacket and was pressing it against the wound.

"Press hard," Karen told him. "There'll be an exit wound on the back and it'll help if you press hard enough to squeeze it against the pavement."

Peter nodded.

"Gone?" Hank asked.

"Bugged out," Karen confirmed, "but they left one behind."

"It was Tommy Leung and his men," Peter said.

"I saw," Karen snapped, standing up. She pointed a finger. "Hank better be all right or I'm going to personally hunt you down and pop you one between the fuckin' eyes."

"He'll be all right," Peter said.

"Where's that fucking EMS?" Karen paced back up to the entrance of the alley. Sirens were curling down the street toward them. "Come on, come on!"

Hank was now becoming aware of the pain in his shoulder, a burning sensation that seemed to be increasing exponentially. He felt a little faint and closed his eyes.

He could hear Peter fumbling beside him and the pressure on his shoulder eased slightly and then was reapplied. Peter had switched to another handkerchief or had added a second to the first one. Or something.

Hank's mind began to wander. Last week he'd been in this same alley, standing on this spot, looking down at the staged corpse of ShonDale Gregg. Was Gregg's ghost hovering around him now, watching to see if he too would die in this place?

No, wait. Gregg didn't die here. He died down at the river. Under a bridge. Was only dumped here. It was Martin Liu who died in this alley, four years ago. Was Martin Liu's spirit hovering nearby, watching him?

No, that spirit was now inside the little boy. Right? Isn't that what had happened? Martin died here, the spirit went off somewhere where spirits go, then came back down to earth to be reborn in the boy, Taylor. Right?

223

"Christ," Hank's mother said, "what took you so long?"

To realize that it was true? Reincarnation? Don't tell me you believe in it, Mother. Does that mean that Dad's spirit is now somewhere else on earth, too, in some little kid's body, slowly burrowing into a new identity? Will that happen to me, now? Will I bleed out in this goddamned alley, have coffee and scones with God and then find my way down to the next life in this sorry, never-ending carousel?

"What's your name?" a man asked.

You mean my current name or my soon-to-be new name? Hank wondered.

"What's your name?" the voice repeated.

"Hank." He opened his eyes a crack but the light was too bright and he closed them again.

"I'm a paramedic, Hank," the voice said. "You've been shot but it doesn't look too bad. We've immobilized your right arm, so don't try to move it. What day is it today, Hank?"

Hank tried to lick his lips, because they felt too dry to speak through. "Tuesday," he managed.

"Close, Hank. It's Monday. Are you married, Hank?"

"One, two, three," another voice said.

He felt himself being lifted up and sideways onto a stretcher. Pain flared and subsided. "Merry," he grunted, then immediately felt foolish.

"Did you say you were married, Hank?" the paramedic asked as they raised the stretcher, locked the legs into place and began to move him out of the alley.

"Lou," Karen said, her voice laced with impatience, "answer their stupid fuckin' questions, they're trying to keep you from going into shock. I gotta stay here for a while, the Crown Vic's trashed and Mr. Mah has a few more questions to answer."

"Merry," Hank said again.

"What?" She bent down close as they stopped at the back of the ambulance.

"Merry," Hank repeated. "Merr'dth."

"Oh Christ, yeah! You're gonna miss that date tonight, Tiger. You want me to call her?"

Hank felt himself smile.

"You're a damned fool, Lou. I'll call her for you."

"Thanggs," Hank said as he felt himself ascend into the back of the ambulance. Then the doors slammed and the paramedics began working on him and he turned his attention fully to the feelings for Meredith Collier that foolishly welled up in his chest.

# 32

He promptly lost track of time. The wound to his shoulder, the doctor explained during one of his brief periods of lucidity after surgery, had been miraculously simple. He chatted about how the bullet had managed to find the small area in his shoulder where it missed everything of importance, including the radial nerve, the overlapping teres major, teres minor and triceps muscles, the scapula and humerus, and the major arteries.

"You couldn't pick a better spot to get shot in the shoulder," the doctor quipped, pleased with his own good mood. He explained that as the bullet passed through Hank's flesh it did not tumble to any degree, in part because it did not meet any serious obstacles on the way through. As a result, the exit wound on the back of his shoulder was not significantly larger than the entrance wound.

"The kind of round that hit you can create enormous exit wounds," he chattered, "so you're extremely fortunate that way. As it is, it kind of pulped the flesh on the way through so we had to do a bit of reconstruction. My old man was a medic in Nam and saw a lot of gunshot wounds caused by .223s. Imagine a round traveling at well over three thousand feet a second. How far away were you from the guy when he opened fire? You wouldn't even hear it coming. Why would these guys use weapons like that in a town like this?"

"You're asking the wrong person," Hank mumbled, not particularly giving a damn.

"Sorry, just curious." The doctor patted Hank's foot on the way out. "Barring infection, you'll be out there ducking more gunfire before you know it. Just duck faster next time, okay?"

Hank had several visitors that he was barely aware of through the evening, including his mother, Ann Martinez and Karen. While Karen was sitting with him, watching a baseball game on the little television next to his bed, Meredith Collier arrived. She chatted with Karen, got an update on Hank's condition while Hank dozed in blissful ignorance, and then left. As she hurried from the room Karen smirked knowingly.

When visiting hours were over Sandy stopped in to pick her up.

"How bad is it?" He frowned at Hank, who slept as though poleaxed.

"He's fine," Karen said, grabbing her handbag. "He's just dogging it at this point."

"Hardass," Sandy said, stepping aside so that she could precede him through the door into the corridor.

"It's not hard," she replied coolly, looking at him. "Just firm."

"You're telling me," Sandy murmured, watching it leave the room ahead of him.

Some time later Hank woke up with his shoulder on fire.

Someone was in the room.

"Time for your pills," a female voice said.

He took the pills and swallowed them with water from a plastic cup. "What hospital is this?"

"Angel of Mercy, dear."

"What time is it?"

"Four oh-six a.m."

"I feel like I've been shot."

"Very funny, dear. Go back to sleep, now."

Obligingly he closed his eyes.


When he opened them again the mid-morning sun was streaming in through the window of his room and a heavy-set middle-aged man was sitting in the chair next to his bed. His thinning brown hair was combed straight back, his nose was large and fleshy, and his watery blue eyes were shot through with red. He wore a charcoal suit under a beige trench coat, brown shoes, and an enormous wrist watch that caught the light and reflected it into Hank's eyes as the man leaned forward and clasped his hands together between his knees.

"Well, well, look who's back in the land of the living."

"What day is it?"

"Tuesday, hotshot."

Hank sighed and closed his eyes again.

"I understand it was only a flesh wound," the man went on, smiling insincerely, "just like in the movies. Most guys'd be up and about by now, but not Hero Man. He needs to milk it a little, first. Had many reporters in to see you?"

"If they've been here, I haven't noticed," Hank murmured.

"Yeah, I bet."

"What the hell do you want, Heidigger?"

Deputy Chief Myron Heidigger shrugged. "Hey, when one of my former boys gets shot in the line of duty, why wouldn't I stop by to make sure he's okay?"

"I'm okay," Hank said. "Thanks for coming. See ya."

Heidigger chuckled. "Still the same old sweetheart. Christ, Donaghue, you'd think that two of the old guard would stick together, look out for each other with all these New Age types around us now in the department, but no, you gotta be the same dickhead you always were, better'n everybody else."

Hank said nothing, licking his dry lips.

"Wanted you to know, straight from me," Heidigger said, "one of my best boys, Cox, has opened up a file on this whole Triad thing you've been

226

messing with. Word is that stuff's been leaking out of the department down into Chinatown, and seeing as you were shot in the presence of a known Triad official, allegedly *protecting* the guy and his driver flunky, we'll see if Cox can add two plus two and get Donaghue."

Heidigger laughed at his own witticism and stood up heavily. "It's been a while, kid. You've had it your way but now the winds are blowing in a different direction. Maybe all your past sins are about to catch up to you."

"I doubt it, Myron."

Heidigger continued to chuckle as he shuffled toward the door. At sixty-one he'd aged badly but the department was all he'd ever known and the only way he was leaving was feet-first. Internal Affairs was independent enough from the mainstream line of command that he'd been able to ride out the changes that had come in waves over the last decade, and he felt confident there were a few battles he could still win.

"Your rabbi Chief White's long gone," he said, "and nobody gives a fuck about you anymore, Donaghue. Nobody remembers the Golden Boy. Trust me, you're my meat. See you soon."

Hank couldn't think of a suitable retort, so he said nothing as Heidigger went out the door. Sighing, he closed his eyes and lowered his head back to the pillow. It was almost like old times, he thought. Do something good and receive Heidigger's fist shoved up your ass as your reward. What a place to work. How he loved and treasured his career.

He heard footsteps in the doorway and wondered if it was Cox, looking for his first interrogation.

It was Karen.

"What did Chuckles want?" she asked, setting a small vase of cut flowers on the bedside table.

"Heidigger?" Hank grimaced. "He's starting up a Hank Donaghue Fan Club."

"What a guy." She sat on the foot of his bed and patted his knee. "He's just all peaches and cream, ain't he? How are you feeling?"

"Like ten pounds of dog shit in a five pound bag."

"That good, huh?" She smiled at him. "So they shaved you."

Hank touched his cheek. "I guess. I was out cold at the time."

"Never mind, it'll grow back."

"Thanks for the flowers."

"You're welcome. They're from Sandy, he's sweet that way."

"Tell him thanks for me."

"Christ, Hank, lighten up a little. They're from me. Sandy never bought a flower in his life. He wouldn't know a flower if it bit him on the ass."

"Well, thanks to you, then."

"You sound real grouchy, but it's just the drugs talking. Inside I know

227

you're happy and pumped right up. It's just coming out wrong." She tapped his knee again. "We've got a line on the Hummers and we'll get the sonofabitch."

"We'd better."

"I'll get him, Lou." She leaned forward and touched his forehead. "I promise."


He was staring out his window at nothing when they came in with his lunch. It was largely inedible. He was flipping a cube of red-colored jelly around in his bowl with his spoon when Peter Mah walked through the door.

Hank put down his spoon.

"How are you feeling, Lieutenant?" Peter stood at the foot of his bed, a light trench coat folded over his arm. He wore a black suit, a pearl grey tie, shiny black shoes, and no gun.

"All right, thanks."

"You look a little pale."

It wasn't quite funny enough to draw a smile. "You weren't hurt?"

Peter shook his head.

"And Benny Hu? Your driver?"

"Benny?" Peter cocked his head in surprise. "He's all right."

"Glad to hear it."

Peter moved up the side of the bed and indicated the visitor's chair. "Mind if I sit down for a moment?"

"Not at all." Cox had probably already bugged the room and was busy in the truck in the parking lot logging the time of Peter's arrival, so what did it matter? One more nail in Donaghue's coffin.

Peter sat down. "I'm in your debt, Lieutenant. I won't forget what you did yesterday."

"I didn't do much more than get myself shot."

"You put your body in the line of fire to protect me," Peter said, "risking your life to save mine. That's not something I'm likely to forget. It's a bond between us that I intend to honor."

"No, no, no, wait a minute now." Hank sat up so that he could turn and face Peter, grinding his teeth at the pain flaring in his shoulder. "There's no bond between us. Let's be clear about that. You don't owe me a damned thing."

"There's something else we have to talk about."

"No, there isn't."

"A problem we have to solve together," Peter said.

It felt as though someone had injected a diluted acid into the blood vessels of Hank's shoulder. He squeezed his lower lip between his teeth.

"Should I call someone? Can they give you something for the

228

pain?"

"I'm all right," Hank gritted. "Say what you need to say."

Peter bowed slightly before turning away to look out the window. "Tommy Leung's business partner was Barry Melton. Melton was the fourth man."

Hank made a noise in his throat. "I doubt that."

"It's true."

In fact, Eddie Leung had told Peter all about it, although only after considerable persuasion. The fool had known about his son's defiance of the brotherhood and had turned a blind eye. Eddie was now in the trunk of the Mercedes limousine, which was currently sitting in a container on a ship en route to the Philippines. The container holding the limousine would be of-floaded at Panama during the passage of the canal and lost among the dock-yards there while all electronic memory of its existence was expunged. Peter regretted the loss of the Mercedes, which had served him well, but it had been used too often. Hank had asked Hu about it, so it had to be gotten rid of. Like Eddie. Unfortunately, however, Eddie had not been able to give him Tommy's current whereabouts. Either he didn't know, or family ties had sustained him to the very end.

"Melton and I share information," Peter said. "I give him Vietnamese gangsters, he keeps me in touch with current events. Very symbiotic. Unfortunately, I didn't realize how deep into our business he was until very recently."

Something registered in Hank's brain. Little Taylor had described the fourth man as a balding monkey, an apt description of Melton. Then Peter had said in the alley he'd *wanted* to know the fourth man's identity. Past tense. As though he'd figured it out from what Taylor had said.

Hank had known Melton off and on for a number of years but knew little about him. He thought about Heidigger's investigation of information leaks into Chinatown and Melton's refusal to run Tommy Leung's name when he and Karen had asked for it. His bullshit story about a multi-agency investigation had thrown them off the track, as Melton had intended.

"I'd need to see evidence," Hank said.

Peter removed a linen handkerchief from his pocket. Within the handkerchief was a small red USB flash drive. He leaned forward and tipped the drive out of the handkerchief onto the bed beside Hank's leg.

"Records of transactions of several offshore bank accounts. Have your forensic accountants look them over and they should be able to tie them directly to Melton. It'll be interesting to see how he tries to explain receiving that much money from known Triad sources."

"I don't understand," Hank said, picking up the drive. "Why are you turning this over when it could end up putting you in prison?"

"Lieutenant, really. I'm just a simple businessman. This information

229

was given to me by an anonymous third party and I thought you'd want it. It establishes a direct connection between Melton and Tommy Leung. Just think of me as another one of your confidential informants."

"But you and Melton have been exchanging information," Hank said. "If this drive contains evidence that you paid off a law enforcement officer you'll be putting yourself in jeopardy. And Melton will certainly want to turn on you if IAD puts the screws to him."

"I'm a simple businessman who believes it his civic duty to cooperate with the police whenever he can. There's nothing he can say that will harm me in any way."

Hank closed his eyes for a moment. "Look, Peter, I'm not quite on my game here, the medication's wearing off and I don't feel so shit-hot, but I don't understand why you're giving Melton to us instead of killing him like you did Gregg and Thatcher. No offense, but I don't get it.

"None taken," Peter replied mildly. "Let's just say I've given my word that I won't harm this man."

"Your word."

"My word, Lieutenant."

Hank opened his eyes. "I'll hold you to it."

"Besides," Peter added, "he's a cop. Way out of bounds."

"There's that, too," Hank agreed.

# 33

On Wednesday morning Hank was discharged from hospital. Karen helped him get his right arm into a sling after he'd dressed, then they slowly walked down to the nurses' station.

"Donaghue," Hank said. "I've been discharged."

"Oh, you can't just walk out," the nurse said, "you'll have to wait a moment." She consulted a sheaf of papers on a clipboard. "Yes, here you are. I'll just call the volunteer to take you down." She looked behind her. "Bob! Chair!"

It was the same volunteer who'd taken Josh Duncan downstairs when he'd been discharged a week before. He brought a wheelchair around to Hank. He looked at Karen and smiled.

"Hey there, Miss. Finally bailing your friend here out of jail, are you?"

"Might be a better idea to leave him in here a while longer," Karen said. "Keep him outta my hair."

Bob guided Hank into the wheelchair. "He's been a bit of a handful, but then again he's a policeman so you got to expect that kind of behavior sometimes, don't you?"

"I've been fully cooperative," Hank protested mildly.

Bob patted him gently on his good shoulder. "Sure you have." He looked at Karen. "Not very often we get a VIP like the Lieutenant here. Should have seen the steady stream of visitors. Some came in limousines, mind you."

"My mother," Hank grimaced at Karen, not wanting to mention Peter Mah.

At the elevators Bob pressed the button. "By the way, my brother-in-law and nephew both send their regards. They're sorry they couldn't stop by to see you."

Hank frowned. "Oh?"

"Sure." Bob wheeled him into the elevator, which was empty, and turned him around to face the doors as Karen moved in beside them and pressed the button for the ground floor. "Adolphus is out of the country right now, but I was talking to him on the telephone and he said to send his best. And Cedric, he's just been appointed by the Governor to District Court as Associate Judge and he's been down at the Capitol for the last week getting things organized. He said he'd be home in the next few days and will give you a call."

Hank was surprised. "Adolphus Post is your brother-in-law?"

"Yep." The elevator stopped and Bob wheeled him out into the hallway on the ground floor. "I married his sister, Belle." He stopped just short of the sliding front doors of the hospital. "Here you go."

231

Hank stood up and turned around. "What's your last name, Bob?"

"Jacobs," Bob said.

The name registered. "Robert Jacobs," Hank said. "You're a lawyer. Criminal defense attorney."

"Was," Bob qualified. "I retired three years ago. I do volunteer work and what not to keep busy."

"Good lord." Hank held out his left hand. "I know of you. Very glad to meet you."

Bob clasped his left hand, smiling. "It goes without saying I know of you, too. The entire family holds you in the highest regard, and it just so happens I knew your father, as well. A little better than I knew your mother. Robert and a few of us would meet for a beer every now and then in a place behind the court house. It's gone now, torn down years ago, but it was a good place at the time. Your father was a fine man. Didn't surprise me that Robert's son became such a hero to the Posts."

"Thank you," Hank said simply.

"You're welcome. Take care, now."

Karen led the way through the sliding front door and out onto the sidewalk that wrapped around the hospital. "Must be nice to have friends in high places, Lou."

The sun felt good on his face. He was alive, walking on his own two feet, breathing the air of the city he loved.

Karen's cell phone purred. "Stainer."

As she listened, her lips parted in a feral grin. "Got it. We'll be right there." She put the phone away and grinned at Hank. "There's a party going on and we're invited."

"I thought you were taking me home."

"I am, Lou, but you'll want to check this out first. Don't whine."

They drove downtown and Karen parked the Crown Vic in a tow-away zone in front of an office building. She led the way to a small group of people standing in the mouth of the alley between the office building and the bank next door. Hank saw that the alley behind them was blocked off by several black Suburban SUVs with federal plates.

A stocky bald man in a cheap green suit stepped forward and shook Karen's hand. "Hey, Stains, you're just in time. Lieutenant Donaghue, how the hell are you?"

Hank nodded at Detective Ellis Edwards of the Financial Crimes Unit. "I'm all right, Ellie, thanks for asking."

"Stains wanted in on this one," Edwards explained quietly, "and seeing as we go way back, walking a beat together, I told her I'd oblige."

"What is it? What's going on?"

"You didn't explain?" Edwards shook his head. "She's such a bitch. It's Barry Melton, Lieutenant. Stains passed us the USB drive and when I got a look at what was on there I called the Feds right away. We put a tail on Melton and here he is, emptying out a safe deposit box. He's already got a plane ticket to Bermuda under a false name and this is his last stop before skipping out. Come on, I'll introduce you."

He turned and caught the attention of Marie-Louise Roubidoux, who stepped forward, smiling.

"Lieutenant Donaghue, how are you feeling? Detective Stainer."

"You've met already," Edwards said, a little disappointed.

"I understand, Lieutenant," Roubidoux said, "that the information on Melton came from you. Mind if I ask where you got it?"

"A confidential informant."

"Inside the Triad?"

Hank shook his head. "I'd rather not say."

"All right, I understand. Maybe I can buy you a coffee sometime and we can talk about it."

Hank looked over her shoulder and made eye contact with IAD investigator Warren Cox, a fat, balding bulldog who leaned against the wall next to one of the Suburbans, by himself, smoking a cigarette. "Maybe," he said.

"This is a Federal bust, Lieutenant," Roubidoux went on as Will Martin joined them. "I assume you understand that. Will and I are participating in an ECTF."

Hank nodded. An ECTF was an Electronic Crimes Task Force operating under the auspices of the Secret Service as authorized by the *Patriot Act*, one of the purposes of which was to investigate crimes against the nation's financial infrastructure.

"We've got big plans for Mr. Melton," Will said. "He's going to be busy for a long time talking to us before you'll get a crack at him."

"I get it," Hank said.

"Son of a bitch can kiss his pension goodbye," Edwards chipped in, looking over at Cox.

Hank had wondered why Peter Mah would put Melton into the hands of investigators who would pressure him for information about the Triad in exchange for leniency, but now it occurred to him that as soon as Melton was in federal custody he'd follow a completely different process than he would have if Hank had arrested him for Martin Liu's murder. The Feds would immediately take him out of the city and sequester him somewhere that he could be interrogated at length by people with no connection to Glendale, its police department, or any other potential source of local taint. The matter was out of Peter's hands, Hank suddenly understood. It would pass to some other Red Pole in some other city whose responsibility it would be to silence Melton for good. In this way Peter Mah could keep his word, in letter if not in spirit.

"Here he comes," Will said suddenly. "Let's go."

It happened quickly. Melton pushed through the glass doors of the

233

bank onto the sidewalk. He lifted his eyes from the aluminum Halliburton briefcase in his hand and stopped dead in his tracks, gaping at the ring of fire-arms pointed at him. He took a step to his left and found himself locking eyes with Karen Stainer.

"Make a run for it," Karen grinned, motioning with her gun. "Come on."

Melton took a step backward, dropped the briefcase and raised his hands. "Keep her away from me."

As federal agents swarmed him, Roubidoux looked at Karen in sur-prise. "He's afraid of you."

Karen snorted. "He wants to be."


She was on a roll. Back in the car, her phone buzzed again. The call was short, and this time her grin was even wider. "We found Tommy, Lou. Ahead of the Feds this time. Let's rock."

They met SWAT around the corner from a building in Strathton that was surrounded by a high chain link fence topped with barbed wire. Two blocks from the waterfront, the buildings in this area had been used as warehouses for more than a century. This one belonged to a company named Yan Yee Trading. The SWAT commander, Lieutenant Pearson, had chosen an approach from the rear. A wide alley provided access to the enclosed paved area at the back of the building. Pearson dispatched snipers to the roofs of surrounding buildings and set up a command post around the corner on Chatham Street.

"The Hummers are inside the compound," Pearson explained as Karen handed Hank her jacket and put on a protective vest over her t-shirt. "There are also two white vans that the targets are currently loading with what looks like electronic equipment, armaments and other stuff. They're bugging out. We've done our sweeps and we've got eleven heat signatures and an elec-tronic security system that's been cut down by about sixty per cent since we got here."

"They're dismantling it and taking it with them," Hank said.

"I'd say." Pearson tapped a finger on the display of his tablet to en-large the satellite photo of the enclosed compound. "We'll stage here," he said, pointing at four dumpsters side by side just outside the gate. "Recon tells us the targets left the gate unlocked, so we'll just waltz in and take the vehicles first, along with the targets loading them. Then we'll sweep the building and clean up the trash. Exit points here at the front," he tapped the photo, "on this side and this side. My men will seal them off."

"Looks great," Hank said.

Pearson gave him an earpiece, glancing at the sling on his arm. "I take it you're going to sit this one out, Lieutenant."

Hank put on the earpiece and nodded. "Unfortunately."

234

"All right," Pearson said, obviously relieved not to have to worry about playing babysitter. "Detective Stainer?" He handed her an earpiece. "Let's move."

"Do your worst," Hank said to her.

"That's what I do best," she grinned back.

The team rounded the corner and moved up the alley to the staging area behind the dumpsters. Karen found herself sandwiched between two team members as the entry team went to work. They passed through the gate, flooded the compound and secured four targets loading the vans. Karen heard the All Clear over her earpiece and followed the others across the compound to the rear door of the building.

One of the men lying prone on the pavement with his hands secured behind his back was a bodyguard who had accompanied Tommy outside the warehouse gate last Tuesday when she and Hank had interviewed him. Karen grinned. "Hey there, Dog Biscuit."

The point man looked at her and put his fingers to his lips. Pearson's voice came over the earpiece directing them to proceed through the door and into the hallway. The elevators were inoperative. The stairway door opened before they could reach it and two men stepped out. They opened fire and were cut down by the team. Karen looked at the bodies as they filed quickly into the stairwell and saw one of the three men who had attacked her at the alley the day before yesterday.

*Taking out the trash.* She followed the team upstairs. Pearson directed them to the second floor, where the remaining five heat signatures were clustered near the northwest corner. As they reached the door to the second floor they heard Pearson saying that two of the heat signatures appeared to be shifting position while the other three remained static. Karen followed her team through the door and down the hall.

This is it, she thought. She wanted that bastard Tommy Leung so badly she could taste it. She wanted the other guy even worse, the one Hank had identified from photographs as the punk who'd shot him in the alley. She was hoping the guy would make the fatal mistake of pulling on her. He'd quickly follow Tang Lei into whatever next world was waiting for pieces of crap like them. She held her weapon at high ready as the team stacked up in front of her. Three guys, she thought. Tommy Leung and two others, hopefully. Four guys in front of her. She'd have to move fast to get in a shot. She controlled her breathing and damped her excitement.

The door opened, the flashbang was tossed, and they rolled inside.

Tommy Leung was already dead.

He lay in a spreading pool of blood with a bullet hole in his left leg near the knee and two others in his forehead. Across the room, draped across a long table holding computer equipment in various stages of disassembly, was one of Tommy's security men. He'd been shot once in the chest and twice

235

more in the left temple. Closer to the door, a third man lay curled in a fetal position, still bleeding out. One of the SWAT members rolled him over and they saw that he had been gutshot and then tapped twice in the head.

It was Hank's shooter.

*Goddamnit all to hell.*

They heard Pearson directing other team elements in pursuit of the two remaining heat signatures, which had moved downstairs. In a matter of moments he'd lost them. Karen hurried down to the basement, knowing it was Peter Mah.

"They fucked off on us, Detective Stainer." The SWAT officer led her into an old boiler room and showed her a trap door in the cement floor. "It connects to the sewer line. Looks like two targets got in and out through here. We're in pursuit but they obviously know where they're going and we don't."

"Goddamn Mah," Karen said. "Son of a bitch." She started for the trap door. The officer grabbed her arm.

"Detective, there's no point. Either my guys'll get them or they won't."

She shook off his arm, adrenaline pumping.

"Karen," Hank's voice whispered in her earpiece, "it's over."

"It's not fucking over!" she shouted. "Not by a long shot!"

# 34

She sat on the wooden bench in front of her locker, her elbows on her thighs and her cheeks cupped in her hands. She was crying and told herself it was just the release of tension, but she'd tried to stop and couldn't so she just let it happen. She was perspiring under the protective vest and wanted to take it off so she could breathe properly, but she couldn't move. She could only sit there, tears running down her cheeks.

On the other side of the row of lockers someone came in, opened a locker, banged around for a minute, shut the locker and went out. Karen unsnapped a buckle on the vest and let her hand drop back down between her knees.

She'd wanted very badly to kill the guy who'd shot Hank. She'd killed three people in the line of duty so far in her career. The first two had happened while she was a patrol officer and the third had been Tang Lei last Thursday. She did what she had to do and tried not to think about it very much, but she'd been so amped up to shoot Tommy Leung and his hired gun it had caught her off guard. She was supposed to serve and protect, not take people out. She was supposed to be better than the scum who pointed their weapons at her; she was supposed to represent a higher value system. But she'd smelled blood in that warehouse, she'd been extremely frustrated when it hadn't happened and now she just felt angry. Angry because she'd been cheated of the payback she wanted for Hank. Angry because she knew she should feel guilty, but didn't.

She stood up, took off her vest and stripped to her skivvies. There was a change of clothing in her locker, a clean t-shirt and jeans, and she put them on. Very deliberately she stuffed her sweaty clothing into a canvas bag.

When she was dressed she closed the locker. On the bench were her badge, ID and weapon. She picked up the gold shield and looked at it.

*"Wow."*

*"I say the same thing every morning when I put it on, Taylor. It's pretty cool."*

She clipped the shield and her ID on her belt. Then she picked up the holstered gun and clipped it onto her other hip.

She walked out of the locker room into a busy hallway and looked around.

*Who else needs their ass kicked?*

# 35

Peter considered Lam's question carefully before replying. "Will I run for *Shan Chu*?" he shrugged. "Perhaps."

Lam shifted his bulk in his chair. The uncles had decided to allow the council to elect a new Dragon Head and it was time for Lam to step aside once more. For good this time, he hoped. "Chow will win."

There was no doubt in Peter's mind that the uncles had discussed among themselves the outcome of the election and that Lam was telling him up front how it would turn out. It was a courtesy Peter appreciated.

"I understand, Uncle Sang. I thought I'd put my name forward anyway, to make my intentions known."

"Your intentions are well known." Lam looked around Peter's office. "Come downtown," he said. "This Opium Wars nostalgia stuff doesn't work."

"I think I will," Peter said.

"Good. This is a boy's daydream. Not appropriate for a man who wishes to be a leader in the twenty-first century." He rubbed his forehead. "Chow will make his own changes."

"I know."

"His own *Hung Kwan* will carry out the duties you've handled for me."

"I understand."

"He'll bury you."

"He'll try," Peter said.

Lam wagged his hand. "Too much killing, too much violence. Chow has to understand his mandate is to heal, not inflict more wounds. Just the same, if you want to survive, you'll need to make some major changes, build a new organization around yourself, get into a business that will increase your influence, change how you're perceived. Can you do that?"

"Of course," Peter said.

Lam heaved himself up out of Peter's chair and patted him on the shoulder. "Get better office furniture, too. My back aches for days after I come here."

"Yes, Uncle Sang."

The old man stared down at him. "Then there's the matter of the police. We'll need Chow to mend things with them downtown." He shook his head. "I don't know how well he's going to manage that. It was a major sticking point with some of us who felt he wouldn't succeed as Dragon Head. We need the police to leave us alone, and Chow has a way of pissing people off." Lam patted his shoulder once more and shuffled out the door.

Peter rose to accompany him downstairs, where his car waited.

"Make changes," Lam said. "Make them now."

"I will," Peter promised.

# 36

It was Peter Mah who ultimately convinced Meredith to visit Taylor Chan, but it took two telephone calls. The first call was short and ended on a somewhat negative note. Peter made the mistake of presenting his idea with too much enthusiasm and failed to detect Meredith's strong reluctance to see the boy until she'd said no for the third time and abruptly hung up. He gave it a couple of days and called again, this time to apologize for his insensitivity to her feelings on the matter and to acknowledge her wisdom in wishing not to revive the emotions that she had reconciled over the course of the four years since Martin had passed away.

Meredith, for her part, apologized for having hung up in his ear and for not considering the good intentions with which he'd proposed his idea in the first place. Once the formalities were out of the way Peter again suggested that it might be beneficial for her to see Taylor at least once while he was still at an age to speak about his past memories.

"How on earth would it be beneficial for me?" she asked, still feeling somewhat vexed about the whole thing.

"The rest of us have heard these things he's saying about having been Martin," Peter replied quietly. "It's something you'll always know happened, that the boy believed he was Martin in his previous life, and it will always bother you. If you see him, maybe hear him say these things, you can judge for yourself and put your mind to rest. If you choose not to believe, then your mind will be made up and you can forget about it. On the other hand, if you choose to believe, your feelings about Martin's death will change and you may find some peace of mind."

Meredith was silent for a long time. "I'll think about it," she said finally, and ended the call.

The visit was arranged for the first Sunday in June. It turned out to be a beautiful day, with a clear blue sky and a warm breeze blowing in off the river. Hank picked up Meredith in a taxi at her building and rode with her over to a school in Springhill that was a block from the Chan home. Michael and Grace often brought Taylor to the football field behind the school to play on the weekends, and Michael felt it might be a good place for Taylor to meet Meredith for the first time.

Hank told the taxi driver to wait for them at the edge of the field. They got out and walked toward the small grandstand where Grace Chan sat reading a book. Hank could see Michael and Taylor down by the far end zone, playing with a football. Taylor was learning how to punt the ball. Hank watched a kick travel about ten yards before it began to bounce, which he thought was pretty good for a three-and-a-half-year-old.

Grace stood up and gave Meredith a hug. Hank gave them a little distance, watching the boy play, and after they'd exchanged a few words Meredith began to walk across the field toward Michael and Taylor. At first she moved slowly, hesitantly. Then Hank saw her head come up and she began to walk more decisively, as though she'd put aside her dread and accepted the fact that she could deal with whatever the next few minutes would bring her.

Hank sat down next to Grace. "How's Taylor doing?"

"Taylor?" She lifted her eyebrows. "He's fine. A typical terrible three, full of energy and mischief. One moment he's doing something wacky, the next he's as grouchy as a bear. He asked his father yesterday if Uncle Peter could come over for a visit because he wanted to tell Peter he was sorry he thought Peter was mad at him before." Grace shook her head. "Michael was very patient. He explained that the rule was, Peter could only visit on Taylor's birthday, so he'd have to wait until November."

"How'd that go?"

"There was a tantrum. Then he got over it. Typical terrible three."

Hank looked across the field at the next street over. A limousine had pulled up to the curb and Hank could see a man leaning casually against the back fender, arms folded, watching as Meredith reached Michael and Taylor and exchanged greetings with the boy's father. Hank shaded his eyes for a better view, but didn't need to bother. He knew it was Peter.

Michael spoke to Taylor for a moment then moved away as Meredith came close. He reached the goal posts in the end zone and leaned against the left one. It was one of those combination goal posts that doubled as a soccer goal, made of four-inch-square tubing. He positioned himself so that he faced the limousine down the street.

Peter did not move.

Hank watched Meredith bend down to say something to Taylor. After a moment she crouched down so that she could talk to him at his level. At first Taylor's chin was on his chest, but before long his shyness seemed to disappear and he had no trouble looking into Meredith's eyes. He shifted his weight back and forth a few times, relaxing, and at one point gestured with his arm as though pointing toward heaven. Meredith lowered her head for a moment, then raised it again. She embraced the boy, held him for a long moment, then let him go and stood up. Taylor skipped over to his father, who pushed away from the goal post and swept him up in his arms. The three of them began to walk back toward the grandstand, but after a few yards Taylor began to twist in his father's grasp and Michael set him down. The football had been forgotten in the end zone, and Hank could see that Taylor wanted to continue playing with his father.

Michael said something to Meredith and Meredith waved goodbye to Taylor, who waved back and then pelted after the football, half-stumbling in his excitement.

241

Meredith nodded to Grace, then she and Hank got back in the taxi. He told the driver to take them back downtown.

"Are you all right?"

She nodded, crying. She removed a tissue from her handbag and dabbed at her tears. They rode for several blocks in silence.

"I need a drink," she said finally, in a low voice. "I need to be around people."

Hank glanced at his watch. "They're serving brunch at the Brass Pump."

"That sounds wonderful," she whispered.

They found two empty stools at the end of the bar and settled in. Meredith had regained her composure, and when Hank ordered steak and kidney pie with a draft of Guinness, she chose the weekend brunch special, which featured two fried eggs and a pan-fried mixture of red peppers, green onions, bacon and sausage with potato wedges. She ordered a Bass, drank it a little too quickly, and ordered another when their food arrived.

When the server had cleared away their dishes and brought them coffee, Meredith took a deep breath. "He said, 'hello, mama.' He said, 'I wanted to see you again but I was scared to ask.' I asked him why, and he said he thought his new mama might not like it. I said Grace was a great person and he said 'I know, but I didn't tell you I love you before I left. I should've said that.' I didn't know what to say, so I didn't say anything."

"Well." Hank really didn't know to say, either. He saw that Meredith's eyes were dry. She was staring straight ahead, lips drawn tight across her teeth.

"He said he hoped I wasn't too upset when he had to leave. He said Shawn and Gary were so mean they never let him go." She looked at Hank. "You said he knows they're both dead now, didn't you?"

Hank nodded. He'd explained to Meredith the circumstances of Martin's death, that ShonDale Gregg had shot her son accidentally while beating him as Gary Thatcher, Tommy Leung and Barry Melton stood by. He'd also explained that Peter had told the boy Gregg and Thatcher were both dead.

"He seemed calm about it," Meredith said. "When he said their names, it was like their memory didn't really bother him any more."

Hank said nothing.

"He said he hoped I wasn't too upset," Meredith went on, "because he went to a really nice place to wait before he went down into his now mama's tummy. He told me God was there and was really nice to him, and there were animals and other nice people, too. Then it was time to go to his new mama's tummy to get ready to be born again."

Hank smiled at her.

Meredith drew in a long breath and slowly released it. "I don't be-

242

lieve in reincarnation. I'm not a practicing Christian. I'm an agnostic. I'm nothing. I don't think about it, deliberately, because it upsets me. It took me four years to get over Martin's murder, almost as long to get over Stephen's death, and now...." She tapped her finger on the bar. "Oh, yeah. He also said when he was in the nice place they told him that his before daddy was sick and was going to go to a new body soon." She looked at him. "Stephen wasn't diagnosed with cancer until several months after Martin's death."

They both turned their attention to their coffee. Finally Hank reached out and patted her forearm. "Are you sorry you met with him?"

"No," Meredith said quickly. "Really, I'm not. Peter was right. Amazing to say, but Peter was right. And when that little boy said goodbye to me, when I was leaving, it was like it was Martin saying goodbye to me, and when I said goodbye back it was like I was saying goodbye to Martin." She shrugged at him. "We had a chance to say goodbye. After four years."

Her eyes filled with tears and she turned away.

"Look who's here," a voice said behind them. Karen patted Hank on the back and slid onto the bar stool next to him. Sandy Alexander sat down next to her and waved. "How's the food today?" she asked, leaning her elbows on the bar.

"Very good," Hank replied.

Karen looked at Meredith and raised her eyebrows at Hank. "How did it go?" she asked, voice lowered.

"It went."

"He was remembering stuff?"

Hank nodded.

"Nice to see you again," Meredith said, moving on her stool to look past Hank at Karen.

"Same here. Are you okay?"

"I'm okay." Meredith's eyes moved to Sandy.

"This is Sandy Alexander," Karen said. "Sandy, this is Meredith Collier."

"Hello, Sandy. Nice to meet you."

"The pleasure's all mine, Ms. Collier."

"Meredith, please."

"Actually," Karen said, drawing out the word until Hank turned around to look at her, "Sandy and I have decided to get married."

Hank stared at her, at a loss for words.

"We're gonna wait for a year," she went on, amused by his reaction. "We found a real nice place down on the waterfront. In fact, it's the building next to yours," she said to Meredith, "and we're gonna, you know, split the rent, mix our stuff together, see how it goes."

"We'll get married in my hometown," Sandy said. "Covington, Virginia. A little church wedding. My parents want to pay for everything, but they insist on having it there. Stains'll be a huge hit back there. They won't know what hit them."

"Say something, Lou," Karen laughed.

"Congratulations," Hank managed. He leaned forward to shake Sandy's hand. He looked at Karen. She threw her arms around him and squeezed.

"Pray for me, Hank," she whispered in his ear.

"Yes, congratulations," Meredith said. "I have a feeling it'll work out just fine. You two seem very comfortable together."

"We do?" Sandy quipped. "Maybe it's because I'm the only male within a hundred miles that isn't scared to death of her. Other than Hank, of course."

Karen turned around and punched him on the shoulder, hard.

"Ouch, glad that wasn't me," Hank said. He reached for his glass and held it up. "Here's to the happy couple. Long may they frolic."

"Here here," Meredith said, tipping her glass.

"Frolic," Karen repeated. "Boy, you have no idea."

Meredith's eyes met Hank's over the rim of her glass. They looked at each other for a long moment, and when Meredith looked away again to say something to Karen, Hank could see the same softening of her eyes, parting of her lips and the gradual disappearance of the little frown lines across her forehead that he'd noticed when they'd first met in the chiropractor's office. Now, as then, it told him she'd resolved an internal question and felt comfortable with the answer.

He didn't have to be a detective to know he'd reached the same conclusion.

# Acknowledgements

I'd like to thank Dr. Jim B. Tucker, child psychiatrist at the University of Virginia, whose book *Life Before Life: A Scientific Investigation of Children's Memories of Previous Lives* (New York: St. Martin's Press, 2005) inspired this story. I appreciate very much the time Dr. Tucker took to review material in this novel related to his work, and I thank him for his patience in correcting my errors. Any further mistakes or inaccuracies concerning the past-life memories of young children are solely my own.

Several sources of information were helpful in writing this book, including Martin Booth's *The Triads: The Chinese Criminal Fraternity* (London: Grafton, 1991) and Gerald L. Posner's *Warlords of Crime: Chinese Secret Societies: The New Mafia* (New York: Penguin, 1988).

I'd also like to thank Carol Ann Driscoll, Larry Sudds, Gwenda Lemoine, Anie Pulsifer and Margaret Leroux for reading the manuscript in its various iterations and providing invaluable feedback.

Finally I'd like to thank my wife Lynn Clark, to whom this book is dedicated, for having read the manuscript twice, for her feedback, her patience, good humor, tact and all the other characteristics that contribute to the makeup of a saint. No wonder I still worship the ground you walk on.

# About the Author

**Michael J. McCann** lives and writes in Oxford Station, Ontario on seven acres of the Limerick Forest south of Ottawa. A graduate of Trent University in Peterborough and Queen's University in Kingston, he worked as an editor before spending fifteen years with Canada Customs. He is married and has one son.

He is also the author of *The Ghost Man*, is a supernatural thriller set in eastern Ontario.

Visit Mike's website at www.mjmccann.com.

COMING SOON!

# MARCIE'S MURDER

the new Donaghue and Stainer Crime Novel by

## MICHAEL J. McCANN

available from The Plaid Raccoon Press

CPSIA information can be obtained at www.ICGtesting.com

235442LV00001B/16/P